THE BORDER GUARDS

THE BORDER GUARDS

a novel by
MARK SiNNETT

HarperCollins*PublishersLtd*

The Border Guards

© 2004 by Mark Sinnett. All rights reserved.

Published by HarperCollins Publishers Ltd

No part of this book may be used or repro-
duced in any manner whatsoever without the
prior written permission of HarperCollins
Publishers Ltd, except in the case of brief
quotations embodied in reviews.

First Edition

HarperCollins books may be purchased for
educational, business, or sales promotional
use through our Special Markets Department.

HarperCollins Publishers Ltd
2 Bloor Street East, 20th Floor
Toronto, Ontario, Canada
M4W 1A8

www.harpercanada.com

National Library of Canada Cataloguing in
Publication

Sinnett, Mark, 1963–
The border guards / Mark Sinnett.

ISBN 0-00-200504-2

I. Title.

PS8587.I563B67 2004   C813'.54
C2003-905644-9

HC 9 8 7 6 5 4 3 2 1

Printed and bound in the United States
Set in Melior

For Sam

Sometimes he wondered with horror whether perhaps she knew everything, whether that complacent face which she had worn since her return masked misery. She said, "Let's talk about Christmas."

—Graham Greene, *The Heart of the Matter*

PART i

DECEMBER 25

A badly bruised Tim Hollins—grieving son, reluctant restaurateur—stands before Granite's long wall of floor-to-ceiling windows and thinks about how he is damn lucky to be alive. He rests his forehead against the icy glass and closes his eyes. His left shoulder is stiff, raw. His right knee throbs and he stands with that leg raised enough that it supports no weight. Like a flamingo is how he feels. There is also a tremendous ache in his lower jaw and a pronounced click when he eats. The doctors, though, are adamant he has done no permanent damage. Give it a week, they say. Right as rain, they concur. They wear similar reassuring smiles but seem vaguely afraid of him, as if they believe the violence and chaos that beset him might well flare up again, or prove contagious. He now attaches their pronouncement experimentally to his actions of the last month—*you've done no permanent damage*—and finds that forced into service this way it sounds like a weak joke, a reassurance that is supposed to serve also as a reprimand.

He tips back onto his left heel and opens his eyes.

Rebecca is puttering somewhere. They have decided to reopen the restaurant, even if it is only for lunch on the weekends. She is probably in the kitchen, sorting through unwieldy architectures of saucepans and cookie trays, stained double boilers and long-neglected colanders. Her family, he knows, will worry about her absence on the holiday, but he is grateful for her staying; it would be unbearable alone.

Off to his right is a leaning stack of dining-room chairs. The wooden legs of one push into the leather seat of the one beneath; he needs to separate them before the indentations become permanent. The linen needs washing, as do the windows and the black slate floor. There is dust over everything, and a heavy ashtray sprouts the bent brown butts of a dozen Dunhills.

The list of chores is long and oppressive; he will have to return to it in a moment. Instead he stares at the sun, heatless and pale in the white sky, like a lemon dropped into milk. Beneath its dim sphere a swarm of islands—Ash and Wallace, Blueberry and Rabbit, Paradise and Wood—are being slowly whittled away by water that today rubs white and frozen at their tough shorelines. There are buildings attached to even the smallest of them, blue and brown and black summer homes that sit jauntily, like Licorice Allsorts, on all the high points. And around those stark, lovely islands is a seemingly random congestion of fishing huts. Some are old and wooden—they lean precariously, like neglected outhouses—while others, those of gaudy scarlet fibreglass, with double-glazed windows and shingled roofs, stand as stiff and erect as Beefeaters. At dawn, men in fleece-lined boots trudge away from the shore to these huts, and then at dusk they retrace their steps. They carry away pickerel and thick, mottled pike. Usually the fish are strung together on a hooked line, but occasionally a man will land a bigger beast and must drape it over his outstretched arms like the recovered body of a child. A turkey buzzard turns lazily in the sky, scans the slope between the fieldstone house and the ice.

Most of the St. Lawrence Seaway is frozen hard now, but a meandering, slush-filled strip winds roughly through its centre, and an occasional channel is visible between distant islands. The Commission has banished the freighters until spring. Farther away, across the invisible border, lie the northern shores of New York State. A mile downstream, the Thousand Islands International Bridge, and the Skydeck, which corkscrews gaudily into the blue, preside over it all—the blue cliffs and brief, sharp tumbles of scree, braids of water too agitated to freeze. It is Christmas Day in Ontario's Thousand Islands.

He is about to limp away, begin more productive work, when a flicker of movement causes him to wheel around. A man, he thinks. Gone now, but a moment ago peering in through the glass panel set into the main door.

Tim crosses the room, navigates around the oak lectern he bought at a Harrowsmith auction to hold the reservation book, now lost. The path that winds between pruned cedar shrubs is deserted and there are no vehicles in the plowed parking lot. The remaining snow is packed hard and resists footprints. A raven lifts heavily from the telephone wire and drops to the ground. It pecks at a brown stain, bounces around it for a better angle. Tim's breath clouds the door.

Finally he turns away. Even if someone is out there, that's not so remarkable. A photograph of him lost in contemplation amid the mess of his restaurant might make a serviceable accompaniment to a magazine article or human interest follow-up story. It is foolish to think there will be nothing else, that the media will abandon him completely. But an alarm has sounded deep in his head. It might be muffled by all the signals that say there is nothing here, calm yourself, you idiot, but still it rings. He paces the perimeter of the room like a wounded zoo animal.

A clanging from the kitchen reminds him that Rebecca is still here. She would not want to see him like this. She would say he is being irrational, that the worst has passed and she needs him to be strong. Her voice would have a desperate, thin edge. He knows these things as clearly as if they have already happened.

And so he begins to dismantle the mountain of chairs. He takes the first and carries it to the far end of the room. He positions its back nearly against the glass. His intention, so far as he has an intention, is to stand them in a long line and to leave the centre of the room empty. Then he will sweep the floor and wipe down the chairs with a damp cloth.

He is untangling the third chair when he hears a car pull into the lot. He goes again to the door. The three spots at the northern limit of the parking lot are obscured by a massive erratic dropped by a receding glacier at the end of the last ice age. A Kingston contractor persuaded Tim's father that, rather than paying good money to have it moved, he should consider it an asset. An added attraction. And so Michael arranged for a thick acrylic plate engraved with the restaurant's name to be attached to the rock by means of two steel rods. A prefatory note inside the menu explained the erratic's origins and also the "knob and hollow" nature of the landscape. The curious diner learned that at last count there were 1,149 islands scattered in the Seaway, give or take, and that when continental glaciation ended, the Great Lakes found a new route to the ocean and the St. Lawrence River was born (in the "hollows"). The islands (or "knobs") are actually the tips of ancient hills.

Tim strains to see around the rock. He opens the door and is assaulted by a surprising wind. The skin on his face and hands freezes instantly, his eyes smart and water. After three tentative steps outside, his knee buckles. He puts his hands out and a spear of pain digs into his neck so sharply that he yelps and smashes helplessly onto his side. He stays there, observing the black sedan tucked in next to the recycling bins. When the back doors open simultaneously and disgorge two men—big men, in black overcoats, with twin buzz cuts—Tim has seen enough. He slithers backwards, hauls himself over the wooden step and staggers to his feet. He closes the door carefully and then bolts it. Already he is breathless. He pushes, nearly blind, between the swinging saloon doors and into the kitchen.

Rebecca is arranging greens on a plate: pushing torn leaves of endive closer together, encouraging its crenellated edges to mesh, placing oyster mushrooms on top of that bright, fresh nest. Expertly she wipes the plate's rim with a spotless white cloth, spinning the china so the cotton between her thumb and fingers acts as a brake to its wheel.

"We have to keep our strength up," she says brightly. "So I thought . . ."

He studies her, incredulous.

"Lunch," she says. "It's nothing special. Not turkey or anything. But maybe tonight. There must be a decent piece of meat in one of the freezers. We really should make an effort, don't you think?"

He nods, but also bites at his lower lip, and he knows that she sees it, as well as the snow on his pant leg and stomach, the trickle of blood on his palm.

She steps from behind her counter, smearing her hands across the front of her apron. She glances at him as she passes. "What's happened?" She nudges one of the doors open and gazes into the dining room.

He knows what she sees. A room, mostly empty. She also hears, perhaps, the tick of the radiators, and the wind whipping around the corner of the house. It is unlikely, given the date, but she might even distinguish the mosquito-ish buzz of a fisherman starting his ice drill, or the scrape as he drags his hut roughly away from the shore. But these are background noises, static. They are not important.

She regards him carefully. "What is it?" She touches his shoulder. "There's nothing out there."

He shakes his head and breaks away.

"Tim," she says, "you're scaring me."

He tells her, "He's sent someone else."

He can see from her expression, how she squints slightly, cocks her head disbelievingly, that she wants to see in him the seed of madness, or paranoia, because it strikes her that those would be preferable, frankly, to the alternative.

He rushes around turning off the sleek Aga grill, the matching gas oven, extinguishing all the flames in case Rebecca is right, because then they will have to come back, and he doesn't want the house to burn down. He is positive they must run, but that doesn't exclude the possibility he is wrong.

"Come on," he says.

Rebecca is shaking her head, fumbling with the knot she has tied in her apron cord. He grabs her arm.

"This isn't happening," she says. "It can't be."

"It is," he says gruffly, obscurely annoyed, and he pulls her to the door at the back of the kitchen, the one that leads into the private side of the house.

He releases her, and she follows him through his office and into the den. He points. "Downstairs."

"But where are we going?" she says.

"I don't know."

They rummage through the basement closet. Tim looks over his shoulder, through the window that gives directly onto the long slope to the water. The sun is obscured now by the outdoor deck that hangs above this level and accommodates another dozen guests in summer, making it necessary to hire more staff.

It has been no more than two minutes. He wrestles a thick green jacket free of its hanger and then dives to the floor for boots. Rebecca has disappeared into a parka with rabbit fur at the cuffs and around the hem, the hood. He wonders how well she will run in that outfit, whether she will slow them down, and despises himself for the thought. "Do you need boots?" he asks.

She shakes her head. "Running shoes," and she lifts a foot off the ground to show him. She is shivering already, and a delicate silver and turquoise earring swings against her pale cheek. He hunts for words that might reassure her, but they would all be lies. Even putting on coats seems ridiculous. They will be dead before the cold gets to them.

"Then let's run." He wrestles with the lock and yanks open the door. A dry pine needle blows into the room. It tumbles, a brown gymnast, across the tiled floor. They charge outside, and he hears the patio door being pulled back. Someone steps onto the deck and the frozen planking creaks. He looks up and sees a man leaning against the balcony railing.

Tim and Rebecca careen down the slope. Where there are gaps in the trees, snow has made white islands in the red-brown sea. His legs are leaden. The cold has already frozen the inside of his nose. Rebecca is six metres ahead, sliding on her backside over a sheet of smooth rock. He was wrong; she is better at this than he is.

They reach a narrow, uneven footpath that traces the shoreline. The air burns in his chest and throat, and Rebecca is panting. She scans the route they have taken down from the house, but there is little to see. The deck is partly visible; the door they emerged from has blown shut, and they have carved a dark, moist track. But no threat, not yet.

"Could you be wrong?" Rebecca asks, hands on her hips, bent forward slightly to catch her breath.

An unfamiliar voice floats down to them: "Down there. Go around."

"This way," Tim says, and they set off to the left.

They scamper along the shore. In the distance, the green iron bridge. On the lake, huts stand guard over the unattended holes fishermen have made. He hears Rebecca's parka rustling, their feet crunching into the snow, and these noises combine to mask whatever chase has begun. At one point, rounding a curve, he catches Rebecca's face in sharp profile against the pure blown surface of the lake. Fear has flooded her. Her eyes look to be focusing inwards, as if she has already stopped seeing the world.

He wants to offer her hope and he considers turning, running towards whoever it is that comes after them, screaming blue murder. Instead he leaves the track and runs down onto the ice. Wind has blown the surface clear. They won't leave tracks out here. And if they can sprint even a hundred metres this way, then cut back into the forest, make it to the road, to a neighbour's, perhaps they have a chance. They will have to time it right. They must head up before their pursuers round the bend and sight them.

They thump, boom across the ice. The skin on the lake here is eight or nine inches. Plenty thick enough. But there are faults, pressure breaks, and they could still plunge through, then rise in a more solid spot. The stuff of nightmares. Massive boulders that poke their heads above the surface in the fall, when the water level drops, are visible beneath them like grey ghosts. He scans the treeline, looking for the best route up. He thinks he hears voices, but he cannot be sure.

And then, suddenly, it is imperative that they hide themselves again. Rebecca veers shorewards, and looks for some sign of agreement.

"Yes," he says, and the word drains him. He follows her. They plow into a drift that has built up between the ice mass and the onshore track. It is waist-deep and eats him up. He will surely die here. They will put a bullet in his brain. The snow will fill with his blood. But then his foot finds purchase on a root and he is up.

Rebecca leads until, on their left, a wide, humped plane of granite stretches away into the trees. The last swooping gasp of the Canadian Shield. He has walked here before, even named this great arcing slab: the Whale Back. They clamber onto its hard-veined nose.

"I felt them," Rebecca gasps. "On the ice. The vibrations. They weren't ours."

"Could you tell how many?"

"At least a couple, I think."

"If we can get to the top of this ridge without them seeing us . . ." he tells her.

"Right."

"We might be okay."

They make it halfway before he hears them. They stop, crouch, and then, hearing the voices clearly, they lie flat. He rotates, crablike, enough to see the shoreline. Four men. Three of them out on the ice, another following the irregular curve of the track. All four with guns drawn, and all moving confidently, as if from habit. Another 30 metres and they will find the spot where he and Rebecca came ashore. They are covering ground slowly, scanning the trees, watching their feet. Only two of them wear jackets. They obviously hadn't expected him to run.

He moves on his stomach, like a snake now. He wriggles and rustles to where the rock ends abruptly in some spots and in others angles down to the forest floor. Rebecca follows him to the edge. They work along the rock, always moving away from the men. Always uphill.

He extends his head over the edge, like a tortoise testing the air. They are on an overhang; the ground here works slightly under the rock. It isn't a cave exactly, more a recess, but deeply shaded, and not an obvious hiding place. He lowers himself gently. Rebecca follows, and he reaches up to guide her. He feels her weight in his arms, notes that he has taken her by the waist, that her toes point at the ground, search for it. It seems to him they are performing the last few moves of a tragic ballet.

They crawl as far under the ledge as possible. The rock forms a forty-five-degree angle to the ground. At first they huddle together, heads bowed uncomfortably, knees drawn up to their chests, shoulder to shoulder. Tim reaches up and touches her cold cheek.

Rebecca whispers, "We should lie down, head to toe."

She is right. By stretching themselves out they will almost disappear into the angle. But it means leaving her side. It means being alone and perhaps never talking to her again.

They do it anyway. Rebecca braces herself against the rock face and he pushes pine needles against her body, tries to erase her from the world. He moves into place below her, his head against her feet, and scoops in more debris, a few twigs, a branch with pine cones still attached. He is convinced these are the saddest moments of his life.

The men climb the rock together. They cough. One of them stops, tries to stamp the cold out of his feet. "It's like deer hunting," he says. His voice is accented, rough.

Another of them replies, "Perhaps they made it into the next bay."

"They didn't have time. No, they're up here somewhere. Search along the edge too."

Tim wants to reach an arm over his head, take hold of Rebecca's ankle. He stares out mournfully into the bleak winter wood and scrub. His home and restaurant have disappeared; they may as well not exist any more.

Two feet in front of him is the corpse of a goldfinch. He must have uncovered it when he raked in the undergrowth. The bird's beak still shines yellow-green and seems fashioned from bamboo. The eyes, though, are dull. One wing is splayed open and shows itself off. Maggots have eaten into the stomach and their excavation has left a blue-grey frozen hollow. The feet are missing. He studies the bird, that frozen two or three ounces, as a man walks out onto the ledge above them.

"I fucking hate this," the man growls, and then he undoes his zipper and urinates onto the ground. A bright stream arcs from the ledge and rains down on the dead finch. Its feathers thaw and ruffle. Piss pours into its hollow body.

PART ii

DECEMBER 1

Ground Control at Newark had ordered Continental Flight 460, arriving from St. Thomas, United States Virgin Islands, to slow its approach. By eleven minutes past five o'clock in the afternoon, rush hour, it had been circling for twenty minutes. The fields below the jet were black and the roads were wet. Drivers had their headlights on, and off to the east New York City was changing into its evening gown of gold and silver. In the north the sky was dark, a storm building at the horizon. Passengers were gathering their things. Struggling into socks for the first time in weeks, tugging sweaters and cardigans over freshly tanned arms. An attendant moved quietly down the aisle collecting plastic cups and half-empty soft drink cans.

In seat 3A, first class, John Selby had his eyes closed. In the seatback pouch in front of him were neatly folded copies of *The Economist* and today's *New York Times*. Early in the flight he had hidden behind them when his neighbour threatened to strike up a long conversation.

He had enjoyed St. Thomas. He had stayed on the north shore in a pretty cottage suite that clung like a limpet mine to the upper reaches of a steep cliff dense with cacti and ferns. From the balcony he could see the island of St. John and, over its forested shoulder, Tortola. At night the lights of ferries and fishing boats glittered in the distance. Most days he contented himself with the tiny beach at the bottom of the cliff. He felt the sun collecting in his arms and legs. He had become, he thought, simply a man on vacation. One morning he walked west along the busy curve of Sapphire Beach and then for a while along the road at its far end. He veered off-road again onto Coki Beach and snorkelled for more than an hour. A cruise ship minivan released a dozen revellers who jostled with him for access to the mild but fish-filled coral canyons.

That same evening Selby sat at Fungi's, a ramshackle beachside bar, sipping Heineken. It was his forty-first birthday. A pelican sat on the nose of a kayak tethered to a wooden pole. An iguana nearly three feet long had stationed itself under Selby's table. A football game was showing on the TV behind the bar, and the bartender plainly didn't give a damn about business.

On the last morning, Selby's cab driver turned out to be a moonlighting island paramedic who drove with his stethoscope draped casually, but also proudly, around his neck. Its silver ear rested on the man's ample stomach and gleamed brilliantly in the sun, like a talisman that contained enough modern magic to protect them both.

"You on your way home?" the driver enquired. "You going back to work now, man?"

Selby nodded. Yes, that's exactly where he was going. "You bet," he said. It had been a year since his employers had called. As promised, they had left him alone. But now, they said, it was time. They needed him again, for something new.

Eventually Flight 460 made contact again with the earth. John Selby was the third person off the plane. The air on the ramp was cold; he could see his breath. Outside, a youth in a toque and swollen down jacket was jumping up and down to stay warm. Selby ambled into the terminal and almost immediately he saw Sonny Rockliff—at a corner table in Starbucks, chuckling at something in *Vanity Fair*.

Sonny looked up furtively from his magazine and when he saw John he grinned, slapped the covers together, rolled the issue into a tight cylinder, and jammed it in his jacket pocket. Then he was on his feet and advancing. The effect was of a retriever puppy seeing its owner for the first time in days. If you loved the dog, John supposed, the sight would warm your heart.

"Well, well. Mr. Selby, I presume," Sonny said. His blue eyes glistened and he held out a soft white paw. He was only two years younger than John, but with his artfully dishevelled blond hair and the scruffy goatee, he could have passed for a man in his late twenties; a college professor, perhaps, or a film critic.

John thought of the pelicans on St. Thomas, how they folded up so carelessly before plummeting into the surf, how every time it happened he thought they would break every bone and die.

They drove along wide, dreary streets. Sonny guided the steering wheel with only the tips of his fingers. He ran his white tongue over chapped lips. "It's not a bad place," he said, as if John had invited the assessment. "Lot cheaper than across the river. Winter's a bastard, but what can you do?" He took his eyes off the road. "Doesn't look like you've had too much to do with winter lately."

They had worked together, briefly, in Atlanta in 1996. Rockliff had headed up an FBI security unit during the summer Olympics. He was ambitious, had climbed quickly in the organization. John was brought home from his Bureau assignment in Berlin to review some of the preparations. Sonny knew this was his chance to shine but was made insecure by the arrival of more seasoned men and women from around the globe. He was mostly unpopular from the start. Inexplicably, he saw John as an ally, and John was careful not to dissuade him from this position. When the games were over, and before John returned to Germany, Sonny had even invited him to spend some days with his young family. John especially remembered a night by their bottom-lit pool. Sonny and his wife Lara had plied him with bourbon, and John had told them how, in a week, he would be back in Berlin, going over transcripts of phone conversations, meeting with union leaders in steel factories, police officers in hidden soundproof bunkers. There would be no more evenings like this, he had said.

John had been mildly surprised to learn a month ago that Sonny Rockliff's career with the FBI had gone well, with good counterterrorism appointments in Seattle and New York. And that Sonny had asked for John personally when a new assignment opened up.

"How the hell did he know where I was?" he had asked Bill Frum. Bill had been John's liaison at the Bureau throughout his sabbatical.

"I don't think he did know," Bill said. "I think you were just the man he wanted and so he put out the word."

"I suppose he knows why I took the year off?"

"Because you were tired? Because you needed some time to recharge the old batteries? Hell, what's to know?"

"That's a generous interpretation. Thanks. So how did he get this new gig?"

"They like him, John. He's keen. Loyal. They keep him mostly at home, but he's a hell of an organizer. Can keep a hundred things going simultaneously if he has to. Very cool under pressure."

"This is the same Sonny Rockliff?"

"Give the guy a chance, John. And he wanted you, remember that.

A lot of men would love to get in tight with him these days. Money's no object; there's plenty of support. And besides, in a couple of months you'll be done. Then you can both decide whether you want to work with each other. As far as I can tell, it's strictly a one-off deal. You're not locked in to anything."

"So tell me about this . . . what is it . . . the BVC? How is it they get to just pluck anyone they want from the FBI?"

"The Border Vigilance Commission, right. Well, there are offices in Newark and Dallas. The Texas outfit deals with the Mexican border, and the Newark site is all about Canada. Their mandate is to make sure Canadian and Mexican procedures are in line with ours. And to make sure those nations understand the gravity of the situation. Meaning we won't hesitate to point the finger should any*body* or any-*thing* unpleasant find its way into our country."

"Wouldn't that be our fault as much as theirs?"

"Don't be a clever bastard, John. The BVC is also, with the full cooperation of the host countries, allowed to place a number of agents on-site. Their job is to root out terrorists, smugglers, your whole range of ne'er-do-well shitheads, and identify them to the authorities. Stop them before they get a foot in the door, in other words."

"You're talking about an expansion of the legal attaché program."

"Exactly. We put agents abroad and connect them to the embassy. They work in tandem with in-place law enforcement."

"And how do Canada and Mexico feel about all this?"

"They're jumping all over themselves to help, John. We're one hundred percent unified on this issue. Just as we should be."

"And what does Rockliff have in mind for me, exactly?"

"You'll have to ask him that yourself, my friend. I'm afraid the loop these days is very small."

And that was it in the way of preparation. John had spent his last free days jogging along sun-blasted curves of Caribbean beach, count-ing out push-ups and chin-ups before dinner because he worried he wasn't ready any more for the rigours of active duty.

Now Sonny Rockliff turned the car onto one of Newark's quieter tree-lined streets. The homes were older, surprisingly graceful. A lit-tle snow clung to the tree trunks.

"How's Lara?"

Sonny nodded enthusiastically.

"And your little girl?"

"Not so little any more."

"I suppose not."

"She misses her friends. She likes the snow, though. And she swims." Sonny looked over. "Oh, you should see Madison *swim*, John. The girl's a regular mermaid."

"I bet."

It was conversation scripted for when there was nothing to talk about, as disposable as Kleenex.

Sonny parked eventually behind a bank building. A locked steel door beside the automated teller machine opened onto a spacious but windowless foyer, with a marble floor that reflected nearly as well as a mirror. An elevator, oak-lined, fast, and silent, transported them to the eighth floor. Sonny said, "We have more public space downtown, but this is where it happens."

They stood behind glass. New York City at the horizon, rising mythically into cloud. Behind them a gas fire and a circular teak conference table. It was Nordic somehow. There might have been skis on the wall. Snowshoes. On the way in, Sonny had acknowledged a young well-dressed man working a reception desk. And along a wood-panelled corridor that seemed never to end John had spied at least two dozen office doors, most of them open. People were moving with enviable speed and efficiency, a strong sense of their collective importance, despite the late hour. There were other rooms with steel doors and guards posted.

"This is a different sort of set-up," he said. "How's the mortgage?"

"Fully paid up. We're free and clear, John. The President wants us thinking with a clear head."

"I can understand that."

"A lot has changed since you went overseas. There are new priorities. Homeland Security is big business."

"I was affected by those events too, Sonny."

Sonny inclined his head. His sideburns, John noticed, extended well below his earlobes and were flecked lightly with grey. "I know you were, John. Absolutely." Sonny made some complicated movements in the air with his hands. "We're in it together. And I wanted to say that right away, first thing. So that you know."

John shrugged. This speech reeked of motive and self-interest, it registered as disingenuous and he didn't like that. He liked least of all that there were already things that needed to be said.

He turned away and stared off at the changed city. He realized with a start that this was the moment, after more than a year, when he had properly registered the terrible absence out there. He stared at the distant oblongs of sky freshly revealed without a clue in the world what it meant, or how it changed him, precisely. He knew only that it did, and to his core. He felt as ineloquent as a baby.

They sat opposite each other at the teak table, ten feet between them. They were strangers, Selby thought, but Rockliff had commanded his presence, had ordered him across a good part of the world to be here. And so it was. Because of the city outside the window and what had happened there.

"How do you feel?"

"Rested," John acknowledged. "I feel rested and ready to work again."

Sonny rooted his elbows to the tabletop and positioned his chin on his intertwined fingertips—a caricature of thoughtfulness. "What do you know about waste disposal, John?" John leaned forward but Sonny wasn't finished. "Specifically cross-border waste disposal. Canadian garbage being shipped into the U.S."

"It's not my strong suit."

"And no reason it should be. Okay, try this for starters. Four and a half percent of the trash dumped in Michigan comes from Canada. Toronto's landfill site is about used up and so everything goes south. Hundreds of trucks every day clog up the border. Eight hundred thousand tons of garbage each year."

"Sounds more like something we'd do to them."

"That's almost un-American of you, John," Sonny said flatly.

"I don't think so. But it does sound like a nightmare."

"How so?" Sonny said.

John smiled. He felt confident here, more so than he had expected. "Off the top of my head, it sounds pretty awful environmentally. So I don't suppose the governor likes it much. Or if he does, I don't suppose the citizens like him. But it must bring in a lot of money."

"About fifty bucks a ton. And he's a she, by the way. The governor of Michigan is a woman."

"My mistake," John said. "But fifty bucks. That's not peanuts."

"Sure."

"And the environment isn't the main reason the BVC is interested, right? More likely you're worried about those trucks crossing the border loaded with unmentionables every day. I suppose you could hide damn near anything in all that trash. You can't X-ray it, you can't expect the dogs to find anything in all that stench, and you can't very well pick through it in any efficient way. So you have to trust the carrier. Or you have to stop the traffic."

"We can't stop the traffic. A 1992 Supreme Court ruling makes it illegal for a state to refuse waste without congressional assent."

"Even international trash?"

"Free trade, John. And a deal's a deal."

"So what about this congressional assent?"

"Dedicated men and women have been lobbying hard for just such a measure."

"And why isn't that working?"

"The waste disposal industry is a powerful monster. A beast. These aren't mom-and-pop operations."

"So what are we doing?"

"Immediately following the World Trade Center we held everything up at the border. It created a backup twenty-five miles long. We checked some of it, we turned some of it back. But you can't do that forever. Free trade is free trade."

"Okay. So how real is the possibility of using these trucks to smuggle something in? What are we talking about—drugs, explosives, weapons, people?"

"People are pretty unlikely. That trash gets compacted more than once. It's not like you can wrap yourself up in black plastic and hop on board. The containers are also closed and locked. The compacting procedures should rule out the other three too, but let's face it, that's a lot of traffic. I've looked at those trucks. It wouldn't be difficult to add a lock-box to the inside. Or you could just give something to the driver. Those guys don't usually get searched. They have to pass a security check just to hold the job, but tell me that's foolproof. Tell me one of those guys isn't having trouble paying the rent and wouldn't mind five hundred bucks in his pocket for carrying a little extra in his lunch box, or for throwing a couple of extra bags into the middle of that shit. It's a goddamn disaster-in-waiting."

"I begin to see that."

"And here's the real nightmare scenario. What if just one truck a year somehow bypasses the compacting procedure, or isn't loaded with trash at all? And what if our inventory control doesn't pick up on that? Imagine for a minute a massive truck loaded with contraband that we don't intercept. That's a shitload of trouble. Christ, it's enough explosive to arm every idiot for a generation, it's guns and passports for everyone and their mother. Enough chemicals to poison every reservoir in the land. It's even a primitive nuclear device, which means game over."

"So what are we doing?"

"As far as the nuclear threat goes, because it's the most serious, we've issued inspectors with radiation-detection devices they wear on their lapels. If that thing starts flashing, all hell will break loose. We've also positioned high-density X-ray machines that give us a pretty decent look inside the containers."

"What else?"

"Mostly we're giving them a hard time. We reserve the right to pull any of your trucks off the road at any time. We reserve the right to turn you back if any of your paperwork is out of order. We turn you back if you can't show us a signature proving you picked up your trash at the allotted place and time. We turn you back if it took you too long to get to the border or if you show up a day early. We kick you out if you look at us funny."

"Sounds okay."

"Sure. But still, it's kid's stuff. These trucks are the size of cargo planes." He rubbed his face with his hands. "And to top it all, there are independents who run a few trucks for the big boys. We have to keep track of them too. It's a full-time job. I tell you, John, checking Canada's shit could run away with our budget, if I were a paranoid man."

"Which you're not."

"Absolutely not. This is a real problem."

"What do the Canadians say? Is there another option for them?"

Sonny scooped a sheet of paper from the tabletop. "Here it is." He scanned the document for highlights. "The Canadians respect our 'need for caution both in regards to the environmental impact' of their trash 'and with respect to the possible security issues it presents.'" He waved the sheet like a flag. "They have an abandoned mine up north. It's a perfect site. Solid bedrock underneath, small local population, plus it's in Canada. They were going to put it all up there, but negotiations went sour. The carrier wanted Toronto on the hook for "unavoidable costs." The city balked. We've got people working on that angle too, but it's a slow process. Something about non-interference in the affairs of a foreign country. It isn't going to happen overnight. And it's now, today, that our nation is worried by this."

"So where do I fit in?"

Sonny pushed up out of his chair and moved theatrically to the window. "One of the independents has caught our eye. We don't like the look of him. The Canadians swear he's just a wealthy immigrant. They say they've done all the necessary checks and we've got nothing to worry about. Can you imagine the nerve—*Don't worry about it*? I whispered two words in their ears. I said to them: 'Ahmed Ressam.'"

"He's the guy who wanted to blow up the airport in Los Angeles? Came across from Vancouver with a trunk full of alarm clocks or some other damn thing?"

"That's right. He claimed refugee status up there, and when that claim failed he went underground. You can imagine how they blushed when I brought him up. I told them if they didn't mind we'd check for ourselves, thank you very much."

"So I'm the checker. Who is this guy you're worried about?"

"This is him." From a drawer hidden below the lip of the table Sonny withdrew a silver remote control and aimed it at the wall. The bottom edge of that wood-panelled surface rose like a garage door and slid beneath the top moulding, revealing a checkerboard of television screens.

"Fancy," John said. "Very James Bond."

Sonny stabbed at the remote and the surface of each screen flickered, then burst into light.

"What are we looking at?"

Sonny was momentarily flustered. "We don't need most of these on, actually." He glared at the instrument in his hand.

"Sure, but where are these places?"

"The top three are the Arrivals areas at the airports. Second row are border crossings. The third is a currency exchange, a car and truck rental, and a swimming pool. The fourth are tapes from yesterday I want to look at again. That man bottom right is yours."

He was in his mid-thirties. A man eating dinner. European. Good suit, platinum cufflinks. Decent teeth, stylish haircut. He needed a shave, or maybe he cultivated that length of stubble. Nails trimmed. Knew how to properly wield a knife and fork. He was eating alone, a newspaper folded neatly to the right of his plate. There was a glass of red wine and the occasional glance off-screen. He read intently and chewed his food slowly. Meticulous was the impression he gave. But with something cruel in the dismissive way he dealt with the waitress. All the better: if you were going to hunt a man down, you had better not find him likeable.

"Tell me more," John said.

"Nikolai Petrovitch. Born 1965, Moscow. His mother was a painter, father ran a bicycle manufacturing factory on the outskirts. Nothing unusual so far as we can tell. But then his parents are killed in a winter car crash and he inherits the bike factory. By selling an interest in that business he was able to raise enough capital to buy an apartment building from the government when it became possible to do so. Within a month he'd sold that building and was able to buy three more. And also a government-run optician's. Things snowballed. It was easy, once you had a little money, a little collateral. The problem for most Russians was getting a foothold, even a toehold, in the market. And others simply missed the opportunities. After all, who would want to own any of these buildings? They hadn't been maintained in decades. The wiring was dangerous. Men were killed because they took hold of the wrong switch. Elevators were plunging into basement floors. The water was brown. So at the beginning, the pickings were easy. The government would call him: "We thought you might be interested in a new property we have decided to sacrifice . . ."

"Within three years he was a wealthy man. But then the government realized, overnight it seemed, what had happened. The concentration of such wealth in so few hands. The influence these men were wielding. And so there was a period when they tried to reverse course. Petrovitch, not knowing what this might lead to, fled the country. He travelled overland to Poland and then Finland, and flew from there to Gander, Newfoundland. Eventually he applied for landed immigrant status. Which, with a healthy bank balance and a promise to establish legitimate businesses and to employ Canadian workers, he received with little difficulty. He still has serious interests in Moscow. Apartment buildings that a half-brother maintains, for example."

"Where did you shoot this video?"

"In Toronto. Nikolai's a predictable man to some extent. He has a favourite table."

"And how recent is this stuff?"

"This is just last week. But the video's a bust. It turns out he eats alone, never reads anything we're interested in, and never talks on the phone from there. We thought it was stupid to leave the equipment in place."

"And he owns a piece of the waste disposal business?"

"He owns trucks," Sonny said. "And the people who have the contract needed more trucks. Petrovitch lobbied hard for that subcontract. Now he leases the trucks and the drivers to the haulage company."

"And why don't you trust him? I get the general drift here, but is there a trigger?"

"A month back we did a regular survey of the week's arrests in New York. Turned up two Russians lording it over Manhattan. They started a fight with some Rangers fans in a nightclub. Beat the shit out of them. Both of them claimed to be drivers for Petrovitch. Just taking a break, they claimed. All their paperwork was in order, and their log sheets. But one of them had twenty-eight thousand in cash in his jacket. The other had eighteen thou."

"A lot of cash for truck drivers to be carting around."

"Both of them were wearing suits worth two grand and six-hundred-dollar shoes. One had a briefcase chained to his wrist. Completely empty."

"How did they explain that?"

"Unsatisfactorily. Which makes it necessary to put someone up there, see what the hell our Mr. Petrovitch is up to."

"What do the Canadians say?"

"Like I said, they've got nothing on him. Petrovitch is well connected, he's made a shitload of money, hangs with a tough crowd, but their most recent security checks turn up nothing significant."

"And when do you want me up there?"

"Within a day or two. I'll show you around the office a bit first. Let you meet some people. Show you the paperwork and explain the entry strategy we've got figured out for you. We've also lined up a contact or two within Canadian law enforcement."

"Entry strategy? You want me to actually make contact?"

"Of course."

"To what end?"

"The paper trail's gone cold. Ditto for surveillance."

"Have the Canadians tried to insert anyone?"

"Not successfully."

"What does that mean?"

But Sonny was up and leaving. There was a new briskness to him. He seemed more self-contained. He was hitting his stride maybe, justifying his salary. "You'll do fine," he said. "And you *will* find something. Understood? I want this man out of the business." He paused, then returned. He moved a chair aside so he could lean on the table. "Where there's smoke there's fire, John. I want this guy's wings clipped. Actually, it's more than that. I want his goddamn wings cut off at the shoulder." He stood up very straight and put his shoulders back. "I want to be able to report that I put an agent in this guy's life and we proved beyond a shadow of doubt he was a threat."

Sonny's run-on metaphors swirled in John's head. "Even if . . .?"

Sonny waved him off. "He's trouble, period. We're worried about much more than garbage trucks here, John. The border we share with Canada is nearly four thousand miles long. That's what this guy has to play with. It's about twice the length of the Mexican border."

John said that surprised him.

"Good. Then this next statistic will absolutely shock you." Sonny stabbed the polished teak tabletop. "We've got about sixteen thousand customs and border guards along the Mexican border. But up here it will be a year or two before it even reaches five thousand customs agents and nine hundred border patrol. A couple of years ago—get this—the total was only two thousand."

John whistled appreciatively, but chose to see the positive side of things. "So we're nearly tripling our commitment. That's good. And we don't have the same illegal immigration issues up here."

"It's not perfect, not nearly, but I can deal with the new numbers," Sonny allowed. "I can make them work. All the same, historically our limited presence up here has been an open invitation to invade, or to set up some malignant import business. Criminals have the mindset that it's easy to get into the U.S. What we need to do is make them rethink that assumption. I honestly believe that's just as important as hiring more guards. And you're dead wrong, by the way, about illegal immigration not being a problem."

John inclined his head slightly, as if bowed down by the weight of Sonny's alarming figures.

"Let me give you an analogy, John. Until a year ago the number of guards along the Canada-U.S. border was equivalent to having only a couple of security guards at each of our international airports. It was fucking ridiculous. It gave the criminal element infinite options. And even now, sure, we can turn Petrovitch and his garbage trucks away at the Peace Bridge every day until doomsday, but if he wants to get in, he'll find a way. He'll drive to Alberta and come across a farmer's field in the dead of night. He'll go to Niagara and swim across the river."

"That sounds a bit drastic."

"Niagara, you mean? It is," Sonny conceded, "because there are a hundred easier ways for him. But thankfully our leaders are now fully cognizant of that reality."

"It all sounds very ominous," John said. "You must lie awake nights."

Sonny shrugged. "As I've said, we're making great strides. It's not all doom and gloom. But not all the work's done. There are still ways to circumvent the system. Which is precisely why you're here. If Petrovitch is abusing his import licence, I want you to find out how he does it, and what he's bringing in. And if he's got other interests, other routes—if he's got accomplices, associates—I want you to uncover those, too. Which is a difficult agenda to work on properly unless we have you infiltrate."

"I'm to plug a hole, then," John said. "That's the assignment."

For some reason Sonny bristled; he tugged at his goatee. "If the work doesn't sound important enough for you," he said, waving an arm, "just let me know right now. Is it not subtle enough, is that it? Are our northern schemes too blunt?"

"No, it's not that."

"We do nearly $1.5 billion every *day* in trade with Canada," Sonny said, still riled. "Think about that number for a second. Think about what it would mean if something happened that necessitated closing that border. The whole fucking hemisphere would grind to a halt, John. There is nothing *small* about this assignment, I can assure you."

This was the Sonny Rockliff John remembered. The defensive, back-against-the-wall posture. The hothead. "You've got me all wrong," he said gently.

"Have I really?" Sonny was suspicious still, and flushed.

"Absolutely. I'm flattered more than anything. I think that's what it is. After all, we weren't working together very long. It's nice of you to remember me, much less bring me in for something like this. I thought my re-entry into active duty might be difficult. I took a year off, and you know how people like to assume the worst."

Sonny pulled again at his beard. "You were in Berlin, John. It's a world away. No one even thinks about you when you're that far away. And besides, it's like banging your head against a brick wall over there. All the goddamn paperwork. All that unnatural *openness*. We fully expect our agents to need some downtime after enduring that posting for as long as you did." He said "openness" as though it disgusted him, as though it caused a bad smell to fill the room. "I don't know how you stood it at all, to be honest. Although I hear it's a bit better now."

"Apparently."

"Perhaps you had something to do with that. You never know." He ran a finger across the teak.

"Now you flatter me," John said. It felt as though they had just made up after a quick fight. It was an awful feeling. John was sweating, anxious, and Sonny looked much the same way.

John pointed again at the screens. "So why the swimming pool?"

"Madison swims there," Sonny said sheepishly. He marched around for the remote control and extinguished the monitors. "You weren't supposed to see that. But it's just around the corner. Every morning. I drop her off and get in here as fast as I can so I can watch her."

"Is there someone at the pool?"

"Yes, but no one's going to watch over her the way I do," he said.

"I remember you saying she has talent," John prompted.

Sonny nodded proudly, comfortable now, and placed a hand in the small of John's back as they left the room together. "She does," he said. "It runs in the family."

DECEMBER 2

As if intent on erasing the event, a thick soft snow had been falling all morning. An old black tractor hunched in the southeast corner of the graveyard like a glassy-eyed dinosaur, the steel teeth on the leading edge of its metal bucket still grimed with earth from Michael Hollins' grave.

Tim had wanted to be the first to arrive. He wanted to stare down into the hole that would soon swallow his father. A light snow settled on the back of his hands, his neck, the bridge of his nose, and on his top lip. He stood beside the fresh still-dark grave. Soil and stone were scattered generally and there was a body-sized mound of earth. A mess of tractor tread was already fading.

They never knew each other, he thought, not really. But there was nothing unusual in that. Many of his friends complained of the same gulf, the same sad space in their lives. Even though they had both lived in Toronto for years, Tim and Michael had grown steadily more distant. Particularly after his mother's early death. But then Michael Hollins was an important man, a widower with little time any more for the intricacies and minefields of family relationships. Before his retirement he had been the best-known lobbyist in a country that liked to think itself above such shenanigans. His name had been attached almost weekly to one project or another, and it hadn't been at all unusual to see his face on the Citytv news broadcast, or even on CBC's *The National*. Michael had been portrayed frequently as a cutthroat negotiator, and he was villainized towards the end of his career. Tim had some sympathy for his father's position that this represented nothing more than a Canadian fear of success, but he also knew that Michael had aligned himself willingly with big business interests and become the point man for some dubious individuals. Tim also saw, however, that Michael was energized by his battles and thought that perhaps history would re-evaluate his contributions. "Canada needs more men like me, not less," Michael had insisted, and sometimes Tim was inclined to agree.

For his part, Tim had been partner for nearly ten years in a catering company, Not Popcorn, that worked mostly film sets and industry parties. Tim was the logistical whiz, the chief organizer. And while his white panel van might not have been as glamorous as his father's BMW, and his television appearances were limited to those occasions when he was caught in the background, tidying shrimp plates or icing down champagne, he was proud of what he'd accomplished. He had never had to ask Michael for help. He took the occasional lavish holiday and he owned a decent wardrobe. He was, he had long ago decided, his own man.

In September 1999 he secured an invitation for his father to the gala screening of a Canadian film in which Tim briefly appeared as a paid extra, and afterwards Michael deigned to attend the party. Tim was working, but the film's stars knew him by name and seemed genuinely to enjoy his company. The evening ran smoothly and the media coverage was impressive. Michael, though, remained unimpressed. "I eat in that room three or four times a month," he'd said the next day, "and you have to bust your balls for years to get through the doors with an apron on." He'd meant it as an observation on the fickleness of the profession, Tim decided charitably, but it ruined the memory. On another occasion, Tim was interviewed by a Hollywood production manager interested in having Not Popcorn set up a satellite operation in northern Ontario for two months, where they were filming a survival epic. The same afternoon Tim ran into his father. Michael wanted only to be given the man's phone number. "Why?" Tim asked him. "What the hell are you thinking? This is an issue of my ability, you know, not your almighty influence."

It was because of this estrangement, this sad lack of understanding, that when Michael retired from public life, Tim agreed (hesitantly) to spend a few months living in Kingston to help his father establish a new restaurant in the pretty village of Ivy Lea. He thought it was a chance to repair damage, perhaps a last chance, and so he took a leave of absence.

Granite attracted solid crowds from the outset. And Tim's enthusiasm for the joint venture surprised him. He rented a small apartment that looked over a steel sculpture along the waterfront. And he was happy. Toronto reviewers spoke of Granite as "an important presence on the culinary landscape" and of Tim as a man who "makes his experience felt." With the restaurant thriving, Michael seemed more inclined to engage his son in substantive conversations, rather than simply dispensing offhand advice, and Tim believed there might yet be a way for them to develop some real affection for each other. When, after six months, he sold his share of Not Popcorn, he did so in the belief that his father would surely offer him a legal partnership in Granite, and Tim was ready to accept. He liked the work, felt a rare peace standing at the long windows watching the cormorant that fished from the rocks at the shoreline and the shifting patterns and colours in the Seaway's waters. He was especially fond of the time he and Rebecca, the restaurant's chef, spent together. They had formed a quick, easy alliance that made the most testing times endurable. Now, with Michael dead, she was the only person he could talk to.

Beyond the low stone wall that traced the cemetery's perimeter, past a hundred metres of thick brush, was a sharp limestone cliff, and at its bottom a churning slush of water and ice. Golden lights were visible from the Thousand Islands Bridge. To the west there was a vague intimation of islands rising. *Dad would approve of this*, thought Tim. Two metres down, the view didn't mean a thing, but up above it was truly lovely. He tried uselessly to track a flake's drift, but the pain rose into his throat and there were hot tears on his cheeks. The last night his father was alive had burned its way to the surface.

The restaurant had emptied of its last customers. Michael was lounging in a chair near the doorway. Tim walked past with a tray crowded with glasses. When he had loaded the dishwasher his father was still there, his eyes closed. Bach's cello suites filled the room. They had installed floodlights at the base of the trees along the St. Lawrence and now they glowed yellow, were reflected nearly perfectly in the black cold water. A brown duck sat at the corner of the deck's railing, its head tucked under its wing.

Tables needed clearing and resetting. A burgundy cloth napkin had wrapped itself around the leg of a chair. The claw of a softshell crab had wound up next to the sliding door, as if, divorced from the rest of its body, it had made a final break for freedom.

"It'll wait," Michael said. "Join me. Please."

Tim sat cautiously. His father's invitation sounded suspiciously like an order, but it might also lead to the offer he had imagined. Together they surveyed the room. It was quiet but still seemed to contain the echoes of the evening's bustle, faint afterimages of men and women living it up, laughing gaily with their families.

His father pulled a cigarette from a pack on the table. He smoked rarely, but when he did it seemed the most decadent behaviour. Rebecca came in from the kitchen. She looked windswept and tired. Behind her was the industrial whoosh and metal grind of the dishwasher, the faint strains of a different music. She smiled. "I thought something must be going on out here."

Michael said, "We were thinking about whisky. *I* was thinking about whisky, anyway, and the silence seemed so companionable, so truly shared, that I can only assume my son was thinking about whisky also."

Tim nodded gently.

"It's settled, then." Michael asked Rebecca to bring a bottle from his office. He had put it aside specially, he said. He told her where it was.

When she returned he raised an eyebrow, seemed surprised, and so she showed him the bottle. It was unopened. "This one?"

He nodded but still seemed puzzled. "It was in the box?"

She assured him it was, then went back to the kitchen and brought them a small blue-ringed plate upon which tumbled a dozen black, wrinkled olives and some bread. A carafe of coffee and three white cups.

They stayed at the table together, mostly without talking, until the cello suites ended. Then Michael got up and began them again. He stood between his son and his chef and put a hand on each of their shoulders. It made Tim uncomfortable; it was as though his father was trying out a new, more physical role. After a few seconds he released his grip. "This goddamn music," he said. "It breaks my heart."

He told them he felt like a drive. "All night," he said, "I've been staring into that sky, thinking, let me at it. And now"—he looked at his watch dramatically—"it's time."

Tim offered to join him. "We could talk. We could go up to the bridge."

"I'm not looking for company, Tim. I want to drive. To feel the road slipping by under the wheels."

Rebecca walked outside with him anyway. And on that cool starlit, moonlit night, his father's old and much-loved BMW started with the first turn of the key.

"Was he okay?" Tim asked her when she came back.

"He seemed fine. Kind of cute, really. All introspective and brooding."

"I'll have to remember you find that an attractive quality," Tim said.

They returned to work. Rebecca wrote out a shopping list for the morning. Tim poured another whisky. They drank out of the same glass. Rebecca tapped a pencil against her teeth while she thought. Tim listened to the hum and tick of the refrigerator. His legs were tired; he could go to sleep, he thought.

At one o'clock in the morning Michael still hadn't returned. They talked about where he might have gone. Rebecca didn't want to leave until she knew he was safe.

"Perhaps he went to Gananoque," Tim said, "or even Kingston." Michael liked occasionally to sit at the bar of Casa Domenico, a favourite Italian restaurant, and swap war stories with the owner.

"That's probably it," Rebecca said. "Should I call them, do you think?"

Tim shook his head. "He wouldn't appreciate that. He'd say, 'I'm a grown man.' I can hear it now. You should go home. He'll be fine."

Rebecca said he was right, but then she fussed for another half hour in the kitchen, and Tim rewired a dining-room speaker that had been crackling all night.

There was a soft knock at the door just as Rebecca was putting on her coat. She would call when she got home, she was saying. Mid-sentence, she jumped back in surprise.

A police officer shifted uneasily from foot to foot in the doorway. And Tim knew—before the cop had begun to run through the routine of things that must be said—what he had come to say. He was also acutely aware of being a little drunk, and of Rebecca beside him, fumbling for his hand.

They were driven to the hospital. In the car, the two of them at separate ends of a blue plush seat, a wire screen hemming them in. Each of them staring out a separate window—Rebecca looking out over the impossible water and Tim over the dark fields that ran away north, the random clutter of sheep and rock, barns and dilapidated clapboards. Then Tim changed focus and saw in the glass the ghost of Rebecca, the back of her head, and even, reflected in her window, her pale, dead-eyed face staring out, staring back in.

Michael was on a gurney behind green curtains. In the next space doctors worked desperately on a young girl who had fallen through a glass door. A blood vessel in her chest had been severed and she was drowning in her own blood. Rebecca cried softly. When Tim moved he felt her hip against his back and they both shuffled a step so it wouldn't happen again.

His father's face was untouched by the crash. A doctor explained that massive head injuries had resulted in instant death, but there was no visible indication of that. Tim supposed that the back of his head had somehow borne the brunt of the impact. That the plumped pillow supported nothing more than a mask, a frozen representation of the man who, only hours ago, had beseeched them to sit with him.

He turned to Rebecca. Her bottom lip wavered and a tic took root in her left eye; she dissolved into sobs. An intern poked his head through the curtain. "Shall we?"

There were forms to be signed, and the policeman wanted another word. He sat them in a cramped doctor's office. The desk was loaded with files; the cop knocked the top of the stack with his elbow and it toppled to the floor. Tim helped him gather up the papers. They were about the same age. Neither of them old enough, Tim thought, to understand yet what it meant that a man had vanished from the planet.

Afterwards they stood awkwardly in the hall. If there was anything he could do . . ., the cop said. Tim thanked him; they shook hands. It was all bullshit. This routine, this play they were putting on. It was shit.

"How is that girl?" he said.

"Which girl?"

"The one next to my father. It sounded touch and go."

"I don't know."

"Will you find out?"

The cop nodded. Did they want a drive home?

"Don't forget about that girl," Tim said.

"I won't."

But he did, Tim suspected, almost immediately, and Tim forgot her too. He'd never given her another thought.

Until now. More than a week had passed. He scuffed a toe through the snow and into the dirt. He peered over the field of leaning, weathered headstones and debated whether the girl was likely alive, whether she ran even now through a suburban house in Kingston.

Rebecca arrived first in her blood-red Lada Cossack. She swung in past the gate and bumped down the track. The stereo Tim had helped her install in the summer blasted the bass notes of a U2 song through the vehicle's thin shell: *Even better than the real thing*. She tugged down the rear-view so she could apply a smear of lipstick. She kicked open the door and slid from the seat. Rock music smashed into the cemetery. She dove back inside and punched at the stereo. Tim fished around for the flask of Scotch he'd secreted in his jacket. Finally it was quiet and Rebecca appeared again, her dark, nearly black hair falling in thick waves over her flushed face. She half ran the two dozen steps between them. With her hands stuffed deep into her pockets she kissed Tim's cheek. "Sorry," she said breathlessly. The snow was like a screen between them. Tim touched his face and checked his fingertips. A trace of Rebecca's lavender lipstick showed up like an old bruise. He smiled. "You smell good," she said, the air clearing again between them. "You okay?"

He handed her the flask. He cared about her more than she realized. Had probably thought more about her the last ten days than about his father. As one flame was extinguished, another had flared. He thought these feelings might prove fleeting or ghostly, but for now he was smitten. And as they stood there like twin ornaments on an iced cake being dusted heavily with sugar, he wished for some mundane misfortune—a flat tire, a too-steep, too-slick hill—that might delay the caravan of well-wishers and hangers-on that surely wound even now through the village.

And sure enough, as Rebecca turned away to take in a sheep that had stuck its head over the wall and bleated, vehicles began to crawl into the cemetery.

They parked in a long line behind Rebecca's Cossack and released their passengers, who, one by one, shook Tim's hand or put an arm around him before staking a small piece of frozen ground for themselves. Someone had brought a Great Dane and the animal loped around the field for the duration of the burial. When the minister had left and the morning had taken on a less formal air, Tim watched for an owner to summon the beast, but eventually the dog leapt the wall and galloped off into the trees.

It was over. There were close to two dozen of them left in the snow. The coffin was in the ground. The minister, a blond boy named Ian who had been born and raised in nearby Rockport, had said not more than a hundred completely forgettable words. Michael wasn't a religious man, and the service reflected that; it felt perfunctory, hollow at its core. When Ian came over to shake Tim's hand afterwards, and began what Tim thought were all-too-standard consolations, it was as much as Tim could do not to argue with him.

Hanne Kristiansen, a friend of Michael's, was pawing at the ground with her boot. In her knee-length fur she resembled a rabbit seeking traction. She bit at her lower lip, and beneath her blond fringe Tim could see that her face was tear-stained.

Donald and Mae, regulars at Granite, were also still there. Donald and Michael liked to commandeer a corner table and sit with a bottle of Barolo. Today he looked older than his sixty years, and he kept resting his head on his wife's shoulder. Mae was taller, much more glamorous than Donald, and she held herself erect and with an ease that evaded everyone else. Earlier she had shared a word with Hanne, and Tim was surprised to see that they knew each other.

Mary Gordon was there from the bakery, and Tony Almonte from Murphy's Seafood. A driver for Linen Supply, the Guinness and Harp reps, and an immaculate middle-aged woman from the liquor board. Tim thought it comical that suppliers would appear to mourn the demise of a restaurateur, and that, without exception, they had managed to ask him what his plans were, was there going to be a reopening?

A pair of Toronto city councillors had made the drive together. "Michael was a decent man," one intoned solemnly, and the other added, "He's right. Your old man wasn't the most popular guy in the city, but he got things done, which is a fuck of a lot more than you can say for most of them, if you'll pardon my French."

There had also been neighbours from Ivy Lea at the service, and friends from Gananoque and Rockport. Businessmen from Toronto and Kingston. There was an actor Tim recognized from an episode of *Due South* but couldn't put a name to. And a woman, Dorothy something, who lived in a trailer on a side road in the hills to the north and sold Tupperware at parties she held in a Tim Horton's coffee shop next to the highway. A dog breeder from Yarker. And Nikolai Petrovitch, an infamous client of his father's, had brought a whole posse of hangers-on.

Tim didn't know precisely what his father had done for Petrovitch, or how willingly, but Nikolai had gained control of a parcel of land at the corner of Bloor and Yonge, Toronto's most expensive intersection, thanks to his father's efforts. Michael had caused the plans of a competitor to be scuttled by the Ontario Municipal Board. He had also gained access to Montreal's ports for Petrovitch and caused his name to appear on the board of directors for the Royal Ontario Museum. He had successfully lobbied in the last twelve months for Petrovitch's grudging acceptance into Toronto's inner circles.

At the same time, Michael had been working for a tobacco company that wanted to be able to sponsor sporting events and an American steel manufacturer that wanted its metal used in Canadian auto plants. And so it surprised no one that Michael Hollins had made enemies in his career. Most of the naysayers managed little more than impotent grumbling in the leather-lined bars of Bay Street and on the op-ed pages of Toronto's newspapers, but there were also union leaders who resented his use of free trade legislation to endanger Canadian jobs, and these men and women were not so easily shaken. In Nikolai Petrovitch, Michael had found a protector of sorts. Petrovitch owed a debt of gratitude to Michael Hollins, and the *Globe and Mail* went so far as to suggest that he had given Michael security, both financial and physical, far above and beyond that required by his contract.

Tim heard a woman's voice complaining that it had drawn a bad crowd, this one, hadn't it? But when he looked it was just a sea of heads becoming less distinct as they moved away towards the gate.

A reporter from the *Toronto Star* was talking to the kid from the *Gananoque Recorder*, and a couple of photographers were stalking the crowd like hyenas. The *Star*'s photographer stuck his zoom lens in Rebecca's face and snapped away. "So who are you, love?" he said. Tim stepped forward smartly and shoved the man square in the chest, sent him tripping backwards, first over hard clumps of grass hidden beneath the fresh snow and then over his own feet. His cameras and lens bounced against his stomach and the man grunted.

Nikolai led Tim away from the grave. "We don't want one of you ending up down there with him, do we?" he said. He muttered something in Russian to a small man in dark shades, and the photographer, down on his elbows, scuttled away backwards.

Tim looked for Rebecca. He had no interest in a conversation with Nikolai. He had received his condolences already—first by telephone the day after the accident, and then again this morning. He didn't think there was any need for them to pretend a relationship more substantial than that. Nikolai, though, guided him to the edge of the crowd, where their nearest neighbours were fishmongers and wine dealers.

"I need to get back to Toronto," Nikolai began.

Tim was relieved. This was to be an excuse for a quick exit.

"Well, it was nice of you to come. My father would have appreciated the turnout." The same inanities he'd rolled out all morning.

Though Petrovitch had visited Granite regularly, he'd never spent any time with Tim, and each time he came Michael would be visibly nervous. Tim asked his father once: "Can he drag you back to work for him?" But Michael had denied it. "He was good to me," he said. "That's all. And you don't want to disappoint a man who's been good to you."

Nikolai knocked one boot against the other, drew his shoulders up around his neck. "I want to send a man up," he said. There was snow in his eyebrows.

"Up where?"

"Here. Here!" Nikolai passed a hand through the air.

"I'm not following. Why would you do that?" Tim squinted. Rebecca and Mae were holding hands. "Everything's fine, Nikolai." Because he had to be talking about sending someone to help manage the restaurant. Tim was well aware that Nikolai owned an interest in Granite, but he hadn't had time yet to go through all the paperwork with his lawyer, to see just how big a stake it was.

The *Star* photographer had dusted himself off and was snapping pictures of Tim and Nikolai without raising the camera from his waist. Nikolai lifted his head slightly and the small man in sunglasses scurried into the photographer's sightline. The stragglers were leaving, and the sounds of car doors being wrenched open and slammed shut were like shots. Ravens shouted to each other somewhere down the slope.

"Your father was doing me a favour. Nothing much, but he was in the right place and so I asked his help." He pointed at Tim. "Look at this. You should see the look on your face. You don't trust me." He put a hand on Tim's shoulder. "You should trust me."

"It's not that."

"It is. And it offends me. Listen. Your father was scouting some properties for me. Somewhere for me to escape to. He was playing real estate agent, just as he played chef. A busy man."

"Rebecca is the chef," Tim said. "Dad worked mostly front of the house." It was important to be precise, although he couldn't have explained why.

Nikolai bowed almost imperceptibly. "It is important that you understand. A man is coming to look around for me. It's that simple. To see what is on the market, what sort of price it fetches. I even thought"—he rubbed a finger speculatively along his lips—"you could put him up for a day or two. Show him around. I'm not looking to interfere." Nikolai brushed his jawline, which was tinted blue in the cold.

Rebecca had freed herself and she stepped gingerly between an old grave and the new one; she took Tim's arm.

"Ah, the cook," Nikolai said, forcing a smile.

Rebecca said they had already met. "A couple of times. You came into the kitchen once," she reminded Nikolai.

"Your domain," Nikolai said. "You must hate me."

"Michael loved to show off his kitchen. I got used to visitors."

"Michael was showing off his cook, not his ovens," Nikolai said. "At least that night. He was very proud of you."

"Chef," Tim hissed. "Rebecca's a *chef*." He felt her grip tighten on his wrist. Ravens, six of them, flew over in ragged formation.

"You know, the last thing I want to do is upset you," Nikolai said smoothly to Tim, and Rebecca said that upset was all any of them were capable of this week. It was good to see him again, she said. Petrovitch thanked her.

"Adams is the man's name," he said to Tim. "I reached him this morning. He's been here before. He loves this part of the world. He's excited to return."

"He can call me," Tim consented. "That's fine. If it was something my father was doing, then I don't see how I can refuse, really." What the hell else was he supposed to do? He resented that Nikolai knew more about Michael than he did, and that Michael had worked so hard cultivating a relationship with this man. But a graceful end was still possible here, on this of all days, and so Tim worked towards that.

Hanne Kristiansen had made her way down to her car. Petrovitch called out, "Hanne. A second." He went after her, and Hanne looked to Tim as if she were about to be eaten. Some of her words to Nikolai drifted up faintly: "I suppose you could . . . I don't know, did you talk to them? . . . No, he doesn't have the foggiest . . ."

The snow had become finer. It fell like Parmesan from a grater. Nikolai bundled Hanne to the other side of her car and they huddled there, or rather Nikolai crowded her.

"What do you suppose that's all about?" Rebecca said.

"He buys paintings from her gallery. Dad said thousands of dollars a year."

"It looks like he's changed his mind about something. Hanne looks about ready to shit."

Tim laughed. "Let's hope she sold him a forgery." He felt the flask against his ribs and he dragged it out. Rebecca told him he'd best not get too drunk, there was the reception to get through.

Petrovitch and Hanne had parted. Hanne rolled down her window as she edged away. "I'll call you," she promised.

"You're not coming to . . .?" Rebecca began, but Hanne had raised the glass again.

"Well, that's one less," Tim said. "Maybe no one will show up."

Rebecca looped an arm through his and together they walked back to the grave. The coffin's brass handles were wet and there was a deep scratch near the foot. Canvas straps still wormed up both sides of the grave. "That other photographer," Rebecca said, "not the one you hit. The other one. He wasn't with the newspaper, you know."

Tim looked at her. "Who was he, then?"

"A cop."

"He had a jacket on. It said *Gananoque Recorder*."

"All the same. I saw him at the supermarket a while back. You remember when that couple from Syracuse drove the pickup through the window and made off with the floor safe? He was the cop investigating that. I remember the scar in his eyebrow. It was definitely him. And he was talking to another guy. It was like they'd come together. So I think there were at least two of them."

So what? Tim thought. Any revelation about his father would add to his disappointment, but it wouldn't surprise him. Not really. All he wanted just now was to get the reception over. His feet were cold. His ears felt brittle. There was nothing he could say. He had lain awake last night thinking he might have to "say a few words," or that when everyone was gone he would need somehow to take proper leave of his father. But, faced with that moment, it had seemed as if he was merely playing to an invisible audience. And Michael couldn't hear him, he was positive of that.

They walked down to the Cossack. He stood by the open door while she climbed into the driver's seat. He expected music to blast forth when she started the engine, and when it didn't he was surprised. They were the last souls, he observed, in the graveyard.

"That's as it should be," Rebecca said. "Last to see him alive, last to see him . . . well, you know." She sighed.

And then she leaned out towards Tim. He thought she intended to kiss him, and his heart punished him for the thought, caused an immediate wraparound ache in his chest. But Rebecca was only reaching for the door handle, and when she had it she waited for Tim to step away, which he did, mumbling an apology.

Her car bumped towards the main road, and he realized with a start that her departure—even though he would see her again within the hour, and even though he supposed he loved his father as much as any son—was the saddest single thing that had happened to him all day.

DECEMBER 3

John Selby had arrived in Toronto the previous afternoon and immediately taken a room at the Airport Sheraton. He took great pleasure from the distant runways, the sight of so many comings and goings. Jets plopping down like ducks onto a frozen pond.

Very early the next morning he collected the keys to his car from the Budget counter. He threw his overnight bag into the trunk of the Jaguar. Something with four-wheel drive made more sense in this climate, but until the blizzards came Selby wanted low-to-the-road, he wanted silky smooth. He was emphatic: it was a brilliant blue morning and he wanted the Jag.

He negotiated the already busy 427 South and then the even busier Gardiner Expressway East. It was rush hour; he had been foolish. He made for the base of the CN Tower and the creamy lump that was the SkyDome. He wanted a taste of Toronto. It was the traveller in him. The tourist. John had decided long ago that he would do well to tame this side of himself, but he was old enough to realize he probably never would. It was time to accept his weaknesses. And if that meant a morning acquainting himself with Toronto's attractions, then so be it.

He crawled north on Spadina; the fruit- and vegetable-laden sidewalks of Chinatown were already teeming. Ancient women with braided steel-grey hair were hunched over metal carts. Men in suits and heavy overcoats headed south, aimed for the bank towers of Bay Street. Some idiot with dreads tried to weave through the frigid crush on his mountain bike. Neon signs for dim sum and ginseng, herbal medicines and cheap luggage.

Selby went east on Bloor Street and then north on Yonge. Under the railway tracks and past the vast Mount Pleasant Cemetery, past St. Clair's cluster of condominiums. He pulled into a metered space near Eglinton Avenue and hurried in the bitter sunshine past bookstores and restaurants. He liked this part of the city immediately. The storefronts were expensively decorated and the sidewalks wider than they were near the lake.

He found what he was looking for quickly. There was plenty of time, it wasn't even ten yet. He took the stairs in the narrow hallway three at a time and surprised the pretty woman at the top. She straightened and beamed at him as if he were her brother, just returned from a war. Her lips were slippery with some sort of frosted balm.

"How ya doin'?" she said cheerfully.

There were three pine-panelled doors to his right and he pointed at the middle one, which was slightly ajar. "Can you squeeze me in? How does it look?"

She looked down at her schedule and quickly up again, as if he might disappear. "All yours."

He held out his arm, showed her the back of his left hand, its ringless fingers. "Thought I'd see about making this last a bit longer."

"You look great," she told him, and came around her desk. "Where were you?"

"Tahiti," he said.

She walked ahead of him. "I didn't realize that was a real place," she said. "I thought they just made it up. You know, like when they rearrange the letters of a word to make another word. I always thought Tahiti was like Paradise all mixed up."

Selby had no idea whether she was serious. Her tone gave nothing away.

"I'll give you a minute to undress," she said. "And then I'll start it up."

He took off his clothes, stretched out on the curved bed, and fitted the plastic goggles over his eyes. The unit brightened and hummed and the lid closed over him smoothly. He stared at the inside of the blue plastic lenses. Soon he could feel the heat on his chest and in the small of his back. He could hear Caribbean wavelets throwing themselves at his feet. He thought of the burning sand and apprehended the coconut scent of Coppertone. It was all so pleasant. But then he was taken by a familiar, jolting nightmare: a man lifting the lid away from him. His goggles slipping away. The sunbed kicking out white heat while his towering assassin smiles, draws from behind a thick leather belt a slim silver pistol and aims at his chest, pulls the trigger. The curved white bed fills with his blood, it laps around his feet, warm as an incoming tide.

"So how was that?" the attendant asked pleasantly, when Selby emerged. "Did you want to buy a package of sessions? It's cheaper and we give you a gold card."

Selby explained that he was passing through, she wouldn't see him again, and she said she was disappointed. He told her he wished that you could believe everything people said, and they both laughed.

He drove back down Yonge to Yorkville. He was still early so he sat at a small table in the window of busy Sassafraz feeling like a million bucks, feeling slightly reckless. He should have been across the street, in a dark corner of Letticri wolfing down pizza. Or better yet, he should have stayed miles away until it was time. But he couldn't resist. It was the same *I am a traveller* business again. Self-esteem gained through expensive meals and seats in first class. An artificially revived tan and a rented Jag.

He bought an off-the-rack winter-weight in charcoal grey at Harry Rosen's, and a tie and shirt at Holt Renfrew. The red-jacketed doorman there greeted him as a long-lost friend, and Selby looked at him suspiciously, paused a beat before marching past.

Now he stationed himself near the door of the International News store. There was a rack there of British newspapers, just as Sonny Rockliff had said there would be, and a good view of the street. John faked an interest in the weekend sports section of the *Telegraph*. He glowered intensely at the soccer scores. "They don't mind a bit if you read there," Sonny had said. "Just wear a decent suit. Yorkville's a swanky part of Toronto. It was a hippie hangout in the Sixties, but now it's the hip who hang out. The visiting film stars, you know—the women who do lunch and the hucksters who prey on them. Prada, Gucci, Tiffany's, they've all got storefronts. A ton of restaurants, cinemas. During the Film Festival you can't move. Pickpockets, prostitutes, waiters and bankers, publishers and art dealers, you name it. Everything you could want if you've got money and you need to spend it. Nikolai sure does. His penthouse overlooks the area. He could spit in your salad if he wanted. The only guy who knows who you are is the driver. And even to him you're just the Good Samaritan."

Beyond the glass doors (only the right one opened) there were two steps down to the sidewalk and from there it was three strides to the curb. No parking was allowed on that side of the street, but it didn't stop a steady stream of BMWs and Jags, all manner of SUVs, from pulling in snug while the driver darted into Starbucks for a coffee, or past him for the latest issue of *Wallpaper**, or the *Financial Post*, the British edition of *Vogue*.

The sidewalks had been cleared of an overnight snowfall but there were still slick spots. Just now a Japanese woman had, to the delight of her boyfriend, lost her footing and then her grip on a Diesel shopping bag that slid into the gutter as smoothly as a bowling ball. She waited, her legs folded awkwardly beneath her, for her suitor to help. Selby hoped nothing like this happened when Petrovitch exited Topaz, a swish underground mussels-and-martinis joint, almost directly opposite the International News. It was Petrovitch's habit, Sonny had said, to lunch there on Tuesdays, to recline a while in one of its cream leather booths with a Bombay and tonic and talk to the owner, or just read over the day's work. "It's a place he goes to hide," Sonny reported. "It's where we filmed him. And when he's done, it's across the street to buy his newspaper. The Saturday *Guardian* shows up that day from England and Nikolai has a copy on order. We don't know why. But he'll be there, regular as clockwork."

Hurriedly John paid for the *Telegraph*—no, he didn't need a bag, thanks—and carried it outside. He had seen movement in the shadows around the steps down to Topaz's entrance. To his right, towards Avenue Road and backgrounded by the Park Hyatt, a yellow, dirt-spattered cab sat idling. Two girls chased a white cat across the road.

Nikolai Petrovitch climbed into the light. He waited for his eyes to adjust. John moved to the curb before that could happen, before it was possible for Petrovitch to have seen him. The cab was inching forward. The driver was wearing a ball cap and leather gloves. He unwound his fingers one by one from the wheel so that he was holding on mostly with his thumbs. It reminded John of Sonny Rockliff's driving style.

Petrovitch wiped his lips with the back of his left hand and then took a step. He stopped to check his watch, but then he came on again. Petrovitch registered the taxi but decided he had ample time and stepped smartly into the road between a canary-yellow Lamborghini and a rusted-out Corolla. He had his head down now, his mind already on other things, as if the next two minutes would take care of themselves. Which wasn't nearly true.

The cab leapt forward, accelerating hard. Petrovitch was at the centre of the road. He looked up idly, still preoccupied. John liked very much how it was working, how the risk might be even slighter than he'd imagined. Petrovitch saw John charging and he jerked upright, twisted his head, and realized the cab was bearing down. John launched himself at Petrovitch's waist and the two of them smacked heavily backwards onto the low hood of the Lamborghini. The taxi clipped John's right foot, pulled off his shoe, and Petrovitch yelped. He had also been hit. They rolled together off the hood and John landed on top of Petrovitch in the narrow space between cars.

John heard the cab's brakes at the corner and knew it was outside Sassafraz, where he'd sat so recently with his stomach churning, wondering how these moments would unfold. Because there was only so much planning you could do. It was shitty to have a man risk his life to get an introduction. He thought it represented a laziness on Sonny's part. There were more subtle ways of getting into someone's life. But Sonny had insisted they didn't have time. And besides, there was less paper to forge this way. "You've already got him hooked on an emotional level," Sonny had said. "They get a blind spot after you save their lives. You know they do."

Petrovitch grabbed his right thigh. He swore and moaned and gritted his teeth, rolled back his lips and screwed shut his eyes. John made it to his knees and from there to his feet. He leaned against the back end of the Corolla. His shoe—where the hell was his shoe? He tested the range of movement in his foot. Just bruising was his guess, but that wasn't to say he wouldn't limp like an idiot for a few days. And the point of this exercise was for them to walk away. Together. Not get shipped off in separate ambulances.

Petrovitch was still on his back, prodding tentatively at his leg and wincing. "What the fuck was that?" he growled.

John affected a weary, pained tone. "A taxi." He indicated the road behind him. "Must've had an urgent call, I guess. How badly are you hurt? You want me to call an ambulance?"

"I'm okay. You?"

John wriggled his foot. "It's still attached, which is a good sign." He said he didn't think anything was broken. Petrovitch rolled forward into a sitting position. A couple of old women, twins, in leather pants and clutching identical pale-blue Birks bags, stood on the opposite sidewalk and gawked. Pages of John's *Telegraph* were being hassled by the wind. "But we're going to attract a crowd," John added. "I don't need a crowd."

Petrovitch wanted to put some weight on his leg. John offered a hand and the Russian grunted upright.

"So?"

Petrovitch shook his head. "That fucker nearly killed us."

"He nearly killed *you*, I think," John said.

Petrovitch pointed at John's foot.

John said it was nothing. "It was you he wanted."

"What are you talking about?"

"That driver was pretty intent on taking you out," John said. "You sleeping with someone's wife?" He hoped he'd managed to find the right mix of consternation and humour.

Petrovitch closed one eye. It was an appraisal he was being subjected to, John supposed. A skeptical, wondering, pirate's gaze. "You've got it wrong," Petrovitch said.

John concentrated on his foot. He made a show of looking for his shoe.

Petrovitch pointed. "Behind you. Alongside the car." He performed a few deep knee bends, accompanied them with a sustained grimace.

As John scrabbled for his shoe, Petrovitch gathered himself on the sidewalk. He brushed himself off. He had the intimidating body of a sprinter. John knelt to retie his lace.

"I need a big fucking martini," Petrovitch said. "What do you say?"

John tugged up the cuff on his jacket and shook his watch down onto his wrist. The crystal on his Tag Heuer was cracked, an opaque diagonal from eleven to two, just as it had been when Sonny provided it. "Shit," he exclaimed, and showed the face to Petrovitch.

"That settles it," Petrovitch said, and he introduced himself.

"Frank," John told him in return. "My name's Frank Coleman."

*

It was an hour before Nikolai Petrovitch thanked him. But John understood that. No one wanted to feel indebted to a stranger. And no doubt Petrovitch was furiously pondering the possibility that someone had just attempted a hit, in broad daylight, in his own neighbourhood. This drink with John was just an obligation Petrovitch wanted out of the way. John would have to supply him with a reason to extend the relationship.

They swapped pleasantries and remarked on the quality of the vodka, the heavy glasses it came in, the creamy leather booths. Finally Petrovitch brought up details of the incident. He was trying to piece it together.

"So, Frank. You are buying a newspaper."

"Right."

"And you come out. And you intend to cross the road. Where were you going? Were you coming here?"

"I was wandering. I wanted somewhere to read my newspaper."

"Which newspaper?"

"The *Telegraph*. From England."

Petrovitch sneered.

"I'm just looking for sports results. Some salacious gossip."

"And so you step into the road?" He wasn't to be sidetracked.

"I stepped into the road, yes. And then I saw you coming towards me, and I saw the cab. I was about to step back when I noticed you had your head down and that goddamn madman had his sights set on you. It's amazing how much thinking you can squeeze into a half second, isn't it? Anyway, it looked like you weren't going to see what hit you." He laughed weakly, remembering Sonny's distant-seeming advice: "See what he rises to, John. Does he like you being friendly or is it better if you're standoffish, devil-may-care? You don't need me to tell you any of this, I know. But you won't be the first stranger to try to strike up a conversation with him."

"And he was definitely after me?" Petrovitch said. He was astonished, outraged.

"I've seen accidents. This wasn't one of them."

Petrovitch shook his head. "I owe you thanks."

John inclined his head. "Oh, not so much," he said. "Now I get to think of myself as a bit of a hero for a day or two, you see. Wander around with my chest puffed out."

"You don't strike me as a boastful man," Petrovitch said.

"Even better."

"What do you do?"

"Travel," John said truthfully. "As much as possible I travel. I flew here yesterday, for instance. My passport is thick with ink."

Obediently—and just as Sonny had predicted and John had doubted—Petrovitch said, "Let's see it."

"My passport?"

"Your passport. Do you have it?"

John produced the battered document. At the Sheraton he had memorized the dates involved and the order of stampings. He had stories for all of the countries, some of them quite true. But he had no memory at all of sitting for the old portrait and wondered where Sonny's people had dug it up.

Petrovitch thumbed through the begrimed pages and whistled appreciatively. "All in the last two years," he said.

"Travel thrills me. More than anything else."

Petrovitch handed back the passport. He dragged an olive from its spear. "More than saving a man's life?"

"You exaggerate. It was a small taxi, a short street."

They laughed together.

"And what do *you* do, Nikolai? It's a Tuesday afternoon. I don't see you punching a clock. I see a nice suit, a man at leisure in a good restaurant."

"I work very hard, Frank. Very hard. And I travel very little."

"We're opposites, then," John said.

"Or two sides of a coin." Petrovitch reached under the table to massage his thigh. His limp when they came in had been worse than John's.

"A very battered coin," John said. He checked the time again, careful to have Petrovitch see the watch. "I should let the busy man get back to work." He pushed his martini glass to the centre of the table.

"You must let me replace your Tag. Or at least repair it."

"Recommend me a good hotel," John said, reaching for his wallet, "and we'll call it even."

*

Sonny Rockliff was worried, which was how John remembered him best. It was Sonny's resting state, his baseline. "I got a report from the driver," he said. "The moron heard a thump. Said he's got no idea who he hit or how badly."

"He was heavy on the gas," John said, the encrypted cellphone squeezed between shoulder and cheek. "Nice to see a man who enjoys his work so much, though." He was flat out on the king-size, his pant leg rolled up and an ice-filled towel lumped over his foot.

"I don't suppose I'd have lost too much sleep if we'd killed Petrovitch," Sonny said. "Accidents do happen."

John grunted noncommittally. Sonny was talking carelessly about an international assassination, accidental or not, and he didn't want to go on record condoning such foolishness.

"So, are you in?" Sonny said.

"Too early to tell. I only just left him. He insisted on showing me his damn newspaper."

"Why?"

"Proving a point, I guess. We hobbled around like two war veterans, holding one sports page up next to another."

"I'd say you were in."

"We'll see."

But when he hung up, there was already a message from Petrovitch, hoping the room was up to John's standards and inviting him, if he was still in the country, to a get-together on the Saturday. "A chance for me to more properly show my appreciation," he said.

DECEMBER 7

Nikolai Petrovitch lived fifty floors up, at the top of a glittering steel-and-glass tower. Three uniformed men patrolled the lobby and restless security cameras swung back and forth. The marble floor had been polished to a high shine. Ditto for the brass doors on the high-speed elevators. Not a smudge, not a fingerprint. Palm trees towered at the corners. Water ran smoothly down the face of a granite wall into an obsidian pond thick with lilies and the fluorescent drift of giant goldfish. One of the guards punched a private code to have the elevator climb beyond the forty-ninth floor and then stepped backward with military precision. John's stomach lurched at the immediate fairground velocity. It's Frank, he reminded himself. Frank Coleman. He puffed out his lower lip and blew a draft of cool air over his face.

The doors drew back to reveal a lavish heaven-high world. A boy of eighteen, nineteen, in a sharp bottle-green suit stepped forward and requested John's coat. There were floor-to-ceiling windows on three sides of the room, and they were a mile away. More marble, but also rugs thrown casually about: Indian, Turkish, and, in front of the wood stove, a baby-blue shag pile cut in the shape of a bear skin. A DJ in skater pants and a reversed ball cap, blue-lens shades, headphones that protruded like the woolly ears of a panda bear, had been established at twin turntables against a brick wall, and he rocked slowly back and forth to a song John didn't recognize. No one danced. The volume was set too low for that; the tempo was too slow. Two women shared a leather couch the colour of cappuccino. They leaned forward over their long legs to draw lines away from a small mountain of cocaine at the centre of a smoked-glass table. A fat man sat opposite, his moustache oiled into a Dali-like curve. Behind him a third woman had her hands on his shoulders, a diamond choker at her pale throat. All over the room there were small knots of people. There were aggressive, spotty young men in sharp suits. A man in a jean jacket with greased hair was on one knee talking to a girl of twelve or thirteen at the foot of a steel staircase. There were even women outside on the deck, all in fur coats, all breathing extravagant plumes into the night. One of them fanned herself as if to cool down. The city was spread prettily in shades of black and grey and white, with sparkles of gold and yellow, blue and red. A Rottweiler sniffed at legs and crotches. It clawed at the edge of the silk rug beneath the coffee table, causing mini avalanches on the slopes of the snowy mound. Two men followed the dog's route, but loaded down with trays of food and fizzing flutes of champagne.

Petrovitch distinguished himself from the crowd, squeezing sideways between two men trying noisily to decide which of them had the best chance of securing a table at the miserably named Sleet. He squeezed John's hand, seemed genuinely pleased to see him. But then, before it began, he excused himself. He had seen someone he needed to speak to. "Enjoy yourself," he advised. "I've told everyone what you did. You're the number-one star here. We'll talk. Promise."

John didn't like crowds. He particularly didn't like crowds of strangers. He was wired for solitude, always had been. He hated small talk. But he had watched videotape of himself in crowd situations—an exercise in which he had to determine who among a crowd of actors was acting the part of terrorist. And the irony was that John excelled. His awkwardness worked for him. His obtuse inquiries and awkward parries, in tandem with his halting body language, made him seem the eternal innocent, a man fundamentally unsuited for undercover work. One on one was an entirely different matter—he was able, confident; but what faced him now was a nightmare.

He recognized only the fat man with the moustache and one of the women outside. Both from photographs shown to him by Sonny Rockliff's team in Newark. "This is who we think you might run into," they'd said. "This one, and this one, and oh yes, him. The Canadians gave us most of these. Known contacts, they call them. Bastards every one. But they still insist Nikolai himself is clean. They say you don't rise that far without attracting some nasty hangers-on. Go figure."

The man's name was Mavlak. He sold credit card information, mostly to associates in Saudi Arabia. He had people all over the city collecting imprints. They worked in the smallest boutiques and the largest department stores, they were biding their time in car dealerships and dry cleaners, photo shops and computer sales, beer halls and tea rooms. He paid them a flat rate and sold the information for ten times that amount. The man's bathroom, apparently, housed a glass case on the wall filled with the platinum imprints of Danny DeVito and Julia Roberts, of Britney Spears and Elton John.

Mavlak's connections were weblike: in government, in business, and even in the media. If someone was busted, roused at three in the morning, and dragged down to Police Headquarters on College Street, Mavlak knew which reporter to warn off the story. He also knew which cop to hound, which lawyer. He knew who to ply with cocaine, who to photograph emerging from the Brass Rail, Toronto's notorious Yonge Street strip club. He knew who would respond to blackmail and who would jump off the Bloor Street Viaduct at the faintest whiff of a scandal. It was this web that kept Mavlak on the street. The RCMP, John had been told, wanted not just Mavlak but the crooked men and women who turned a blind eye, or made the unethical phone call, the insider trade. His knuckles, John noted, were fat and soft and sprouted a wiry black fur.

The other familiar face, the woman outside, was Nikolai's partner, Ruby. She was a pretty thirty-something business loans officer for the Bank of Montreal and the primary reason the Canadian security forces had decided Nikolai was clean. She handled Nikolai's finances, which made it easy to check them. When Sonny had raised the possibility that Nikolai was using these transparent records to distract attention from other more incriminating accounts, the Canadian Security Intelligence Service swore it wasn't happening. "They're just not paranoid enough," Sonny said. "That's their problem."

Nikolai had real estate holdings in Moscow. "I told you about some of that," Sonny had said. There was also a confectionery factory in Warsaw, and two warehouses at dockside in Gdansk. An import-export business that shipped mostly foodstuffs, cheap clothing, and luggage. Wines from Bulgaria and Hungary: thick meaty Cabernets with unappealing labels. In Toronto there were unsurprising and unalarming interests in restaurants and condominium developments. The land at Yonge and Bloor was worth millions. He had established dry-cleaning outlets in Mississauga and Hamilton. There were a few discount CD outlets, a jeans shop in Montreal. In winter he flew in roses from Peru. He imported linens from Egypt and containers full of antiquities from the Middle East.

The RCMP had sent a woman to talk to Ruby. Months later the same woman returned to the bank. "Keep in touch with us," Ruby was told. "That way if something happens we can help you. You're on the right side." Ruby had tried to throw the woman out of her office. She'd lodged an official complaint, and John had read a copy of that. She had been insulted, she said, but not surprised. The strategies were so obvious, she said. Eventually an apology was issued and a short time later an official internal order to back off. The decision had been made. Nikolai Petrovitch was all right. He was as clean as the next guy.

Selby watched Ruby interact with the other women out on the wintry deck. He could feel that Mavlak was watching him watch her. There was a circle of attention. And somewhere, it was a safe bet, Petrovitch watched all of them. A flash filled his side of the room and a woman squealed with delight: "Oh I *love* photos!" she said. "More, *more!*" It was one of the women rooted to the couch. She dropped the disposable next to her and dove again for the cocaine.

Selby experimented with lines for the travel article he imagined writing when this was over. A new career, far from the Sonny Rockliffs and Nikolai Petrovitches of the world.

With Lake Ontario at its feet, sparkling Toronto might easily be mistaken by the jet-lagged traveller for a coastal city, rather than one of the most inland metropolises in the world . . .

He'd have to check that inland part. Or maybe he should open on a dramatic note.

One of the great miracles in Toronto is that more innocents aren't mown down by the motorists who accelerate frighteningly in their mad rush to pass the streetcars before their doors swing open . . .

Or a mildly comic one.

Toronto's pint-sized mayor is often seen mugging for the cameras, leaning on any of several life-sized fibreglass moose left over from a recent art project and now loitering in front of civic-minded banks or hotels, their antlers broken off, their flanks dented by reversing taxicabs . . .

He needed to jot this stuff down somewhere. Work on it later.

Petrovitch was at his side again. "We can go up to the roof." His breath was strong but the scent unplaceable. Anchovy maybe. Or caper.

Selby trailed him across the room. The dog licked at his hand and Selby smiled as if to reassure the animal.

They climbed the stairs, past a man in black turtleneck, crew cut. Someone fresh off a Russian sub, Selby thought. A man on shore leave. He amused himself with the notion that submarines might be able to navigate the St. Lawrence Seaway, end up in Thunder Bay, or train a periscope on a very surprised Duluth.

They passed a bedroom. The young girl Selby had seen earlier was now asleep. A dark-haired woman was collecting clothes from the floor.

"Why outside?" Selby asked. He thought it must be for the privacy, the freedom to talk, but he was willing to hear Petrovitch expound on a theory of open spaces, on a human need to congregate beneath a canopy of winter stars. He would have welcomed that. The cold moved quickly through his clothes, gathered at his throat and his wrists.

Petrovitch shrugged. "I can't stand all that fucking noise."

There were dead palm trees and a purple go-kart with a two-stroke engine near the low wall. A dull roar emanated from four circular fans behind a thick wire mesh. A jet making for Pearson International was low enough that in daytime, Selby imagined, you might see hopeful faces in each of the windows.

"You are enjoying yourself?" Petrovitch wondered.

"You have one hell of a home," John said, dodging the question. "The world at your feet."

"Ruby is fond of it."

"And you aren't?"

"Too many men come up here and say, 'You have the world at your feet.' The symbolism is too easy. It makes me think our being here is vulgar somehow. I picture an island, Frank. A seaplane. My mail and my news delivered by a man in a boat. Those are the things I would enjoy."

"You must be a hands-off sort of man, Nikolai. Otherwise that wouldn't work."

Petrovitch shook his head. "A dreamer," he said. "I want that which would ruin me. I want the impossible."

Sounds from the party buzzed around the door. There was a slow leak of the druggy festivities.

Petrovitch leaned out into space and then pushed back from the rail. He walked a tight circle, knocking his hands together.

"You've got something on your mind," John said.

"I am grateful to you, Frank."

John laughed. "Is that all it is? Then, forget it. I'm not the sort of man to hold that over you."

"But still. I feel an obligation."

"Don't. I don't need your guilt. I'll wish I'd taken a step backward instead of forward." Good one, he thought. Remind the man of his debt while at the same time denying it. Very nice.

Petrovitch stuffed his clenched fists in his pockets. "What are your plans, Frank? Tell me that."

"Ambitions, you mean? Where I see myself in five years. That sort of thing?"

"Immediate plans. How long are you in Canada?"

"Oh, I don't know. Not long, unless it warms up some."

"But for Christmas. Where will you be? You must have a wife. Children somewhere. Every man thinks about where he should be at Christmas. Every man with a choice."

"Not this one," John said. "I might be here, or in Fiji or, hell, I might be in Iceland. I've heard good things about Iceland. I like the idea of being able to say in January, that's where I was."

"I thought you might tell me some stories. A well-travelled man like yourself. A man of varied experience. Perhaps one evening soon when I am without so much obligation."

"My stories may bore you, Nikolai. I have a suspicion they would pale next to your own adventures."

"I don't know," Petrovitch said. He smiled, a man about to let the cat out of the bag. "I have never been to prison, for instance. Certainly not for a ten-year stretch."

And there it was. Petrovitch had fallen for it.

John produced his look of astonishment. Traded it for expressions of indignation, betrayal, hurt. Finally he looked just plain mad.

"How the . . .?" he exploded. He pointed a finger, put it close to Petrovitch's chest. He stared upward, as if to pull down an answer from the heavens. "My goddamn passport," he stammered finally. "That's it, isn't it." He turned away, took a step towards the door.

"Ah, don't be so melodramatic," Petrovitch cajoled him. "Every time you cross a border your history flashes on the screen. I bet you've caused some serious lineups. It is a wonder to me that so many countries allow you in."

John turned. Petrovitch smiled sweetly. That was a good point. But surely Sonny was cognizant of the apparent contradiction between invented life and purported travel history. "We all have to shoulder responsibility for our pasts," he said.

Petrovitch pulled a fresh pack of Camels from his pocket. He unwound the Cellophane, cast the wrapper into the night sky like a golfer testing the wind. "The *past*, you say. Are those days really behind you?"

"Prison sure the hell is," John said. "That was a long time ago. A different Frank Coleman."

"A Frank Coleman who lost most of his twenties to a drug bust."

"You're not impressing me any more," John said. "I'm sure you know all about it: me hopscotching north from Colombia in a small plane. Stopping at various Caribbean islands, Mexican villages. And then busted in Florida. Ten kilos, that's all it was. That's all we had left by the time we reached the U.S. I served one interminable year for each of them."

"*We?*" Petrovitch seemed surprised. "I thought it was a daredevil kid flying solo."

John shrugged, then grinned. He'd practised this. He wanted it to communicate that he considered this a small victory. "There were two of us. A friend was waiting at the landing strip. I guess we surprised them. They'd decided I'd use one runway and I came down on another. They were too damn sure of themselves to secure both. They were soon after us, though. We saw the dust coming off the road; we knew it was trouble. I threw my friend out. They didn't think to look for someone else. They thought they'd got me cold."

"Who was he?"

"She," John said. "It was a she. A friend from college. I told her I'd put her through med school. I didn't need her help, really."

"You were just being a good guy, Frank. Is that it?"

"Stupid is more like it."

"Where is she now?"

John shrugged. "We lost touch. It happens."

Petrovitch smoked his cigarette. "That's a sad story."

John didn't know whether he was being called a liar. There were always moments like this for a man who travelled with false passports, claimed a life that wasn't his. Petrovitch launched the glowing butt into space and they tracked its end-over-end.

"But you still haven't answered my question," Petrovitch said.

"What question is that?"

"Is it really in your past, Frank, or do you still . . . *tinker?*"

"Why don't you tell me what *you* do, Nikolai? Not every man can turn a passport into a resumé. An American passport, at that."

There was the sharp slap of leather-soled shoes on the steps, the laboured breaths of a man not used to climbing. Petrovitch swore, pivoted on the ball of his left foot, and glared into the empty doorway until someone appeared.

The new man was tall, broad-shouldered, in pinstriped suit and wide red tie with a gold pin speared through its heart. His hair was dyed black and combed back. Green eyes. The nose thin, impossibly long, and the lips equally severe. John had seen him downstairs, his face blanching when it took the full blast of the camera flash. His head must have been eighteen inches top to bottom, and it should have been cartoonish, a caricature, but all John could think was: film director, playwright, sculptor.

"The party is downstairs," Petrovitch said. "Oleg should have told you."

"My name," the new man said in heavily accented English, "is Viktor Laevsky."

"Charmed. But everyone is to stay downstairs," Petrovitch said. His smile was unconvincing.

"I have arrived"—Viktor was struggling for calm words—"to see only you."

Petrovitch cleared his throat. He tapped another cigarette free of the pack and placed it between his lips. He made no attempt to light it. He was annoyed. There were men downstairs who would catch hell for this. "*Yob tvoyu mat*," he muttered.

Laevsky merely tossed his long head in John's direction. A strand of hair came free and fell over his face. "You don't want this guy around for this, do you?" His tone was accusatory.

Petrovitch reached out as if he wanted to pull Selby into the frame, but his hand flailed uselessly. John moved in anyway. He introduced himself.

Petrovitch was leaning back against the wall, his hands braced against its top edge, his legs crossed in front of him, only his heels touching the ground. It was a way of saying: *You don't frighten me*, or, *I trust you not to harm me*. His knuckles, though, were white against the stone lip.

Laevsky said, "You should send this man downstairs, I think."

John said to Petrovitch, "We can do this later."

"Thank you, Frank. A couple of minutes, I am sure."

John nodded curtly at Viktor. He entered again the hallway that led past the child's bedroom and to the staircase. The submariner posted downstairs would have no idea he had come in. He pulled the door almost closed behind him and checked that his shadow wouldn't be thrown underneath it.

He concentrated on the argument that had erupted outside. Laevsky had launched into a furious tirade in Russian. Petrovitch tried several times to interrupt. As far as John could tell, he was denying a charge being levelled at him, but Laevsky wouldn't be persuaded. Their speeches became shorter and shorter until finally there was a brief silence. Petrovitch began to say something and Laevsky cut him off. "I have not come across this world because I suspected," he said in English, the words slow, deliberate. "I have come because I know."

"You know nothing," Petrovitch insisted. "I suggest you take in some of the city's sights. Otherwise you will have wasted a week of your life. I can suggest an itinerary, set you up with some lovely girls."

Laevsky sputtered furiously, an engine running out of fuel, and John backed away down the hall. The little girl's door was closed. The guard appeared at the bottom of the stairs, a swirl of guests behind him moving into new arrangements. John took a breath and descended.

He accepted a flute of champagne from one of three women in turquoise evening gowns who were working the room with silver trays and made his way to the kitchen. Groups had congregated near the stainless-steel refrigerator and around the massive butcher block. He pulled down a cookbook and leaned against the stove. He flicked idly through its pages, trying to listen in, and at the same time trying to look unapproachable, a man lost in a book.

At the refrigerator it was casting calls and "that fucking dimwit at the other end of the phone. I mean, have you ever actually tried to have a conversation with that man? God, I hate him. All I was trying to do was line up an audition. It wasn't like I was trying to direct the fucking thing." The woman was abruptly silent. And then, "Oh shit, here's Oleg. He going to be all over me again, you watch."

Oleg was apparently the guard about to catch hell from Petrovitch, for he wandered casually now into the middle of the room. He whispered into the ear of a man at the butcher block, and then took the man's spot. Someone made a crack about shift changes and Oleg seized an untouched beer from between them.

John read with negligible interest that cream of tartar was the key to a decent meringue. As well as a good stainless-steel beater.

"Niki seems good," someone said. "Determined, but good."

"Now that Hollins is out of the way," Oleg said.

"Too bad that didn't happen here."

"Why?"

"The more visible the better, don't you think?"

Oleg shrugged. He looked around the room, and John ran a finger down a list of ingredients. He rhymed them off, let his lips move a little.

"Leave it alone," Oleg muttered, and wandered away.

After a decent interval John followed him back into the main space. People were leaving. Mavlak's unattended cocaine glowed, seemed almost to hum at the centre of the coffee table. John put a hand on the back of the couch. The disposable camera was wedged between the cushions and John scooped it up casually and pocketed it. No one gave a damn.

He surveyed the room one more time. A red wine spill on the blue bear rug resembled a bloodstain. Two women were still outside. One of them looked directly at him. It wasn't a calculated move—she was only looking to see who remained—but his heart lurched, and her mouth dropped open. She murmured something to her companion and hauled back the patio door.

He wanted to run. He wanted to scream *Fire!*, create a panic that would drive them apart. He wanted her to have been mistaken about who she had seen. Most of all he wanted her not to greet him loudly. To that end he walked at her rather than turning tail. He had read that to diminish the power of a punch you should always move towards it. It was a lesson he thought must be nearly impossible to put into practice, and furthermore he doubted the physics. But here he was, moving forward. They met in the centre of the room. The DJ had his eyes closed, was swaying to something he had announced in a whisper was "Pan-American, boys and girls, the late-night crossing, lights down, seats in the fully reclined position."

"You don't know me," John breathed. He smiled innocuously. "Frank Coleman," he said. "Awful nice to meet you."

She looked well. How long had it been, four years? She parted her lips and then sealed them again.

He said, "I was just leaving. Can I see you out?"

"I can't leave yet," she said. "I have to talk to someone." She tipped her head to one side. "What did you say your name was?"

He told her.

"Jesus Christ."

"I have to go."

There were steps on the stairs: Petrovitch, and Ruby was with him. John felt as if he was lurching from one disaster to another. He knocked his glass against Hanne's and made for the door.

Petrovitch caught him while he was waiting for someone to return with his coat. "You are escaping our clutches," he said.

Ruby slapped his arm. "He has a terrible way of putting things," she said brightly. "Half the time I don't know if it's the language or if he's doing it on purpose. You must be Frank." She took hold of his arms and squeezed as she kissed his cheek. "Well, thank you, Frank."

She smelled of cigarette smoke and champagne and something mildly floral.

He wriggled into his coat.

"Forgive the interruption," Petrovitch said.

"I was relieved, to be honest," John said. He smiled bravely. "And anyway, you're a busy man."

"I told Ruby I would like to buy you lunch. She said she would like to join us. How do you feel about that, Frank?"

He said he would think about it.

Petrovitch pressed for the elevator and the door opened. "It is all a man can ask," he said pleasantly.

John felt Hanne's gaze on him. He smiled, but self-assurance had left him. The muscles in his face contorted into wretched unappealing shapes. "Nice to meet you," he murmured at Ruby, and again she touched his arm. But John was already stepping backward into the opening, praying as he did so that the elevator had actually arrived.

DECEMBER 8

"I quit." It was the next morning, and John was talking on the phone to Sonny Rockliff.

Sonny said he was watching Maddy swim lengths. "I'm actually at the pool. No closed-circuit bullshit for me this morning. My shoes are getting wet. Tell me I'm not the happiest guy in the world."

"I quit, I said. You must not have heard me."

"Oh, *man*! You should see her turns."

John hung up and waited for Sonny to phone him back.

He was in the shower when the call came and he didn't bother to chase it. Sonny's gung-ho attitude towards this assignment—and towards his daughter's swimming, towards his life in general—didn't sit well. This need Sonny apparently had to see dramatic results, and to see them instantly, worried him. If you were over-anxious you were liable to miss something. And you were going to put your own people at risk.

Ten minutes later the phone rang yet again. John carried it to the window and propped his coffee on the radiator. His room faced south, over the Royal Ontario Museum and Queen's Park, as well as assorted university buildings and snowy quadrangles. A hospital chimney released thick smoke into a bitter blue sky, and almost directly south the CN Tower's sky-high spike appeared to divide Lake Ontario in two.

John repeated his plan. He was tense and his neck ached. "I'm booking a plane this morning. I'll do you the courtesy of a stopover in Newark. You can debrief me and then I'm gone."

Sonny was now in his car, being driven back to the offices. He didn't understand. "Tell me about the party," he said. "What happened?"

"You know damn well what happened."

"Of course I don't."

"You had to know she was here. It's why you picked me. Don't lie to me, Sonny. I know how these things work."

"Who was there?"

John held the receiver away from his ear. He was tempted to throw it across the room. A small plane lifted off from the Toronto Island airport, circled back towards the tower, appeared to fly below the level of the observation deck. Sonny was still talking: ". . . because unless you tell me . . ."

"Hanne," John barked. "Hanne Kristiansen was there, and if you claim you didn't know that was a possibility, I'll hang up again and that will be the last time you speak to me."

"Hanne *who*?"

"Tread carefully here, Sonny. Bear in mind that I know how closely you must have gone through my file before offering me this assignment. I know this isn't coming as a surprise."

Rockliff repeated her name.

"I don't want you strategizing while I'm talking, Sonny. What is her connection here?"

"_____"

"Well?"

The admission finally escaped Sonny like a sigh. "She sells him art," he said.

John dredged up a memory of Petrovitch's apartment and noted for the first time that the walls had been well covered with paintings and drawings.

"Mostly Russian art," Sonny said. "She set up a gallery in Yorkville a couple of years ago. Well, we were fairly sure you didn't know where she was. Right? Anyway, she struggled. The Toronto scene is like everywhere else, you need contacts. Hanne didn't have those. But Petrovitch suggested, we think, that if she were to bring in some Russian artists he would be interested. Well, she must have a good eye, because she's doing well now, by all accounts."

"You knew we would meet."

"It was a possibility we entertained."

"And yet you sent me in there as Frank Coleman. That's a bomb just waiting to explode."

"We didn't see it that way."

"What do you mean, *We didn't see it that way*? That's the way it is."

"We saw it as an opportunity. You know that's how the Bureau works."

"You don't work for the Bureau any more, Sonny."

"The BVC saw an opportunity to gain deeper penetration faster."

"What the hell sort of talk is that?"

"You and Hanne have a history. A bond. We thought you might benefit from that bond. Your investigation might benefit."

"You meant to exploit it, is what you mean."

"We thought if anything went wrong Hanne might be able to warn you."

"She sells him paintings. Why would she know?"

"Look," Sonny said. There was an exasperated edge to his voice. "Look, all I thought when I saw her name was, John Selby should get this assignment. That's it. It's why I went to the fairly extreme trouble of requesting you, John. I could have let you languish in Virginia. They had you up for some sort of desk-bound rehab, did you know that? Minimum of six months checking licence plates or wading through court transcripts. I thought you'd be pleased. And I don't know what you're going to find. She's not suspected of anything. I'd tell you if she was. But come on, if Lara's name came up, *I'd* want the job."

"We're not the same." John paced in his cage. "You don't know me. And you sure as hell don't know *her*. What made you think you could predict how she would react? *I* didn't know what she was going to do, for Christ's sake."

He tried to stop it from happening but his head filled up with images of her as she was then, in Germany. Arguing with a ticket agent at the train station, her terrible, comic German betraying her. Asleep in his bed while he tiptoed around her, the covers riding up over her legs, and one of her feet, as always, hooked over the end of the mattress. Whispering in his ear that she was bored, or tired, or aroused, at the movie theatre three blocks from where they lived. And then the sprint home with her through the grey-green streets in a spring thunderstorm, Hanne shrieking as she leapt through rushing gutters. And the final awful vacuum that was his apartment when she left him. The walls screaming in at him. The cruel spatters of paint on the floor where she had stood her easel.

"I commissioned a report on her," Sonny was saying. "And I kept track of you, John, after Atlanta. You two were close. Everyone in Berlin remembers her."

"Not everything would have been in your damn report," John said, freshly angered. "You don't reduce it that way—to words."

"I hear you," Sonny said, and there was something about the jocular phrasing or the blatantly false camaraderie that caused John to hang up on Sonny one more time.

*

He took a brisk but painful walk along Bloor Street and dropped the camera off at a developer's. He ate lunch at an Indian restaurant tucked down an alley just off Yonge, next to a subway entrance. And then he returned to his room. He sent away the woman who wanted to pull the bed together. "It's too late," he told her without opening the door. The cart squeaked along to his neighbour. He picked up the cellphone.

"Tell me one thing," he said to Sonny. He was holding up one finger in pointless illustration. "I understand you not telling me in advance. I would have run the other way, and you knew that. I'm not saying what you did was right, but we'll say for a minute that I understand."

"Okay." John could hear that Sonny was tapping away at a keyboard.

"The Frank Coleman name tag. It could have got me killed last night. It might still."

"It's a fuck-up, John. Plain and simple." He sighed. "I thought you should get the job. I felt strongly about it. And I guess that means not everything else was thought through to the degree it should have been. I'm sorry. I'm prepared to bring you back. We'll find something else for you."

It was bullshit. Something Sonny had cooked up that afternoon. There might even have been a meeting to iron out the kinks. But it was what he wanted to hear. When he said he would stay, Sonny was appropriately quiet in his thanks and obvious in his relief.

"We're going through one of his trucks tomorrow," Sonny told him.

"Where?"

"Just outside Toronto. At the old dumpsite."

"I'd like to be there."

"That's fine."

"Good."

"So tell me about the party," John's boss said.

And John, a man who knew he had returned rather meekly to his flock, did as he was told.

DECEMBER 9

"How the fuck can it be raining?" John asked. "It's too cold for rain."

"You want me to answer that?" Sonny Rockliff said cheerfully. "Because Madison asked me the same thing the other day. Next morning I was online finding out."

"Finding out what?"

"*Rain*. How does it rain? How does an internal combustion engine work? How do you catch a cold? Why is the sky blue? It's all right here." He tapped the side of his soaked head.

They wore canary ponchos, rubber boots. The rain was severe, and complaining gulls tipped and wheeled through the storm.

"This is full," Sonny said, indicating the massive dump site in front of them. "Those grass hills are all full of garbage. Everything you see going on here is aimed at locking the gate and walking away."

"Really."

"Well, not literally. You have to ensure the runoff isn't contaminated. You have to vent this stuff properly and take core temperature readings to make sure there isn't a fire raging down below. But its days as a receiver are over." He was shouting to make himself heard over the rain.

"Except for today."

"The RCMP called the mayor."

"So they'll just bury this load here when we're done?"

"Sure. What's another hundred tons when you've been generating nearly two million a year?"

John whistled and water ran into his mouth. He had decided not to mention Hanne this morning. If he did, their conversation would have a bad outcome. Sonny would defend himself poorly, in all probability he would lie, and John would be forced to either walk away or back down. He indicated the silver tractor-trailer parked fifty yards away. Men in black rain gear and surgical masks, thick gloves, were working to remove its load.

"So this is one of his rigs? Where's the driver? I don't need to tell you how bad it would be if he were somehow to identify me."

"We've got him drinking coffee with the gatekeeper. Half a mile away."

"And you're going through other rigs, or just his?"

"Three others over the next week. Different contractors. I won't be here, but it will look the same."

Two of the search party ran towards them, both holding their plastic hoods by the brim. Their faces were streaming. Water made a web of their eyelashes.

Sonny made the introductions. "This is Matt Hart. He came up with me. And Tom Pernice, RCMP. Those are mostly his boys doing the dirty work. This here is John Selby, he's just joined us in Newark."

Pernice said they had pulled maybe 20 percent of the contents from the trailer. "It's been compacted, you understand that?" he said. "It's a tough slog. Where exactly are you thinking you might find something?"

"We don't know," Sonny said. "Your guess is as good, you know."

"Well, this is going to take all morning. Maybe even all day."

"That's okay."

"What's the weather forecast?"

"Snow."

"Snow?"

"By midday."

Pernice and Hart, grumbling, went back to their sifting and sorting.

John said, "I don't think they're happy to be out here."

By noon the container was half empty and the rain had changed to sleet. They had found nothing. Three men were examining the inside of the container with powerful torches. John clambered up into the cab. A creased photograph of a brunette was attached to the sun visor. A paper coffee cup crushed on the floor. The seat was thick with dirt, and where it joined the backrest were dozens of pistachio shells and gold toffee wrappers. A November 1–7 *TV Guide*, a *Toronto Sun*. In the glove compartment a sun-browned copy of *Siddhartha* and a jumble of filthy cassette tapes—Shania Twain, The Tragically Hip, Poco. A logbook (everything in order), insurance documents, a Canadian passport identifying the driver as Mita Potoshkin, forty-three.

"Find anything we missed?" Sonny's head was at the window.

"Can you imagine living like this?" John said.

Another hour and they gave up.

"Send it out," Sonny commanded. "The driver's getting restless. He says he's a family man and doesn't want to get stranded overnight in the U.S. He wants to get out of here and reload. What do you think, Tom?"

Tom Pernice was all smiles. "I think I'm glad we didn't find anything. I'm relieved. You?"

"Absolutely. It doesn't mean it's not happening, though. And while we don't want Petrovitch taking this search personally, at least he knows we won't make it easy."

Pernice was almost apologetic. "We've paid him some attention because that's what you wanted, but we've still got nothing. His friends are assholes, I'll grant you that. And he does fuck-all to discourage them. But all the same. Maybe we should lobby for some surveillance money."

Sonny said their actions were being driven by an abundance of caution, nothing more, and he didn't see it was necessary for the Canadians to go out of their way just yet.

"But you've inserted John, am I right?"

"He's met the man, yes."

Pernice looked at the two of them in a way that said he knew they wanted to run their own operation and quite frankly that was fine with him. He was less territorial than Sonny Rockliff would be if the situation were reversed.

There were handshakes all round. Promises of further cooperation. Matt Hart was sticking close to Sonny's side; he'd had enough of hands-on work for the day.

Sonny rode with John back to his hotel. They entered separately, but then John took him up to the roof and pointed out Petrovitch's apartment building.

"What do you do next?" Sonny said, staring intently, as if he might see Nikolai moving behind the penthouse glass.

"I've got names for you," John said. "Hollins."

"Doesn't ring a bell."

"Well, check it. Someone at Petrovitch's place expressed a relief at Hollins being out of the way."

"Okay. What's the other one?"

"Victor Lefsky, Levski, something like that. A Russian. Petrovitch was surprised to see him, and not pleased."

"I'll get on them."

"Until then, I wait for him to get in touch," John said. "He wants to do lunch."

"Cozy."

"And I get my pictures back this afternoon."

"We should do that together," Sonny said, rubbing his hands together. "I've got a keen eye."

"A keen eye?"

Sonny shrugged cheerfully. "You know what I mean."

"Not a clue," John said. "Not the faintest."

DECEMBER 10

Tim Hollins was on the couch in front of the fireplace, his backside sinking slowly between the cushions. The fire sputtered and flashed. An ember spat free and died on the oak floor. One wood attacking another.

He was restless, and when it was dark he got in the car and drove. He liked the way headlights lit into trees, and how the darkness crowded in. His father's death hadn't changed that. His every turn, every rise and fall, was amplified by the twin beams.

He crossed the one-lane land bridge to Scorpion Island. On his left was black open water. It never froze because warm water from an industrial parts factory hidden in the hills entered the Seaway here through a steep-sided culvert. A green light bobbed in the distance. The island's sharp cliff rose precipitously ahead. A white skirt of ice clung to the rock face. The road climbed from the water, veered steeply between towering velvet firs.

He wanted to talk to Bill Sumner, who lived in the only house on the island. Bill was a friend of his father's, someone he had met after his retirement. Bill hadn't come to his father's funeral and Tim was curious why.

This stretch of the Thousand Islands was full of characters, his father had told him once. They'd been scaling the Bridge en route to a wooden boat show in Clayton. The restaurant hadn't opened yet; Michael was still trying to decide on the name. He had pointed out innocuous-seeming specks of rock, half-acres of berry bramble and sumac that nearly vanished whenever a storm swept in. "That place, or so I've heard, is home to a man who saved a lot of lives in Nicaragua."

Tim had told him, "I'd feel a bit isolated out there, I think."

There were others, Michael had said. A woman who worked in New Zealand for the Canadian government. A husband and wife team who taught English in the former Yugoslavia for nearly twenty years. There were hoteliers, he'd said, and bankers; there were mystery writers and retired politicians. The list had gone on for miles.

Tim worked the car through the trees, worrying all the while that he wasn't going to be made welcome. Bill Sumner was a big man, bearded, very private. He had worked for many years in Spain, and one Sunday morning he'd lost an arm in an explosion in a terrorist attack on a hotel lobby. He had been on Scorpion Island seven years now, doing some freelance consulting work for Trade and Industry.

The island's heart was as flat as an airfield. During the Second World War pilots had practised grass landings here, dropping precipitously over the water before bouncing noisily to a stop, the undercarriage slashing through wheat grass. These twenty-some hectares of grassland were ringed thickly by evergreens. From the water it was deceiving, it looked densely forested, and from the air it looked uninteresting. But Bill had built an impressive home on the edge of the cliff where it pointed most clearly towards open water, a modernist experiment in glass and steel.

He shared the island with two buffalo. Tim had seen him once sitting in the waving grass, his new arm resting in his lap. A big man adrift with a pair of behemoths he had adopted from a bankrupt petting zoo.

Tim rounded the last hairpin. His headlights swept pleasingly over the trees and into the centre of the pasture. The halogen beams locked onto nothing. The road split left and right. Both routes led around the perimeter to the house. The left ran past the barn and boathouse, but he chose right and didn't know why. Perhaps because there was nothing to be seen in the dark. Or perhaps, he thought, because by choosing the counter-clockwise route he kept the field, the heart of the island, closest to him, and the cliff farthest away. It was possible he felt infinitesimally safer that way.

When he knocked, no one came to the door. He circled the building on foot. Every six metres he entered the range of another motion sensor and was caught in its harsh cone of green-white light. As each one clicked off, the next kicked in, so that there were only half seconds of darkness trapped between them. Each time the beam held him, his own reflection stared wide-eyed from another of the dark windows. Bill's decrepit Jeep sat idle in the middle of the turning circle, kindling stacked in the torn back seat. There was no smell of a fire.

Tim walked up behind the house, through bare alder and cherry, past the white hammock that drooped moon-like between two trees, and he scuffed through the fallen, still-crisp leaves. There was light in the western sky from Kingston, thirty-two kilometres away. A few clouds floated grey in the sky.

The fierce volcanic light of the explosion reached him before the concussive wave could storm across the field and knock him onto his back. He sat up, his hands splayed out behind to support him. He was aware of a peculiar acuity to his vision, as if he had just surfaced from muddy water. A pink mushroom of smoke was chased into the stars by flame. He scrambled to his feet and ran. The field was hard and uneven. He stumbled and staggered, his ankles nearly giving out.

The blast must have come from the boathouse. He reached the edge of the field, crossed the sandy road. A footpath led through the trees to the barn, a narrow corridor of frosted rock and wood. But already, at the base of a tree, a lick of flame had taken root. A second explosion knocked him off course and heat bored into him. There was the whistle of something pressurized exploding, screaming into the sky. He brought his hands up to his face and kept going.

The barn had been built at the top of the cliff, and an iron staircase descended in an elongated Z from its back end to a sleek steel-and-timber home Bill had made for his speedboat. But that end of the barn was gone. Its dark frame roared viciously. The blast had obviously come from below, and Tim had no idea how to get down there. Black smoke poured along the underside of the barn's roof and funnelled through the front doors.

He was coughing, choking, his lungs were filling with the heat and the smoke. He wavered at the edge of the cliff. A side panel of Bill's boat had been carried a good distance offshore. It lay ripped and buckled in oil-slicked water, the heat of it melting the ice. The roof of the boathouse had disappeared and fire raged in the steel box that remained. It chewed at the rest of the boat's carcass and wrapped itself, like red tinsel, around the staircase. Two paint cans surpassed their limits and fired high into the sky. The trees would catch next. He called out: "Bill!" But it was an exercise, a reflex. If Bill was down there, and Tim thought he must have been, he was dead now.

Tim raced once more around the barn. The fire gleamed through the gaps like the light inside a Hallowe'en pumpkin. He dashed back and forth until he was sure there was nothing to be done. Then he edged along the cliff in the lit darkness, hunting for a way down.

A terrible bellowing sounded behind him. One of the buffalo charged from the barn, a thick length of rope around its neck like a leash. It bucked, hooves flashing, and nearly stood on its massive head, throwing itself about as if the heat were an unwanted rider. Smoke wafted from its back, and at first Tim thought that's all it was, but then the animal bucked again, spun around to reveal an acre of flank in flames, fire cooking its side. The miserable beast tipped onto that side, tried to smother the fire. Tim ran halfway to it before he realized that was crazy. He took another step and the buffalo saw him, trained its wild eyes on him, then roared again, snorted, and fought its way to its feet.

A crash of timbers sounded from inside the barn and then the cavernous, sick bellow of another animal. For fuck's sake! The second buffalo ripped free of its tether and plowed, it seemed, into the side of the barn. And again. Finally, it blundered through the door. This one fully aflame. Only its short horns and the wet, fat splash of its snout had been spared. It streaked into the trees, caught an old pine head on and bounced away, pinballed along the forest fringe. At first it moved generally away from Tim but then it veered right at him.

The other animal had sunk once more to its knees. It moaned terribly and tipped again onto its side. It crackled dully. That noise of it cooking, not quite dead, was separable somehow from the rest of the cacophony. Tim backed away, stumbling, a hand out behind him. There was nothing between him and the second animal. There were certainly smells in the air now—of wood and gasoline, and noxious heavy fumes from the boat's upholstery. The smell everywhere of meat. The buffalo charged him, its mane and chest aflame, its flanks smouldering. Tim threw himself to one side and the animal missed him, careened instead over the edge of the cliff, seemed for an instant cartoonishly suspended there, as if some suddenly alert God might yet rewind the film. Tim crawled forward in time to see the collision of buffalo and ice, to see the ice give, great milky plates sinking under the animal. It thrashed at the surface, its fire doused, but already aware of the new threat. It smacked at the edge of the ragged receding lip.

Nudged it again and again. If it had swum for shore it might have made it, at least to shallow water. Then perhaps Tim could have helped. But instead it struck out heavily for a green light that blinked benignly, way off in the channel. For ten minutes Tim watched. He lay on his stomach, in tears, as the buffalo beat against the edge of the ice, mooed desperately, then swam a little, then rested. Finally its head sank under the white shelf. For a while it appeared it might remain that way, its great length of furred spine breaking the surface. But then slowly it sank. A dark island sinking into a much greater, permanent darkness.

*

The open-cockpit RCMP launch smashed its way to shore and trained a concentrated light on the remains of the boathouse. Two divers in neoprene suits moved about stiff-leggedly, like monsters, on the wet deck, as a third person fiddled with the valves on their oxygen tanks. Eventually they leapt over the side and entered the gelatinous water feet first, right hands holding their mouthpieces in place. Their lights revealed them below the surface: yellow beams that poked again and again into the pilings. Up top, an Ontario Provincial Police cruiser and a fire engine bumped around the field. A hose was aimed at the barn. A constable had given Tim a blanket, even though he wasn't wet and it was impossible at this blaze to be cold. She asked him to explain himself, who he was, why he was there, and for ten minutes he indulged her; they played their roles under the stars. She doesn't know what to do, Tim thought, watching her take notes nervously and look around for direction, the angle she should most properly take. This was all new to her. To all of them.

They discovered Bill's burnt body wedged between the wrecked melted hull and a support beam for the shed. One of the divers explained to his superior: "It looks like the explosion threw the boat this way, and *smack!* he was crushed. We freed him, no problem, but most of his guts are floating around like snakes." The diver's red, towel-dried hair stood on end. Someone else shone a light onto the body, which lay uncovered on the deck. A brown fluid leaked from Bill's neck. Tim, not able to look away, saw Bill's metal arm against a backdrop of torn jacket. He took in the duller gloss of his exposed skull where the hair and skin had burned away. The dead-fish gaze of his eyes.

Eventually the sky began to lighten and Tim became restless. The cop said she would walk him to the house. Others would want to talk to him. A satellite moved steadily across the morning sky. The noises behind him were terrible. The extended scrape and splinter of wood on metal as another beam in the barn gave out. People running and shouting, occasional exclamations of horror. A crane arrived and stretched its arm over the ruin. It was a Goya back there, Tim thought. It was a Francis Bacon.

At the house there were two more OPP cruisers, a red Pathfinder and a black sedan, and tape had been strung across the road to block access. There were men inside the house. One was on his hands and knees just inside the door, another was down the hall talking on the telephone. From an upstairs bedroom the flash of a camera blasted out into the trees. All four doors on Tim's battered Toyota were open and the contents of the glove compartment lay on the passenger seat.

A burly man in a stained black jacket and faded jeans puffed across the gravel. "We were going to put it back together for you," he said.

Tim nodded. There was no point saying anything unless he had to.

"What were you doing out here, Tim?"

"Bill was a friend."

"A friend of yours?"

Tim shrugged. "Sure."

"And you thought you'd drop by."

"On a friend. Sure."

The man's stomach hung over a worn brown belt, and a small V of doughy flesh poked below the bottom button of his cheap white shirt. "You see anyone else out here? You meet anyone?"

"No."

"Only, there's a set of tire tracks on top of yours. Someone left after you arrived."

"How can you tell?" Tim asked. "Surely the fire truck, the cruisers, covered everything up. Didn't they?"

The man shook his thick head. A latex glove poked out of a pocket in his jacket. "Not everything, Tim. We checked. You can't be too careful."

"Tell that to Bill," Tim said. "So you think someone else?"

"I don't know what we think. I'm wondering about you."

Tim cast his mind back. It was difficult to say what he thought.

The man pointed at the house. "And someone was in there." He struggled for breath, as if even speaking tired him out.

Tim told him he had circled the house when he'd arrived and hadn't seen anything. "But I set all the lights off." He squinted up to the roofline, hunted out the motion sensors that had caught him snooping. He found them spaced evenly along the side of the house, suspended from the underside of the eaves like bats. "So anyone in there would have seen me just fine. But there was no car. Nothing. Just Bill's Jeep. So I figured he had to be around somewhere. That's why I went up into the field." He spun around. "Well, that's it," he said. "Of course."

"What is?" The cop looked at him curiously, tried to figure out Tim's sudden enthusiasm.

"Bill's Jeep was here when I arrived."

The cop didn't answer but seemed instantly more alert. He turned and gestured to someone in the house. They waited. Scarlet cinders twisted and frothed into the sky. The muscular sound of the Coast Guard boat surged across the field. A tall, skeletally thin man emerged and walked towards them. He seemed fragile, mechanically unfit for the act. The first man's physical opposite. The two of them stood before him like ghouls.

"Tim, this is Des Boyle. He's in charge here. He's with the RCMP. We both are."

Tim nodded. "We know each other. We've met, anyway." They shook hands. It was like taking hold of a small and surprisingly soft glove, picking it up in a high-end store and being impressed by its feel.

Des said, "Are you okay?" His voice was strong, sonorous, one you might hear on the radio introducing Puccini or Mozart.

Tim's hand had begun to ache. There was a cut across his palm. "Ah, you know," he said vaguely, not at all sure how to describe what he felt. Aware only of the sensation of floating—his feet floating above the ground, and his brain doing the same but in the very centre of his head, unsupported by the spine or any necessary fluid.

The first time Tim had seen Des Boyle was at the reception after Michael's funeral. It wasn't much of a party. They had put some bottles of decent, but not too decent, red wine on top of the bar and Rebecca had pulled a mile of Saran Wrap from two trays of elaborate hors d'oeuvres. When Tim had approached, openly curious, Boyle had identified himself and bowed his head fractionally; he might even have closed his eyes, said how sorry he was for Tim's loss. The same words had been living in everyone's mouths.

Tim had asked him whether he was there in an official capacity. "Rebecca says she saw you at the cemetery," he said.

Boyle said, "No, I'm not. Not really. I'm just interested in the death, that's all." That was the word he had used: *interested*.

"You had a photographer there too," Tim suggested. "Wearing a *Recorder* jacket."

"We did indeed."

"How come? Did you know my father?"

"Well, he was my age. And I watch the news. I'm always interested in how another man makes use of his time on this planet. It's a nasty way to die, is all. I'm obliged to take a look at it. I don't expect to find anything. So it's official and at the same time it's not, you know."

Tim said, "What exactly do you look at?"

"The car, for one thing. Its brakes. The steering."

It was as far as they got. Rebecca must have thought he might need rescuing and she had glided his way, linked an arm through his, and led him to the window, where they'd stared out together.

Now he stood in front of the house on Scorpion Island and tipped forward onto his toes the way Rebecca had in his memory, then rocked back onto his heels, connected again with the ground. His boots were cold. The fat cop said, perhaps not for the first time, "Tell Des what you just told me."

"I told him that Bill's Jeep was here when I arrived."

Des lifted an eyebrow and it made his eye seem perfectly round. "That's right," he said, unlocking a memory. "Bill had an old Jeep. Completely unroadworthy."

Tim nodded. "It was loaded with kindling. The back seat was piled high with the stuff."

Des Boyle and the other cop exchanged a look. There was a patch of stubble along Des's jawline that the razor had missed. He said, "He had wood in the back of the Jeep?"

"Exactly. It was over there when I arrived." He pointed.

"Were the keys in it, Tim?"

Tim shook his head. "Sorry."

Des unexpectedly touched his arm. "Not to worry. We know a lot more than we did five minutes ago."

"I suppose *you* do," Tim said.

Des turned to the other cop. "Check on that, Jerry," he said. "Okay? Get us a plate, and get the word out."

Jerry puffed away to one of the cruisers. Des said, "I hear you got a glimpse of Bill's body over there." He shuddered. "Are you sure you're okay? I can have someone drive you home if you like."

"To keep an eye on me, report back on how I acted?" Kindness wasn't what he wanted. He needed desperately to sleep.

Des smiled kindly, and the corners of his mouth seemed to reach most of the way up his cheeks. "If I thought you were involved I wouldn't be letting you go, Tim."

Two men were carrying out a rolled-up carpet. The photographer was still working. A man with latex gloves was on his hands and knees beneath a window, a flashlight between his teeth.

Tim said, "There's no way this was an accident, is there?"

"Our friends in the Coast Guard say it was a bomb. And that Bill was already dead."

Tim looked at him carefully. "That's not what I heard them saying."

Des said calmly, "There's no smoke in his mouth, Tim. That's the latest word. His tongue is pink as a salmon steak."

"Maybe he was killed instantly."

"Maybe. They're pretty good, though. And this tongue thing seems to satisfy them." He stuck out his own tongue, reached up and waggled it a few times. He let it go and it darted away. He indicated Tim's car. "You should go home. Get yourself some breakfast, or some sleep. I'll get someone to hold up the tape for you." He shook Tim's hand. "Right, then. We'll be in touch."

Boyle headed back towards the house and Tim watched him go. The detective was skin and bones, he saw; there was almost nothing to him.

DECEMBER 11

The phone call came at seven in the morning. John Selby had been under water; he assumed it was St. Thomas. He was weightless above a luminous coral landscape. And he could breathe. In fact his lungs had never worked so well. He looked up and saw the water-air divide, a shifting silver foil, and the sight left him ecstatic. Only now the phone was yanking him from those waters as unceremoniously as if he had been fooled by an angler's lure.

He forced himself, as he rolled, to appreciate the three hundred thread-count sheets, the cat-in-heaven purr of the humidifier. A wafer of golden light lay at the bottom of the door.

He heard: "Your cellphone is off, John. Do you know that? We've found Hollins."

"Where?" He saw the coral, its rough crevices. He tried to fix it in his memory so he could return to it later.

"The Islands."

"Which islands?" *Come on, Sonny*, he thought. *Don't play games.*

"The Thousand Islands. Three hours east of you. In the St. Lawrence Seaway."

Selby was coming around. He stared up at the stippled ceiling that had to be, what, twelve feet away? "Who is he?"

"Who *was* he. He's dead. Car crash. Three weeks ago."

Selby threw off the duvet and swung his feet around and over the edge of the bed. He caught sight of himself in the mirror over the walnut bureau. He was doing okay, he still looked pretty good. Sonny hadn't said anything else yet; there was only the hum and whistle of the distance between them.

"What are you doing?" John asked.

"Waiting for you to wake up."

Selby opened the soft pouch of coffee with his teeth. He brought water from the bathroom. "I'll call you back," he said. "On a better line."

He dressed while he waited for the coffee and then took a mug down to the lobby. He had woken with a new fear: that Petrovitch had the room wired. The battery on his cellphone, though, had run down and he had forgotten to recharge it during the night. All the technology in the world couldn't save him from absentmindedness. He took the pay phone farthest from the elevators.

"Okay. Shoot," he said. "Was it an accident?"

"So they say. Why? Did you get the impression it was a hit?"

"This guy—this Oleg—wasn't specific." He racked his brain to check the truth of that statement. "He just said they were glad to have Hollins out of the way. Who was he?"

"A lobbyist. Worked out of Toronto. Did well for himself. But made himself unpopular along the way. Not exactly a liberal. More a mercenary. Sniffing after the almighty dollar. Didn't care who his clients were. Worked for Ontario Hydro one day, the cable company the next. He nearly always got what he wanted."

"Did he work for Petrovitch?"

"Funny you should ask. Mr. Michael Hollins was responsible for securing the garbage deal for Nikolai. The mayor didn't want it to happen. Said there were any number of better-qualified outfits, some of whom contributed to his re-election campaign, by the way. Council didn't want it either. Seems they anticipated some of our concerns. Not with Petrovitch per se, but just with the fact that he wasn't a pro. He'd got his hands on some trucks, that was it. I've got a press report here. Some clever bastard said that having a fleet of big rigs didn't qualify you for cross-border drops any more than having a physics degree made you Einstein. I like that. Too bad no one listened."

"How did he end up in the Thousand Islands?"

"He retired last couple of years. Nikolai owns the paper on a waterfront building that Hollins turned into a restaurant and home."

"Was it a payoff?"

"Sort of. Petrovitch retains a controlling 51 percent. Still, there's a son, Tim, and his share alone is worth three-quarters of a million."

"That's a heck of a thank-you."

"We think you should go down there. Nose around."

"I'm not sure I follow. He's dead. All the players are here."

"Last night another man died."

"No shit."

"He was blown up in his boathouse."

"How does he tie in with Hollins?"

"They were practically neighbours, for one thing. For another he was a regular at the restaurant. It's called Granite, by the way. And the island this guy lived on—it's less than a mile from the border and he had a good speedboat. Past tense, of course."

"You think there's a smuggling operation going on."

"There are several smuggling operations going on up there, John. In fact, there have been several smuggling operations in those islands for hundreds of years. Booze, cigarettes, drugs, guns. Chinese migrants headed for restaurant kitchens in New York. You name it and it's been spirited across that strip of water. We sink an increasingly large amount of cash into policing that stretch of river. Until recently it's been impossible to do the job properly. It's a maze of islands and channels, deep passages and impassable swamp. The good guys haven't stood much of a chance against an old-timer with a head full of knowledge. It's even worse when that old-timer gets his hands on a speedboat. The border's just a crooked line running through the middle of a thousand islands."

"Hence the name," John said. "But maybe someone else killed them. You said yourself Hollins wasn't popular. Made a lot of enemies, I bet. Who was this other guy?"

"Bill Sumner. We don't know much yet. Retired. But this is all happening very fast. I'll have more later in the day."

John watched a doorman chase a panhandler outside. They stood beyond the revolving doors yelling at each other.

Sonny said, "You remember those two Russians I told you about? The ones we picked up in Manhattan after a brawl? Well, they're back in Russia. The New York Police charged them with disorderly, some run-of-the-mill battery stuff, and they made bail. Next thing you know they're in Moscow."

"Why the hell would they bolt like that?"

"No idea, John. But they're Petrovitch's men. So our best guess is he ordered them out. Said don't come back. Can you imagine the clout he has, if he can change their lives that quickly? Maybe you should ask him. When is that lunch of yours happening?"

"I don't know yet. Have you had any luck with the photographs? Or with the other fellow—Viktor whatever-it-was."

"I should have something for you this—"

John didn't hear the rest. The panhandler had been bustled from the frame, but spinning through the brass roundabout was Nikolai Petrovitch, with Ruby on his tail. They released into the lobby laughing. Petrovitch spun around to greet Ruby and the two of them staggered in each other's arms across the gleaming floor as if it were the ballroom of an ocean liner.

John hung up. They hadn't seen him yet. Perhaps if he turned . . . But then Ruby's face lit up and she stabbed a finger repeatedly in his direction. The shock of seeing him had robbed her of his name.

"Frank." Petrovitch clapped his hands together. "My God, you have ruined the surprise."

John cleared his throat, moved away from the telephone, but too late.

Petrovitch said, "Is the phone broken in your room? You should make them move you. Whenever Ruby and I go away we change rooms at least once. Something is always wrong with where they put you."

"I was on my way to breakfast," he lied.

"But you didn't make it," Ruby said helpfully. "Good. We wanted to take you."

"Take me?" It was appropriate to be openly wary, he thought. Hostile would be overdoing it, but a bit hurt might still work to his advantage.

"To breakfast," Petrovitch said. "Ruby thought of somewhere. She can't make lunch. Come on. Can you go? Are you ready?"

He patted his back pocket. "My wallet," he said.

Petrovitch shook his head. "Your money is no good this morning, Frank."

"You don't know how I spend money, Nikolai. No, I need my wallet. And a coat. Wait for me."

"We want to see your room," Ruby said, pouting.

John looked pained.

Petrovitch said, "She is kidding! She hates hotel rooms. But rush, Frank. Rush! Ruby has to be at the office."

They took him in Petrovitch's Land Rover south on Bay Street. The towers of the financial district blocked out the sun. John held on to his knees and sat very upright until he decided it was an arrangement that didn't match the impression he wanted to make. He leaned against the glass, rubbed a hand over his unshaved chin.

"I was thinking about Spain," he said, wanting to appear unconcerned, otherwise engaged. "Of moving on to Spain. If you go far enough south it's quite warm, even now."

"You can just about see Spain from where we're taking you," Ruby said. "Isn't that right, Nikolai?"

"You can certainly see at least halfway," Nikolai agreed amiably.

He guided the Land Rover west along Front Street and south again on Blue Jays Way. They passed below the SkyDome's frantic gesturing gargoyles and parked next to The Roundhouse, home to a microbrewery.

John knew where they were going. Had known since Ruby's crack about Spain. The CN Tower. At the base, the kid selling tickets nodded, waved them past. They were guided one by one through an illuminated security arch that examined the molecules around them for signs of explosive, and then by a beaming and relieved usher into the confines of the elevator.

The joint up here revolves, man. John had his nose to the elevator's glass front as they rose at a disconcerting speed and the reflections were hard to concentrate on. He couldn't tell who it was talking behind him. *It goes around and around. I don't know how they do it, man.*

The SkyDome was a cotton-ball below. Three excited children jumped around their father and a woman with a passing resemblance to Meg Ryan. The children rushed the glass and Ruby caught her breath. John worked his way to the back of the cage. Back to the wall, that was the plan. Thick cloud swallowed them and then, contemptuously, it spit them out again; they were above it and still climbing.

When the doors pulled back fifty-five seconds later, he thought, for an instant, he would step onto the deck of the Starship *Enterprise*. He walked the platform alone. Completed a full circle. The sun above, the patchy cloud below, the horizon endless. He knew it had to be an illusion but the earth's curve seemed visible, even from this relatively modest height of 1,150 feet, apparently 665 feet shy of the spire's tip; the edge of the world appeared to curve at both ends like a downturned lip.

"I'm starving," Ruby said. She rubbed her stomach and arched her back and groaned.

John said, "I thought it went around. Someone on the elevator was talking."

"The fancy restaurant. That's what goes around. Once an hour. Like a big clock."

They stood shoulder to shoulder, the three of them. They were like gods stationed high above the earth. It was an irresistible thought and he shared it with them.

Two boys, eleven or twelve, were sprinting laps, screaming: *North, East, South, West. North, East, South, West.*

"I need to eat," Ruby said.

Thirty feet away a man in Kodiak boots was staring between his feet, as if he expected to be able to see the world turning beneath him.

Petrovitch guided John and Ruby into the café. They sat in a line at the outermost edge of the circle. It was as if centrifugal force threw everyone out to the glass.

A waitress with a name tag that identified her as Mandy brought their breakfasts, and Ruby said, "Thank God. I thought I was going to have to leave without eating. I have a meeting, Niki. You know I can't miss it. I probably shouldn't have come, but Niki said you might not be so keen to see just him. It sounds like he was unpleasant with you, Frank."

"I was only saying we had things to talk about," Petrovitch grumbled.

Ruby made excuses for him. "He's hungover, Frank. It's another reason he had me along—to make conversation while he hydrates himself." She called for the waitress. "Can you put this in a bag for me?" She wiggled a finger over some unbuttered toast. "I know it seems ridiculous but really, I *have* to go and if I don't eat . . ."

She gathered her coat and released the hem of her pants where it had caught on the heel of her shoe. "Go easy on him, Niki," she said. "Okay?"

Petrovitch grunted. He tipped his head back so she could kiss him.

And then she was gone. They had said less than a hundred words to each other. She'd only been the bait to get him there.

Petrovitch swallowed and wiped his face roughly. His beard stubble shredded the delicate paper napkin. Cars and trucks were visible beneath the clouds, moving along the congested streets.

"Ruby is sweet," John said, looking for an avenue.

Petrovitch scooped more potato onto his fork. He wasn't going to be rushed, and John suspected he had a speech to make; he wanted John apprehensive.

Petrovitch called Mandy over and ordered soup. John still had food on his plate. It was a little after eight in the morning.

"What's with that?" John said. "Soup? *Now?*"

"I don't want to be eating all day," Petrovitch explained. "But you have to eat enough. It is a complicated balancing act."

For the first time John thought Nikolai Petrovitch might be mad. "I suppose you have to be careful," he agreed.

Mandy delivered a bowl of lurid orange purée. In the centre was a small clump of what looked remarkably like grass clippings. Nikolai created figure eights in its slick surface. "What is it?"

"It's mango," Mandy said. "A curried mango lime."

"And this?"

"Coriander," she said. "You want me to take it away?"

He pushed it towards her. "Just bring us the bill."

He stared down, disconsolate, into the churning cloud, the city beneath.

"Gods," John reminded him. "Like gods." But Petrovitch fiddled with his cellphone, the cuffs on his shirt. John pulled out cash for the bill and Petrovitch tried to wave him off.

"No, no, I've got it," John said.

He found Mandy at the cash register. "Does he come here a lot?" he said, indicating Nikolai.

"Oh yeah, him, he's okay," she said. "A bad day, I guess." She counted his change out and eyed John hopefully. He passed her a five-dollar bill.

Petrovitch was already outside on the observation deck. He was tucking his shirt in properly and hiking up his pants. He saw John approaching. "So," he began.

John smiled, held out his hands, palms up, wanted it to signify that he was in no mood for another interrogation, that he wasn't going to be a pushover.

"New Jersey Water and Power," Petrovitch said, undeterred. There was nothing pleasant about his tone.

"New Jersey what?"

"Water and Power." He enunciated every syllable, which was fine with John because he needed time to think.

"It's not ringing a bell." But it was, and he knew exactly how Petrovitch had come up with the firm. The pay phone in the hotel lobby. He also knew that because Petrovitch didn't have an access code he would have been shunted through the system slowly until finally he would have been given an opportunity to leave a voice-mail message.

He squinted, took a tough step forward. "At the hotel when I went upstairs."

Petrovitch looked at him steadily.

The real New Jersey Power and Water Corporation had the same number Sonny's group used. This was a dead end. "I was paying off an old utility bill," he said angrily. Sonny would make the appropriate records appear by day's end.

"Your passport shows you out of the U.S. most of the year."

"I keep a base. An apartment."

"In New Jersey? A man who can live anywhere decides to live in New Jersey?"

"To each his own," John said. He held his ground, experienced the familiar surge of chemicals that proved he was in jeopardy. The Kodiak-booted man was still thirty feet away, pretending to take in the view. Of course, he was part of this too. Whatever *this* was. And it couldn't be more than a warning. They were at the top of the world, a confined barred space; there was too much traffic. Just around the curve the elevators were releasing two dozen sightseers every ten minutes. Take it easy, John told himself.

"You are one paranoid son of a bitch," he said to Petrovitch. He ran a hand along the frigid guardrail. Christ, it's beautiful up here, he thought. And then, What's Hanne doing tied up with this guy?

Petrovitch shrugged. He looked at his feet and shuffled them over the concrete. "I don't deny that, Frank. And for that reason it would be better if you left Toronto. Go to Spain."

"Look, I didn't ask for this date, or for the invitation to your party. And I certainly didn't ask to be there when that cab came after you."

Petrovitch bent his leg at the knee and massaged the muscle. "Do not get me started on the taxi, Frank. My mind runs amok."

John pointed at his own, still aching, still black and blue and yellow foot. "If you're suggesting I arranged that, I'm happy to show you the bruises."

"I am undoubtedly wrong," Petrovitch conceded. "But you have come too fast, Frank. Your entry is . . . What is it? . . . It is *questionable*. And I cannot have questionable men around me."

"Your goddamn party was full of questionable men. What are your questions, Nikolai? Not, you understand, because I have any interest in being around you. I'm a man of leisure, not a man interested in a new friend who takes me to the top of tall buildings so he can threaten me. I've met men like you before. The stress gives them ulcers and makes them enemies. But you want my New Jersey address? My account number with the utility company?"

"I want you to leave," Petrovitch said. Rather than raising his voice he had lowered it. "I am scared of you, if you like. I am scared the stories you told me would all be false. It would pain me to listen to them, not knowing."

"I'm not much of a storyteller anyway. I told you that." Thinking now to retreat safely. To exit gracefully, with Petrovitch's mind put at ease. This wasn't the rarest scenario: a cover not quite trusted. It beat the hell out of a cover completely blown.

"And anyway, look at you, Frank," Petrovitch said, moving a gloved hand smoothly up and down in front of John. "You are a man used to sunshine. So little of that reaches the ground in Toronto in the winter. A man could freeze to death. It is a meteorological fact. Now Spain, there is a country a man can relax in."

"Well, I don't have any plans yet. To stay or otherwise."

"I think, then, you should make some." Petrovitch smiled charmlessly. "Here, let me give you an example of how my mind plays tricks on me. Okay?"

John signalled his agreement.

"Good. Here you go, then. Ruby"—he checked behind him to see if his mentioning her might cause her to reappear—"lost a camera the night of the party. She lent it to a friend who swears she put it down only for a minute. And now I worry that you might have picked it up. How ridiculous that is. I know what you must think of me. But these things add up in my head. They worry me. The tanned man who arrives and suddenly my life is different."

It was time to leave, if he could. John threw up his hands. "It must be tough. Living like this."

"It can be."

"But as you like," John said. He held out his hand, but at the same instant Petrovitch turned his head away so smoothly, gazed so concentratedly out over Toronto, that John couldn't be positive the slight was intended. He began to walk away.

Petrovitch shouted after him, "I am sorry, Frank. Truly."

John waited for the elevator. There were children around him, one with a stuffed bear under her arm, another with a cast on his left arm. The innocent and injured had arrived to protect him. At the rail Petrovitch was talking with his help. He was clearly angry at something. How he had handled this, John thought. It could be that. He stared at the silver doors. He was leaving the bridge. To his left a woman leaned as far forward as she could, looked straight down at the ground. She was on tiptoes, and through her thick black stockings her calves lengthened and defined themselves. The man in Kodiaks sauntered towards him. His lace ends were left too long and two great loops, like rabbit ears, drooped from each boot.

The doors slid open and all of them boarded. The floor of the elevator was transparent. They sank quickly into the clouds, which had thickened since the ride up. Eventually the city revealed itself again, soft-sided blocks of colour that hardened as the mist gave them up. The man was studying John's reflection. The elevator slowed sharply and Selby felt his organs shift inside him.

The man spoke. His accent was thick, Russian. At odds with his appearance. "Shithead," he said, and marched away. It was ludicrous, the impotent verbal attack of a man whose parking spot has just been stolen, whose mail is late. He vanished in the long tunnel that led to Front Street, to the train station, to the SkyDome, to the Convention

Centre. It led everywhere. He was gone, and John stood there mute, with sweat running all the way from his armpits to his belt.

*

When Tim got home from Scorpion Island he was dazed. His hand throbbed. He couldn't think. He kicked off his boots, his wet, stretched-out work socks. It was past nine in the morning.

He pushed at the door of the kitchen and he heard her moving around in there a fraction of a second before he saw her. He tried to gather himself. Rebecca had her back to him. He hadn't seen her since the grim post-funeral reception. She was whisking eggs and she kept her elbows tucked in next to her body, her left knee bent and crossed in front of the right, pressed lightly against the counter. He could see the sole of her left foot, the dry, rough skin at her heel, the pink Achilles tendon burrowing beneath the frayed hem of her Levi's. The way her hair caught the light as she moved.

"I heard your car," she said. "I hope it's okay I'm here. I still have keys." She lifted the steel bowl from the countertop and cradled it against her stomach. "You must be hungry." She turned to face him, but concentrated on the eggs. A small pile of grated cheese rose from the sand-coloured wood, as well as a matching pyramid of chopped red onion; there were a few mushrooms, a little spinach.

"Why must I?"

She looked up then and immediately gasped, raised a hand to her face. The beater dripped a long string of egg to the floor in front of her. "My God! Tim, what happened?"

"I'm okay." He was frazzled. He had talked to so many people in the last twelve hours. "Let me take a shower, then I'll explain."

Rebecca nodded. She held out the bowl. "Will you want this later?"

He tried for a smile.

"Good." She was pleased. Some of the awkwardness slipped from her face. "And you don't mind?"

"Your being here? Christ no," he told her. He indicated his clothes. "Anyway. I should . . ."

"Of course," she said. She waved the whisk in the air. "I'll be fine."

He put himself under the hot water, leaned heavily into the wall, and let it rain down on his neck, pour over his shoulders. His mind filled with the details: the acrid death-stink of the buffaloes' fur. The water rising over his boots once the firehoses had made a swamp of the ground. Des Boyle's spectral thinness in dawn's ground-hugging mist. The thrilling sight of Rebecca making herself at home in his house, her neck stretching as she tipped her head to one side.

Getting dressed—the faint smell filtering in of omelette, of potatoes—he wondered how old she was. His age, maybe a year older. He had never asked her. The absence of facts saddened him. They had poached her from a restaurant in Kingston. She had trained in New York. "I'm ambitious," she'd said. "I want to warn you right up front. I probably won't stay long." Michael had loved that speech and he'd left her alone; he respected her talent. He also had a wonderfully laid-out restaurant, and the kitchen—"It's *your* kitchen," he'd said to her, throwing open his arms—was a small marvel. Michael Hollins and son might have been novices in the restaurant business, but she knew they had set things up right.

She had set a place for him in the dining room. "You're not eating?" he said. He wanted her to eat. The balance was wrong if she didn't.

"I am, yes. I forgot." She rushed away, then reappeared with another plate before the swinging doors had even stopped their oiled back-and-forth.

He told her what had happened out at Bill's.

She looked at him skeptically, as if he were being deliberately cruel. He thought perhaps she didn't believe him, but when he stopped she wanted to know, "What is going on in this world?" She pushed the food around on her plate. "All this death." She leaned away from the table.

"We're just a little closer to the action at the moment," he said.

Rebecca shuddered. She prodded at the yellow fold of her omelette until cheese oozed from it. She put her cutlery down. "Do you think it's connected?"

"To Michael?"

"Yes."

He said, "Of course not."

"Really?"

"Really."

"I keep hearing the scream of the engine," she said. "You know? After the impact."

"You have to stop that." He reached over the white field of tablecloth and rested a hand on her arm. "That's a bullshit way to think. And cruel." Tim had driven out to the site, run his hands along the rock face, seen the paint flecks from his father's BMW still attached.

Rebecca focused again. "I don't mean to be cruel."

"Not to me. To yourself." He felt the egg in his mouth, its pale warmth, all the air turned into it so expertly. He was hungry. He didn't know what Rebecca was doing. It annoyed him a little. It was time to move on.

He stared through the window. It had begun to snow. The ice had crept a little farther from the shore, islands were being connected to each other. In the narrow all-white passage between Madawaska and Virgin, a man was inching a fishing hut away from the shore.

Rebecca regarded him freshly. "I almost forgot," she said.

"What is it?"

"There was a man here when I arrived."

"Who?"

"Adams," she said brightly. "Adams Denver. That's quite a name, isn't it? A movie name."

"Where is he?" Blood was filling his head, like a dam had given way.

"I passed him in the doorway. He said he had to pick some stuff up and he'd be back."

"What else did he say?"

"That it was a fine way for a host to treat a guest, you not even being here to greet him. He said he had to break in downstairs." She laughed lightly, and he realized she must have liked Denver. Her face darkened, her brow knotted up. "He's the man Nikolai Petrovitch was sending, right? He is supposed to be here, isn't he? You did say in the end it was okay."

"He didn't say when he'd be back?"

She blushed. "He said he'd be a while. 'I'll give you lovebirds some time alone,' he said. Can you imagine?"

Tim tried to hide the fact that, yes, he could well imagine.

They cleared their plates and then worked together for a while in the kitchen. There were mouse droppings in the flour and forgotten potatoes had gone green and sprouted translucent feelers that wrapped themselves around a broom handle. Rebecca sorted and organized and Tim dutifully carted away the garbage.

"I can't believe you saw him," Rebecca said after a particularly long quiet. Tim was on his hands and knees, coaxing bread crumbs, onion skin, over the lip of the dustpan. She meant Bill Sumner. She was hooking a stockpot to the ceiling rack, and a slim expanse of stomach showed itself between her jeans and navy T-shirt. A tremendous warmth welled inside Tim, moved from his centre to link itself irreversibly to his every organ, wrap itself around the thousand miles of ligament and tendon, artery and vein. He felt the hot shame of it in his arms and his hands. He turned away; the debris in his dustpan tipped onto the floor. He swore and kneeled down to try again.

"Are you okay, Tim?"

"I do want to reopen this place, you know." It was all he could think of.

She smiled.

"In case you were wondering."

"I was, as a matter of fact. I have bills. And I think we've got a good thing here."

He was relieved. "We should take out an ad," he said. "I'll put something together this week."

"Did Bill have a wife?" she said. He looked at her. "I was just wondering."

"No, that was another trait he shared with Dad. Both of them were widows."

"The poor bastard."

A car pulled onto the gravel. A car door opened and shut. They waited. The bell rang and then the door creaked open. "Anyone home?"

Rebecca jumped.

"He's just coming right in," Tim said, alarmed.

And as if that were his cue, Adams Denver threw open the door with gusto. He set full grocery bags on the bleached counter and rifled through them. He produced a bottle of Scotch. "Ta-da!" he said, brandishing it like a club, before diving back in. A bronze baguette in its waxed white sheath. A handsome wedge of Stilton. Three plums that rolled the length of the counter and stopped just short of the edge. Adams watched them go. He seemed entranced by their antics. He clapped his hands together. "Brilliant!"

Adams was in his thirties too, but his hair was thinning quickly and he was very pale. He wore a grey ribbed T-shirt with very short sleeves, and the bottom edge of a tattoo poked out just below his left shoulder: poppies wound around an iron railing. His nose was pointed and bent. A white scar on the centre knuckle of his left hand looked like a gull in flight. A large steel watch, black denims, and black Doc Martens. And most noticeably, even from the half dozen words he'd heard, it was obvious Adams was English. Working-class English. It was ludicrous but he wanted Rebecca to have told him that. Or if he had simply been told by Nikolai Petrovitch, "I am sending a man. Imagine a soccer hooligan. Imagine a man who worries you from the outset, a man who likes to use his feet in a fight, likes to drink whisky and calls women 'birds.'" Then Tim would have felt better. He would have seen this coming.

Denver grinned. His eyes lit up, they gleamed. They were, Tim thought, a pure mercury grey. "Timmm," he said, stretching the syllable extravagantly. He laughed, a great roar that clattered out of his mouth like a metal bird and filled the room. He advanced quickly and embraced Tim, lifted him centimetres from the ground. "Great to see you," he said. "Absolutely lovely." He put Tim down and took a step backwards. "My God," he said, "let's have a look at you, then." It was absurd. He put a finger thoughtfully to his chin. "You look really *well*," he said. "All things considered you look absolutely fucking *lovely*. Shame about the hand, though. You all right, are you?"

Tim looked at Rebecca. She was enjoying this performance more than he was.

"Nah, don't look at her," Adams said. "Although I'm sure she'd confirm it for you. Wouldn't you, Becky?"

"I would," she said. She hated having her name shortened, but he had got away with it somehow.

"I'm glad," Tim said.

"I was hoping you'd wait for me to arrive before you cleared off. Didn't Niki tell you I was coming?"

"He didn't say when. He said he'd call."

"Well, there's your problem, then. Did she tell you? I had to break in! You should take some precautions, Tim. Piece of cake it was."

"I'm sorry about that. Something happened last night."

"I know. I heard. People are talking about it in the village. Some old codger blew himself up tinkering with his boat is what I heard. They said you found him. Christ, mate, that is tough."

"Word gets around fast."

Adams laughed, grabbed one of the plums and bit into its side. "That's the beauty of being in Canada. All the openness. In America they'd be treating this like Kennedy died. Being hush-hush and very serious all day. Can you see America from here, then?"

Not quite. You have to go up towards Rockport."

"Well, we'll have to do that, won't we? Can't come all this way and not see America. You're all right, though, are you?"

"He's okay," said Rebecca.

"Well, he would be, wouldn't he? A lovely lady like you around to take care of him."

"Rebecca's a friend," Tim said firmly.

Adams put the rest of the plum in his mouth, talked around it. "I know that, mate. Rest assured. Rebecca made that quite clear when we ran into each other earlier. A lovely first impression that was, I can tell you."

Ten minutes later, Rebecca left to clean her own apartment. She had let things slide, she explained. "It's getting beyond serious," she said. "There must be a law against the kind of mess I've made. I'll see you later."

Tim, freed of the need to be polite, lit into Adams. "I told him I wasn't keen," he fumed. "I said I'd had enough, that I wanted to be left alone. And now you just *show up*."

They were still in the kitchen. Tim didn't want to let him roam the house.

Adams raised his hands. He looked sheepish, but also vaguely amused. He said, "Word never reached me, Tim. God's honest truth. If I'd known, then maybe, you know . . ."

"So you'll leave."

"Well, it's a bit late for that now, Tim. Not a lot of room on the schedule for changing homes."

"This isn't your fucking home."

"Not entirely yours, either, though, is it?" Adams said.

If he hadn't looked quite so unpredictable, so accustomed to violence, Tim thought he might have stood closer to him to drive home the point. Or even accused Adams of lying, because the last thing he looked like was a real estate agent. He might have poked a stiff finger into his chest and ushered him into the cold. Any number of things. But Adams Denver didn't come across like a man who would appreciate those tactics. Or respond well to them. What the hell was he doing here?

"You're right there, Tim, it's not my place. I'm sorry. But what's done is done, right? I mean, not a lot of point getting yourself worked up."

"That's a real persuasive argument," Tim sneered. "I'm bowled over."

Adams advanced a step on him. "Listen," he hollered. But then he stopped abruptly and walked himself to the other side of the kitchen counter. It was unsettling. The metal refrigerators and freezers crowded around, like an audience egging them on. "I need a rest, mate. I think that's what it is. A bit of a lie-down, you know. Don't mean to be such a contrary bastard. Up here to help, you know?"

Tim looked at him.

"So. Is there a place for me?"

Tim said he would pull something together; give him a minute.

"Lovely," Adams Denver said. "I'll just make myself at home here while I wait, then."

*

John took the Jaguar up to eighty miles per hour. Then pushed it a little higher. After Oshawa, thirty miles east of Toronto, he had the road almost to himself. All the same, he pulled off at a truck stop and watched the off-ramp for a tail. Ten minutes later, confident he wasn't being followed, he headed east again. There were intermittent sightings of Lake Ontario, and low snow-covered hills were patrolled by a thin scattering of sheep.

An hour in, Sonny Rockliff called. John was listening to Diana Krall on the radio and was mildly embarrassed by how much he was enjoying it. It dated him, he thought. *'S wonderful*, he'd been crooning. *'S marvelous.*

"I've got news on your photographs," Sonny said. He sounded excited, pleased with himself.

"He threw me out," John said. "I'm gone."

"What do you mean you're gone?"

John told him what had happened, and what he needed in the way of additional backstory. "I need an address, an account with New Jersey Power."

"You've already got them. It's part of the package. When did this happen?"

"A couple of hours ago."

"Well, it's good that he wasn't positive of anything. And where are you now?"

"Going east. I should reach Hollins' place before dark."

"Is that your smartest move? If he gets wind of you up there, he'll have no more doubts."

John told him he wanted to try a conversation with Hollins' son. Just to see. Maybe the kid had all the answers, he said. And then they could talk again. "If it doesn't work, I can cross the border and be in Newark by lunch tomorrow. You can bring someone else into the Thousand Islands."

"Let me think this through. Call me before you talk to this kid. I'll see if we have anything more for you. If it's a go, I'll give you the news on those photos."

John exited at Kingston. Wal-Mart had taken root there, as well as the usual car dealerships and fast-food joints. He could have been driving into any of a thousand American cities. A fantastic red-roofed prison reminded him of Disneyland. There were low-slung telephone cables and a cop sitting beside the road at its lowest point, his radar gun aimed at the crest of the hill. Billboards that advertised steak houses and Marlboros, winter getaways in Cuba. No wonder the Americans were losing so much of their film industry to the Canadians.

Princess Street, the city's main drag, was more English than American, sleek boutiques and restaurants inserted into the ground floors of impressively detailed limestone and brick nineteenth-century buildings. In the market square behind City Hall a woman in a black apron decorated with paintings of bumblebees and sunflowers sold winter tulips. An antique car had been painted scarlet and a dragon's head, breathing fire, had been airbrushed onto its side. And at the bottom of the street, next to the lake and the ferry to Wolfe Island, a typically bland Holiday Inn and a sprawling limestone pub, the Merchant MacLiam, with some sort of Celtic greyhound painted onto the cream sign over the thick sunken door. A pint would be so welcome, John thought. What he wouldn't give for a half day with nothing on his plate.

He pushed on, past Fort Frontenac and the National Defence College, behind a ten-foot limestone wall. He thrummed over the iron grating of the LaSalle Causeway, which crossed the Cataraqui River, and skirted the Royal Military College. At the crest of a major hill was a fully restored Fort Henry, built in the 1830s by the British but never used for battle. And then the army base, stretching away to both sides. Most of Canada's armed forces, past and present, it seemed, had taken root here.

Twenty minutes of running parallel to the St. Lawrence Seaway and he was welcomed into "Gananoque, Gateway to the Thousand Islands." He parked in front of the liquor store and bought a bottle of Australian shiraz.

"Nice wheels," the girl at the register said, snapping her gum and tossing her head. "They yours?"

"Rental."

"That's too bad," she said.

"It is," John said. "It's a crying shame."

He tossed the wine on the back seat and walked down the street. A miniature version of Kingston. Maybe five thousand people. Obviously not a boom town now, but he bet it had done well at the turn of the century. Logging was his guess. Then tourism. And smuggling, according to Sonny. There wasn't much heavy industry that he could make out. A pretty but depressing village was his opinion. Dead in the winter and crawling with tourists, mostly American, in the summer, all of them here for a ride on one of the tour ships he'd seen half tarped at lakeside as he turned off the highway.

He crept into Bellini's Family Italian Restaurant and ordered some garlic bread. There was a pay phone in the back corner. A length of red velvet attached to a brass rail with curtain rings would give him some privacy but no view, so he left it open. His garlic bread arrived and he balanced the plate on top of the phone.

"We think you're okay to talk to Hollins' son," Sonny said. "Everything we have—although it isn't much—says he and Petrovitch don't care much for each other, so I don't think they'll be swapping stories about you. Our best estimate is that the boy isn't involved, but he might still have some inkling of what his dad was up to. I assume that's your feeling."

John said it was.

"Okay. So who are you? I don't think we want you knocking on his door in any official capacity today. We might be dead wrong in our assumptions, and I'd rather this was a scouting mission than a full-on interrogation. Let's leave all our options open."

"I'll think of something. Friend of the father. Old associate. Something like that." Selby bit into the garlic bread and warm olive oil flooded into his mouth. He wasn't eating enough. A meal this ordinary shouldn't excite him so much. "Tell me about the photos."

"Well, Mavlak you already know," Sonny said. "A credit card thief. Your basic one-dimensional slimeball. Credit card scams are typical eastern European fare. A lot of the others we couldn't identify. Which is a positive sign. One of the men plays hockey for the Toronto Maple Leafs. His girlfriend is on TV. One of our people recognized her face from an American Express commercial. The DJ showed up too, on a record label Web site. There were a couple of local politicians and even a member of provincial parliament. Something to do with Trade and Industry. We'll red-flag him. The kid collecting coats has an assault conviction. And the one you identified as Oleg worries us because he's obviously an insider and yet we can't find a damn thing. We saw him on the surveillance tapes, but we've no idea who he is and neither do the Canadians. Which we don't like much. It's always nice to identify the inner circle."

John ate more. So far the bread was more remarkable than the news. "Anything more on the guy in the boathouse?"

"Not yet."

John waited. Sonny was holding something back, like a kid saving the biggest birthday present for last. It wasn't proper operating procedure. John wanted whatever it was, now.

"A lot of nobodies with brush cuts," Sonny said. "Muscle."

"So he has enemies."

"Your man on the rooftop might well be one of them."

Finally. Here it was. "Victor, you mean?" John said.

"Viktor Andreitch Laevsky is his full handle." He spelled it out.

"Who is he? A rival?"

"Mr. Laevsky is shift manager at a mine in northern Russia."

"So what's he doing in Canada? How does he connect?"

"It's a diamond mine, John."

"That's an interesting turn."

"It sounds like it, doesn't it? Except we don't know what he's doing here. The Arkangel mine doesn't sell any of its product in North America. It goes to the markets in Antwerp. De Beers controls most of it. They buy 800 million in Russian rough every year. When Laevsky arrived he claimed it was a pleasure trip. That's it. All we've got."

"And how big a player is this mine in the Russian market?"

"Russia produces about 20 percent of the world's rough. That's somewhere in the vicinity of 14 million carats each year. Arkangel mines about 4 million of that."

"And are we talking Black & Decker drill-bit diamonds, or Tiffany engagement rings?"

"Mostly Tiffany. The very best Russia has to offer. Sure, some of it ends up in India, being ground up for tools or fashioned into trinkets, but a lot of world-class stuff comes to the surface."

"And how much is that good stuff worth?"

"A one-carat cut stone of great colour, flawless, would fetch anywhere from fifteen to thirty thousand. A flawless three-carat stone, though, might go for anywhere from a hundred thou to half a mil. It's a jungle out there. You need a degree. It depends too on where you bought it, how it was set."

"The Russian government lets the owner keep it all?"

"They'd love to nationalize the industry but it's too late. They do demand that some stay in the country, and some of the best get put in a Kremlin vault for a rainy day."

"How powerful is Laevsky?"

"We don't have any idea. They're bringing some lovely stones out of the ground in the Northwest Territories in Canada, and the same job up there might command eighty, ninety thousand a year."

"So not a pittance, but hardly a fortune. Does he have access to the diamonds?"

"The million-dollar question. The short answer is, we don't know."

"Any theories as to why he's so pissed at Petrovitch?" John wiped a finger through the bread crumbs and salt on his plate.

"It could be that he steals diamonds and Nikolai's moving them for him. That's the hypothesis we work with, I think. We talked to our men and women in Russia and they say the owner is above-board. And the official line is that Laevsky is a man on holiday. Maybe it's true. Or maybe Petrovitch screwed Laevsky's sixteen-year-old daughter, or his wife. Maybe they crossed paths when they were both in Russia. Maybe Petrovitch just served the wrong caviar at the shindig you were at. We don't know yet."

"But with bodies showing up, and Laevsky taking the time to visit Canada, we should press ahead."

"A few of those diamonds buy a lot of guns, a lot of explosives. Who knows what he's thinking, what drives a man like that. Maybe he's planning some grand political statement."

John had discovered grains of sand in his pocket. He rolled them between thumb and forefinger. So far, he had a lot of information that led to no natural conclusions. It was like looking at a map of the world and trying to decide where to take a holiday: the possibilities were bewildering.

John said, "I'm just down the road from Hollins' son. I thought I'd go over there now."

"Fine, but bear in mind he's the volatile type. I've got a report of him assaulting a photographer at his dad's funeral. A funeral Petrovitch attended, incidentally. We can't dig up any photos of him and his dad together, but obviously they were enough of a team to start the restaurant together, so be careful. For Christ's sake, make sure Petrovitch doesn't have someone watching the place. Okay? Just because he didn't follow you down there doesn't mean you're in the clear. And by the way, I've also told the local RCMP that you're carrying a weapon. You are carrying a weapon, John? It's not in the trunk of your car, is it? Wasn't that your habit?"

"You've done more homework on me than I realized," John said. "But yes, I am." He smiled at the waitress as she removed his plate and mouthed a thank-you.

He let Sonny provide him with a further ten minutes of detail on the family Hollins. By the time he hung up, though, he was in a fog. He had drifted—irresponsibly—into travel journalist mode: *A visitor to the Thousand Islands is afforded a modest welcome at the splendidly down-home Bellini's. That such an establishment still exists so close to the magnificent Islands . . .* He'd have to check out "the magnificent Islands" first, he knew. But wasn't that the way all great travel writers worked, at least some of the time—getting it down and then confirming their facts afterwards?

*

Tim was hiding in the restaurant's kitchen, listening to the radio and scrubbing saucepans that had been put away dirty two weeks ago when all that mattered was closing the doors. He went through the tin-lined drawers, taking inventory. He crawled around on his hands and knees, peering into the black space beneath the refrigerator, looking for evidence of mice. For a long while he simply sat on a tall chrome stool nursing a beer. He let his mind drift back and forth over recent history, hoping a pattern might emerge, or that he would see it with a clarity that had so far eluded him.

He needed to open Granite's doors before it was forgotten. There had been gushing reviews. Important people had driven considerable distances to eat in that wood-panelled room above the water. They'd booked weeks in advance. A few of the regulars had even called to offer condolences. Strangers professed to be mourning Michael's death and the restaurant's closing.

In the dining room the tables were still set but the cutlery had dulled; grey circles of dust had settled in the wineglasses. He tugged at the sliding glass door and the air that fluttered in smelled of the earth and the water.

He retraced his steps, left the kitchen, and walked through the office into the private half of the house. He located a thick roll-neck sweater on a shelf beside the fireplace, put it on and went outside.

His father had fashioned a garden beside the house. He had laboured long and hard on a rose bed, and had knocked together a trellis arch over which Concord grapes draped themselves in summer. A few woody stems still clung to the crossbeams. There was a twelve-metre square of lawn, now yellow and threadbare with blotches and humps of snow. A stone bench. The slim limbs of a locust tree cast a lacy shadow. Another bench at the bottom of the lawn, wooden and more comfortable, looked over the Seaway. He sat at one end of that, as if expecting company. It was zero Celsius, he estimated, or a shade below. A freighter seemed to sit squarely on the horizon's blue line, just visible between Georgina and Surveyor islands. Another steamed a kilometre behind it, and east of that a third. The mad dash to beat the Seaway's closing had begun. He trudged back to the house and pulled the telescope out of the den. He carried it outside and established it squarely on the flattest part of the lawn. The first ship was flying a Panamanian flag, and the second was registered in South Africa. Deckhands were tossing a football.

A car pulled into the lot. A Jaguar. The driver's door opened, metallic blue, and a man climbed out. He stared up at the house, unaware that he was being studied. He was in his early forties and wore an open-necked black shirt and a grey jacket. His brown hair swept back in elegant waves from an angular, nearly gaunt face studded with small but brilliantly blue eyes. The man had been in the sun recently and he stood confidently, one brown hand resting on the top of the door frame. His cuff rode up and his watch caught the sun and flared like magnesium. The man turned slightly to take in more fully his surroundings. A suit bag hanging in the back of the car had "Harry Rosen" written across the chest. Money, Tim thought. Money from Toronto. The man raised his head to the sun and closed his eyes, drew in a breath and appeared to hold it. He remained perfectly still. Finally he looked directly into the garden and saw Tim. He waved brightly.

"Hello there. Tim?"

Tim rose from his bench. He lifted his beer to his mouth and let the liquid fizz gently against his lips.

The man gestured at the garden. "You mind if I come aboard?" He stepped away from his car and closed the door.

Tim didn't say anything. Insurance, he thought. Banker. Something, anyway, to do with his father's death. The new arrival spread his hands in front of him, palms up. A gesture evidently intended to save himself an awkward repeat of his question. He smiled broadly.

"Come on in," Tim told him, and took a little more beer. The man moved easily across the lawn. No mean feat when you were being so obviously scrutinized. He gestured at the bench, and when the man sat, Tim remained standing.

They looked at each other.

"You've got the world watching you," the man said, and Tim knew he meant the cluster of TV trucks up at the main road. He had walked up there and seen a CBC satellite truck at the side of the Parkway, a woman with a cellphone gesticulating at the trees. Next to it another truck from CJOH in Ottawa and a white Jeep emblazoned with the Kingston channel's call letters. "You're going to be famous."

"What can I do for you?" Tim said. He wondered where Adams Denver was.

"Selby. My name is John Selby."

"Should I know you?"

"We met once. Through your father." John pressed his hands together as if he were about to pray.

"I don't remember you," Tim said. Michael's life was as full of unreadable spaces as the locust tree's shadow was full of sunlit holes. The two of them faced each other.

In a sheltered deep cove off Tunkhannock Island, a yacht had been anchored. Ice was moving around the point to greet it. It was madness to be out there this late in the year, but there it was. For two days Tim had watched through the telescope for signs of life. He was turning into a voyeur. But how had it got there? Through which hidden and still-open channel? He wondered where John Selby's tan came from. He knew exactly how it looked: two men sizing each other up. He had seen his father out here, talking to strangers where a conversation couldn't be overheard, where the wind could be relied on to carry the words away, to hide them forever in the trees, or bury them at sea.

"I thought I'd stop by is all, Tim. I wanted to pay my respects."

"You missed the funeral. It was on the second."

Frustration seemed to creep into Selby's face. "I was out of the country." He stood up and paced to the very edge of the lawn. He held his hands behind his back as if he were an admiral on the bow of his ship, wondering, as Earth sailed on, what he could expect of his men when the trouble came.

The beer tasted stale in Tim's mouth. The breeze had picked up. He remembered the forecast: Cooler near the lake. He made for the house, swinging his empty bottle. He knew he would be followed. But he wanted four walls around him. And the opposite was probably true for this man.

He surrounded John Selby, whoever he was, with steel freezers and a line of butcher's knives stuck by the flat of their steel blades to a thick magnetic strip on the wall. He drained the sink as casually as he could and stacked the clean, wet saucepans noisily on the counter. He wiped his hands, and Selby watched him.

"So were you friends? You and my father?"

Selby nodded absentmindedly, as if a memory, some minor evidence of their relationship, was moving through him.

"And did he like you?" Tim hiked himself up onto the counter, swung his legs a little. Let him know whose home it was, he thought.

Selby focused on him. Now he shook his head. "You never know, not really, do you? But I've followed his career. He left quite a mark." He reached out and grabbed a leg of the stool. He dragged it, bumping and tipping, across the floor and climbed onto it, throwing his legs too wide, like it was a horse.

"Tell me what you want," Tim said.

Selby looked around casually. He whistled appreciatively. "This is a hell of a set-up." He ran a finger over the counter. "It's all grade-A beautiful, isn't it?"

Tim pushed off from the counter. "That's it," he said. "Come on. You work for a newspaper, right? Or one of the TV crews. Well, fuck off. You're trespassing and I want you to leave."

Selby recoiled, jostled unintentionally the row of knives against the wall. "Hey, I'm sorry, okay? I met him in New York."

"When?"

"Way back. We were both young. Both trying to secure the same contract. Bathroom supplies to a hotel chain. It seems stupid, doesn't it? But think about it. Two hundred rooms per hotel. A hundred hotels across the nation. That's a lot of shampoo. And all of it needing to be replenished every morning. Anyway, your dad had a client in Toronto and I had one in Boston. We were there to schmooze with the hotel execs."

"So you became friends? You bonded over *soap?* Is that your story?"

"I liked him. He was straightforward, respected that we were peers, not enemies. It's a hard distinction to make when a six-figure bonus is riding on your efforts. And then I read that he died."

They lapsed into a companionable silence. After a while Tim took another beer from the refrigerator. He held the door open. "You want one?"

They settled on the deck. John had his feet up on the railing; the front legs of his chair were off the ground. He belongs in Barbados, Tim thought. Near warmer islands. His ease, his wardrobe, the way he was letting the day slide by without getting to the point, the slight unplaceable accent, the faint drawl, all spoke of a different climate, of a man on vacation.

Eventually John said, "I didn't see him after he retired. I feel bad about that. I promised him I'd come up and try the food."

"You kept in touch, then?"

"Not much. Last time I saw him he was working for that Russian fella—Petroleum, or some such. Nasty piece of work, I heard. Strange, seeing as how Michael was always such a straight arrow. Must've been tough on Michael, getting tarred with the same brush, as they say. None of my business of course."

Tim shook his head. "My father did nothing wrong. He was hardnosed, maybe even bullheaded and unpopular, but he was always honest. As honest as he could be, given the type of work. I don't think his reputation had much to do with his association with Nikolai Petrovitch."

John Selby touched his nose with a finger. "Petrovitch, that's right, that's the man's name. So did Michael do any work for him after he retired? You know, did he keep his hand in, so to speak? He and this Petrovitch were partners in this restaurant, weren't they?"

"I guess," Tim said. "But Nikolai was always a silent partner."

"And you hope he stays that way, I bet. Will you buy him out, Tim?"

"Maybe."

"No fun dealing with your old man's business associates about now, I'm sure."

Tim allowed the hint of a smile to work a change in his lips.

"That includes me, doesn't it?" John said quickly, laughing and patting his chest. "See, I told you I wasn't as good at this game as your father. But you say they did work together, after his moving down here?"

"I didn't say that, no," Tim said. "But I'm sure there were details to iron out. The sorts of deals they worked on never seemed to really close."

"What deals were those?"

"Oh, I don't know. The stuff that made the news. You probably understand it better than I do. That was his world. And maybe yours. It sure wasn't mine."

"And it was more high-stakes stuff than I was used to, Tim. All that cross-border negotiation's not for me. I'm too lazy. But your dad did his homework, I'll give him that. He knew the legislation inside out. Me, I've always been more inclined to bullshit my way into a deal. A good meal and some free T-shirts, a round of golf or some Cuban cigars. Not Michael, though. He worked damn hard. You must have helped him a bit, eh, Tim?"

"Not at all," Tim said. We saw things differently."

Well, someone must have. I just figured it was you because he never had much in the way of a secretarial staff."

"He worked alone," Tim said. "And we didn't see that much of each other until he retired. Since then it's been all about Granite. So no, I didn't help him. I think you're wrong; I think he did it all himself."

"That's a heck of a talent, then. You sure it doesn't run in the family?"

"Positive," Tim said. "Which might be why I don't remember you. When did you say you met me?"

"Close on twenty years ago, it must be."

"Where?"

John reflected on that. After an eternity he said, "In Toronto. Your dad was rushing you off somewhere. Maybe it was a baseball game. It was summer, I remember that. It was a long time ago, Tim."

Tim didn't believe him. He had no memories, not one, of walking Toronto's streets with his father. Besides, twenty years ago he'd been in Europe with his mother. They had spent the summer in Italy. She'd been sick even then, but hadn't told him yet. "Twenty years ago, you say?"

John said he wasn't positive on the date, no.

Tim wanted, oddly, to punch this stranger who seemed to embody the worst traits of his father—the evasiveness, the self-importance. The smug way he sat with his feet up, his hands knotted in his lap.

"I should do some more work," he said. "It's getting dark out. Where are you headed?"

"I'm between jobs, as they say, Tim. Another starts up in the new year, but for now I'm killing time. I'm due in Atlanta for Christmas. That's it, though. Thought I might hole up along the border here for a few days."

"The restaurant won't be open, if that's what you're thinking." Atlanta made sense. The accent might be right for Atlanta.

John smiled. "I'm thinking to get out of your way," he said. "That's all." He put his beer on the ground. "I'm intruding, aren't I. Being too nosy. Don't tell me I'm not, I can tell. I wouldn't get very far if I couldn't read at least the basic state of a person."

Tim said, "You know how you put a fire out and hours later it flares up again? This is like that." He ran a hand through his hair, grabbed a handful at the back, tugged hard enough that he could feel his scalp pulling away from the bone. "I'll see you out," he said. "Sorry you wasted a trip."

"I don't feel that way at all. Truly."

They walked out to Selby's car.

John opened his door and rested a hand on top of it. It was the same pose he had struck when he'd arrived—it was how he wanted to be seen. He put a foot up on the frame. "Will you be able to manage the place on your own, Tim?"

Tim felt he was being accused of something, laziness perhaps. He thought this man, John Selby, might really be cut from the same cloth as his father. But John apparently realized the inference he had made, because he raised his hand and thumped lightly on top of the Jag. "How stupid of me," he said. "I only meant that you must be up to your eyes these days."

"Pretty much."

"And your dad was the same, I bet. Not a lot of time to take it easy. How long a day would you put in, keeping an operation like this going, Tim?"

"When it was open we'd start about eight in the morning. We were lucky to finish before midnight."

"Seven days?"

"Seven days, yes."

"That's a damn shame. A man should have some time to reflect on his life. But it's what he wanted, I suppose. To be busy again." Selby's features arranged themselves then in a way that made Tim think he might have been ambushed by a deeply felt and unsettling memory. A quick, fierce scrunching of muscles, a bearish darkening of the brow. He climbed behind the wheel, lowered the window, and looked straight ahead, as if he expected the right words to come from that direction. "Awful stuff. That's all I know. This whole business. And this other fellow just down the road? I think I road he know your father too. Bill something."

Tim leaned to see properly into the car. "Bill Sumner. Yeah. They were friends."

"That's a heck of a coincidence. I mean, I'm not saying . . . not a bit . . . but . . ." John smiled weakly, showed off one more time the startling contrast between his perfect, white teeth and his shaved, sunned face. It was obnoxious. "I'm sorry. It's the James Bond fan in me, I guess. Always looking for my life to intersect with some real intrigue. That sounds just terrible, doesn't it? I'm sorry again, Tim." He smiled broadly. His teeth were impossibly even. "I'll come back when you reopen, then. You can show me what your dad did with the place."

"He did everything," Tim said and walked away.

John touched the accelerator and the tires spun for an instant before grabbing. He put a hand out the window and waved apologetically. And then he was gone.

DECEMBER 12

Adams Denver was killing them at shuffleboard. They couldn't touch him. None of the regulars at the Stone Street Tavern had seen anything like it. Bill Stinson, a tough, barrel-chested septuagenarian who worked sports for the *Recorder*, grumbled, "It's a crime, the wrist action on our Mr. Denver."

Adams was bent over the table and scooping up sawdust from the worn felt gutter to cast, like a farmer's seed, over the wooden surface. When he grinned at Stinson, his ground-down teeth were a vivid yellow in the twilight.

He had been in the Stone Street Tavern since noon. He loved the sight of the familiar, sweet taps all lined up: Guinness and Harp, Smithwicks and Tetley's. There were some others, Canadian he assumed, that he didn't recognize and didn't trust—Moosehead, Creemore, and, at the end, Keith's.

He had cozied up to the bar on a tall stool topped with a deep mound of red velvet. A lady's chair, he'd thought, but he'd stayed where he was. The bartender was a middle-aged woman, her unkempt curls going grey, her face red and her hands fleshy and white. Her name was Rosie.

"You pour a good pint of the dark, Rosie?" he'd asked. She had assured him she did. "Go on, then, show us, love."

It was midway through the third of those (because she was right, she poured a fine one) that he'd decided on a spot of shuffleboard. He'd played alone for a while, getting into the hushed, smooth rush of the stones and the satisfying collisions at the far end. He'd even nosed the inside of his glass for a soapy scent, something to get worked up about. A way of finagling a fresh pint.

Bill Stinson had sidled over and asked him did he fancy a game. So had Terry Bishop, a waiter on his day off. He'd slaughtered them both, and laughed off their faint praise. They liked him. He could see that. But of course they did. It was easy, in these foggy stale rooms, to fit in.

He excused himself, examined a display case mounted high on the wall. It was decked out with some stringy gone-brown moss, a bit of dry bark. A bad painting of a pagoda with a red sun setting behind it. *Peking Duck*, the brass tag said. The opposite wall was studded with slabs of poorly stained pine on which fish had been mounted. Above the door, a muskellunge that had apparently tipped the scales at forty-five pounds, eight ounces and been caught by one Bud Grimley. "It's lost a bit of weight, by the looks of it," Adams said to Rosie.

She wiped her hands on a Newcastle Brown bar rag and said cheerfully, "Best not to say that too loud. Bud's mighty proud of that fish." She was from Sussex, she told him when he asked after her accent. "But more than half a lifetime ago. This is home now."

He ordered the bangers and mash because he couldn't remember the last time he'd had a full meal, and sat in front of the projection television watching a basketball game. The image was fuzzy, the colours too separate from each other, as if what he was seeing were the molecules that made each player up.

He ate moodily, with all his fingers wrapped around the fork. He made a small spear of it and harpooned the slick overstuffed casings hidden in the potatoes. Dragged them into the gelatinous puddles of steaming gravy and hacked at them.

Adams enjoyed his work and he hated it. He hated the petty deceptions it called for. *Real estate agent!* For fuck's sake. Because that's essentially what Petrovitch was asking him to pass for. And that was demeaning. He knew every job required that he not declare his intentions—he wasn't a fucking idiot, was he?—but what no one realized was that it took its toll. The effect on him was cumulative. Each job broke his defences down a little more. And no one seemed to remember: he did it for them because they didn't have the stomach for it. Sure, they dressed it up, but that was its essence: *he* did it because *they* couldn't.

Rosie appeared at his shoulder. Her scarlet lips parted over perfect dentures. "Your plate, love. Was it all right?"

He took a new pint to the pay phone. Angie answered immediately, as if she had been waiting for his call. He listened to her tender "Hello," and knew there was nothing he could say. He had been gone too long for them ever to discover a way back to each other. He also knew his silence wasn't going to fool anyone, but he needed the connection. He examined the transatlantic hiss and buzz for some sign of his growing boy. Or another man in Angie's life—surely there was one by now. She said hello again, but she knew it was him and her tone had changed. He thought she was probably pacing the living room of the flat she shared with her sister, Shelley, looking up at the ceiling perhaps, fighting back a tear either of sadness or anger. He hung up, disgusted with himself.

He took the bar darts and lobbed them underhand at the battered cork, and then he looked about for his pint. Another man had moved it, carted it back to the shuffleboard. A big man, a bear with an extravagant grizzled beard and thick eyebrows shading dark eyes. Hands like dinner plates. A forest-green jacket lined with creamy fake fur, and under it a plaid shirt open at the neck, revealing a thatch of black hair.

"Who the fuck are you?" Adams said. "Never move my pint, mate. You hear?"

"I'm a friend of Nikolai's," the man said. "From Toronto. Steve."

"You're no friend of mine, then, are you, mate? I'm afraid I don't know what the fuck you're on about."

"You're a fast one, I see. But then Nikolai said you were quick."

Adams told him to go fuck himself. "I know when a man's taking the mickey," he said. "And I don't stand for it. I don't give a toss whose friend you are." He grabbed his drink. "And like I said, don't move my pint."

"You need to calm down."

Adams repeated his instruction that Steve could go fuck himself.

Steve had his own pint of Guinness and he took a long meditative sip that left a tan stain in his moustache. "I'm on my way across," he said cryptically. "Our Mr. Petrovitch thought it would be nice if I stopped and said hello." He had lowered his voice, the implication being that Adams should do the same.

"If you've got a message, give it," Adams told him.

Steve said, "He doesn't want to attract a lot of attention. It seems like you might be doing the opposite."

"What, in here? I was having a laugh," Adams said, sizing Steve up, thinking the big man was referring to his unorthodox approach at the dartboard, and wondering also what it would take to bring him down.

"Well, this is work," Steve said. "You can have your laugh when it's over."

Adams didn't appreciate being lectured on protocol. Methodology was his end. And anyway, attention was what his work created. The space vacated by a man always filled up with scrutiny.

Steve played with one of the shuffleboard rocks, had it skate back and forth over a ridge he'd made of sawdust. "Nikolai has business up here," he said. "Imminent business. And all this *fuss* is making it hard for him."

"I don't see how that's something I can control," Adams said. "I'm checking out summer homes, right?" He waited for Steve to acknowledge the fact.

"It's all the peripheral noise that bothers our friend."

Our friend. That was priceless. "So what would *our friend* like me to do?"

"He just wants you to go about your business quietly." Steve tipped the rock onto its edge and balanced it like that. "He also wants you to check on Hanne. Make sure recent events haven't given her cold feet."

The man was pissing him off: *do this, do that.* "I'd be happy to leave right now, if that would make *our friend* happy," Adams said belligerently. "You could do the work yourself, for instance. I don't mind at all." Adams had come a long way, no one was going to sack him just like that. Replacements were hard to come by.

"He doesn't want you off the job. He just wants you to avoid the grand dramatic gestures."

Rosie was watching them from behind the bar.

"But that's all my job is, really, Steve, if you think about it: one grand dramatic gesture after another."

"You know what I mean." He polished off his pint smartly, stretched his jacket around his plaid gut and hunted for the zipper. "Shall I tell him it's okay, or shall I tell him you were an argumentative bastard and he should send you the fuck back where you came from?"

Rosie was making her way around the bar tentatively. She

couldn't have heard their conversation, but it didn't take a genius to read her body language—she expected trouble from them. Adams pulled himself together. When in Rome, he thought. When in fucking Rome. This was just the standard bullshit. There was always something, and here, apparently, it was Steve. He stuck his tongue in the roof of his mouth, because it calmed him, and he gripped the edge of the table.

Rosie said, "I don't know either of you's. And I'd like to keep it that way."

Steve apologized. "Have yourself a pint on us," he said, and he handed Rosie a ten. She seemed absurdly satisfied by that and bustled away, whistling and twirling her bar towel.

Steve said he was leaving anyway. "I've done my bit," he said. "So check this art dealer's not having a nervous breakdown, can you? He'd appreciate it."

"Why don't you do it?"

"He wants a fresh face," Steve said, walking away. "She's too scared of me."

Adams went to the can. He grinned idiotically at his own reflection in the chipped mirror. Look at that! He had a fresh face. Shit, he was the most fresh-faced person he knew. "Pleased to meet you," he said. "Adams Denver's the name." And he held out his hand.

*

John Selby tapped his foot impatiently in the RCMP waiting room. You didn't keep the FBI waiting. And to his mind the BVC *was* the FBI. And yes, he knew how that sounded. It smacked of superiority and arrogance. But it was true. And true also that men were dying; the border's integrity was being compromised. The Canadians had pledged their cooperation, and yet the nation's intelligence service, CSIS, had yet to offer any substantial assistance or even show interest. He flicked irritably through the dishevelled fan of outdated magazines on the steel-and-glass tabletop. He was, perhaps, a little dehydrated. Last night, after leaving Tim at Granite, and after booking a completely adequate room at the Northern Lights Motel, and after talking one more time to Sonny and eating too much of a Pizza Hut pizza, he had become depressed and drunk the bottle of shiraz. The fact that it was now the middle of the afternoon didn't seem to help.

Sonny had been pleased with John's conclusion that Tim Hollins was probably in the dark.

"We've got an eye on Laevsky, the mine manager," Sonny reported. "He's holed up at the Windsor Arms with a bodyguard. He hasn't seen Petrovitch since that night."

"What's the Windsor Arms?"

"It's a hotel. Very close to where you were. A bit more exclusive, I think. But close to Petrovitch."

"So he's throwing around a bit more cash than your average shift supervisor would. And how about Sumner? Any news?"

"Nothing yet. But this is the cop dealing with the case." He gave him Des Boyle's name. "He looked into Hollins' accident too, *and* he's our liaison vis-à-vis border security over there."

"A multi-tasker, then. Does he think they're linked?"

"Ask him yourself. We've set up a meeting." And then Sonny, in a further demonstration of his fondness for saving his most startling news for last, said, "An interesting tidbit on Hanne for you, John."

"What's that?"

"Now don't go assuming we knew this in advance, because we didn't."

"Get on with it, Sonny."

"Hanne Kristiansen has an art gallery in Kingston. It has the same name as the one in Toronto—the Hansen Space. Cute, don't you think? Anyway. There it is. Make of it what you will. Have you seen her since the party, by the way?"

The last question, John knew, was a test. Had he been holding out on them? Was he working on his own agenda? No, he told Sonny. There was no point in complicating her life needlessly, he said. Which he hoped would register as a jab.

"Perhaps you should," Sonny said. "It's a heck of a coincidence, don't you think? No stone unturned, okay?"

John didn't know what Hanne's presence in Kingston meant. Or Laevsky's in Toronto. Or Sumner's fiery death. Or the yellow Volvo he had seen pulling into Granite as he'd left, its driver craning to see as much of John's face as possible. What he needed now was for Des Boyle to shed some light.

Finally a painfully thin man beckoned from behind a decrepit and dehydrated potted palm and Selby followed him down a long corridor with orange water stains blooming in the ceiling tiles. Behind one open door a filthy sink was nearly hidden under a jumble of coffee mugs. They sat on opposite sides of a cheap and well-organized desk. A Céline Dion tune trickled from a digital clock radio, and on the ground behind his desk a humidifier gamely fogged the air.

Des Boyle bit into a plate-sized pastry and some of its see-through icing fell away in heavy flakes. He was glad to have this opportunity, he said. It was long past due, he thought: the forces of both countries truly working together.

"I don't know all the details, because there hasn't been time," John said. "But I'm told you're the point man for border security this part of the world."

"I'm the Canadian coordinator for the Thousand Island Integrated Border Enforcement Team," Boyle said. "Quite a mouthful, isn't it."

"It puts you on a hot seat is how it sounds," John said.

"It's not so bad. IBETs are a good idea. They're only a couple of years old, but basically they're multi-agency—and multinational—law enforcement teams that target cross-border criminal activity. We try not to keep secrets from each other. The idea is to make the border seamless. How can you argue against something like that?"

"And who's involved?"

"On your side? New York State Police, U.S. customs, Border Patrol, the U.S. Attorney General's office. Over here it's mostly the RCMP, which is how I ended up with the grand job description, but we get assistance from First Nations law enforcement agencies, the Ontario Provincial Police—even CSIS calls me up once in a while."

"And how's it working?"

"It's all good news so far. No more duplication of services and surprisingly little bickering. I was expecting everyone to fight over who would get credit, but in practice I've seen no grandstanding at all, it's been a treat. We work together well. We ran down smugglers in the main channel together a couple of times this summer. It's a kick, I've got to tell you, knowing that the bad guys can't just tack back and forth across the border to evade arrest."

"My people tell me there are now acoustic and seismic sensors set up through the islands, and they're supposed to detect any suspicious traffic."

"That's about right," Boyle said. "And we talk to each other on encrypted hand-helds. The smugglers can't listen in any more."

"Like a spiderweb, then."

"I've heard it described that way, yes."

"Are there any holes?"

Boyle smiled tolerantly. "Bill Sumner's death might lead one to that conclusion, I suppose."

John told him it wasn't an accusation, he was simply wondering if smuggling remained a problem in the area.

"Sure it does," Boyle said. "It's an incredibly complicated geography. The number of routes through the islands is in the hundreds of thousands, the millions even. And if we chase someone into a shallow passage in a speedboat that rides too low in the water, we're in trouble. It's not always a simple seek-and-intercept exercise. But we're getting there. There's money coming down the pipe these days for us to hire more officers, and that's our main deficiency, so I'm optimistic."

"I feel safer already," John said.

Boyle held up the remains of his pastry as if to toast their meeting. He said, "Well, now I've given you my credentials, I hear you talked to Hollins' kid."

"I hope you don't mind. I should have told you first, I suppose, in light of all you just told me—no secrets and everything."

Des shook his head. "I don't mind. You played an old friend of his dad's. Have I got that right?"

"I thought I might catch him unawares," John said. "No point frightening him."

"Yes, but are you sure he didn't see right through you? He's no dummy."

"Neither am I," John said. "He doesn't have a record, I assume?"

"Nothing. And he's well liked. A positive addition to the community, I reckon. His dad could be a bit prickly sometimes, and Tim was able to soften the edges a bit. I think he and Rebecca Rae—she's the chef out there—deserve most of the credit for Granite's success."

"I had the same gut feeling about him," John admitted. "So what about his father, then? What's your take on him?"

"Well, his restaurant raised the profile of Ivy Lea, not that the village needs much help in that department. But he did get some of Toronto's money down here, and that's nothing to sniff at."

"But there's a casino up by the highway now," John said. "So I don't suppose attracting cash is a big problem."

"Yes, but Granite was seen as a classy joint," Des told him. "Something to offset all the fuzzy dice and the plaid-panted gamblers. An upscale attraction to put in the brochures next to the dancing girls and the tour boats."

"And you never suspected him of anything?"

"Nothing more insidious than a thirty-dollar lamb chop," Des said.

"And the accident remains an accident?"

Boyle said, "I've driven that road a lot, John. And it's just plain stupid the way the road surface leads you inland at the same time the curve wants you to go the other way. It's like it was built expressly to fool people." He shook his head and polished off the Danish. "He was also drinking beforehand with his son and Rebecca. God knows why he thought he'd go for a drive. Idiocy is what that was. But there was no autopsy."

"Why not?"

"Hollins isn't the first man to buy the farm right there. It didn't seem necessary. We didn't know then what we do now. Hindsight says it was a bad call, but . . ."

Selby said, "You've checked the car, though?"

"We had it in isolation for a week. The brakes were good. Time for the steering. At least until impact. We're confident of that."

"And you're confident it was the impact that killed him."

"You should have seen him. Yeah, I'm sure."

"But—"

"I know what you're suggesting. No, he was alive until the crash.

He lost control, drunk or sober. He was driving too fast. It's a sad but unoriginal story. Sorry."

"Okay. What about Bill Sumner?"

"Bill's a different story," Boyle said. There was icing on his lips. It made him look frostbitten, ghostly.

"Any leads?"

"Not yet. Bill was a loner, pretty much, even though he's lived here for years. He knew Hollins, I'll grant you. That's why it's so tempting to look for some big plot. But we can't put Bill and Michael together in any substantive way. Can you?"

John said, "Only that Tim was there when Bill was blown up. Which is pretty weird. His story holds up, but still. And Sumner, we'd never heard of him. We're still doing a background."

"He kept buffalo out there. Did you know that?"

John said he had read about it. He assumed it was an accident that they were killed too.

Boyle said, "It's a sick bastard we're looking for if it was done on purpose."

"You think it's just one person?"

"We haven't decided that. We found Bill's Jeep out by an old quarry. Whoever killed Bill used it for getaway. I don't know why they didn't push it right in, drown it. But there it was. Wiped clean. Nothing. Like someone had taken a Shop-Vac to the front seats. The back was still full of kindling. Tim Hollins reported seeing it loaded up when he arrived. So we assume a maximum of two passengers. It's not much to go on."

"Did you find tracks out there? Presumably they had another vehicle."

"Some Michelins. But it's a common tread. A snow tire. These were fairly new, came off a regular-size wheel, no big scars. I use the same tire myself."

"Okay." Selby didn't want to interrogate Des Boyle. He wanted him not to feel pressured. "What do you do now?"

"We still have a team out at Sumner's boathouse. Hopefully that will turn up something."

"He had a powerful boat out there, didn't he?"

"He liked to tool around some, yes."

"Any smuggling, do you think?"

Boyle leaned back in his chair and put his hands behind his head. "Back to this," he said. "Let me guess. The President wants to know if our Bill Sumner was moving Stinger missiles across the Seaway on weekends."

"I don't think it's that, exactly," John told him. "But you admit this is still a weak spot. That makes it a legitimate concern for us. It should worry you, too."

"I think it's a legitimate concern if you're worried about Jack Daniel's and cheap smokes," Des said. "There's certainly work to be done in those areas. But our government has always recognized that. They even reduced taxes on cigarettes a few years back, cut their price in half, because it was the only way they could think of to stop the massive traffic."

"Did it work?"

"Some, sure. But prices are back up now, so we're already seeing a resumption of that business. Or at least they're trying. I think they're surprised how much more difficult it is."

"What about people?" John said.

"Which people?"

"Migrants. The thousands that end up in New York every year. The Chinese and the Koreans and the Vietnamese. They're not all going over the border hidden in vans at Vancouver and Windsor. A lot of them are being whisked across by your cigarette smugglers. My research indicates that there are three people-smuggling rings active in this area."

"It's true," Des admitted. "And you're right. That's a terrible worry. For you especially. And we understand that. It's what we're focusing on. But a lot of your problem is at the airports. The no-visa-required policy that allows those people to just waltz into Canada. And even some of those arrivals who do have visas are getting them by bribing officials abroad. There's a problem, I'll grant you. But I truly believe the solution lies elsewhere in the system, not here at the water's edge."

John said, "All I know is there's a fire we need to put out, and it's my hope we can do that together."

"Of course," Des said. "I don't think we're arguing here."

"No, neither do I. How about another question, then?"

"Shoot."

"The casino. That must bring a whole new slate of worries."

"The usual. Some drugs, some prostitution. Some con men and some dark-alley thugs. But most of it stays up at the highway. I don't have any indication that Michael's or Bill's death is connected to that."

"Did either of them have a stake in it? Or gamble?"

"The casino's run by the government. The inside work is contracted out, and neither of them look to be connected to that. And gambling? I don't think so. Both of them were pretty much homebodies. I think Michael's weakness was for food and single malt whisky. Bill's was those two buffalo." Des leaned over and played distractedly with the controls on the humidifier. "You know, this thing right here scares me as much as anything we're talking about," he said. "I keep thinking about legionnaires' disease. Some godawful bacteria or virus blowing in my face all damn day. One day I'll probably just keel over like one of those cruise ship passengers."

"So turn it off," John advised. "Isn't that the answer?"

"You'd think so," Des agreed, "but then my lips chap and hands crack. It's not pretty. I'm just worried is all." He turned the plastic machine down a notch and the fog pouring from it thinned some. John wondered if it was responsible for the faint mildewy scent in the room. He liked Des, he decided. The man was quirky, and odd to look at, but he took his work seriously; he was conscientious and not afraid to take a stand.

Des pulled a Kleenex from a flowered box on his desk and blew his nose. He said, "So what are you after, John? This Sonny Rockliff told me some, but I'd like to hear it from you, too."

"Fair enough." John told him it started with a Russian named Nikolai Petrovitch. "I was supposed to infiltrate his Toronto operation. But then word reached us of Hollins' death, followed so damn closely by Bill Sumner's. It seemed to us that it was worth coming up to take a look. Particularly because Petrovitch established Michael here. We're worried, I suppose, that a pipeline of some sort is being established."

"That's what I was told. Any idea what might be going across the river?"

Selby said it could be anything. They didn't know yet. "Our latest possibility is diamonds."

"Diamonds. Well, that's a new one. Your Mr. Rockliff didn't say anything."

"It's a hypothesis based on one overheard argument."

"About diamonds?"

"I don't really know, the argument was in Russian."

Boyle raised a skeptical eyebrow. He scooted his chair to a steel filing cabinet, withdrew a black binder and from that binder a stack of photographs. He tossed them across the desk and they spread apart like a deck of cards. Boyle ferreted through them and pulled one away from the rest. "Is this him?"

"Where were these taken?"

"Hollins' funeral. When you described him it made sense this was the same man. I was told by higher-ups to put someone there. We're always worried we might miss something in our own backyard."

"Let me see the rest of those," John said, enjoying himself now. His head still pained him, and his foot, and his heart sank at the thought that Hanne would appear around one or another of the corners he would have to brave in the coming days. But this, he thought, this meeting was going well, and the prospect of conferring with a reasonable colleague, seeing him occasionally, rather than hearing only a tinny voice at the end of a phone line, pleased him out of all proportion. He fanned through the photographs. Tim Hollins. Tim Hollins. Petrovitch. Again. Again. A large brown dog. Hanne Kristiansen. He stopped and stared at her.

*

It was almost dark when the electronic door chime sounded in Hanne's office at the back of the Kingston gallery. She had been projecting slides onto a blank wall. According to the handwritten index she was, at that moment, staring half-heartedly at an oil painting titled *Lingua*. It comprised solely a reasonably accurate depiction of an *Oxford Dictionary*, shaded panels of royal blue and a discreet static of scarlet and tree-green in the upper-left and bottom-right quadrants. It bored her. She couldn't focus. But that was nothing new.

When Michael died she had wanted to close the gallery and fly away.

She felt crushed beneath the weight of the realization that it could have been her. Everything hung by such a thin thread. For two days in Toronto she had paced. Then she had driven to Kingston and done the same in the gallery there. She'd intended to visit Tim, but in the end she'd simply driven home to Toronto again. Nikolai had requested that she visit him at his office, a renovated loft space on Avenue Road, but when she'd arrived he hadn't been there and she'd left hurriedly. Later, he'd called her and said she should have waited. But she wanted never to have to talk again; she wanted to run from her life again.

The day of the funeral was the worst. She had worn her fur hoping to hide inside it. All morning she'd been on the verge of tears. And when Nikolai cornered her, when he leaned against the door of her car so that she couldn't escape, she would have traded places with anyone in the cemetery, including Michael.

Nikolai had followed her afterwards to the gallery. It was middle of the afternoon but the room was dim. One of Nikolai's men, a dismal, cheerless man who wouldn't take off his sunglasses, leaned against the limestone wall and didn't move.

Nikolai hadn't liked the way she was at the funeral.

She summoned indignance. "And what way was that, Nikolai?"

He ignored her question. Did she have it? he wanted to know. Had it arrived? Not a word about Michael, about the funeral they had just left. Only: did she have it; was it here?

She told him it was. He did want it to come to Kingston rather than Toronto, didn't he?

"Where is it?"

"Downstairs."

He said something in Russian and disappeared, leaving Hanne to stare gloomily at the walls. When he returned it was with a painting gripped in his left hand like a suitcase. His thumb pressed squarely against the canvas. "Have you seen it?" Nikolai asked her.

"Of course not. They are yours."

He held it up for her.

"It's nice," she said. "She is good, I think."

"I hate it." He tossed it to the man against the wall, who straightened and caught it by its ornate wooden sides. Nikolai smiled. "But that is okay. It is a good investment, isn't it?"

"I believe so, yes. It's what you wanted, then?" Hanne said uncertainly.

"It is fine. Better than fine. When did it come?"

Hanne thought about it. "The day after . . ."

"Michael?"

She nodded.

"Even better."

That chilled her. She wanted her coat again. She even looked around for it, forgetting for a moment where she had put it. She crossed her arms and shivered.

Nikolai said, "The light is going."

She stared outside.

"The thirteenth we will be back, I think. I have left everything here."

Hanne nodded.

"You will be here."

She didn't know if it was a question. "I can be," she said.

After he'd left, she'd wept. She'd checked that the basement safe was properly locked and then she'd slept in the office.

And then there'd been the party at Nikolai's. Holy shit, the party. And John. As if she didn't have enough to worry about.

Seeing him had just about given her a heart attack. She couldn't breathe. It had shocked her as much as Michael's death. She had strained to see who it was in Nikolai's apartment that reminded her so much of John Selby, FBI agent, old lover. The likeness was uncanny. She had stepped closer and then frozen.

Leaving him in Berlin had been reasonably easy. She had simply taken a taxi to the airport and waited for the next available seat on a flight to London. In case he tried to track her down she'd holed up under her mother's maiden name on the third floor of a bed and breakfast in Bloomsbury. She didn't want to deal with him falling in love with her, it was that simple. He was so *serious* about everything: about the state of the world and the progress of their relationship. He wanted *clarity* all the time. He said the world was muddled and his desire was for some sort of order. When they argued she was cruel, she called him an obsessive, a fascist; she told him life was meant to be messy and he was going to end up an unhappy man, which made things between them predictably worse. She'd been gone a month before she'd realized perhaps she could have tried harder, been a little more flexible. After all, a painter and a spy getting involved in Berlin, it just *sounded* like something that should be given every chance to succeed. The sex was great too, and when John relaxed, when he could be coaxed away from politics and global geography, his stupid fantasy of becoming the next Bruce Chatwin, he could be charming, even suave. He had a mischievous sense of humour, and a vanity she found endearing.

She'd flown to Italy then, and begun to paint again. She was offered, and quickly accepted, a position on a cruise ship that sailed the west coast of North America from Seattle to Juneau, Alaska, attempting to show seniors how to paint icebergs and churning diamond seas. Two months later she'd moved onto dry land and into a small apartment in Vancouver. She'd walked aimlessly most evenings in Stanley Park, had finally decided that she wanted her own gallery and moved to Toronto. She rented a vacant storefront north of Yorkville and filled it with new work that she didn't think was very good. Some of it even embarrassed her, but if she could sell enough to pay a couple months' rent, and if she networked like crazy, then perhaps she could fashion a life for herself among Toronto's most successful artists and business types. Nikolai was one of her first customers. A week after he bought her most expensive work he returned with a proposition.

Hanne looked up and it was December again. Cars had their headlights on. The sky had taken on a purple tint; the temperature was dropping. The chimes had rung and someone had entered the gallery. Hanne swore under her breath. She had meant to lock up.

She eased the office door open. A very white, very scruffy man was standing before a large abstract in greys and pinks. He swayed gently back and forth. At first Hanne thought he was trying to find the right focus point. That he must believe that at a certain distance, if he screwed up his eyes, a realistic painting of a cliff or a donkey or a beautiful woman would suddenly reveal itself. Then she realized that he was, in fact, drunk.

He had heard her, and yet he didn't turn immediately to face her.

He screwed his face up as if he had smelled something unpleasant and cocked his head at an extreme angle. He had on black boots of the sort favoured by skinheads, and his black jeans were faded.

"It's really lovely, this one," he said. "I like it a lot. I had a blanket that colour as a baby. Do you think that's what she was after?"

"The artist's name is Dominic Aitchison," Hanne said. "Dominic is a man, and I doubt highly that he had your baby blanket in mind when he painted this, no." She smiled, but firmly.

"A fucking *bloke* painted this?" The art critic turned his head towards Hanne for the first time and he nodded seriously. "I am absolutely flabbergasted."

"Why is that?" Hanne said. There was no point being provocative. A couple of harmless sentences and she could point him in the direction of either the taxi stand or the Merchant MacLiam. It was amazing how often her gallery was mistaken for a pub.

"Because a guy would not normally use these colours together." He pointed vaguely at the work. "This is weird for a bloke."

Hanne said, "And yet you had a blanket very similar."

"Oh Hanne, Hanne, Hanne," the man said.

Hanne stopped. She had intended to move around the man and open the door for him, point out the late hour. Force a smile and hope he responded well.

"How do you know my name?"

"Your name? Your *name?* Oh, I know a lot more than your name, Hanne."

"Who are you?"

"I'm Adams Denver, love."

"And who is Adams Denver when he's sober?" She was still hoping he was nothing more than a punk. Some bar drunk who had heard her name during some dartboard gossip.

"A friend of a friend," Adams said. He staggered a step towards her. Gathered himself and took two more.

"Which friend?"

"Mr. Niki Petrovitch is the man I had in mind," Adams said. "Ring a bell, does it?"

He was close enough she could smell his breath. He put out a remarkably steady hand and touched her hair. She couldn't move. He looked at his hand touching her hair as if witnessing a miracle.

"Our man Nikolai asked me to check up on you," Adams said.

"Hanne shook her head. "I don't understand. I've spoken to Nikolai."

"Not fucking today you haven't." She felt his spit on her cheek. "He said I should drop by, make sure you were holding up okay."

"Did he say you should terrorize me while you were here?" She twisted away and made it to the door.

"I'm not leaving just yet, love," Adams said. "I thought I'd warm myself up a bit first. Get to know you."

"If you have a message to deliver . . ."

"He said I should check that you had it together. That you didn't look like you might fall apart. He said you've been under a lot of pressure lately. A lot of things going on in your world, Hanne. Is that right, has it been tough for you?"

"Not until very recently," Hanne said through gritted teeth.

Adams laughed. "Like the last five minutes, is that it? Very clever. I do love it when strangers try to impress upon me just how much cleverer than I am they are."

"Nice sentence," Hanne said. She regretted the sarcasm the minute it escaped her.

Adams leapt through the space between them. They were at the door. The glass door. Anyone walking by could see them. Adams didn't care, obviously, because he put a hand to her throat and pushed her back against the glass. His thumb was exerting pressure next to her ear. "He said I should make sure you understand how important it is that everything is ready for him. He's coming up, you know."

"I know he is."

"Soon."

"I know."

"And you're ready for that?"

"I was." Hanne wrapped a hand around as much of Adams' wrist as she could and tried to wrench his arm away. When it was clear she wouldn't be able to, he let her go.

"So I should tell him you looked lovely, then? Calm as can be? Pleased as punch? Ready as ever?" Adams stuck a hand in his waistband, yanked his shirt around.

"You can tell him that, yes."

"Lovely."

"You still haven't answered me. Did he tell you to scare me?" Hanne asked. Because she didn't believe Nikolai would do that. At least not like this. He demanded a military discipline from the men who worked for him. They only drank on days off. "I'm curious."

"He said I should be firm, yeah."

Hanne pulled open the door. "I'd like you to leave," she said. "You're drunk. I'll tell Nikolai you came by, and how you acted."

Adams put his face close to hers. "Threatening me is not the way it works, see. I come and lean on *you*, right? Not the other fucking way around." He touched the end of her nose very lightly with one finger. A sobriety test, Hanne thought. A sobriety test all screwed up because he was so damn drunk. She was terrified. She gripped the door frame tightly because it stopped her arm from shaking. She waited. She wasn't going to say anything.

Adams swayed backwards and then loomed in. He had taken hold of the door frame as well, his hand just above hers. He stuck his nose next to her neck and left it there, breathing deeply. "That's a lovely smell right there, Hanne," he said. "Shalimar, I reckon. Am I right? Is that what that is?"

Hanne ducked under his arm, escaped to the top half of the room. She was breathless, her vision seemed subtly altered, the edges of things weren't crisp. "Go!" she commanded. She was amazed when it worked. Adams lurched in the doorway, snow, blown from the ground up around his legs, swirling into the gallery.

"Right, then," Adams said.

His attitude had changed slightly. There was a self-awareness in his eyes, a doubt, and Hanne was overjoyed because she thought it must mean this was almost over. "You can go now," she told him.

He pulled a wallet from his pocket. But it wasn't a wallet. Hanne had mistaken the cross-hatchings on the black steel for leather, the grip of the pistol for a billfold. She gasped, and apparently that was all Adams wanted, because he promptly stuffed the weapon away again.

"You don't have one of those, eh?" he said. "I didn't think so. Which is why you should keep the lip zipped, darling. You know what I'm saying? But of course you do." He grinned—it was maniacal, that expression, Hanne thought; it was exactly the brainless grin you would expect. "We all set, then, love?" he said, and Hanne nodded. "Good stuff," Adams said, pleased as punch with the afternoon's work, by the look of him. "Keep your chin up, then, eh," he said. "See ya later, darling." And he tottered off cheerfully into the squalling white mists.

DECEMBER 13

Tim woke that morning at six, disoriented. He heard steps in the hall and in the confusion of half-sleep he had been sure for a second or two it must be his father. He lay on his back and listened, disappointedly, to Adams pad into the living room. He could hear him singing quietly. Something by The Sex Pistols. The man was a hood. This wasn't an act, Adams really was a lout. He was nothing like Michael Hollins, who was more likely to move through the morning to the sounds of Benjamin Britten, and who might once in a long while hum but would never break into song.

Last night Adams had returned late, smelling of beer and whisky. He could barely talk.

"Where were you?" Tim had asked him. "How far did you drive like this?"

"Best not to ask, really," Adams had said, ignoring the sarcasm. "A nod's as good as a wink, and all that, if you know what I mean."

Tim had given him the spare room he had been using since his father's death, when he'd given up his small apartment in Kingston and the daily half-hour commute. He'd then slept in his father's room for the first time. There were pictures of them together. And in an ornate silver frame that opened like a book was his mother in a fur coat, standing before the Parliament Buildings in Ottawa. His father's clothes still hung in the wardrobe; there seemed no reason to rush them off to Goodwill. Adams seemed thrilled at how little had changed.

Adams was peering glumly into the fridge when Tim entered the kitchen, his body bathed in the yellow electric glow. "Must be weird," Adams said, apparently wondering what might be hidden behind the purple swell of eggplant. The hairs on the back of his arm were lit as if from within, like neon filaments. "Your kitchen being the restaurant kitchen too. Mixing business and pleasure like that."

Tim reached past Adams and grabbed a grapefruit. He set it on the counter and put a knife to it; the two halves tipped away from each other. "It's not real estate, is it?"

"That's answering a question with a question, isn't it, Tim?" He raised a hand to his temple. "You got any aspirin?"

When Tim returned, Adams was breaking two eggs into a pan. Tim told him he was making a mistake. "Heat the pan first. Then add a little oil. *Then* the eggs."

Adams turned on the gas under the pan. "Fuck off." The whites hardened slowly. Adams took the painkillers and tossed them hard into his mouth, swallowed them without juice or water. He scraped at the side of the pan with a knife and the eggs broke up awkwardly.

They sat in the dining room together and Tim repeated his question. "You're not up here looking for a house, are you?" He dug at his grapefruit.

"Course I am. What you need in here is a television, by the way. Show a little footer now and again. Attract a wider crowd, you would."

"Because it makes no sense," Tim insisted. "It's the wrong time of year, for one thing."

Adams shook his head. "You need to know if the place is properly winterized," he said. "A lot of your Island cottages advertise themselves as such and you buy them in July thinking, 'This'll be lovely for Christmas, all of us gathered around the tree in our jammies,' but then the snow comes and you're freezing your tits off. No, Tim, this is the perfect time to buy."

"But you're not looking to buy a cottage, are you?"

"No, a house, mate. You think Nikolai wants to worry himself with a cottage? No, he wants a decent-sized place. Which is another reason. Those places don't come on the market very often. You have to be ready."

"Houses are all winterized, though," Tim said. "You wouldn't need to check that."

Adams stabbed at the heart of one of his eggs, but the yolk was set and nothing happened. Tim attacked the second half of his grapefruit. He sipped his coffee and it tasted, he thought, of a small victory.

Adams let his cutlery clatter loudly onto his plate. "You are fucking lucky I'm here is all I'll say. Really fucking lucky."

"Funny. I don't feel that fortunate lately," Tim said.

"You are fucking lucky to be alive." Adams blinked furiously, as if astonished at what he'd said. "Maybe," he added limply.

Tim waited. There had to be more. Even a maniac like Adams knew he couldn't leave a remark like that just hanging.

"You've got a guardian angel is what you've got," Adams said. "You should consider yourself blessed."

Tim chuckled.

"Don't you fucking dare," Adams said. "I am dead serious. If it wasn't for Nikolai taking an . . . an interest in your welfare, I don't like to think what might happen."

"You're going to have to explain that."

"He was worried about your safety. That's all I'm going to say."

"Does he think my father . . .?"

"He just wanted to make sure you were okay. Your old man was good to him. So my advice is that you should shut the fuck up and be grateful I'm here."

"What were they doing, my father and Nikolai? It had to be—"

"Men get jealous," Adams growled. "They see another man doing well and . . . boom!" He smacked his hands together.

"Bullshit," Tim said. "That has to be bullshit."

"I'm not getting paid to convince you of anything. I'm paid to see you're all right, down here on your lonesome." He got up from the table. "And so I should do my job, shouldn't I, lovely as this is."

Ten minutes later Tim heard the distinctive diesel buzz of the Volvo as Adams headed up to the Parkway that wound prettily along the bank of the St. Lawrence Seaway. From there he would go east, towards Kingston, or west, towards Montreal or the bridge to the United States.

The world had frozen hard. A woman on television stamped her fur-fringed boots and shivered dramatically. Her lips were blue. "That might have been it for the warm weather," she reported. "Game over until April." She grimaced bravely for the camera. The bloated, scarlet anchor back in the studio laughed amiably. A lightspeed look of impatience betrayed her. She hates him, Tim thought. In the office she ignores him.

There were more fishing huts on the ice, and most of the passages had grown at least a thin skin. If it remained calm and cold for three or four days, the full army of winter sportsmen would move in to join these foolhardy advance scouts.

Tim sat on the floor beside the fireplace, trying to reread the local newspaper reports concerning Bill's death. "Police are still on the scene," he read, "and expect to be there for several days. The fiery explosion was witnessed as far west as Wolfe Island and as far east as Rockport."

Rebecca telephoned and he told her about John Selby and how something about his coming bothered him. But he felt manipulative somehow, as though he wanted his retelling of recent events to bring about a change in his relationship to her.

"So what do you and Adams do?" she asked.

"Not much. I glare at him. He's gone most of the time."

"Where does he go?"

"No idea."

She wanted to come over but he said no.

Ten minutes later she called again with nothing to say.

"Come on, what is it?" he said.

"I just wanted to make sure you were still there," she said. And then, after a pause, "I'm coming over tomorrow, whatever you say."

"Adams might be here."

"That's okay. I'll see you."

He pictured his father at the stove, stirring with a red spatula a frying pan full of onions. His dirty white running shoes and white trouser legs rolled up over his shins.

Adams wasn't back at noon. Tim moved restlessly through the rooms. He felt like a man between jobs. He poked around downstairs. There was still mud on the bottom of his father's hiking boots. His deodorant was still beside the clouded Listerine and the aspirin he took religiously, every day, to ward off heart attacks. A half-done bottle of port. A stack of *New Yorkers* off the end of the couch. A thousand insignificant proofs that Tim would remove over the coming days and weeks. The benign clutter of a life.

He certainly didn't mean to ransack his father's files. He had intended merely to move a stack of old invoices—all stamped "Paid" and pinned to the desktop with a fist-sized and rough lump of dark granite—into the bottom drawer, where he knew there were others. But his intentions changed. He wanted to be the first to know. He wanted a chance to change things before Adams finished his fieldwork and began, maybe, to tear into the house.

He found other bills—from Mary Morgan for bread, from a fish-monger in Montreal, a butcher in Kingston. Dry cleaning and adver-tising receipts. Anything that might come in handy at tax time. Tim had seen much of this stuff before. But in the bottom-most envelopes he discovered photographs, as well as scribbled notes, old CAA maps of British Columbia, Ontario, New York State, an expired driver's licence, two lime-green plastic paper clips, an invitation to one of Hanne's art openings, fifty-six cents American, the label from a bottle of French wine. He tipped everything onto the floor and made a loose collage of it. The photographs he mostly recognized—a trip in the winter of 1996 to Quebec City, his father leaning in a dark doorway with a cigarette drooping from his bottom lip; the view from his Toronto apartment; Rebecca shopping in Kensington Market, a ludi-crous vinyl hat pulled low. There were a couple of men he didn't rec-ognize, but no sign of John Selby. He supposed that was what he was looking for.

He worked through the rest of the material quickly. He was wasting his time. He fed everything back into the envelopes, pulled open the top drawer of the four-drawer cabinet and rifled through the beige files. Nothing. Visa bills and warranty information on the sound sys-tem, the refrigerators. He pulled those same files forward and stood on tiptoe so he could see into the back of the drawer. Nothing.

He badly wanted a drink. And why not? He was the grieving son. He could do whatever the hell he wanted. He spied his father's Scotch next to its ornate cardboard tube and popped the cork. He drank straight from the bottle because it would have given his father fits. He realized he was grinning for absolutely no reason. No, that wasn't true. It felt damn good, that was why. He took another, more modest belt, and reached for the tube, slipped off the metal lid, and dropped the bottle in. Except, it didn't fall all the way home. The neck jutted above the rim. He extracted the whisky and tipped the obstruction onto the desk. A Ziploc bag full of folded paper tissue. Stupid. He was about to open the bag, or toss it, when he heard Adams pull up outside. Instead he stuffed everything in his pocket and slammed the file drawers shut. He ran through the house and launched himself at the couch.

Adams was flushed. Things were heating up, he said; he wanted to go through the office. He'd told Tim that, hadn't he? He was a man possessed. A whirlwind.

"That's my dad's stuff," Tim said. "You've got no right." He felt guilty, transparent. Once, as a boy, he had snuck into his father's room, believing Michael was in the bathroom. His intention had been to steal some change from the night table. His hands were on the money before he saw in the mirror his father's rumpled head poking above the sheets, taking it all in. This was the same feeling. He wondered if Adams had been skulking around outside, peering in windows.

"Actually, if it has to do with the restaurant, it's Nikolai's," Adams said.

"What are you talking about?"

"I'm talking about 51 percent. That's what. Niki owns that much of this joint. Didn't you know?"

"I knew it was . . ."

"You just didn't know it was a controlling interest, is that it? Well, I'm not surprised your old man was mum about that part."

Tim left him to it. He didn't know what else to do. He would need to see his lawyer. He had no idea if Adams was telling the truth. Which was terrible. "I don't suppose you'll find much," he said. "I'd be surprised."

He tried watching television but found that he was listening not to the embarrassing guesswork of the game show contestants but to the rubber wheels of the filing cabinet drawers running back and forth in their steel tracks. He had discovered that there were objects wrapped within the tissue paper in his pocket but he was afraid to open the bag until Adams was gone.

Adams returned eventually to the living room. "Nothing there," he said. He was carrying a bottle of Scotch—a fresh bottle of his own—and two glasses.

"Is that right?" Tim was laid out on the couch. It had begun to snow and he was watching the soft white flutter and drift of it against the pines. He had started a fire.

"Your dad was conscientious in his record-keeping, I'll give him that."

"Glad to hear it."

Adams poured two drinks. He had evidently decided to try a different approach.

"You never went through that stuff yourself, Tim? I mean, the temptation must have been enormous. It would be for me."

"But we're not very much alike, are we." Tim sat up.

"We're all essentially the same," Adams said. "Every one of us."

"Not really."

Adams peered into the glass as if trying to calculate how many ounces of the toffee-brown liquid there were, and what effect he might reasonably expect them to have on his thinking. "We all want to be happy. That's at the bottom of everything."

Tim said, "Going through the files in there, knowing I'm out here hating every second of it, does that make you happy?"

"It makes others happy."

"So it's okay?"

Adams shifted easily in his chair. "You'll get over it," he said. "Your dad wouldn't want you out here sulking. He'd want you on your hands and knees helping me."

"I think it's a mistake to think you have to carry on the work of your parents."

"I reckon your old man would be disappointed to hear that." He lifted his glass, showed it to the corners of the room. "Wherever he is."

Tim looked to the television, the garish spinning and clicking wheel, the hidden words and phrases. "Are your parents alive, Adams?"

Adams kicked off his running shoes. "They're somewhere about. Hartlepool, I think."

"You're not sure?"

"We're not proud of each other, let's say, shall we?"

"Does that make you *un*happy?"

Adams said, "Is this a trap, then, Tim? Prove me miserable? Prove me a liar? Well, let me tell you something, son. I am fucking ecstatic with the way things are turning out." He offered a mirthless smile. A crooked line of not-nearly-white teeth.

"That's good," Tim said. He was alarmed all over again by Adams' sudden fury, the way this younger man had called him "son."

"I am a world traveller," Adams said. "The things I do for people make a real difference. How many people can say that? Eh? And when I do something, a week later, or a month, or a year, I see the consequences of it showing up in the papers. I see the revelations that shock the world and I know that I played a part in all that. I was privy to the mechanics." He rubbed his hands together. "Here, I'll give you another way of looking at it: *You* see the balance of power shift suddenly, mysteriously, and you're confused, shocked, whereas to *me* it's no mystery at all. I was the one who did the paperwork, see? Or the legwork. I have a hand in things, Tim. Not everything, I'm not God, and I have no desire to be God, that would be a big job."

"All I see is people dying."

Adams shook his head. "Yeah, but the TV cameras up at the road. They *know*, Tim."

"So you're the man who's going to save us from ourselves?" It was ludicrous, delusional.

"You taking the mickey?" Adams stood up sharply. He put an arm on the mantel and posed there, the punk lord of the manor. He gazed for a moment at the limestone chimney, appeared to examine its grey surface for hint of fossil or history, all the while muttering under his breath like a man possessed. But when he spoke again it was very calmly, deliberately. "I just don't understand our not getting along."

Tim mumbled that he didn't get it either.

"We're on the same side," Adams said.

It was the Cold War reduced to absurd dinner theatre.

Adams poured them more whisky. He pulled the cushion from his chair and plumped it. When he sat down again he bounced around like a child before settling in. The air filled with bright dust filaments.

Finally it was over. They sat in the dark and watched the fire die. "I've enjoyed this," Adams said. "Considering the circumstances, I'm pleased."

Shortly Adams rose, patted Tim on the knee, and disappeared into his room.

Tim wanted to heave a chair through the window, bring the winter indoors. He was swimming upstream here. No, it wasn't that ordinary. It was more like he had fallen through ice not strong enough to support him. The water was setting around him, like amber. There were people in the distance who might have been able to help, but they didn't see him. They were too busy with their own stories.

*

He met Rebecca up at the road. When he saw her headlights he hid until he was sure it was her.

"Don't come down to the house," he had said to her. "I'll walk up and meet you." He'd been half drunk, whispering into the telephone.

"What is it?" she had said.

"You won't believe it."

He directed her off to the side of the road. She killed the engine and he climbed in.

"You okay?" She put a hand on his arm. "You smell of whisky."

He was shivering. The Ziploc was clenched in his blue fist. He unfurled his hand.

"What is it?"

He teased out the tissue paper. Handed it to her. "Careful." He put his hands beneath hers, ready to catch.

"I need more light," she said. "Can I?" She reached for the interior light. It turned their skin to gold.

"Quickly then," Tim said. "Unwrap them." *She thinks they're alive*, he thought. *She thinks it's something that might bite.*

Rebecca pulled away layers until she found them. The fourteen stones glinted disappointingly. Tim knew what they were. He was confident. And although their existence scared him, he wanted them to *glow*, damn it. He wanted drama. Because this *was* a dramatic turn. He wanted to see the evidence of that in Rebecca's palm.

"Diamonds?" she asked quietly.

He nodded. "Big fucking diamonds! They're like marbles."

"Where on earth did you get them?"

He had difficulty hearing her. She brought the diamonds closer to her face.

He said nothing for three minutes, four, just watched her, and then he told her where he had found them. "I think he wanted us to find them."

"Michael?"

"Remember that last night? How adamant he was that we drink this Scotch rather than the stuff from the bar? The funny look he had on his face when you didn't say anything, just brought the bottle?"

Rebecca shook her head. She was staring at the stones as if she expected them to vanish if she so much as blinked.

"Well, I do. He was going to explain them. I'm sure of it."

"So if I missed them, why didn't he just get them himself?"

"I don't know."

He tapped one of the diamonds with a fingernail, tipping it over. With no facets ground onto it yet, and with its asymmetrical, nearly unattractive shape, it was hard to understand all the fuss. But his heart thumped as if a rabbit were trapped behind his rib cage.

"Are they real, you think?" Rebecca said. "They look . . . weird."

He shrugged. They had to be real. It didn't make sense otherwise. "I'm sure it's what Adams is looking for."

"Why? Michael might have had them for years. Maybe they were your mother's. An heirloom."

He said he didn't think so, but couldn't tell her why.

She asked him what he was going to do, then. "Are you going to call the police?"

"If they were Michael's, they're mine now. I don't see what that has to do with the police."

"Tell them Adams Denver is after them."

She was calling his bluff; he knew that. Ferreting out the illogical strands of his argument.

"What if Michael got them illegally?" she said. "What if they're connected to his death?"

"We don't know any of that. And I sure as hell don't want to be the one responsible for labelling my dad a thief." Whatever the truth was, it had to be more complicated than that. You didn't find diamonds with your whisky every day. "I don't know who to talk to," he said. "I thought it should be you."

"Then, don't talk to anybody else yet. Hide them. Wait for a few days. Let's see what happens."

"Will you take them?" he said. "Put them somewhere?" He was asking the world, he knew.

Rebecca covered them up again. She stuffed them into the plastic bag and sealed it. She opened the glove compartment and tossed it in, like it was a cassette tape she'd finished with. "How about there?" she said. "For now. Until we decide."

*

Des Boyle was dropped off at Kingston's small airport by his wife. John glimpsed her freckled face and red hair through the open door of the Toyota Camry. She leaned across the passenger seat to say something and Des bent down to kiss her. His shirt was untucked and the lace on one of his oxfords came undone as he galloped, like a giraffe, across the floodlit tarmac.

John apologized for the short notice. Des turned and waved to his wife; he blew her a kiss. "It's okay. What's going on?"

John took Des's overnight bag. "In a minute. Come on. We're boarding."

It was a forty-minute flight to Toronto, and when they were in the air and land had fallen away, John said, "You remember I told you our theory was that Petrovitch might be moving diamonds?"

"Sure. An argument in Russian."

"Well, the reason for that speculation was a man named Viktor Laevsky."

"I'm listening."

"He's shift manager at one of Russia's largest diamond mines."

"Which one?"

"Arkangel."

"I'm familiar with them. I was sent to a weekend seminar in Halifax."

Below them Lake Ontario and the string of pretty, glowing towns along its Canadian shoreline resembled, oddly enough, an unclipped diamond necklace. But the scene also reminded John of numerous flights between islands in the Caribbean. He recalled nostalgically the wave of hot scented air that rushed up the stairs to greet him every time he landed, and how sad it would feel to land now in frigid Toronto.

"You were sent on a seminar? A seminar about Arkangel?" It sounded ludicrous. "Tell me what that means."

"Well, we've long recognized that diamonds attract organized crime. They're hard to trace and easy to sell. Plus you've got a huge profit-to-size ratio. Maybe the best part is that diamonds aren't like drugs. Drugs are always illegal. You sell cocaine, it's still cocaine. But diamonds are different. You have no way of knowing when you buy your pretty diamond ring in Toronto whether it has been mined legally and sold legally, or whether it was stolen, whether people had to lie and cheat and even die for that diamond to make it to market." He laughed lightly. "What does that say about love, that its most precious symbol is so often tarnished this way?"

"It says love is blind, perhaps," John said. "So why did they send you in particular on this seminar?"

"The United States consumes 50 percent of all the diamonds produced in the world each year. Presumably the bad guys try to exploit that fact. And with my country rapidly becoming a force in the diamond market, it just made sense to have those of us who work along the border brought up to speed. The thing is, the security at Canadian mines is considered as good as any in the world. There's not a single case of theft yet reported. What we mostly expect to see is blood diamonds from Angola being rerouted through Canada."

"And?"

"We haven't seen any, not here, not as yet. They do arrive occasionally, though, at Montreal, or Halifax. And especially Toronto. Melted into the middle of Belgian chocolates, or some such. I'm sure some make their way to New York. But I don't see that it's happening through the Islands."

John laughed. "Jesus, you're a regular professor," he said. "Maybe you can take the lead when we get to Toronto."

"Because we're going to talk to this Laevsky fellow?"

"Precisely. He's in jail."

"On what charge?"

"Vehicular manslaughter."

"Wow."

"He rented a car this afternoon, then parked it and went for dinner at a place called Susur. You heard of it? Anyway, afterwards he was driving back to the Windsor Arms and he hit a woman in an intersection. He blew twice the legal limit."

"He was drunk?"

"Quite pissed, apparently. And belligerent to go with it. Said something about diplomatic immunity, but your people are dismissing that as raving right now."

"And what do you hope to get from him?"

"What he's doing in the country, for one, and what his beef is with Petrovitch. Was he carrying stones? Whatever he wants to get off his drunken, guilt-ridden chest, I suppose."

The plane was descending already. The lights were thickening on the ground.

"I'm not a fan of landings," Des said, and, as if to prove his point, he clutched at the armrests as the small plane jostled through some thin cloud cover.

*

Des was only too keen to make the necessary introductions at the police station on Dundas Street, a sprawling building of unappealing white brick and thick opaque glass. The lobby smelled of fresh carpet, and when John touched the footrail along the bottom edge of Reception a spark jumped across the space to meet him.

They were holding Viktor Laevsky in an isolated cell. "As per your agency's request, Mr. Selby," the bearded and barrel-chested desk jockey said ingratiatingly.

John told him how much he appreciated the cooperation.

"What's happening with this diplomatic immunity business?" Des asked him, and the sergeant perused his admission notes.

"You'll be wanting to talk to the arresting officers on that matter," he said. "Only, they're at the hospital as I understand it. Filing a report on the deceased. Their feeling, though, I can tell you, is that it's all bullshit. He's Russian and he thinks that's enough to get him off. I don't think anyone's taking it very seriously."

"Seriously enough that you're checking it out, though," Des said.

"As fast as we can."

"And we can see him?"

"I've been told to cooperate fully. Anything you want."

John nodded, pleased with the smoothness of their progress, the lack of obstacles. But then Des said, "Have you got some duty counsel kicking around here somewhere? I'd like them with us. Just to be on the safe side."

"He hasn't asked for a lawyer."

"All the same," Des said.

"I'm sure I can rustle someone up."

The sergeant got on the phone, and John raised an eyebrow at Des, who shrugged. "This is an unusual situation. I think we need a witness in there, that's all."

"I can take you down there," the sergeant said, replacing the receiver. "There's a lawyer just finishing up on the other side. She'll meet us there." He snapped his fingers and a baby-faced corporal materialized from behind a burlap-sheathed room divider. The sergeant led them across the new carpet and along a concrete-floored corridor that ended at a steep, painted stairwell. Two floors below ground level they followed the sergeant through a maze of tunnels that seemed always to work south, away from the road.

"I suppose if someone got out of their cell the thinking is they'd get lost down here," John said cheerfully.

"We found one of our own just last week," the sergeant agreed. "I thought he'd been transferred three months ago."

Viktor Laevsky was asleep on his thin grey mattress. A spotless steel toilet in the opposite corner. A camera next to the ceiling. Cinderblock walls. All standard issue. The same as any the world over, except perhaps for this one's obsessive cleanness. The lighting was dim and green, and Laevsky's massive head, with its open mouth and sallow complexion, the drooping shadowed eyes, gave the emotional impression of a painting by Edward Münch. The knowledge that he had caused a woman's death that evening only added to the monstrous effect.

They turned to await the lawyer's arrival. They could hear her footsteps echoing off the walls, but it was fifteen seconds before she rounded the last turn and marched towards them—a smart, attractive woman in a blue suit and low black heels. Her hair tied back in a ponytail that was thrown from side to side with each step. She had a battered black briefcase, and a small leather purse slung over her shoulder. A friendly smile; altogether unimpressed by the presence of an American agent. John liked her immediately, and realized that that positive snap judgment was something she was very used to.

Staying outside the cell was fine with her, she said. In the absence of Laevsky expressing a firm wish otherwise, she was happy to simply observe. "But you'll have to ask him up front what he wants," she said. "And I'll tell you if you cross a line."

The sergeant unlocked the cell, and John and Des slipped sideways through the narrow opening. Another cop appeared with two straight-backed chairs and placed them in the centre of the cell. John and Des sat on them, deliberately making noise, and still Laevsky didn't wake.

"You smell that? The champagne?" Des said. "Only it smells like cheap apple juice now."

Viktor Laevsky rolled onto his side and groaned. He half opened one eye and held that position for a long time. "I know you," he said, and cleared his throat. His English was remarkable, almost without an accent.

John shook his head. "You think you do, perhaps."

"You were at . . ." He waved a finger loosely at John, trying to stir up a concrete recollection, a name.

"I was. But that doesn't mean what you think it does."

"I think it means you are a prick."

John threw up his hands. "My mistake, then. It means exactly what you think it does."

Des sniffed, covered a grin with his cuff.

"You've created a world of trouble for yourself here, Mr. Laevsky."

"If that is your only message, you can fuck off." Laevsky belched loudly. "Run back to your master," he said.

John introduced himself, as well as Des. He told the lawyer he didn't know her name, and when she told him he repeated it for Laevsky. "She's a lawyer," he said. "But if you'd prefer someone else, we can—"

Laevsky cut John off. "No. Who the fuck are you? Really!"

John said, "I think you heard me." He repeated his introductions.

Laevsky pushed his shoulder into the mattress and heaved himself up into a sitting position. He rubbed heavily at his face and let his head droop between his shoulders. His hair was matted and his scalp showed through.

"You killed someone tonight," John said. "A young woman."

Laevsky stared at the floor. "*Polny pizdets,*" he said.

"We hear you're of the opinion you won't have to face charges," John said, assuming the Russian would translate himself.

"I may have been jumping the gun," Laevsky sneered. "It is a serious charge."

Des asked him, "Where did you learn to speak such good English?"

"In England, at school. Four years."

"What did you study?"

"English, of course." He laughed at them. He leaned back and crossed his arms, positioning his closed fists behind his biceps so they seemed to swell. It was like sitting with someone from the circus, John thought. A huge-headed performer of brutish secret acts. Laevsky grinned and there was, from deep within his mouth, a golden glint.

John looked around the room, gazed high into its clean white corners. He was focusing, wiping the slate clean so he could remember every detail.

Viktor kicked gently at the metal bed leg. He said, "So why were you at Petrovitch's party?"

"He pisses me off," John said. "Just as he pisses you off."

"Why *does* he piss you off, Mr. Laevsky?" Des said. "You see, I wasn't there. Why don't you bring me up to speed?"

Laevsky wrapped his fists around the edge of the bed and put a little weight on them. It looked as if he might try to stand up, but the sergeant barked at him and he slumped back down. "It is none of your business why I was there," he grumbled. He needed a shave and a shower. His clothes were rumpled, and, now that they were talking, the room had filled up with the scent of rotten fruit.

"Did you come to Canada expressly to see him?" John said.

"I came for the weather," Laevsky said. "And for the warm hospitality."

"Because if we discover that—"

Laevsky held up a meaty palm. "You are already charging me with manslaughter," he said. "How much worse can you make it?"

"I think more to the point is, can you make it *better* for yourself?" Des told him.

Laevsky eyed him suspiciously, then scornfully. "Fuck off," he said.

"That," said John sarcastically, "is where a good education gets you these days. It's very sad."

Laevsky lay on his back and closed his eyes; he folded his arms across his chest. "Talk to me in the morning." He belched extravagantly.

"SIT THE FUCK UP!" It was the desk sergeant. He had moved into the doorway, and even John wondered whether he might charge into the cell and grab Viktor Laevsky by the throat.

Laevsky grumbled, muttered something in Russian, but he sat up again. He adjusted the way his shirt disappeared into his pants.

"Is Petrovitch a business partner? Is there some joint venture you're cooking up?" John asked him.

Laevsky said nothing. Then he spat in the direction of the toilet. The spray slid slowly down the outside of the steel bowl. "Piece of shit," he grumbled.

"Is he an investor in the mine?"

"_____"

"Are the two of you stealing from your boss, then? He seemed a bit surprised to hear you are in Canada," John said.

"You are lying," Viktor said wearily. "It is a bad strategy to lie to me, when I so clearly know the truth to be otherwise."

"Are you here at his request?" Des said.

"Whose request?"

"Anyone's," John said. "We don't care. Nikolai. Your boss."

"I am the last person Petrovitch should want to see."

"Why is that?" John said. His backside was going to sleep, but it was a rule that you had to appear completely at ease in these situations. The discomfort had to affect only the prisoner.

Viktor shook his head.

"Because Nikolai likes to run his own show," Des said. "Am I right? You do your thing and he does his."

"Petrovitch couldn't run a flea circus. Are you joking? No, you are not right," Laevsky said.

"He stole from you, then," John said. "From the mine. And you've been sent to . . . I don't know . . . shoot the bastard. Talk some sense into him."

"Run him down in a drunken stupor is more like," the sergeant said and paced away.

Laevsky wasn't going to talk to them. He had sobered up too much to be tricked into a stupid mistake. Even at this early stage that much was clear. They might as well leave, John thought.

But Des leaned forward in his chair. "If your mine is typical, then between one-quarter and one-third of your production goes missing," he said.

"I know what happens at the mine," Laevsky said.

"But you don't know how Petrovitch did it, do you? And now there's a lot of pressure on you, I'm sure. They have so many tricks, don't they? They eat them, they stuff them up their behinds, they hollow out their teeth, they tie them to the legs of homing pigeons. It's a wonder any of them make it to market."

"We lose very little. And anyway, Petrovitch couldn't sell stolen diamonds, not in Canada."

"That's why I'm here, isn't it," John said cheerfully. "In case he's sending them my way. To the good old U. S. of A. and all its free markets."

Des said, "You insult our intelligence, Mr. Laevsky. He can sell them in Antwerp or Tel Aviv or New York. There are thousands of buyers out there."

"Are these likely to be rough diamonds?" John asked Des, cutting Laevsky out of the loop. "There are people who can cut them in New York?"

"Two or three hundred," Des explained. "In Antwerp five times that number. In Tel Aviv three thousand. In Bombay everyone is a diamond cutter. This is a massive business we're talking about. Diamond polishers sell more than ten billion dollars in diamonds every year. Pedigree and provenance is next to impossible to prove in a market that large."

Viktor sat back and watched them. He was holding his head. "You two should get a TV show," he said. "It is all so very entertaining."

Des ignored him. "De Beers sells five billion in diamonds every year in London. There are rooms full of stones, other rooms full of money. If Petrovitch has diamonds, or if Viktor here was trying to sell some to him—because that's another possibility—they could be absorbed easily."

Laevsky was amused, when what John wanted was to intimidate him. "You are so stupid. Like schoolboys trying to impress the teacher. Now get me a real fucking lawyer."

"Do you have someone in mind?" Des asked him. "What's wrong with her?"

"Get me a list," Laevsky snorted. He spat again, this time at the wall. The sergeant bristled and grabbed at the bars.

John had had enough. He put his hand on Des's knee. "Let's go. Give him his list."

It was Laevsky's last chance to be forthcoming. But he merely sighed, as if mildly pleased that the badgering had ended and he would be able to sleep again.

"Don't forget you killed someone," the sergeant blurted, as Des and John filed out. He turned the key in the lock. "Someone's wife," he said. "Someone's mother, you asshole."

They gathered again in a small office the desk sergeant had found for them. The lawyer asked if they needed her. Her name was Lily. John said no, they were good. But had they jeopardized anything in there, did she think?

"I'm not sure he'll even remember the conversation," she said.

When she was gone, John asked for Des's opinion. "Did you see anything there? Any reaction to any of our questions?"

"On the one hand, I think we told him more than he told us," Des said. "He knows our suspicions now. But we do know he's here with his boss's blessing, and I don't think any of us believe he's on holiday. From what you said, he sought out Petrovitch as soon as he arrived. And calling him a piece of shit doesn't exactly lead me to believe they're partners. He wasn't faking his distaste for Petrovitch. No, my guess is that if anything's going on—and we've got nothing in the way of paper to prove there is, yet—it's that some of the Arkangel diamonds are ending up in Petrovitch's pocket, and Laevsky's been sent to investigate. Which isn't the same as saying they end up in Canada or the U.S., mind you."

"Why wouldn't Arkangel just contact you?" John said. "The RCMP's rep is as good as any force in the world. They could have got you guys to play the heavy."

Des shrugged. "Makes sense to me. But hey, if Petrovitch has people operating above the law in Russia, maybe the thinking was that he would have the same immunity here."

They grabbed a cab back to the airport, and because there was no flight back to Kingston until the morning, they took two rooms at the Sheraton. They shared the elevator. At the fifth floor Des held the door open. He said he had to call his wife. What was John going to do?

John said there was something Des should know.

"Yeah? What's that?"

"Hanne Kristiansen. She imports art from Russia." The disclosure pained him.

"Well, she's our next stop, then," Des said, nodding.

John asked him to hold on. He muttered something about having a history. Would Des mind if he went in alone first?

"I'll wait for your word," Des said, seeming to realize that a gracious step backward was what the moment required. "You go ahead, if that's how you want to handle it."

John thanked him awkwardly. "I'll, um, I'll let you call your wife."

"Thanks. Get some sleep."

It was so familiar a thing to say that it made them both laugh. John continued up to the eighth floor. He could sleep until the new year.

While he undressed he flicked on the television. An overnight low of minus 25 Celsius, the announcer predicted. He pointed at the snowflakes all over his map. "And plenty of the white stuff in the next few days. So dust off those shovels, folks. It looks like it's going to be a long one."

Don't I know it, John thought, and clambered stiffly under the soft sheets. He pulled them up to his neck and lay like that a while, staring at the pristine stipple until his eyes watered from the strain and he had to look away.

DECEMBER 14

Later in the evening a thug named Oleg would say to Donald Graves: "Your wife looks a lot like Anna Karenina. All the snow behind her." Gesticulating like a filmmaker with a fabulous plan. He would frame Mae's fifty-four-year-old face in a squarish arrangement of thumbs and fingers, sigh foully. "She is beautiful, Donald. Beautiful." And everyone aboard would know his interest in Mae was in no way literary.

But now, Karenina was the furthest thing from Graves' mind as he steered his boat through the dark rock- and ice-strewn narrows of the Lost Channel. When he and Mae cast off, it was a frigid cloudless night, the sky saturated with stars. A dangerously thin strip of black open water perfectly still between the litter of islands and the thick, creeping fields of ice. The rumble of trucks over the International Bridge above them was a noise he and Mae were so used to that they would have sworn there was no sound at all. Donald steered west and south, even though he wanted to go east. He worked around the tip of Georgina Island, with Bratt hulking off to starboard, Himes behind it, and Rabbit barely visible, seeming more a sweet protrusion from the much bigger Hill Island. They said nothing. Then Donald worked east into the Channel. It was safer to go through the islands this way, in case anyone was foolish enough to follow an expert into this nearly solid labyrinth. At any time, though, they knew they could find the route impassable.

The bridge soared ahead of them, strung with festive white lights. Mae stood in the bow staring down into the impenetrable depths. Donald knew she could see only a distorted reflection of herself, the humbling spray of stars, the fast-gathering cloud. The water here was deep and gave nothing away. No sign, for instance, of the British boat and the fourteen sailors aboard who had disappeared in this channel August 7, 1760. The *Onandaga*, armed escort to a nine-hundred-strong flotilla of smaller boats en route to Montreal, had been ambushed downriver by the French. It launched a smaller boat so it might head back and warn the *Onandaga*'s sister ship, the *Mohawk*, but that boat vanished. The search went on for a week. Donald had guided thousands of tourists and fishermen through this maze, and had told variations of the same true story every time. And it never failed—all his paying customers fell silent and leaned over the gunwales, believing against reason that they might find that which had successfully evaded two centuries of prying eyes.

Small cottages and spectacular mansions, all abandoned until spring, were plainly silhouetted. A miniature copy of the bridge linked two small islands. A barbecue grill was stationed on a grassy point like a sentry, its perfect snow cap being unstitched by a fresh gusting wind. Among the trees on Constance was a half-deflated soccer ball. And slow-turning whirlpools churned directly beneath the bridge.

They pushed farther east. They had come little more than full circle. Taken twenty minutes to make a quarter mile.

"Where did the stars go?" Mae complained. She looked back at him.

"This is the last time," he reminded her, trying to shrink into his down jacket. "Petrovitch said this is it."

It had begun in September. Tim was busy in Granite's kitchen with Rebecca, experimenting with a soufflé recipe. Or perhaps it was the oven they were fooling with, arranging shelves in it to find where the heat was most even. At any rate, they were out of the room and Michael was all business. He began by apologizing. He had no right, he said, to involve Donald. To think he might be interested. Donald told him they were grown men. "You can't live here without thinking about smuggling," he said. "It gets in the blood. It's something in the water."

For many years Donald had scraped by as a historian and a guide. But Michael's scheme would pay them five thousand dollars each run. A maximum of six runs to an island just across the border. And if all went well, a bonus of twenty thousand at the end. It wasn't booze they were moving, Michael said, but it wasn't heroin either. It was nothing that would get a man killed.

And Donald and Mae had talked about it, because they shared everything. Mae had said it was stupid. But she agreed they needed the money. An ice storm had taken the roof off their house and the repairs had set them back. Plus it was going on all around them. Donald had made a name for himself as a guide. Men were offering him money all the time. Booze and cigarettes. People looking for a fresh start. Damn near everyone here got something out of the smuggling that went on. Why not them for a change? Mae said they should worry more because of what Michael had done for a living—he was a powerful man, and dangerous, maybe—but Donald argued that that should make them rest easier. He was a professional; he knew how to minimize risks. And he was their friend. Michael Hollins was a good man. They recalled how he had refused to let them pay for their meal on their wedding anniversary. But Mae was torn between sympathy and anger. "He didn't tell you who these people are," she complained. "And he wants to put us at risk. It's not what friends do. We just haven't known him very long. We should say no. Why are we even considering this?" Donald thought she was right, but still he fought. And in the end Mae stopped arguing because she saw that he wouldn't be moved. They offered their services. And no, they didn't want to know details. Details, they said, could sink them.

It was too late now, anyway, to beat themselves up. This was the fourth run and apparently the last. Michael was dead and they were frightened. They had to get this trip behind them so they could relax.

They were in the wider Canadian Middle Channel. Buck's Bay on their port side, Reveille Shoal solid to starboard. Then Watch Island and Club. Beaulieu and Redstone as they approached the tiny village of Rockport. The open water as narrow as a country lane. A fine snow fell. There was no weight to it. It was a mist that drifted in front of them, moving from north to south in white washes that reminded Donald inexplicably of hot-air balloons coming in over a field to land.

St. Brendan's Roman Catholic Church, apparent guardian of the ninety-six winter residents, appeared like the ghost of a building. A yellow light burned in the living quarters attached to the back, and also in the house across the road where it was possible in the summer to rent scuba gear, or buy worms measured in a tin mug they dipped again and again into the busted chest freezer that Amy Bannon insisted her husband keep right next to the back door of the mud room.

The smaller tour boats had been hauled ashore and lay around the boarded-up ticket booth like bony cattle. A man was walking his dog up the slick hill away from them. At the sound of their motor he stopped and strained to make out a name on the boat. He would have no luck because not an hour earlier Donald had draped white plastic sheeting over the side, held it in place with an invisible line of water-proof putty. Nothing intentional, of course, if they were questioned: *We use this to keep the seats dry, officer. Just wasn't thinking tonight, I guess.*

He stayed close to shore, pointed the boat into the Tar Island Narrows until they saw the coded flashes of light he knew were coming. Three long, two short. Repeat as necessary. Donald handed Mae a flashlight and she returned the signal. He let the quick current push him at the shore. Willow branches drooped over the boat. Mae sat down and dropped a hand into the water.

There was no ice here, the water ran too quickly. It made life easy and it made things difficult, too. He didn't want to tie up; he wanted Oleg and whoever was accompanying him this time to scurry down the bank. But it didn't happen, and so he cut the engine. The stern wanted to pull around but Donald grabbed the willow, and that way they were able to hold their own against the river.

A gravel road petered out here, at the ruins of a clapboard farm-house. Donald had suggested it in the fall when Michael had pointed out that the proper boat ramp in the village was too risky. Through the trees, the roof of a car was visible. The silhouette of a man's head and the red glow of a cigarette. Another figure in the back seat.

Donald wanted to lean on the horn. Mae lifted her hand from the water and put it to her cheek. She looked surprised at how cold it was. Donald adjusted his grip on the tree. An animal moved on the ground. The driver's door of the car opened and the inside of the sedan flooded with lemony light. The two men met at the trunk. One of them removed a soft-sided bag. The driver climbed back inside. The first man started down the slope. Oleg called him back. "Lushin! The bag." Lushin scrambled back for the duffle bag and began his descent again. With his free hand he grabbed at saplings that were like spears in the ground. He came down the slope sideways, grunting, swearing. He didn't acknowledge them. The sedan pulled ahead, pushed its nose under the trees, and the driver climbed out again.

There was more movement in the leaves. A small cat—white and brown—appeared, moving slowly, lifting its feet daintily. Lushin kicked out a leg. He caught the cat with his boot and it rose surreally into the air, like a plastic grocery bag inflated by a breeze. He swung his leg a second time but missed. The cat was clotheslined by one of the saplings and then crunched into the ground. Mae was on her feet. "Donald!" she gasped.

Lushin raised his bag. "Stay!" He regarded the ground around him angrily. The cat shook itself and clambered gingerly over soft snow. It sank in and leapt forward, sank in again, and then was gone. Probably it had hidden, Donald thought, beneath the wheels of the sedan.

Lushin had now reached the bottom of the slope. He wore a black turtleneck, black ski jacket. Hiking boots with yellow laces. He looked to Donald like an alpine cat burglar. Donald took Lushin's bag and then his hand, and hauled him aboard. The man smelled of Turkish tobacco. The boat rocked, and Lushin looked for a handhold. He collapsed onto the bench seat, spread his arms along the back of it, like a man settling in for an evening of entertainment. "Oleg is coming," he said. "Wait for him."

A man similarly outfitted, only with a black toque stretched over his skull, climbed skilfully down to the shore. He grunted when he saw Mae and fell on to the bench next to Lushin.

They cut across the Middle Channel at twenty-five knots, circled Cleopatra Island and Yeo, quite close to the border. Nothing. There was room to move, and that was reassuring. They held steady for ten minutes, the engine purring, the snow gone on ahead and the waters calm again, even a few diluted stars above. Neither of the Russians had said a word since coming aboard. Michael had told them that at the beginning: "They're not big talkers, so don't take it personally. You're a taxi driver, that's all."

They darted across to Ball Island, went once around it, Donald's pulse climbing, Mae in the bucket seat beside him biting her nails but smiling bravely. They reached Zavikon, the island closest to the border. Donald pointed. "The finish line," he said. "Manhattan Island. The United States of America."

"That is no finishing line," Oleg said dismissively. "Look at all the ice. How do you know we can make it?" He concentrated his gaze on Mae.

"You have to trust me," Donald told him. But then Oleg compared Mae to Karenina and Donald just wanted it over with. Mae's smile was watery and she was, Donald observed, a woman drowning.

Donald said, "The two ahead are Douglas and Deer. If we can get between them, and do it without attracting any attention, we're okay, we'll be at your man's island." He visualized the route. "It's almost over," he promised, talking much more to Mae than he was to Oleg. What had he been thinking when he let her come along? But she had insisted—"I want to be there for the end of it"—and she had stuck her chin out defiantly, a pose Donald had long ago realized meant that it was a waste of breath to argue with her.

There were no boats foolish enough to be out with them. And no sound in the air, either of seaplanes or helicopters. Lights on shore at Alexandria Bay to the southwest were to be expected. Donald pulled back on the throttle. A freighter chugged away in the distance to the east, but it was already so far downstream that its wake had disappeared. Oleg tipped his head back and closed his eyes. The duffle bag was trapped between Lushin's feet. Michael had always said that if the worst happened and they were caught, one of the passengers would do all the talking. He would claim to be an American fisherman whose boat had run aground in Canadian waters. He was hitching a ride with Donald; here was his passport. Donald was to say he had met the men in Ivy Lea wandering around looking for a telephone, and that he had decided, against his better judgment, to be a good Samaritan. It was an impossible argument at this time of year. But no one knew the waters better than he did. And anyway, they were only going a hundred metres across the border. A navigational error. Mistaking one island for another. He would be turned back at worst. He knew the patterns followed by the boaters and the Coast Guard. The ice, though, frightened him, the way it penned him in and limited so drastically his options.

Lushin was on his feet before they hit land. He bounded from the boat like a gazelle escaping the zoo. A house lit up between the trees. Oleg unzipped the duffle bag and pocketed two sheaves of cash. He re-zipped the bag and threw it to Lushin's feet. Lushin struggled up the slope. The experience of watching him was eerie, so clearly did it mirror his recent appearance on the Canadian shore. It felt to Donald almost as if time might fold back on itself and free them from the consequences of what they had done.

Oleg hollered at them, "Let's get away from here. You idiots. Get away."

Donald cleared his throat but did as he was told. He was too old for confrontations, let alone shootouts. He stole a glance at his wife and resented greatly that she looked frightened and that he felt he couldn't take her hand. Donald turned away. Fuck him, he thought, and Mae fixed her gaze on the bottom of the boat.

Oleg produced the two bundles of cash." Here," he said, "twenty thousand." They had done well, he said. "It was good to be in America." He laughed in a way that made Donald shiver. *We didn't do this for you*, he wanted to say, only he wasn't sure exactly who they *had* done it for. Was it to honour a promise made to Michael? Or was it for the contractor who had fixed the roof? The truth was, he supposed, that they had done it for the same reason anybody else broke the law: because they were greedy. Privately, Donald also believed that it made him part of the history of the Islands. Perhaps in two hundred years tourists would follow his and Mae's route, look at their (hopefully flattering) portraits in their Palm Pilot guidebooks.

Donald indicated the lights of Rockport, the absence of anyone between them and shore.

They concentrated on their approach. It was, Donald realized, the only common ground they had—a desire to make it home. When the boat nudged and scraped against the bank, Oleg managed the slope up to the road easily. The interior light came on in the sedan and then the purr of its engine. He might have waved—Mae claimed later that he had raised his hand, but Donald was doubtful.

Donald reversed the boat some ten feet. He smiled grimly at Mae and pulled back hard on the throttle. He was worried. He should have been relieved it was over. But he couldn't shake the feeling that any second, yellow-toothed dogs on the decks of sleek warships would fight against leashes to get at him. He expected the clouds to part and reveal squadrons rappelling from the stars.

Mae put her cheek against his. "I didn't like that very much, did you, Donny?"

Donald wanted to weep. He squeezed her hand.

"Good," she said mildly, laying her head on his shoulder. "I hoped it wasn't just me. That makes me feel better, then."

DECEMBER 15

It was a vicious night. The wind screaming out of the north, bending the pines double. Adams had checked the route the day before, when he'd met Lushin and Oleg down on the shore. Oleg, because he wasn't the one who had to make the trip, had said, "It looks fine. What are you complaining about?"

"I'm saying there's no way of knowing. If I get halfway across and it starts cracking and buckling under me, I won't be a happy sodding camper."

Which had made Oleg laugh, and Lushin too.

"Don't laugh, mate," Adams said. "This is serious shit. There's a lot of open water on the other side. If you send me to my death I'll be coming after you."

"Then, thank God I'm an atheist," Oleg said.

Adams thought it really did look solid, Oleg was right. But he wanted them to acknowledge that what he was doing was no piece of cake. "I'm not big on ice," he told them. "Where I come from, you don't see a lot of ice thick enough to support a man. Let alone those stupid houses out there."

Oleg suggested he was scared, and Adams just looked at him. I'll show you scared, he thought. "I can go right now," he said. "He's over there, nothing's stopping me." But Oleg said he wanted to be hundreds of miles away, and Adams would have to wait.

Overnight, snow and wind had been added to the bone-snapping cold. There were six new inches on the ground and drifts of over a foot. Visibility was awful. This was Shackleton and Sir Edmund, Adams thought, as he stepped away from shore. This was fucking *Arctic*.

The island was less than a hundred yards away. Some of the time Adams could see its smallish pine-covered hump, and some of the time it was just the damn snow. He put his head down and charged. There was no point pussyfooting around. He didn't know how to test ice, and you couldn't see the ice anyway. And so he raced lead-footed across the divide. Nearly there he tripped, came down on one knee—

it hurt like he'd gone down in a parking lot. Snow up his sleeves, for fuck's sake. He got up and ran again. It was like speed bumps. Up and down and then up more consistently and into the trees, thank Christ.

He leaned into the trunk—it was as hard and unbending as steel—thinking to catch his breath, bring down his pulse, but it was too cold. It was dangerous out here; a man could die in this. And that at least made him smile.

The trees acted as a middling windbreak, and a gentle, curving track was still visible. You'd get a nice shade from these trees in the summer, Adams bet, slogging towards the cabin at the top of the slope.

The walls were stripped logs laid on top of each other with thick belts of cement between them. He stood on the lip of the concrete foundation at the rear, where the ground fell away, so that he could get a look in the high, small window. Cowley was facing away at an angle, reading in a leather chair. He was older than Adams had imagined, maybe sixty-five. This was going to be easy. Cowley had a tartan blanket draped over his lap, and a fire grooved in the wood stove. A battered rifle lay on a red-flecked couch. A hound of some sort dominated the floor. It was a painting come to life: *The Pioneer Spirit. The Endurance Of Man.*

The dog stirred, cocked an ear. Adams hated dogs. They were unpredictable and they were fast and some of them were man-strong. And every last foul-breathed one of them was inclined to bite. He didn't care if it was the mildest-looking golden retriever or your drooling chocolate Lab, all dogs were the same.

This one, though, rose and wandered from the room, its tail between its legs. There was a door Adams could use to lock it out. The rifle was on the way to that door. He worked through all the possibilities. Adams jogged around to the front. He took the door handle in his own nearly frozen paw and turned it.

He was half in before Cowley saw him. And Cowley's look was of gentle surprise, nothing more. Adams moved decisively into the room. Reached over the back of the couch for the rifle, keeping an eye on the old man. Adams hooked a toe around the interior door and kicked it closed, separated this room from the dog's. A breeze from somewhere deeper in the cabin pushed it open again. Adams re-closed it and the same thing happened. The two men studied the door. Adams fingered his gun. If he wanted to, he could shoot with-out even drawing it from his jacket pocket.

"Broken," Cowley said. He smiled. "No real need to fix it out here."

Adams didn't get this man's casual manner, his apparent lack of interest in why Adams had trekked in a blizzard across a frozen river. Which meant he knew full well why, was Adams' guess. Well, good for you, he thought. Because he had no interest in holding a question-and-answer. He held dear the idea that the less he knew his victims the better. He didn't want to discover Cowley had a wonder-ful radio-friendly voice, because then it became more difficult. He had, in Australia once, actually apologized to a victim. "I like you," he'd said to the man. "I really do. I could see us down the pub knocking back a few." The man had tried to laugh, but he was already crying, and the combination was awkward, girlish some-how, and he sputtered that he would like that too. He was begging really, and the whole scene had made Adams sick. He had shot that man in his Brisbane bungalow and then, if memory served, he had chastised himself for the amateurish swell of sympathy. That evening he had watched *Trainspotting* at a rep cinema, drifting from the screen's chaos into a contemplation of his life. He never wanted to experience that sort of doubt again, that nearly despondent state.

That said, a man had a right to know why he was going to die. He didn't want some cinema drama where he revealed the reasons for a man's downfall only to be overpowered by his victim. But he did think Cowley should know.

"You stole something that didn't belong to you," he began, and pitifully, predictably, Cowley shook his head. He put his book down on his lap. He looked like someone's grandfather. "Yeah, you did. The name Nikolai Petrovitch ring a bell, Grandad? How about Michael Hollins?"

"Michael is dead," Cowley said quietly.

"Well, ten points," Adams said. He pushed the door shut one more time and leaned against it. He dragged a three-shelf bookcase along the wall and stepped away, pleased. Sometimes there were simple solutions to things. Without intending to, he saw titles and authors lined up on the top shelf. Jack London and Zane Grey, Robertson Davies and Margaret Atwood. *Survival* and *Herzog*.

"I don't know this other man."

"Sure you do. You met him at lunch with Hollins. Hollins and Bill Sumner, the four of you. At the restaurant. You swapped war stories. He says you told some pretty colourful tales. Banks you'd robbed back in the sixties. Jobs you did time for, and others you never got caught for." The dog sniffed at the bottom of the door. It whined and scratched. "He starts howling and he goes first," Adams said. "Nothing worse than a howling dog."

"No one can hear him," Cowley said. "Not out here."

"It's not that. It's the noise itself. It gets inside my head and shit."

"Luke, it's okay," Cowley called. "Lie down." The dog whined once more and then there was the soft thump of it hitting the ground.

"Very nice," Adams said appreciatively. "A lot of people can't control what's theirs."

"I don't understand what I'm supposed to have done. I don't know why I told those stories. Because Michael was boasting again about his successes, I suppose, and your friend said some things about bodyguards and penthouses and women, mostly about women. I guess I was just trying to keep up."

"It left an impression is what I'm saying."

"I see that."

"And in the end he put two and two together."

"What did they add up to?"

Adams was put off by Cowley's refusal to panic, or beg. It was unusual. "He said you and Sumner and Hollins were close."

"We got along."

"Better than that, Nikolai said. He realized that you must have been in on it. Probably one of you put the idea in Hollins' head. Because Hollins was fine in Toronto, it was only when he moved here that he crossed over. Didn't you say you smuggled booze across from New York?"

"An overstatement."

"All the same. He was impressed. And cigarettes?"

"I lied about that. I'm too old for that. But the natives bring them in through the reserve, a ways up the river."

"You made it up?"

"It was that sort of afternoon. We were shitting each other, that was all. I was shitting them, anyway."

"But the bank jobs?"

"I was just a kid. It was forty-five years ago. The time in jail was real enough."

"This seems like a sort of jail—the fucking winter howling outside."

"I can leave any time I want."

"Not any more," Adams reminded him.

"So now you will punish me for telling stories at lunch? Did you pay Bill the same sort of visit?" He arranged the blanket over his thighs, brought it a little higher over his stomach.

Adams couldn't take it. What was he supposed to say? He knew where this was leading and he didn't like it and certainly didn't want to hear it in detail. It sounded like Petrovitch had maybe got it wrong. He just wanted to make sure he got everyone.

"You don't have a clue, mate, do you?"

Cowley smiled and shook his head.

But a job was a job. And so here, in the middle of this small Ontario cabin, with a dog sleeping behind the door and a bashing wind outside, he pulled the pistol from his pocket and he shot Cowley in the chest.

The old man had been about to say something. The word caught in his throat and was replaced by an awkward gulping noise that galloped out. He tried to stand and instead he tipped forward onto the worn carpet. There was blood against the back of the chair and there was a scrabbling sound against the door. The fucking dog. If the latch gave he would kill it too.

He tossed the rifle back onto the sofa and backed away, towards the main door. He felt behind him for the handle. Saw ahead of him the thinner inside door rattling on its twin brass hinges. And then, as the bookshelf tipped, he saw the grizzled grey snout of the mutt halfway up the door. A paw with its black dry pad and long clicking yellow nails reaching around. But Adams got his own door open and a northern winter night enveloped him, dragged him outside so the dog could live on in misery.

DECEMBER 16

What should you expect of a woman who ran away from you one morning and hid in another country? You should expect, John thought, when you find her, when you stumble upon her in the rooftop lair of a gangster who is quite possibly using her somehow, that she will run again. That she will refuse help and will deny everything. Which doesn't change the fact that she must be confronted. That speeches must be made.

He slid back to early spring, 1997, in Berlin. He had been in the German city for most of the previous three years. It was considered a plum assignment. It conjured, for all the men and women fresh out of Quantico, images of slick tunnels riddled with big secrets and bigger rats, distant footfalls and looming noirish shadows. A city where every phone call was monitored, every wall veined with plastic-coated wires that led to primitive listening devices. But the reality was more routine. The city struggled with the usual problems. An underfunded infrastructure, a populace unhappy with their tax bill. And Selby's work required much more of his time than it did of his brain. The Germans were fanatically protective of civil rights and privacy and equally suspicious of all intelligence organizations. Tracing a bank account, the movement of money, could take weeks. A letter had to be submitted to each of Germany's three thousand banks. Selby knew, as did many of his German peers, that terrorists loved to hide in this skittish, spooked country. His duty was to map the location and organization of elements that might harbour dreams of European and American destabilization. Find the bad guys.

He'd arrived thinking it would be an intense but straightforward procedure. But the data-protection laws made him feel permanently handcuffed. For the first few years he was in the country, wiretapping homes and offices was illegal. This despite the fact that most of the expertise and ingredients Saddam Hussein used in his chemical-weapons industry came from Germany. And so much of his information was gleaned from newspapers and wire-service reports. He skulked around right-wing meetings and collected photographs of concerts at which skinheads raised hell. His superiors lobbied for changes, new sets of laws that would respond to a world they saw heating up. They were sternly rebuked. The German authorities pointed out that foreign terrorists were not active in Germany, there were no bombs exploding, no kidnappings, no unsigned letters arriving at parliament. John indiscreetly suggested that this was because the terrorists knew they were on to a good thing and preferred to use Germany as a home base while exporting their expertise. It made him unpopular, and he was told by Washington to establish a lower profile. There were other men, better placed, he was told. He asked what that meant and was told he should know better. To rest assured that his was a valuable contribution. This faint praise made him feel that his talents were being wasted, that he was a decoy, and the real intelligence work was being conducted underground. He wondered what he had done to deserve such a posting. But then he met Hanne.

Hanne Kristiansen, a Canadian artist, had arrived in the city in the fall of 1996 from Rome. She was living in a semi-converted warehouse space in a part of the city that boasted absolutely no services, and promises of an influx of similar-minded artists and hipsters had not materialized. She was feeling isolated.

"I get work done," she said, "but it feels like an experiment being conducted in space."

They were at a blue-lit bar. It was nearly three in the morning. Selby had been sipping on the same cognac for an hour. They discovered they were the same age, and it seemed enough to prolong their conversation until the sun appeared at the bottom edge of a cracked, dust-filled window and the bartender threw them out, pleading fatigue. They went home together and she never left. Until it was for good.

Now he had arrived at the Hansen Space near Kingston's waterfront. He sat with the lights on and the engine running, watching people dash into Minos, the Greek restaurant across from the gallery.

He should have told Sonny, but this felt personal as much as it felt business. And so when he'd reported in, after the meeting at the police station with Viktor Laevsky, he had left her name out altogether. Sonny would twig to the omission—of course he would—and would order John to put his personal feelings aside, talk to the woman, damn it, but it would take a couple of days, and by then he would have acted on his own initiative. Because the worst scenario was being *ordered* to talk to Hanne. And Hanne was no criminal, after all. He knew her.

Or he *didn't* know her. Maybe that was the problem. He knew her body, and some of her habits, her skills and her deficiencies, her taste in music and art, but those don't add up to much. Not really. If he had known her, he wouldn't have gone to work that morning a little more than four years ago in Berlin. He might not have lost her.

He braced himself. The door scraped and plowed through the snowbank and he cursed as if the car were his own. Thirty-six bracing and still-painful steps and he was inside again. Not nearly enough time to formulate a proper plan or even to run through a few lines.

He saw her before she saw him. She was at the back of the space, working in the pool of light cast by a green banker's lamp. He hated those lamps, always had. He stood very still. He had heard the chime when he came in; she knew someone was there. But she was immersed in whatever she was writing and hadn't registered the sound. He waited for her to offer a weak smile perhaps, some indication at least that she wasn't altogether unhappy to see him again. A man could die, he thought, if he held his breath too long.

She approached him as if afraid he might be someone else. She checked the street over his shoulder. She paused before rushing towards him over the high-shine floor and down the two steps mid-gallery—and then right past him as if he weren't there. She locked the door and set an alarm, wiped her palm over a bank of light switches, threw them both into a grey half-light that John chose to see metaphorically as the twilit limbo her disappearance from Berlin had cast them into.

"Jesus," she hissed and took his arm, dragged him to her office, her hand exerting real pressure. She indicated the empty seat and obediently he took it. She was the high school principal, he thought, and he was about to get a dressing-down for some adolescent mischief.

"What are you doing here? It's been more than a week. I've been going nuts here, waiting."

Which was a lot to throw at him. He wasn't sure where to begin. She examined his face for a clue, tried to read his answer before it became words.

"It's good to see you," he said.

"John!"

"It is," he insisted. "I'm shocked to see you, or I was, that first night. But it's good. Really."

"That's not what I mean. What are you doing here?"

"Can you tell me how you are, first? Can we do that? Before it becomes business."

"I'm fine."

She wasn't. She was torturing a paper clip, wrenching it into a rough line then snapping its back. She kicked the office door closed with a heeled boot that had been hidden under jeans that flared sharply from the knee. A panic in her eyes, though, took any pleasure out of the visuals.

"You look like you thought I might be someone else," he said.

"This is a gallery, John. People come in and out."

"So it's me making you act this way."

"Yes." She stared him down. "No. No, it's not you. It isn't and it is. I'm happy to see you too, I am, it's just so . . . unexpected. And at the same time I've been totally expecting you."

"You locked the place up. Should I be flattered?"

"No, you shouldn't. I was going to close early anyway," Hanne said.

"It's not even noon."

"You didn't come to tell me how to run my business."

The pause between each of them saying something was a fraction too long. The effect was of listening to a United Nations speech that needed translating deep in the inner ear before it could be understood.

Hanne said, "What is it?"

"I was just thinking this isn't how I imagined it."

"You've imagined it?"

"Many times."

She arched an eyebrow.

"You know what I mean."

"Are you still with the FBI? Who the hell is Frank Coleman, anyway?"

"He's a drug smuggler."

"You've gone up in the world. You must be very proud."

"They thought it would sell well with Petrovitch."

"They? So you are still with the Bureau. They've put you in Canada now?"

"Sort of."

"Sort of? Well, this is going well," Hanne said. "I expect you'll expect me to be a lot more precise in my answers, won't you? Do you think that's fair, *Frank?*"

"There's something new." He explained the BVC, and she blanched. He explained Sonny Rockliff sending John because Petrovitch had the garbage contract and that had people worried.

"Sending you in undercover is a pretty elaborate response."

John shrugged. "The Canadians couldn't give us much. It's huge trucks crossing the border every day. These are very different times, Hanne."

"Thanks for letting me know."

Sarcasm. There was no reason for it. Or maybe there was. He was trained to analyze people, to make quick judgments about intellectual capacity, about body language, about truth and deception, armed or unarmed, risk and benefit. He was also trained against personal involvement, and this situation was a perfect example of why.

"Are you okay?" he said. He would have touched her if the table had been smaller.

"I told you."

"Then, tell me how the hell you got involved with someone like Petrovitch."

She eyed him bitterly. The circles they were talking in were getting smaller and smaller. Soon they would have nothing left.

"Do you know anything?" he said. The question frightened him. It was the question Sonny Rockliff had wanted him to ask. This was why they had sent him. In case the answer would come from this simple question.

"About what? Hiding things in his trucks? Why? Can you see me out there in a pair of coveralls, with my hair tied back, trying to stuff a pound of hash into an abandoned washing machine? Come on, John. Really."

"That's no answer." It was time to be stern. To turn the tables and play principal to her student. "Because if you are involved"—God he hated this, hoping to intimidate a woman he'd once thought he might love—"you have to tell me now." Sometimes clichés were all you had left.

The phone rang and they both jumped. Hanne patted her chest and blew hair out of her face. She checked the display. "A client," she said. "I'll call him later."

"Not Petrovitch?" John said, and Hanne told him to fuck off.

He looked around him. Took in, for the first time, the limestone walls and the stack of wrapped canvases leaned against a wooden scaffold. A coffee maker and a bean grinder. A small refrigerator and a coat rack. A pair of running shoes with the laces still tied and with a white ankle sock stuffed into each one. A small television on a wooden shelf. "You could live in here, just about," he said.

"I keep a house here."

"Really?"

"Yes, really. Why so surprised?"

"I didn't know about it, that's all."

"You've been investigating me."

"Don't be coy. You know how it works."

"So you wouldn't be here otherwise?"

"I didn't say that. But I wouldn't be in Canada if it weren't for Petrovitch. I never would have known you were here. It's also true that if I'd just seen you on the street somewhere I would have run after you."

"I'm not sure I would do the same if things were reversed."

"You left me, so I'm not surprised."

"You're pleased to see me," she said.

"It was the first thing I said when I got here," John said. "I'm delighted to see you. Worried, yes, but delighted." He was aware of heat in his shoes, as if there was a radiator somewhere close, and a tingling in his lower back. He would need to move soon. He was finding it difficult to simply look at Hanne. The act of concentrating on her face was proving more and more tricky. There was a sense that she was only a mirage and might shimmy into nothing.

"You didn't have to leave," he said. "Not like that."

"I felt I did," Hanne said. "But let's not talk about that. Please, John. Not now. Talking won't change anything. I had to go."

"You would do it again?"

"I'm not the same person now. Neither are you."

"Where did you go?"

"I called you from London."

"After that."

"Europe again, then Canada."

"Were you ever tempted to look for me?" He cringed inwardly. It sounded so *weak*.

Hanne shook her head. "What we had didn't last that long, John. And to be honest, I don't think we saw it the same way." Then she laughed. She stood and reached across the desk. It was the move he had found too daunting earlier, and yet she managed it so easily. She put a hand to the side of his face and held it there for two seconds, three. "It doesn't mean I wouldn't have liked to see you. It didn't have much to do with you at all, really."

"Perhaps when this is over."

"A drink or something," she said, sitting down again. Rearranging herself. "Yes. Perhaps a drink. We'll see."

And he thought he saw it again then: fear. Something flickering in her face.

"You import art for him," John said. Wanting to get the ugliness over with and also, he knew, inviting a confession.

Nothing. Anger, though, a heat in her eyes. Indignation, dislike even, in the arrangement of muscles around her mouth. He pressed on. What choice did he have? Didn't she understand?

"From Russia," he said. She was going to make him spell it out when he didn't want to say it at all.

"He's quite discerning," she said. "He knows what he likes."

"Can you explain to me how it works. What's the process involved?"

"Shouldn't you read me my rights or something?"

"Hanne."

"John." She threw it at him, sticking her chin out. "Where are you going with this? How does this tie in to his having a garbage contract?"

"I have to ask" was all he said.

"And I have to tell you what your question implies," she retorted. "And that it discounts right away any possibility that I work damn hard as a dealer in fine art, and do a good job, and work independently of my clients. And have a good reputation in the community. Holy shit. I mean, I thought you knew me better than this."

John reminded her painfully that not five minutes ago she had told him they *didn't* know each other, and that when she'd called him from London and he'd been alone and drunk in their Berlin apartment, she'd told him they had *never* known each other. "At least two people are dead, Hanne. I think that gives me a right to push a little." Anger nudged him in the back. He put an elbow on the desk. "Screw the fact that we were involved, to be honest."

"You're talking about Michael," she said.

He said he was, and he thought he saw a tremor in her right eye. She put her hands on her hips, perhaps to steady them. She wanted him out, she said. It was her way out of a jam. He might not know her well, but he knew that when she was cornered, Hanne lashed out.

"Seriously, John. I don't have to listen to this shit any more."

"If you're scared, don't you think it would make sense—?"

"Now you're going to patronize me. Jesus!"

She was out of her chair and throwing the door open wide. She couldn't hide the worried glance she took at the front windows, but she stood her ground. "Come on, I haven't got all day." Which was comical, he thought, her relying on his respect for her busy schedule.

"Hanne," he began, "it's not that easy, I'm afraid."

"Of course it's that easy. Out. Get out of my office. You think because we slept together, I'll open my life for you? I don't think so, John."

"But I can't just walk away like this. You know it doesn't work that way. If it were just you and me—"

"It is just you and me."

"No, I mean if it were just *about* you and me, but it isn't. It's important." Which was to understate the case by a lot.

"Fine. I get that," she said. She was nearly breathless. "Just fucking fine. But not like this, okay? I need to get over the shock of seeing you."

"That's weak," he told her.

"I don't care. I can't talk to you now. I have to get back to Toronto. I have commissions to pay out. A show to organize."

"We have to talk."

"You'll have to give me a day or two."

He told her that before he came in he had guessed she would disappear again rather than admit anything or suffer the consequences.

"That's ludicrous."

"It's not," he said. "It's what I have to go on."

"Will I be followed?"

He told her, "Yes, you will." He thought she seemed almost relieved.

"They'd better be good," she said. "If he sees I'm being followed . . ."

"He won't."

"Give me a number. Can you do that? If I don't call, you can haul me in, bring out the rubber hoses. You might enjoy that."

It was the wrong thing to do. Every instinct told him he would regret this. But if she thought she was being tailed . . . He looked at her, really looked. It was so *weird* to have her in front of him like this. He got up and squeezed past her at the door, noticing that she didn't move aside at all.

She followed him outside. In Germany she would walk him out most mornings, already in her own uniform—the oversized and paint-spattered shirt and the thick black tights she'd cut the feet from. Her hair tied back and, if she'd already been in to prepare her studio and brushes, the smell on her hands of Varsol. He had cared for her back then, it wasn't a trick he had played on himself. And feelings like that don't just evaporate. At least *his* feelings hadn't evaporated. Hanne, though, seemed much more resistant to the idea of a shared history.

He sat in the Jag and wondered whether it meant anything that she hadn't said goodbye, just "See you." A chaste peck on the cheek. It was possible to feel sixteen again, he had discovered. To make the irrational, or just plain dumb, decisions of a teenager, and then to sit in a dark cold car worrying about them.

DECEMBER 17

The telephone rang, waking Tim. It might have been a fire alarm, a siren.

"Something has happened," he heard. Her voice was breathless, strangely pitched.

"Rebecca?"

"Of course it's Rebecca. I'm coming over. Is *he* there?"

"Denver? I don't know."

"Okay. Just wait for me."

The house was cold. He hadn't stoked the fire properly before turning in, and he had forgotten to turn up the heat. He twisted the thermostat and waited for the hum, the subtle vibration of the floor.

When he peered around the door of Adams' room, he saw him buried there under the blankets. His head was vaguely green against the white pillow; the stubble along the line of his chin was red. You can see in his face where he comes from, Tim thought. The history of an island in the shade of the skin. The bad haircut.

"Oh, I see you," Adams said, his voice muffled and unpleasant. "You might think I don't, but I do." He threw back the covers and lay there naked, blinking, like a monstrous worm dug from the dirt. "May as well get a good look while you're here, eh?"

"I was going to make coffee," Tim said. "That's all. I thought I'd see if you were awake."

"Brew on, then, Timmy. I'll be there. Just give us a sec."

Adams paced into the kitchen a few minutes later, wearing an old robe of Michael's, cinched recklessly at the waist. He reached inside and scratched absent-mindedly at his ribs. "I don't know how you make it through these sodding winters," he said. He collapsed onto a stool as if the world had disappointed him, let him down. "I couldn't live here," he said. He had cut himself shaving, and a fleck of dried blood clung like a scarlet tear to his neck. Tim handed him a mug of coffee and tried to go back to a book he wasn't really reading.

"Cheers," Adams said. "Let me ask you a question. Do you believe in fate?"

"Why?" Tim said. Thinking, though, about Rebecca.

"I just thought it might make this damn country easier to take. If you thought it was out of your hands, you wouldn't feel so picked on." The robe had fallen away from his thin white thighs; each knee was like three ping-pong balls lashed together. He took a swig of his coffee.

Tim regarded him curiously. "I want you gone, you know," he said. "I want to get on with things. You've had enough time."

Adams ignored him a while, but finally he said, "Did you like your old man, Tim? Really get along with him?"

"Why would I talk to you about that? How about I do it to you? Do you have kids?" He put the book on the corner of the cold stove behind him. Wiped a scattering of bread crumbs onto the floor.

"Fine," Adams said. "But I know where you're going with that. You're picturing my little boy all grown up and cursing me the exact same way I slam my old man. Am I right?"

"What's his name?"

"Aidan. He's with Angie, his mum."

"Does he know where you are? What you do?"

"We're separated. He doesn't need to."

"He'll ask questions, won't he? If not now, then later."

"Maybe." Adams peered into his coffee as if it were a telescope trained on a choppy brown sea. "But what do I tell him? I walk down a lot of snowy driveways. Have a lot of pointless conversations in barns with old gits chopping wood who don't want to talk to me and laugh because I want their snarling dogs tied up. I'm a nosy neighbour. I dig the Volvo out of snowdrifts."

Tim grabbed at his own shoulder, massaged it. He recognized it as a tic, a way of thinking, chewing into the muscle of an idea, seeing it for what it was. "Do you suspect my dad of something, Adams? Does Nikolai suspect him?"

"No idea what you're talking about," Adams said. "I've explained all this to you, Tim. He's worried about you. Not that I'm finding anything that would give you a reason to worry. Your old man took a curve too fast. Sorry to say, he was no fucking Emerson Fittipaldi."

"So you can leave, then."

"Well, if it was all about you, maybe. But there's other interests here, see. Just because you can sleep like a baby doesn't mean there isn't work to be done. And I'm a bit shocked you don't seem to give a shit about anyone else's welfare."

"Now you can definitely leave."

"Oh, sit yourself down. You're getting all hot under the collar for nothing. Drink your coffee."

Tim shoved Adams in the chest. He remembered doing the same thing to the photographer at Michael's funeral. It was his technique; the way he fought. Adams' feet jerked up and nearly caught Tim square on the jaw. The robe fell open and flared up over his bare hips. It was a graceless comic tip. He was still sitting on the stool but it was up on two legs and Adams fought for his balance, his arms wind-milling. Tim hit him again and watched him smack to the floor. The wind jerked out of him.

"You little cocksucker," Adams howled.

Tim wanted to run. He felt stupid. He'd defended his honour, he supposed. Gone through the motions of that. But now Adams was scrabbling on the floor.

"You little prick. I'll fucking *do* you!"

Rebecca entered the house moving fast. Nervous. She rushed in, breathless, and didn't for a few seconds notice the brawl about to break out. Then she stopped.

"What are you guys doing? Were you fighting? Tim?"

"It's nothing. Let's go to the dining room." He glared at Adams.

"You're fucking lucky," Adams sneered.

Rebecca turned Tim around and pushed him between the saloon doors. "In here."

They huddled at a table by the window. It was cold. Warm air from the vent ruffled the bottom edge of a tablecloth.

"What's going on?"

"He said something about my father. It was nothing. I'm just sick of the guy."

"But you didn't tell him?"

"What we found? No." He told her she looked completely freaked out.

Gananoque was crawling with reporters, she said. "You haven't heard?"

"No, nothing."

She chewed at the inside of her mouth. A certainty was changing inside her, becoming more complicated. She twisted uncomfortably at the waist, chased down the beginning of what she had to say.

"Do you know Hinton Cowley?" she said. She looked again towards the kitchen. At any moment the doors might swing wide and green-headed Adams would shuffle in, a cloud of sleep and fury.

"Another Islander, right?"

"One of the Admiralty Islands. The town council tried to force him off. Said he was going to die out there."

"Because he didn't have a boat. I remember."

"Exactly. He was completely dependent on people going out to see him. And in the winter they have to wait for the ice to thicken enough that they can get to him."

He looked past Rebecca out the window at the ice around all the islands. Winter had taken hold, and the windows had collected fantastic blooms of frost at their corners. "Should be no problem getting out there now," he said.

"He's dead."

The phone rang. Rebecca waited for him to get up. "Ignore it," he said, and eventually it was quiet again. Tim didn't say anything. Rebecca wouldn't have come if Cowley had had a heart attack.

In the kitchen Adams coughed. They heard him spit into the sink and turn on the water.

Rebecca said, "He was shot." Her eyes filled with tears. She clutched his arm with both hands.

Adams appeared in the doorway, his bare feet and shins visible beneath the swinging doors, his head, its stick-up mop of hair cartoonish above. "Becky!" he said. "Nice to see you again." As if the kitchen scene had never happened. He had changed and had on a pair of white Adidas shorts with blue stripes down the sides and a blue, short-sleeved soccer sweater that read "CHELSEA."

"Have you got a game later?" Tim said.

Adams acknowledged the hit. "Very clever, Tim. I like you more and more." He kissed Rebecca on the top of the head and sat down. He beamed, apparently oblivious to Rebecca's tears.

The telephone started up again and Tim swore. This time he ran across the room to answer it.

"So Tim told you all my secrets," Adams said.

Rebecca shrugged.

"I thought as much," he said. "You don't seem nearly as pleased to see me."

Tim clapped his hand over the receiver. "Every time I try to warm to you, you act like an asshole," he said. "I mean what I said: I want you gone."

Adams rolled his eyes. "I just don't want my loved ones being too hurt when I move on. And I love you two, I really do." He put a hand theatrically over his heart.

Rebecca concentrated on Tim, who was suddenly very focused. He faced the window and closed his eyes. "Fine," he said into the telephone. "Soon." He hung up. "Someone else is dead," he said to Adams. He felt like a newscaster.

Adams placed his fingertips on the very edge of the table. His thumbs dangled free. "Who?"

"Hinton Cowley."

Adams shook his head. Tim thought he was communicating that he had never heard of the man, but Adams said, "Guess I won't be talking to him."

"You were going to?"

"Who knows?"

Tim offered a mildly accusing glance.

"He orders food once a week from the IGA," Rebecca said. "Then he either picks it up, or sometimes they'll send someone over."

"Like Robinson Crusoe, but with a delivery service," Adams said.

Rebecca sniffed. "I was in there today. His order didn't come in so I guess they tried calling him, but there was no answer."

"Doesn't this bloke go anywhere else?" Adams said. "Couldn't he be in Toronto? Or off fishing somewhere? Maybe he's in one of those mad little huts out there."

They all studied the gathering population of huts on the ice. They made out men on stools in some of the doorways.

"That's fucking stupid, that is," Adams said. "You walk out onto a frozen lake and drill a hole through it. Un-fucking-believably dumb."

"Not if you know the way ice works," Tim said. He hadn't a clue how ice worked, and he would have been inclined to agree had it been anyone else across the table.

"He was shot," Rebecca said. "Cowley was shot in the chest."

Adams seemed surprised. "They found him, then."

"They're bringing him ashore this morning." She focused on Tim. "I think you should talk to the police."

Adams thought that was a bad idea.

"Why?" Rebecca said. "Tim was there when it happened to Bill Sumner. They'll want to talk to him again. Don't you think?"

Adams pushed noisily away from the table. "Stupid, I'm telling you." The back of his shorts had a faded grass stain on them. A sliding tackle, maybe. Tim pictured him thrashing about the field. Someone you wanted on your team only so he didn't direct his tackles at your ankles.

"No, that was Des Boyle," Tim said, indicating the telephone. "You're right, Rebecca. He wants me to come down."

*

Tim rode the brakes down the precipitous, iced road into the village of Rockport, population 502. In front of St. Brendan's Catholic Church, a snow-white statue of the Virgin Mary cast its cold gaze south. A man in a suede Stetson walked stiffly along the shoulder of the road, a folded newspaper under his arm, a brown dog trotting ahead. A porcupine humped casually down the centre of the road and they crawled along behind it.

"I thought they hibernated," Tim said, but Rebecca appeared not to hear him. She merely stared as the animal lumbered ahead. "Shoo," she said quietly. "Shoo."

A police van was at the top of the boat launch, its engine running and a bearded man at the wheel reading an Ian Rankin paperback. A small crowd had gathered in the parking lot next to the information booth. Reporters and technicians busied themselves around a CBC satellite truck. Others were there from Global News and WWNY Watertown. Thick rubberized cables snaked over the ground. A woman in an RCMP windbreaker recorded their arrival with a video camera. White ribbed concrete angled sharply down to the ice. There were thick gouges from the sharp bottom edges of fishing huts. Those huts were everywhere. In the distance, between two small islands, were four men in white coveralls. They pulled a sled loaded down with gear. There were other men, in black overcoats, but too far away to be identified.

Tim and Rebecca stood shoulder to shoulder. Rebecca linked an arm through his and he tried not to think too much about what that meant. She held him more tightly as the men came closer. The upper branches of a leafless birch tree knocked noisily against each other.

When the assembled gathering realized, as one, that the sled was not loaded down with gear at all but with the body of Hinton Cowley, wrapped in a blue tarpaulin and strapped to the bed of the sled, a murmur of shock passed through them like a current. A woman crossed herself and tugged at a plum-coloured scarf around her neck, pulled it up over her mouth, as if to protect herself from a plague.

One of the men coming ashore was Des Boyle. The rest were strangers. Reporters and TV crews jostled for position. The sled's metal runners grated over the ramp. Once it achieved level ground everyone stopped. There was a sense that they didn't know what to do next, that they had crossed an invisible finish line. Their faces were uniformly grim.

Des came straight over. He pulled off a fleece glove and shook Tim's hand, made him the centre of attention. He heard camera shutters, feet moving around him. Boyle did the same with Rebecca. "Des Boyle," he said to her.

She lowered her head slightly.

"I'm glad you came," he said to Tim. He ushered them away from the crowd and down the ramp. They stood together at the bottom, at the rough seam where ice met concrete. Boyle said, "We don't want our every word broadcast on the six o'clock news, do we?"

Tim told Boyle that Rebecca had guessed he'd want to talk. "She said Cowley was shot. And because I was at Bill's I figured you'd want . . . hell, I didn't know what you'd want, but . . ."

Boyle smiled gratefully. "And we like to think our methods are beyond the understanding of outsiders."

The driver of the police van climbed out and opened the back doors. The sled was brought around. Two of the men lifted the body carefully into the back. The tarp bent heavily in the middle. One of the men in coveralls climbed in back and the doors were closed behind him.

"Did you know Hinton?"

"We were talking about that. I'm not sure."

"I'd like to see if you recognize him."

Rebecca had come to him again and he took her arm. He wanted her closer. Because if they were together it meant, in some obscure fashion, that he hadn't done anything wrong.

"I'd like you to take a look," Boyle said. "Would you mind?"

"A photograph, you mean?" Tim said, recognizing it as stupid as soon as he'd said it.

Des shook his head. "Not a vain man, it would seem, our Mr. Cowley. Not a photo of him to be found."

Tim shivered. His legs were weak. He had been standing still too long.

"Shall we?" Boyle said. When Tim agreed, the words caught in his throat.

Inside the van there were metal benches against both walls. Tim and Boyle sat opposite each other, the wrapped body between them. A dark square of window framed with a rubber seal showed the front cab. The driver was immersed again in his mystery.

Tim tucked his feet under the bench. There was so little room, and his knees ached. He shifted, tried for a different angle, but his feet were jammed. With his hands against the bench, he lifted himself slightly. He tried to move his foot out a little. Suddenly it came free of the metal floor and he delivered a solid kick to Cowley's midsection.

"Christ," he said. "I didn't mean to do that."

Boyle said, "He won't hold it against you, Tim."

Tim put a hand to his forehead. "All the same."

Boyle undid one of the straps. "You'd think we'd have taken a bag over with us. It would have saved this guy a final indignity. Wrapped up like a goddamn turkey." He wasn't talking to Tim. Just angry at the way his day was going. He pulled the strap free from under the tarp and rolled it up neatly, like a tape measure. It took forever and felt like torture. Boyle tried to unwrap just the very top section of the tarpaulin. He cradled the head.

"Sorry, Tim," he said. "I wanted this to be easy for us." He slid off the bench and straddled the body, fumbled with the second strap, which was fastened across what had to be the waist. He rolled the body onto its side. Tim pulled his feet up onto the bench. Boyle was sweating. The van smelled of that sweat, and of dirt, and plastic.

Finally Boyle paused. "Are you ready for this?"

Tim tried to gather spit in his mouth. "How could I be?" he murmured.

Boyle nodded and sweat dropped from his forehead onto the plastic cover. He pulled back the cover. "Here we go, then."

Hinton Cowley's face was sunken and mottled grey and purple. His head was one bruise. He had fresh grey stubble and his eyes were closed. The eyelids lay flat over the sockets, as if the eyeballs had collapsed. His nose had been flattened by the tarpaulin and gave the impression that this man had been beaten in a boxing ring.

A dried Rorschach of blood had grown at his chest around a hole in his blue plaid shirt. The stain spread up to the neck and had dried on Cowley's skin. In the other direction it reached nearly to his waist. His arms were stiff at his side, the fists clenched. He lay at attention. There was a further tear in his right sleeve, and when Tim steeled himself, then bent in for a better look, he saw that there was blood inside, and a series of puncture marks. He sat back as much as he could and looked at Cowley in a general way, tried to summarize what he felt. "That's a hell of a hole," he said.

Boyle said, "The saddest thing is the arm, though. His dog tried to wake him up, we think. That's what those are. Teeth marks. Hinton here had been dragged around. We thought he might have been moved by whoever shot him. But no, it was the damn dog. It wouldn't let him alone. Destroyed any evidence there might have been."

"Where is the dog now?" Tim said.

"Still over there. It wouldn't let us near him. Someone will go back." He shifted. "Have you seen enough?" He draped the cover over Cowley.

Tim felt his back stiffening. He could still see Cowley's hand. The hairs on the back of it seemed of the purest black, and Tim recalled reading somewhere that fingernails continue to grow after death.

"So. Is he familiar?" Boyle said.

"He is." He saw the eagerness on Boyle's face. "He was a friend of my father's."

Boyle whistled gently, almost noiselessly. Then he said, "Do you know how, why?"

Tim said he had no idea. He thought of Rebecca out there in the cold.

"What do you know about him?" Boyle said.

"That's it. He was a friend of my father's. But I was never introduced. I saw him at the restaurant. He had a favourite seat, and Dad got a big kick out of showing him to his table. He was in fairly regularly."

"Did your father sit down with him?"

"Did they huddle, you mean? Did they pass maps across the table? That sort of thing."

Boyle drew in a breath. "Maps? Why maps?"

"I'm making shit up," Tim said.

"So are my bosses." There was an impatient edge to his voice. Boyle moved along the bench, towards the back of the van. "I need fresh air," he said. He grabbed at the handle. Sunlight and cold wedged itself into the narrow gap and widened it.

They stepped down, and it was farther than Tim had expected. A memory jarred loose: "He was a friend of Bill's, too." He saw Rebecca. She hadn't moved. She looked worried. Tim strained now to hear any of what Cowley had said to his father, to rescue it from memory. He made out murmuring. And laughter. A certain lightness of mood that brightened their faces. But there was no concrete detail.

Rebecca joined them, and Tim tried to explain to her who Cowley was. She said she wasn't sure. The confusion showed on her face. "I'm in the kitchen most of the time," she explained.

Boyle wanted to know what they talked about; could Tim remember?

"I'm trying," Tim said. "But I had no reason to pay any attention."

"Of course not."

Rebecca squinted at Boyle, and then more sympathetically at Tim. "Are you okay?"

"I'm cold," he said. "You must be even colder." He touched her sleeve.

Boyle said, "I might have to call you again, you know."

Tim said that was okay. Any time.

"I've been meaning to get in touch, as a matter of fact," Boyle said. "Things have been crazy and I keep forgetting to follow up on this. I'm sure it's nothing."

"Oh yes?"

"You've got someone staying with you."

Tim shrugged. He wanted it to seem nonchalant, but his heart raced, his chest filled up with toffee and it poured into his arms.

"He was at the pub the other afternoon," Boyle said.

"I don't know anything about that."

"He was throwing darts around," Boyle said. Tim could tell he was being checked more closely. "He damn near took out a reporter's eye. The bartender says he did it on purpose."

"He's a friend. Well, sort of." Tim felt he was being set up.

Rebecca shuffled nervously.

Boyle seemed satisfied. "None of my business, really," he said. "Just something I heard. I thought I'd pass it along to you. They said he had an English accent."

"That's right."

"That would explain the passion for darts," Boyle said, and he laughed invitingly.

"I'll tell him to take it easy," Tim said.

Boyle shook his hand, and then Rebecca's. He seemed not to be listening now. He gazed instead out at the lake. The wind had picked up and clouds of loose snow were being whipped around. He was thinking about Cowley, perhaps, and how he was going to have to make the long trek back out to the island.

"It's no good," he said. "This damn wind. No wonder he didn't come ashore very much."

"Right," Tim said.

Rebecca said she had one question. "Are you still sure Michael died in an accident? I mean, you're not rethinking anything in light of this?"

"A hundred percent sure," Des said. "No question."

"That's good, then. So this is . . ."

Des smiled. "I don't know what this is, honestly. But it doesn't change how Tim's father died."

Des Boyle left them. He was shaking his head. He was going down the ramp; his legs were like sticks, even bundled up. He was on the ice again. Alone this time. And going back for more.

*

Adams was still at the house. He had ransacked the fridge, made a towering sandwich he had no interest in eating. He was thinking about Angie. Near the end she had said constantly that it was impossible for her to understand him. "I just don't *get* you any more, Adams," she'd say. Moving her hair out of her eyes.

The memory had given him an urge to talk to her again. It was like the urge he felt for a pint some nights when he'd decided to take a night away from the bottle. He could do it; it was just a lot easier on the system if he gave in.

He also needed out of this house soon. Tim was hiding fuck all. Tim was just too close-mouthed, that was his problem. His head would explode soon. He'd have an aneurysm. He knew Rebecca saw it too. She fancied Tim, that was Adams' guess, and she wanted Tim to realize it without her actually saying anything. Adams' problem was the opposite: he said too much. He didn't have the right filters installed in his head at birth. He was probably missing, he thought, the head gasket. He should say that to Angie. Head gasket. *Head*. Get it? Only, she'd say that didn't excuse the way he was with her, the way he ran away. Or maybe she wouldn't. Maybe she'd laugh.

He pretty much ran to the Volvo. He drove up to the Parkway and pulled off at the first rest stop. Left the engine running and pumped the heat.

He dialed her number.

"Hello, love," he said. It was a start. A good one, he thought.

This time it was her doling out the silent treatment. There was a low whistle buried in the connection, a wind that wrapped itself around the wire.

"I said, 'Hello, love.'" Smiling in a way that made his face ache and was a defence, he knew, a way of hoping she simply hadn't heard him, and any second they would talk freely, as if the bad things had never happened.

Nothing.

"*Fuck.*" Said under his breath, the receiver held away. A steel trash can right outside the car, mounted to a concrete platform. A Big Mac box open on the frozen ground like a clam, pale strands of lettuce still inside. Down in the trees an empty vodka bottle, one blue sneaker. The radio barely audible. The sunlight a glare in the frozen puddles.

"Angie."

"_____"

"Ah, come on, love. It's me."

"_____"

"I want to talk to you." He heard, he thought, a car drive by outside her apartment. "Is that your sis?" he said. Thinking she might be returning home from work. "Just let me know you're okay," he said. "And our boy, too."

"Piss off, Adams."

It wasn't Angie. The relief made him sweat. "Shelley. Jesus. I thought you were—"

"I know who you thought I was."

"Is she there?"

"Just sod off, okay?"

"Come on, Shelley."

"I mean it, Adams."

"I know you do, love, but can I talk to Angie?"

"She's not here."

"She's out, then?"

"You heard me."

"I did, love. But—"

"She's not here. You understand? This is *my* place now. So don't call."

She hung up. He stared at the gone-dark telephone, the radio with its lit-up scale. There was news being announced that attached to him. He listened for clues. Were they working on a theory? Bits of information he could use. He liked that he was the answer to all the questions. What was "a mysterious death" to everyone out there in Radioland was as clear as a shot in the head to him. It was a solace, he guessed. England might be a total mystery these days. And Angie certainly was. Her whereabouts today, for instance. How her hair looked. Whether she wore the same lipstick she used to—Hyper—and the same Jam T-shirt with the tiny split in the seam under the left arm and Paul Weller looking real sharp on her chest. All of it had been taken from him, rendered as unknowable as if she were dead, a ghost. But then death, and some of the ways it came at you, he understood.

DECEMBER 18

Sonny Rockliff was watching television. To be precise, he was watching twelve television sets at once. A flickering matrix of inspections. Tired travellers shuffled past tense-looking or bored security guards, or lined up at a nondescript grey counter. An endless stream of cars and trucks filed under steel scaffolds at the border. A dozen scenes of mild inconvenience and elevated blood pressure.

Sonny was thinking about John Selby. The man knew what he was doing. But there was a grey vibration around even their most perfunctory communications. A suspicion. He wondered if he had made a mistake recruiting him.

Sonny had received numerous phone calls in recent days about the border situation. The *New York Times* had picked up on the deaths. They pondered "the still-porous border." They wondered if a turf war was being waged, and mentioned bike gangs. They dragged out the Thousand Islands' colourful history, its tales of bootleggers' shipwrecks and people-smuggling rings. Men closer to the President had asked Sonny for his opinion, men from Homeland Security who worked out of the White House. They threw around terms like "dirty bomb" and "compromised perimeter." They talked of deployment and timeliness as if they were coffee and doughnuts. He told them he was monitoring the situation. And he was. But privately he worried.

Lara was telling him he was an absent father. That she appreciated he was stressed, but he needed to compartmentalize some of that. He thought she was beginning to sound a lot like them.

"Do you have anyone on the inside?" he was asked.

"I do, and I expect answers from him imminently."

"How worried should the President be?"

"Selby is a good man. He hasn't indicated this is anything serious."

"We hear diamonds. Which is good in the short term."

Sonny wondered who in the office had leaked that; the list of people who knew was short. "I hope that doesn't hit the newspapers, sir," Sonny said. "I'm not sure that wouldn't jeopardize things."

"Do you need anything from us?"

Sonny pictured Black Hawks over the Seaway, assault forces mustering at Syracuse. "Not at present, sir."

"Well, let us know."

Sonny reflected nervously on his good fortune. How the President was aching to spend money. Throwing it at him so he could make a splash.

He raised John Selby on his cell. They hadn't uncovered any hint that Petrovitch might have the capability to intercept, let alone descramble.

Selby was in the Jag. Sonny had wondered privately whether the luxury car was necessary or wise, but he had learned long ago that you don't call agents on the small details. Not in these days of fiscal extravagance.

"Can you talk?"

Selby said he was on the way to Hanne Kristiansen's gallery.

"Which one?"

"Kingston."

"And?"

"Hanne's not here. She's in Toronto. Setting up the gallery for an opening."

"So what's the plan?"

"The gallery here is closed," John said.

Sonny put John on the speakerphone. He sat at the head of the table and stared down at the telephone set in the centre, like it was a vase of flowers or a candlestick, part of a formal setting. "And you're going in?"

"I hope so."

Sonny told him this business was making waves south of the border. He drifted. Through the window and a half-hour distant, ten million people went about their business. It was amazing, he thought, that you couldn't hear that. That so many people didn't make a racket loud enough to be heard around the globe. That their sound died out pretty much before it even got across the river was a shock to him. Because the shit that was happening out there was unbelievable.

John Selby, waiting for Sonny Rockliff to expand on his news, was of the opinion that his boss was on drugs this morning. Distracted didn't begin to describe it. But after a few seconds Sonny said he'd only been thinking.

Selby was motoring slowly down Princess Street, Kingston's dividing line, the slim neutral zone where the city's fortunate and less-so met to shop or to panhandle. Away to his left stretched the crumbly brick and aluminum-clad homes of the working class, the down-on-their-luck, the newlyweds and the mechanics, the pizza delivery guys and the dental assistants. Also that way were the police station and a couple of strip joints, the abandoned, polluted waterfront. Off to his right, though, were the shaded streets of Sydenham Ward, its Victorian mansions and its university campus, its students and teachers, its hospitals.

He passed the Gap and Windmills Café. Novel Idea and Shoppers Drug Mart. He reached with his right hand to turn down the music, obliterate the man's serenade: *I'm dreaming of a white Christmas.* But after the music came the news, and he twisted the volume the other way. He told Sonny to hold on.

"*There are still no leads in the death of another resident of the Thousand Islands who was murdered two nights ago. Sixty-two-year-old Hinton Cowley was discovered shot to death in his island cabin. Police are releasing few details at this time. This follows the death of Bill Sumner, who was killed when . . .*"

"What's going on?" Sonny wanted to know. "You're hoping to find some proof inside?"

"This is clearly why you pull down the big salary," John said.

He drove along the waterfront, past the Hansen Space and past City Hall. He would circle back rather than sit conspicuously outside the gallery. He had already read the plaque, the brochures in Tourist Information. He knew that the imposing limestone building on his right had been conceived in 1841, by a mayor anxious that Kingston, when it was the nation's capital, should have a grand municipal building. John Counter was the man's name. Selby's head was full of the unnecessary; it teemed with the facts appropriate to a career sideline that was all vanity, to a fanciful future in which he lived and worked near a perfect crescent of beach and at a rough-hewn desk before a window that looked over a turquoise ocean.

"So does it surprise you?" John said. He needed to hear that this part of the operation wasn't foreseen weeks or months ago, during a committee meeting. That his real mission wasn't to either incriminate Hanne or "flip" her, have her work for them. Hearing it didn't mean necessarily that he would believe it, but it would tamp down, for a while, his suspicions.

"You having to go into Hanne's gallery? Of course it surprises us, John. I wouldn't lie to you."

"I don't expect I'll find anything," John said.

"Nothing would make us happier." He cleared his throat. "And by the way, we've done some research. Des Boyle's numbers were bang on regarding the number of diamond cutters in New York. He also knew what he was talking about when he said that stolen diamonds get mixed in with legitimate. Happens all the time. The main problem is war diamonds from Angola. Both sides in the civil war use profits from diamond sales to finance their war effort. Just about every government says they're doing what they can to stop the traffic in these blood diamonds. When this situation is defused, I think maybe you and I should spend a day or two bending some ears on the Hill. It's a terrible scene, John. Terrible. Every time I look at Lara's hand I wonder."

John drove along the lakefront and past a martello tower. *One of four planned by the British Royal Engineers to protect Canada from the Americans.* Through the park behind him and at the brow of a long gentle slope loomed Frontenac County Court House. *Built in 1858. Designed to be seen by ships and boats sailing past, to remind them of the law, to frighten them into good behaviour.* He doubled back and parked a block away from the gallery. He could afford no mistake this afternoon. It was against Canadian law—it constituted break and entry, unlawful search—which meant he wasn't supposed to be even considering it. Besides which, Hanne would hate him for it.

He took a window seat at Minos, ordered a Greek salad without taking his eyes off the window opposite. Penetrating as best he could the darkness at the back of the room where Hanne's office was, hunting some shadow of movement. He took a long time with his coffee and an age working out the tip. When he was positive there was no life inside the gallery, he walked as casually as he could across the street and attacked the lock. He felt, whenever he did this, that he was back in Quantico, an instructor hovering with a stopwatch. He gripped the doorknob with his left hand and inserted the first of the hooked key rods with his right. *Feel the click in the knob and work towards the front.* All the while acting out the charade of a man who can't remember which key is which. A confident, trustworthy smile. A friendly nod. A hopeful twist and . . . Bingo!

He locked the door behind him and punched in the alarm code just as he had seen Hanne do. At the green light he scurried back to the office and shut himself in. He sat in her chair and waited again, this time for his heart rate to return to normal.

He tried to work methodically through her office. It was like reading his lover's diary while she was out buying breakfast. He was sweating. Clumsy.

He lifted the carpet and tested the wide pine floorboards. He unzipped the cushions on the chairs and felt around inside. He scrutinized the backs of canvases and pulled out the drawers on the filing cabinet. He found Hanne's Palm Pilot in her desk but gave up trying to guess the password after punching in *Hanne* and *Hansen* and *Berlin* and *art* and then, desperately, *John.* He lifted photographs from the wall and he emptied the tiny icebox in the refrigerator. He looked in her coffee beans and deconstructed her fountain pen. The phone rang and he froze, stared it down and caused it eventually to stop.

Taking some masking tape he crossed to the small washroom. He found two black garbage bags and opened the door to the basement. Flashlight in his free hand, he descended the wooden stairs. There was a small window on the east side of the building at the level of the sidewalk. He folded each of the garbage bags in two and taped them over the glass, then turned on the overhead fluorescent.

Beneath the window there were twenty-three wooden folding chairs stacked neatly on a square of green indoor-outdoor carpet. Two card tables supported four boxes of wineglasses and two stacks of napkins. A corkscrew. An industrial coffee maker. On plastic trays beneath the tables were three dozen Ikea coffee mugs and the same number of steel spoons. Beside the card tables a sump pump had been inserted into a two-foot square cut into the concrete floor. The pump was unplugged and the mud at the bottom of the hole had grown a skin of ice. Straight ahead, leaning against the limestone wall and resting on wooden pallets to keep them off the ground, were wooden packing cases, enough for several paintings. He ran a hand over the wooden angles. The corner screws had been loosened and John scraped a length of skin from his right palm. He swore and wiped the blood onto the leg of his pants. He turned his attention to the workbench.

A length of steel, fifteen feet long and supported by six solid and ancient timbers. Six small steel drawers of a size that might accommodate filing cards. John inspected each of them, and they were as clean as if they had been vacuumed. A digital scale comprised a tiny steel basket resting over a digital readout. John turned it on and rested a fingertip in the basket. He felt it hit bottom and the readout displayed a line of madly flickering hyphens. Too much weight. He bent down to the floor and pried a minute concrete pebble from a crack that ran the width of the room. He dropped it into the basket: 200. Next to the scale a microscope. Not a particularly impressive machine, more something a boy might receive at Christmas along with a box of slides that held butterfly scales and insect parts. But good enough. Magnifications of one, two, and three hundred. Tweezers and needle-nosed pliers. A lamp on an impressive steel arm.

He was broken-hearted again. He hated Hanne for denying everything. For laughing at his insinuations. How cruel it would seem to her, that it was he who threatened her comfortable existence here. Not Nikolai Petrovitch, but John Selby.

He worked one more time through the room. And then he extinguished the lamp over the desk and the fluorescent, and peeled the garbage bags from the window. A giggling and bundled-up couple ran along the laneway outside. He craned to see more of them than their boots, and managed the hem of her coat, her stockinged knees, and the collection of gift bags. It was little more than a week until Christmas.

DECEMBER 19

Rebecca lived in an apartment above Delaney's five-pin bowling lanes. From the outside, the building resembled a Hollywood version of a Mexican jail. High, small windows and curvy battlements. Peeling white stucco and a broken marquee. But her apartment was a beautiful, Californian space. Tim felt disoriented moving from the stairway's murk, its buzzing shadeless bulb, into these rooms of high vaulted ceilings, of skylights and beams of bleached pine. The furniture was leather, the electronics were black. The kitchen proved to be elaborate, a hive of copper-bottomed pots and aerodynamic tools, steel appliances, and German knives. He had imagined something very different: piles of good books with ripped dust covers, yellow flags inserted at favourite recipes. He had thought dust in the corners and a favourite blanket strewn over a sagging couch. He had seen Ikea, not Bauhaus.

She saw his puzzled look. They were at the front of the building, directly above the shoe rental counter. A square window looked down on Main Street. It had begun to snow again. There were black tracks on the road. A blue neon martini glass, framed by pulled-back pink curtains, blinked in the window of Bellini's. A pickup truck idled in front of the video store. Down the street and across the frozen park, the town hall's busted clock was stuck at eleven-fifteen; it was nearly noon.

"My parents," she said by way of explanation. "I receive an income."

"What do they do?"

"They own hotels. In British Columbia mostly. Mountain lodges, faux-French chateaux. My mother's parents started them. It was in my grandparents' will that quarterly cheques be distributed to all of us. That way I'm not beholden to Mum and Dad. Dad signs the cheques, he's the administrator, but I don't owe him anything."

He asked her if she had worked in these hotels growing up. It made sense; it would explain her career.

She said something he didn't catch, a few words that drifted upwards and wrapped themselves around the crossbeams.

A grizzled man in workboots and a green cap approached the idling pickup. He opened the passenger door and a collie jumped out. The two of them set off towards the park.

Rebecca stood with Tim at the window.

"You know," he told her, "when I went out to Bill Sumner's I walked around his house, staring in the windows. I was snooping. Seeing what he had in there. If I'd headed straight over to his barn, who knows, none of this might have happened."

"Chaos theory," Rebecca said. "One small change in the sequence and everything comes out differently."

"Exactly."

"You'll drive yourself mad that way. You can't see around the corners, Tim. You can't just stay in bed."

She turned his way. He could feel her doing it; he didn't have to look. It was as if the air in the room moved out of the way to allow the rotation of her head. Tim felt for an instant as if he were in sync with the subatomic movements of everything. He was tuned in to the finest frequencies.

"It could be Denver," he said. It seemed to him undeniable. He waited for her. The man came back up the street with his collie. He had a stick in his right hand and the dog leapt at it repeatedly.

Rebecca grabbed at a white cord that Tim hadn't seen and a venetian blind descended from behind a moulding. She let it fall, and then she moved across in front of Tim and closed the blind's louvres. They sat close to each other on the couch. Tim could have leaned into her and slept.

"It just fits," Tim said. "He arrived the night Bill Sumner died. Imagine I went to the police. They would check it out."

Rebecca conceded the point. "But it makes a hell of a lot more sense that he's looking for those diamonds."

"Maybe he thought *they* had them—Bill and this Cowley guy. And now he's going through my father's things."

"And when he didn't find them he killed them? Then, how come you're not dead? I mean, come on. I do think he's weird. And he's crude and all sorts of things. But do I think he's a cold-blooded killer?

No, I don't. He's here to search the place. And even that we don't know for sure. Maybe he doesn't have the foggiest that those jewels even exist. And maybe they're not worth much. We don't know where Michael got them, or what he meant to do with them. We need to get them looked at, sure, but not yet. Not until things settle down."

"Then, why is he really here?"

"I don't know."

The telephone rang. Rebecca checked and saw that it was Granite.

"That's him," Tim said.

Rebecca got to her feet. "*So*? Of course it's him. He's concerned." She disappeared, and he heard glasses being knocked against each other. She came back with a bottle of wine, uncorked it easily, and poured him a glass. "You're acting irrationally," she said. She held her glass up to his, tapped it lightly. "Cheers."

"God I hope you're right," he said. He let his shoulders drop. He felt deflated and relieved at the same time. Unconvinced but desperate to believe her. "What about the fact that Adams said he hadn't talked to Hinton Cowley yet? Remember? He made it sound like he was going to."

"He's a bullshitter, that's all. Listen, I know what you're doing. Everyone wants to catch a murderer," Rebecca said. "Everyone sees the sketch artist's drawing on TV and wants to think perhaps that's him in the car on the highway, or sitting opposite in a restaurant. It's a quest for immortality." She laughed at herself. "Well, maybe it's not that. But people want to solve crimes. It makes them feel safer."

He went to the window and lifted one of the slats in the blind. Snow rushed towards the glass but always seemed at the last minute to dash off in another direction. "I just figure three people are dead," he told her, "and we're sitting on a bag full of diamonds. If Dad had those for years, and if there's nothing illicit about them, why the hell was he hiding them under a bottle of Scotch? And why didn't he sell them and pay off the mortgage on Granite? Did you know Petrovitch owns 51 percent of the building?"

Rebecca shrugged sadly. They were hungry, they decided, and the sense of imprisonment was making them irritable, so Rebecca followed Tim out into the late afternoon. The snow had stopped and a plow carved its way towards the lake. He pointed at the window of

Bellini's and they filed in and sat themselves down in the window. The blue light of the sign flickered over their faces.

She asked him what he was thinking about.

"About death and greed and how fucking weird everything is," he said. "How I don't trust anyone's motives, not even my own. I don't know what anyone's up to, or thinking, or what I should do. I feel about six years old."

"You want to know what I was thinking?" she said.

"Something reassuring, I hope."

"I was thinking that if we act on these feelings we have"—she paused, studied the grain on the wood panelling—"these feelings *I* have and that I'm pretty damn sure you have too." She stopped again. "Are you with me so far?"

He nodded slowly, felt the blood slosh about in his head.

"I feel that if we act right now I wouldn't know. This feels like it might be one of those situations where two people fundamentally wrong for each other are thrown together by circumstance. Some cornball *From Here to Eternity*. And I don't want that."

Tim placed his hands down on the table, spread his fingers wide. All the synapses were gumming up. "I always thought . . ." he began, but he didn't know where that line would take him and so he simply left it there, unfinished.

She took one of his fingers and held it. "I'm happy," she said. "I guess I just want to acknowledge that. And I'm scared that if I don't say it now, it might never get said."

Tim knew that moments like this, those that, even as you experience them, reveal themselves as permanent, life-altering, were rare. This one held the promise of a future that might stretch all the way to the horizon and even ride the curve a little farther. That was what he wanted. But as he looked at her then, the velvet shadows over her shoulder and the wet sheen to her lips, the sentiment that rose to the top was this one: That damn martini sign is driving me nuts. He felt along the wall with his foot for the plug. And when he found it he kicked at it. Once, twice, and then it pulled away. The light in the window failed and they were alone.

They ordered food because it had been all day since they'd eaten. And they agreed to wait, to not act until the world sorted itself out.

There was a disturbance at the bar. The bartender had cut off the only customer. Tim recognized both of them. The bartender had approached him in the market square a few months back, wanting a job. His name, he had said, was Trout. Which had sealed his fate, right there. The customer's name was Daryll something; he owned all four taxis in Gananoque, but had lost his driver's licence after knocking a woman from her moped.

"Ah, come on. Give me another one of these." Daryll held up his glass, tinkled the soft-sided ice cubes.

"No can do, man," Trout said. He smiled broadly and wiped his hands on a towel. "Tomorrow maybe. Get yourself some dinner somewhere."

Daryll put his glass down on the bar, pushed it from one hand to the other. He was building up to something. Trout sensed it too. He reached for the glass, but Daryll snatched it away. He brought his arm back and then whipped it forward, launched the glass at Trout's head. Trout somehow dodged the collision. Tim waited for him to explode.

Daryll regarded the bartender uneasily. He swayed from left to right, as though the exertion had robbed him of stability. Trout strode to the end of the bar, where there was an opening. A boy aimed at a man twice his age. He nodded at Tim and Rebecca as he rounded the bar but showed no sign of recognizing them. Daryll struggled to his feet and Trout promptly took hold of his head and, using it as a battering ram, he pushed open the glass door and deposited Daryll on the pavement outside.

When he returned to the bar he offered to buy them a drink. "No one should have to see that sort of thing," he complained.

Tim said to Rebecca that he would pay a lot of money for the uncomplicated sort of life where a drunk being thrown out of a bar was a story worth retelling.

They returned to her apartment and Rebecca took him straight to the bedroom. She threw a towel over the bedside lamp so the light was muted. They didn't need coffee, she said. Or anything else to drink. And they sure as hell didn't need to talk any more, because that was all they had done, for too long. "We need sleep," she whispered in his ear. "Are we agreed?"

He tried to raise his head enough to nod but she pushed him down again. "So sleep," she said. "No argument, okay? I'll take the couch."

*

Adams Denver bet Tim was with Rebecca. It was what people did when confronted with death. They huddled together. And he had no problem with that. It kept them out of his hair. They'd be up over the lanes in her swanky digs. He had been to her apartment himself, days back, checked it out when he knew she was out.

He liked her taste. Rebecca had done the place up nice. He'd like the time and the focus to do the same thing with a place of his own someday. He'd settled in Spain for a bit, in a whitewashed stone walk-up on a cobbled street. It had tiled floors and strings of beads hanging in the doorways. It was lovely, but he had little attachment to it, save for his boom box and his CD collection, a couple of photographs—Aidan and his mum in Trafalgar Square, Angie in a leaky piece-of-shit rowing boat he'd rented for them in the Lake District.

Rebecca had some of the same music. He liked that. Sure, there were some very dodgy albums tucked into that wooden box and sorted alphabetically, but there was also Blur's *13*, one of his all-time favourites. Damon wrote those songs when he broke up with the woman from Elastica, and Adams was of the opinion it was the finest breakup album he'd heard. The raging, the pain, the fuck-you beauty of it all. He had slipped the CD from its case and meant to listen just to the opening minute or so, just up to the first words—*tender is the night*—but he'd made it all the way through to the end, and louder than he should have. Finally he'd heard a scraping in the hallway and hightailed it out the back window. He'd left Blur in the cradle, but he was okay with that. She'd think she'd done it herself.

He'd tried to call them earlier. He wanted to hear what they made of it all. Were they weepy or suspicious, vengeful or scared shitless? Talking to the cops or whispering to each other under the covers?

His plan was to leave tonight. He'd worn out his welcome. The cops would twig any minute. He would have left yesterday, but then Nikolai had called with his stupid plan to send Oleg up. It wouldn't work very well, would it, he'd said, if Adams were gone and they had to break into the place? "Turn on your charm," Nikolai had said. "I just want

Oleg to check for a couple of things." And so he'd done his best. But it was getting old. There was way too much interference on this job.

And here he was now, watching Oleg rifle through the same damn drawers Adams had gone through days ago. It was enough to drive a man off his rocker.

Oleg insisted it wasn't a matter of trust. "You have your realm of expertise," he said, dumping a wastebasket onto the carpet, "and I have mine."

"It's tricky work," Adams agreed. "I'd have screwed that up right there. It can't be as easy as it looks."

Oleg ignored him and Adams stewed on the couch. He didn't care much for this Oleg; he seemed to find something civilized in his own behaviour that was missing in Adams'. But that was about the *only* thing he was likely to find, Adams noted with considerable relish, standing in the doorway to watch the thick-necked bastard plunder a bedroom closet.

They sat afterwards in front of the fireplace. Adams' bag was packed and next to the back door. He was ready to go. Oleg, though, was on hold, waiting for Nikolai to get to the phone. He and Adams stared each other down. Then Oleg started to speak into the receiver, quickly and in Russian. Adams fucking hated that. And Oleg was enjoying himself, laughing uproariously. He winked at Adams at one point and that was almost it. A fever rose in Adams, a murderous rage. He wanted Tim to show up. Then he could make out that Oleg was here for Tim, and Adams, heroically, could blow the guy away.

"Let me talk to him," he said, and Oleg put a hand up.

"Give me the goddamn phone," he said. Oleg turned away and stuck a finger in his ear so he wouldn't have to hear Adams.

Adams had had enough. It was like he wasn't even there! He was up and on Oleg before the bigger man realized. Adams wrestled the phone away. "Stay there!" he yelled.

Oleg raised his hands, this time in mock surrender, and sank back into his chair. A satisfied smirk on his face. *"Poshol ty na khuy,"* he said casually. "Go fuck yourself."

"Nikolai? So what's the meaning of this, then?" Adams demanded. "I mean, I went through this place, days ago."

"I needed to be certain. It is nothing personal. You can understand. There is a lot at stake, and I have kept you busy with other matters. But there is pressure on me. I need to be careful."

"But he didn't find anything, did he?"

"No, Adams, you did well. And your most recent work: did everything go equally well?"

"Piece of cake."

"Did he say anything?"

"Did he admit to it, you mean?"

"That is what I mean, yes."

"Well yeah, he did," Adams lied. "Not in so many words, you understand, but it was the last thing I got out of him."

"What was?"

"Regret," Adams said. "He said they should all have been happy with the original arrangement. He said he loved his little house and why the fuck did he think he could change that by putting more money in his pocket."

"Did he give you any other names?"

"No," Adams said, "it was more in the way of a final confession. Getting his own sins off his chest."

"And no word where the materials went?"

"I tried to persuade him, Nikolai, but he wouldn't be moved, you know."

"I am satisfied with that." Adams waited for Nikolai to follow up. What the fuck did that mean: *I am satisfied?* He'd better be satisfied. Adams didn't do what he did for the sheer screaming joy of it. Well, not often. He did it because he was asked to, and Nikolai needed to be straight about that.

Nikolai said, "I would have preferred those men go undiscovered until spring. We discussed having them disappear under the ice. That way it would have been months. Not this sudden big bang."

"The buffalo guy went under the bleeding ice," Adams reminded him. "Okay? And as for the last one, you should see the thickness of the ice around his place. If you think—"

"Fine."

"No, really," Adams said. "It's not my fault they went looking for him so soon, is it? I'm not blessed with a load of time up here. And

I'm nobody's lackey. Do this! Do that! Changing the contract as we go along, making up new rules. You understand?"

"Give me Oleg," Nikolai commanded.

"No more fucking Russian, then," Adams said.

"I don't understand."

"Make him speak in English. I want to understand what he says."

He returned the phone to Oleg, who had preserved his smirk. Oleg listened carefully for a long time and then he said, "Yes, he is, isn't he? It's very cute," and Adams nearly killed him.

"Give that back to me," he said. "Come on, hand it over."

Oleg muttered something into the receiver. He listened and then he handed over the phone.

"What is it?" Nikolai said.

He sounded impatient and Adams almost didn't tell him. He almost said he'd made a mistake, but then he thought better of it. "There's another guy up here snooping around. I forgot. Tanned guy, about forty, drives a Jag. You know who that might be? He was pulling out as I came in one day. And then yesterday I saw his car parked outside the cop shop, so I figured he was bad news. A Jag, though. So he's not your regular cop."

Nikolai swore. At least Adams assumed the barrage of Russian was laced with obscenity.

"You do know him, then?" Adams waited. Oleg was poking gingerly at the fire with a stick. A shower of sparks fell to the carpet. The Russian jumped to his feet and began to stamp them out. "You're a great dancer, Oleg. I'll give you that," Adams said nonchalantly. "That it, then, Nikolai? Because your man's a bit tied up. I should go lend a hand before he burns the whole house down."

Nikolai grunted and Adams hung up and watched Oleg.

"Help me," Oleg cried. And he was right. The embers had taken hold. Licks of flame jumped from the rug.

Reluctantly Adams joined in and the two of them performed a strange jig in front of the hearth. Adams started to laugh. "If my girlfriend could fucking see me," he said, "she'd wonder what the hell I was up to with you."

"Really?" Oleg said. "Your girlfriend? That surprises me. I was sure you were gay."

*

Hanne played with the heating controls in the Jag and watched the condensation shrink away from the vents. John was still in shock that she had called, and he had admitted as much to her on the phone.

"I told you I would," she had said. "As soon as I got back." But something had happened. She needed to see him. Could he pick her up?

He drove them to a brick rowhouse on Earl Street, just north of King. Across the street were larger limestone residences with warped glass windows and dark shrubs. She could walk to the gallery from there. She was lucky, she said. In the summer the trees were full of songbirds, and the backyards were full of faculty from the university, or old men bent over tin-spoked rakes. He said it looked like she was doing well for herself; this was a long way from their old apartment in Berlin, wasn't it?

"Don't do that, John."

She made him tea and changed into sweatpants and a white T-shirt so stretched at the neck that when she leaned to work at the fire John saw the pale curve of her breast nuzzled soft against its own shadow.

She sat at the end of the couch; he was on a chair twenty feet away. Above the fireplace was an oil portrait of a man that Hanne had found in the attic. "It isn't very good," she said.

He asked her how she knew.

"It seems rushed," she said. "Sketched in. The nose sits awkwardly on the face, the eyes are dead, the skin is green."

"I like it all the same," John told her, thinking she must too, since she had hung it so prominently. They studied it together, from their chairs.

"Are you going to tell me?" John finally said.

"This other man," Hanne said. "Hinton Cowley. Is he connected?"

"I assume so. I actually hoped you could tell me."

She shook her head. There were tears on her cheeks. "I've never heard of him," she said. When John looked at her skeptically, she said, "I swear."

"There are some things I should tell you," John said. Hanne tucked her legs underneath her, and John stared at the soft pink soles of her feet, the crease in the skin on her smallest toe. "I've been in the basement."

Hanne looked around, focused on a door beside the entrance to the kitchen. "Here?"

"No, at the gallery," he said. "I saw everything." Which she must know; he was simply trying to head off any denial. He waited for her to speak. He could imagine the torrents inside her. The confusion and panic. He wanted to calm her. Why didn't she start from the beginning? he suggested. Did she want to do that?

Finally she rose and pulled very thick velvet curtains at the window. She walked through to a narrow dining room with a pine table in it and she drew similar curtains at that window. She returned to the couch and picked grit from the soles of her feet. She leaned over the armrest and retrieved her mug. She played with its handle and finally she said, "Okay. Fine." It was the petulant compliance of a schoolgirl.

"You're doing the right thing," he told her.

"I'd rather you keep quiet than try to persuade me with limp platitudes," she said. "Let me just give it to you without you interrupting, okay? We can go back afterwards. If I don't tell you all of it at once I might never get it out."

She braved a smile. There was an intimacy that had been absent before.

She told him: "Okay. So all of us paid roof to him. *Krysha*. Protection. No one is exempt. Even though I was already helping Nikolai."

"Helping? How?"

Nikolai had come to her, she said. She had already sold him an expensive work of hers. And so she felt indebted, which of course was what he wanted. He told her he was a proud Russian. He had business there still, and family. And he had developed a passion, he said, for art.

"He blamed it on me," Hanne said. "My painting had moved him to tears, he said. I was flattered beyond belief. I was gullible, I wanted it to be true." She gulped her drink and poured herself more. "He said there were artists in Russia he admired and he was interested in acquiring some of their work. Maybe I could help him. He had no knowledge, he said, of how that world worked, and I did, surely. Well, I lied and said of course I did. And I suppose if I had said then, 'I haven't the foggiest, Nikolai, not a clue,' perhaps he would have picked on someone else. I doubt it—I think he picked on me precisely *because* I didn't know which end was up—but it's possible.

"And so I began. I talked to customs officials and other art dealers, and after several weeks of trying to make myself understood by people in Russia who were supposed to speak English, eventually we discovered that it was best if we wrote to each other, outlining what it was we needed. I was so excited when the first works arrived. Much more excited than Nikolai. I mean he *was* pleased, he congratulated me, but it wasn't the jumping up and down that I wanted."

"What happened next? He asked for this, what did you call it, *krishna*?"

"*Krysha*. Yes. He sent a goon over. I thought I was exempt because of what I was doing, but they laughed. Their excuse for collecting from me was: You represent Russian artists. You profit from their toil. It was my privilege, they said, to give something back. I told them I was already giving enough, but they would have none of it. Everyone else on the street paid, they said. How would it look? I should be grateful for the services they could offer me. I asked them to explain these mysterious benefits. They said that my mail would arrive on time. That my alarm service would be unnecessary because they would protect me. They said my 'premiums' meant I could walk the streets safely. There would never be a fire. Or an audit. And if I didn't pay? Well, then I couldn't walk the streets at all. I would have to find a new location for my gallery. Somewhere farther away from the film stars, all that money from New York and Hong Kong.

"I paid them $750 a month. I considered myself lucky. Others were forced to provide services for them. Accounting, or storage. A phone line. If they came to me for that, I thought, I would have to say no. Can you imagine? How stupid I was to think I was clean, even then. But eventually Nikolai came back. A change in the plan, he said. And I heard him out, and then I said yes. Just like that. This was just before Michael and I met. What they wanted seemed so easy to accommodate. But am I boring you, John?"

John opened his eyes. "Far from it. You know that. I'm concentrating. How did it change?"

"Dramatically."

She was playing with him. No one could resist their own story, he thought.

"What more did they want you to do?"

"He wanted to help me. 'I want to make you a tycoon,' he said. I knew I should say no. I *knew* it. But they are so dangerous. Part of their game is keeping you off guard. They want your imagination to run riot. It saves them the trouble of actually doing anything. And there is always enough real event to keep you in line. A body suddenly outside a nightclub. A stabbing. A mysterious fire. The police come and say they know we are paying protection, they can change that. But it's bullshit. We know, and so do they. They don't even think it's Nikolai. He's that smooth. Anyway, it becomes your world, John. You don't imagine any other system is possible. And it's like a tax. You learn ways to write it off. They even tell you how to do that.

"But one day Nikolai said he wanted to offer me a change of scenery. He told me about Kingston. He wanted me to open another gallery, he said. He wanted to buy property down here because it's such a lovely part of the world, and this way he could get art shipped straight to Kingston. He wasn't even trying to be plausible. He has such confidence. He's frightening that way. I told him I wasn't sure, but he said he had a space in mind already and he would take me to see it. I asked, 'When?' and he said, 'Now,' and clicked his fingers, and just like that we were on our way. It was horrible but exciting too. I was being offered the chance to be a force in the Canadian art world. He knew exactly what he was doing. You've seen the gallery. It's beautiful. I fell in love with it immediately, and the price seemed so reasonable—just the occasional shipment of art from Russia. And remember, I thought those shipments were all completely above-board. Oh, I see that look, John. You think I was deceiving myself. That I should have known there was a catch. Well, I said that to him, and he said only that he was a generous man. Too generous. Instead of helping me he should be doing his own art shipping. 'I am a fool,' he said. 'But I like you. I like to help people.' And that was that."

"Hardly."

"It was how we started. He even sent me to Russia on a buying trip. It was marvellous. At least until I got back and he knew which flight I had been on, and which hotel I had stayed in, even which room. Not so extraordinary, I suppose, but I had made my own arrangements. He even told me where I had eaten dinner one night and what I had ordered. I think that was when he began to turn the screws a little. It was then I thought I might have been better off staying in Toronto and paying the damn protection. Or sailing up the west coast teaching remedial art to a bunch of pensioners. Anyway. Then Michael showed up."

"You didn't know him before?"

"In Toronto? No. Not personally. He showed up one day and introduced himself. I recognized him from TV. Not his name, but I knew who he was. I was stupid. So stupid. I told him that Niki scared me. That I thought there must be more to the art than I was seeing. God knows why I opened my mouth. The next day he was back with Nikolai. And Nikolai said, I was suspicious, was I? I was scared, was I? He took me by the arm and dragged me into the back office. Michael just looked on, horrified. I don't think he realized what he'd done. He certainly wasn't expecting that. And anyway, Nikolai sat me down in my office chair and made me watch while he tore into the work I had picked up just that day."

"Let me guess," John said.

"Right. Diamonds. Hidden in tiny pockets in the frame. One pocket beneath each of the corner screws. The screw acts like a cork. There are a few dozen carats at each corner."

John felt his palm, the scab from the cut he had suffered from a frame in Hanne's basement. Of course. "You must have panicked."

"I thought he might kill me right then and there. I couldn't figure out why he was showing me."

"No shit. And why was he?"

"He said I was a part of it now. I had been in Russia. There was a paper trail. Every step of the journey had my name attached to it. That he didn't want to hear any more that I was suspicious, or frightened, or wanted nothing to do with it. He said that there were only a few shipments that would carry this sort of 'attachment' and then it would be over. He said he would close down the Kingston gallery and I could go back to Toronto a free woman. He said there would be a grace period in my payments for contributing so handsomely. I should save my tears, he said. Tears didn't work on him. I thought he might hit me, but he just yelled. 'Do you understand?' he kept yelling. 'Do you get it?' What else could I do, John?"

"You could have gone to the police. They would have believed you. When was this? And what about Hollins?"

"August. Oh, Michael was so awkward. They left together. But he was back the next day with flowers. The biggest bouquet I'd ever seen. Apologizing profusely."

"Was it a trick?"

"I don't think so. I think he was just trying to impress Nikolai by telling him what I'd said. Afterwards he was always trying to make it up to me."

"I bet he was."

"No, not like that. We barely knew each other, even at the end. Despite everything."

"So how did it work?"

"Michael handled the delivery. He wanted to protect me, I think, and so he spoke about it very rarely. I wasn't involved."

"But you must have some idea."

"He had friends, apparently, who took it across the St. Lawrence for him. Petrovitch has a buyer who lives on an American island."

"Which island?"

"Manhattan, I think."

"There's a Manhattan Island?"

"There were supposed to be four trips," she told him. "The fourth was last week."

"Four trips in total, or four trips this year?"

"In total. But who knows? When the Seaway melts maybe he was planning to start again."

"And was Sumner one of the boaters?"

She didn't know, she said. And John believed her.

"How about Cowley?"

"The same," she said. "But it's over, whoever it was. I'm sure it's over and done with."

"Except, everyone involved is dying. Is that why you called me?"

"It's partly that," Hanne said. "Well, it *is* that, of course. But Michael's death isn't the same as the others, is it? I mean, that was an accident still, wasn't it?"

"I think so."

"And this last one—Cowley—I don't know how he fits in. So part of me thinks I must be okay. But if it's over, and Nikolai is killing everyone who knew, then . . ."

"You think you might be next."

"He wants to see me. He has ordered me to meet with him."

"When? Where?"

"At Chez Piggy. It's a restaurant."

John knew that. "I've heard of it. One of the Lovin' Spoonful owns it," he said. "The guitarist, I think."

Hanne looked pained. "Zal Yanovsky," she said. "But he died. A week ago maybe."

"How?"

She shook her head. "A heart attack at home. Trust me, he's not involved."

"That's very sad, then," John said. "He was young, wasn't he?"

Hanne shrugged. "I guess."

"Well, it's good it's a public place he wants to meet," John said. "That bodes well. Petrovitch wouldn't set up an appointment if—"

"Can you come?" Hanne said. "Can you sit somewhere in the back, just in case? He has some thug up here. If he shows as well, I don't know if I can handle that."

"You forget he knows me," John said. "I'd end up as dead as the others. Who is this thug?"

"Adams something. He's English."

"English? That's a weird turn."

"I guess. He came to the gallery once. He was really drunk and said Nikolai had sent him to check up on me. I assumed he came up from Toronto."

Hanne was exhausted. She moaned and stretched.

She was using him; she wasn't using him. He couldn't decide, and it made him anxious. Anxious to console her and touch her, but anxious also to have her strapped to a polygraph machine. To have someone else sit in on their conversations. A chaperone.

"You think I'm terrible," she said.

He denied it.

"Stupid, then. Wilfully blind."

"At the very least," he said. "It's a mess."

She struggled to sit up. "Sit here."

He took the far end of the couch and immediately she shifted closer. She lifted her face to his. For an instant he might have been able to turn away, but that instant passed and he lost himself in her. The months and years were wiped away. He was in Berlin again, steel light cutting in through the tired lace curtain, her hair brushing his face, her breath in his mouth. He pulled away, dizzied by time's compression and the sensation of her perfect hip beneath his hand.

"Don't," she said, but it was too late, he had his head in his hands. "John, come back." She tugged at his arm and he resisted, because if he fell now he couldn't trust himself to stop again. She kissed his neck and pulled his collar away so she could get at his shoulder. He studied the empty chair he had inhabited so recently and wondered at the vast distances involved in moving from there to here.

"Lie down," Hanne whispered. And so he did.

After a while she led him upstairs. She said it was what they needed, both of them, and he thought that was probably true. Hanne because she was scared and she wanted to hide for a while under the covers. And John because he wanted to connect the past to the present, repair all the frayed ends.

Hanne pulled back the covers and John followed her in. The world and its problems could wait. He was happy again. Whatever it was she told him, he would find a way. Together they would work it out.

DECEMBER 20

Sonny Rockliff had his hands full. A wilderness outfitter from Kenora, in northern Ontario, had tried to smuggle eight shotguns into Minnesota. When the customs agents found the guns—duct-taped to the underside of the liner in the bed of his truck—the fool took a swing at someone, a female trainee from Grand Rapids. And now a database search was showing that this man had been across the border eighteen times in the last six months. The locals were doing the math and starting to fret. But what had landed this incident on Sonny's desk and not one of his operatives' was that the hunter in question had spent six months out of the last twenty-four in Jordan and Syria, and couldn't explain to anyone's satisfaction exactly why that was. It also turned out he had a graduate degree in urban geography and three minor convictions, for trespassing (on an army base— he claimed to be looking for golf balls on the military's golf course) and for public intoxication. Sonny didn't think it was going to add up to much—there were almost invariably mundane ambitions and motives at work in even the strangest-sounding of cases—but it was taking up his morning, when what he dearly needed was half an hour to organize his thoughts.

John Selby had been in touch, looking for assistance in a possibly hare-brained scheme that involved his ex, Hanne Kristiansen. Sonny knew damn well John was taking a circuitous route to justice in the hope that Hanne would benefit from her cooperation. It wasn't what Sonny had envisioned when he'd brought John aboard. But perhaps he should have. It was naive of him not to see that people always try to protect their loved ones. And he understood that. It pissed him off, but he understood. He only wished he had foreseen the possibility three months ago.

The problem was that John had already set things in motion. He had made Newark's involvement pretty much a necessity. True, it wasn't the worst plan Sonny had ever heard. It was just the motivation behind it that made him jittery. That and the fact that Arlon

Trent, a high-up in Homeland Security, was in New Jersey that morning and would want a briefing. The original plan had been for Trent to visit the FBI field office two miles away at 10:00 a.m. and then meet with Sonny at 2:00. But the schedule had just been reversed. Trent was due any minute, and Sonny's desk was still littered with briefs on bear hunting and truck modification data. He pulled all the paperwork together at the front edge of his desk, opened the top drawer, and slid everything in.

Arlon Trent was a man who, in the face of rapid advancement, and handed immense power and influence, had not succumbed to self-importance and ego. He always swept into an office like a localized storm system, yes, and staff were rendered either desperately mute or risibly sycophantic, but his schedule required such entrances. And the country demanded it. Sonny liked him, respected him, and thought the sentiment was widespread among the upper echelons of intelligence. It could so easily have been otherwise, and each of the four times Sonny had met Trent he had tried to discern a little more precisely what it was that impressed him so much.

This morning Trent appeared in a blue suit two shades brighter than Sonny would have dared to sport. His handshake and smile were warm, his gaze unwithering. He led Sonny into his own conference room (a reversal of protocol that Sonny found unnerving) and the two of them sat side by side, rather than opposite each other, at the massive teak wheel.

There were only the most meagre of formalities, a series of brief inquiries: How's the space, Sonny? And the staff? The FBI boys around the corner giving you all you need, are they? Anything new on the radar this morning?

Sonny told him about the shotguns. The half year in Jordan.

"And you say he took a swipe at one of ours?"

"A woman, yes. She's new."

"And rethinking her career choice about now, I suppose. What do you think, Sonny?"

Sonny told him he was still reviewing the notes that had been faxed to him. Weighing up whether to fly there himself, so he could sit in the room while the man was interrogated.

Trent suggested—lifting his hands from the table; making it clear it was Sonny's business—that he view the tapes of the initial questioning before making that decision. "In the meantime, maybe we'll unearth some of this idiot's friends. I doubt there's anything there."

Sonny said he was inclined to agree.

"Fine, then," Trent said. "On to the main event." He rubbed his hands together, then linked them and reversed them, stretched them away from him so that his knuckles cracked. He relaxed, apologized for the rush this morning, and shared the observation that the times required it of men like them, didn't it? Sonny felt the absurd glow that accompanies such recognition and wished that Lara could somehow be present to witness these companionable moments.

"John Selby is the man up there," Sonny reported.

Trent nodded. "I recall you saying."

"He reports that Petrovitch is using an art dealer to smuggle large quantities of rough diamonds from the Arkangel mine in Russia into Canada. From there they move across the St. Lawrence Seaway to an island on the American side of the border. Fenton Mossine is the man who owns the island. We don't have a complete file on him yet. Hanne Kristiansen—the art dealer—believes that he sells them for Petrovitch, or arranges for their sale, most likely in New York. The fact that Mossine's name doesn't show up on any of our screens makes me think he's just a middleman."

"We have *something* on him, surely."

"He's a tool and die maker from Pittsburgh. In '92 he won $11 million in the state lottery and bought himself a little bit of paradise. But that's it. He's clean. He flies to the Caribbean every winter for a couple of weeks. He's divorced, and the ex is in Florida. There are two kids. It doesn't get any more interesting than that."

"Okay. So what's Selby thinking?"

"He's thinking to lure Petrovitch to the island. Spark some sort of confrontation between the two men where they say more than they should. Because right now we have nothing against him on paper. *Nada.* And he says Kristiansen can only testify to Petrovitch's illegal importing, which won't net him a long enough sentence."

"So we get him for illegal entry. Put him in a cell while we prepare our case against him. It's a start, I suppose. Better than letting the Canadians lose him. What else?"

"There's a mine rep from Arkangel in Canada at the moment. Selby thinks he's there trying to recover the diamonds. Trouble is, he's not talking. Won't even confirm that Petrovitch is, in fact, stealing from them. Which isn't helpful. He was just busted for a drunk driving incident up there."

"So our theory is that Arkangel is simply the aggrieved party. And you say this rep is in a Toronto jail cell? Well, at least he's not going anywhere."

"Actually, he made bail. We're trying to keep up with him." Sonny fidgeted in his chair.

"So this plan of yours, will it work? Will this bastard take the bait? The last thing we need is an embarrassing fuck-up."

"I think so. I'm sure it will. But it's pretty elaborate and pretty expensive. And it has to be noted that when Selby was stationed in Berlin he was involved for a while with this Hanne Kristiansen. We believe he's trying to protect her somewhat."

Trent raised an eyebrow. "How about some good news? Do we know where these diamonds are, where they ended up? Or even how many of them we're looking for? And is Petrovitch motivated by profit, or are there darker forces at work here?"

"The short answer to those questions is, no, we don't know. All the more reason to get him in a room talking."

"What about going to the source? Can we not talk to the mine's owners, or to the Russian government? Better still, what do our Russian experts say? Worst case is we find out that we're wrong and Arkangel knows damn well what Petrovitch is doing, that they control his every move."

"We have talked to them. Arkangel is pretty convincing in their denials. And our people back them up. They say they can't see a good reason for Arkangel to involve themselves in a scheme like this. Even if they did want to siphon off some of their production and sell it in the U.S., there are easier ways, more direct ways. No, I think Selby is right in his assessment. This is all about Petrovitch having someone steal stones for him. Or maybe he's a fence for Russian Mafia interests."

"Okay. And the murders in the Thousand Islands?"

"I believe we can nail Petrovitch on those eventually."

"You mean the Canadians can nail him."

"That's right. But who knows how long it might take, and what damage Petrovitch might cause in the meantime. We need to find out what he's doing, what he's already done. I don't think we can wait."

"So when would this takedown happen?"

"Christmas Day."

"That's a lot of overtime. A lot of unhappy families and kids."

"It is." Sonny waited. He glanced at the distant city through the window, its shimmering blocks of grey and gold.

Trent was on his feet. "Fine. I'll read the rest of it over lunch. But for now let's say it's a go," he said. "Put in your manpower requisitions today, so that no one's breaking the bad news to their wife on Christmas Eve. But go easy on the specifics. I don't want to see our intentions broadcast on CNN. I'll talk to the President tonight. We'll work out the legal end with Ottawa, but you can handle jurisdictional issues with Canadian law enforcement."

Trent paused a second at the window. He hung his head a second and sighed, and then he was away. There were members of his support staff waiting at the door, and some of Sonny's people hovering back in the middle distance.

Stopping in front of the elevator, Trent shook Sonny's hand again, as if there were news photographers stationed in the ferns and behind the photocopiers. He did up his jacket and punched impatiently at the button his assistant had only just released. For seven, eight seconds, they waited with nothing to say to each other. But Sonny Rockliff had just lobbied successfully for a military action along the Canadian border, and Arlon Trent had authorized it. They were men with a lot to think about.

*

Des Boyle and John Selby were at Fort Henry, on one of the ramparts that looked out over the narrows between the mainland and Cedar Island. Behind and below them lay the parade square where, in summer, university students in full regalia re-enacted the lives of a nineteenth-century regiment. Today, though, only the grey-haired quartermaster made his lonely walk to his corner workshop, where he oiled the original rifles to protect them from rust.

Men had drowned trying to swim that gap, Boyle said. Deer went down every year. There were powerful whirlpools and a hard current. It was one of the last passages to close every winter. He said the British must have loved having it there—a first line of defence against the Americans. John tried to work every word into a paragraph worthy of Condé Nast.

They stood shoulder to shoulder, like sentries on watch duty. John would have been happy to peer for a long while out over the ice and the frost-encrusted Murney tower with the sun climbing over its broad shoulder. Off to his right the ferry from Wolfe Island churned along its wet track towards Kingston.

"I was over at Tim Hollins' place before I came here," Des said.

"Oh?"

"I've had reports of some character staying there. Tim gave me a line about him being 'sort of' a friend. It didn't sound right so I dropped by."

"And who is he?"

"He's gone. His name, though, is Adams Denver."

"Adams?"

"You know him?"

"Hanne got a visit from him."

"Well, he works for Petrovitch. Tim says he was up here looking into Michael's death. Tim didn't know whether to buy it. Now he's disappeared, but Tim says he gave his place a good going-over first."

"Do you like him for the murders?"

"I'd sure like to put him in a small room for a while."

"But you've no idea where he is."

"We've got all our boys on the lookout for his Volvo. Canary yellow."

"Volvo?" John told him about the Volvo that had pulled in to Tim Hollins' drive just as he left, way back on the tenth.

Boyle said, "That's the day after Sumner took his last swim."

John said that all fit with what Hanne had given him.

John had already told Des about the delivery system for the diamonds, and about Michael's involvement. He'd given him everything he had, including the meeting Hanne had lined up with Petrovitch at the restaurant. Des said he was confident that his people could wire the place before Hanne arrived.

A young girl in a lavender snowsuit chased her cocker spaniel over the white slopes far below. Des tapped his wrist. "It's time," he said, and they marched along the parapet to the stone steps that descended into the parade ground. A man on a mountain bike rode into the square. He locked his bike to an iron grille on a window and went inside.

"A time traveller," Des said. "That's what he looks like."

John laughed. "And we're the weary foot soldiers."

Des slapped him on the back and jarred loose a little more guilt. They reached the parking lot. "You called me from Hanne's. Last night, I mean."

John paused.

Des said, "One of our boys saw your car parked outside her house. He phoned it in. Not sure why, really." Boyle smiled and they climbed into his modest dark sedan.

*

Hanne arrived soon after Chez Piggy opened. John had warned her: "You won't see us. You'll have no idea where we are. And there'll be men and women in there with you, but don't go looking at them all, trying to pick them out. You'll scare him off. Just wait for the signal, and when it comes, you get on the phone and act your heart out. After that, if he reacts badly, we have men and women everywhere. If he pretends not to have overheard, which is most likely, you just keep him talking."

Hanne ducked into the stone laneway that led to the main entrance and disappeared. John was so close to her he leaned away from the Op van's tinted window as she passed.

"She'll be okay," Des said.

A technician tapping at her laptop glanced at him and then away again. "Let me know when you want volume," she said.

"Give it to us now," Des said, and as the gathering hubbub built within their steel box, Des told John, "There's a microphone in the bookcase behind them and one in the light fixture overhead. Both invisible. Four SRT men on-site in case we decide to take him."

"Or in case he does something stupid."

Des nodded.

Hanne's voice silenced them both. She was only asking for tea, but all of them were rigid.

The dining room took on more passengers. The snow-white van parked two hundred feet away on King filled up with their noise. Sounds and voices divorced from the visuals. John saw her anyway—ordering a mineral water, her waitress loading up a wicker basket with bread. Hanne fiddling with her teaspoon and moving the napkin fractionally left, then right.

An unfamiliar voice rose up and dominated. "I threw them out on their ear, that's what. Damned ingrates."

"And you got away with it?"

"Got away with it? My lawyer thumped me on the back, bought me dinner. First time that's happened in thirty years. Course I got away with it."

"Well, Stewart, it's just that—"

"I built the damn company. I won't have some damn union take it away from me."

"They'll outlive you, Stu. You know that, don't you? That's their revenge."

Des said, "I know that guy. Old-timer. I see him running through the university campus. Painful to watch."

The technician picked up another voice on her headphones. "Wait. The subject has arrived. He's at the desk," she reported urgently. "Shall I send word up to the dining room?"

"Let him start up the stairs first," John instructed. "He has to hear her."

"He's doing that now. Second stair, third. He's thirty feet away from her."

"Then, quickly."

She spoke into her microphone, and John knew that a man in brown tweed would now shake open his newspaper and Hanne would recognize the signal.

They heard her voice, quietly at first, but quickly getting louder: "I don't care, it has to be the twenty-fifth . . . I don't think you realize how much . . . no, the paramount thing is . . . Listen, you take them to Manhattan Island at eleven . . . Yes, you heard me. I know it's Fenton, but he works for me too . . . Listen, he pays you the money, you're home for

Christmas dinner . . . No, I don't think . . . there's far too much at stake . . . Just take them there, you hear me? . . . He's waiting for them, okay? . . . Good . . . Yes, I think so too . . . Great . . ." By the end, she was nearly shouting. There was no doubt Petrovitch, if he was on the stairs—and the technician assured him he was—would have heard every word.

John said, "Petrovitch must be right there. If he goes ballistic, your men had better be ready."

Des said, "They are. Christ, listen to how quiet it is now. She sure shut everybody up with that performance. He's going to know she faked it."

John didn't think so. "He hasn't said anything because he was listening. I think he bought it."

The technician scraped her stool around. "He's there," she said. They hadn't heard anything, just the murmur of conversations being resumed. The clink of china and, deep in the mix, a rumble from the kitchen. "The other chair," she said. "Someone just pulled it away from the table.

"I didn't see you," Hanne said, startled.

"I'm glad. You mind?" It was Petrovitch.

"No. Of course."

"She sounds scared," Des said.

"So would I," John said.

The waitress arrived with bread and said she would give Hanne and Nikolai a minute to decide. She rhymed off a couple of specials for them to think about. The technician muttered that she was partial to lamb herself, and Des agreed with her.

For ten minutes, fifteen, Hanne Kristiansen and Nikolai Petrovitch swapped tense small talk. Which was what John had told her to do. "Nothing will arouse his suspicions as much as you trying to work the conversation," he'd said.

Shortly their food arrived. And a while later their plates were taken away. Still nothing. Petrovitch was toying with her, John thought. He had demanded her presence and now he had nothing to say to her. Even after the phone call. It didn't make sense. John wanted to be able to see her. Second-hand reports couldn't come close.

"You look distracted," Hanne said. "Checking out the room that way. Is something wrong?"

"She's trying to send us a message," Des said.

Petrovitch said, "Where will you be for the holidays, Hanne?"

"I don't know. Jamaica, if I have my way."

Des raised an eyebrow. "Not if I have mine, you won't." But then he apologized. "Sorry, John."

Petrovitch said, "I can picture the two of us there. It is not the worst image."

Hanne laughed awkwardly. "Ruby might think differently."

"They're flirting, for God's sake," Des said.

"More like he's about to trap her," John said.

"Ruby knows where I live," Petrovitch said.

Hanne sniffed. A teaspoon clattered in its saucer.

"And how would you pay for this trip?" Petrovitch wondered. "There is money put aside?"

"I'm joking, Nikolai. And anyway, I'm not talking about Australia, am I? Just a little getaway."

"Because if you had a lot of money put aside . . ."

"I don't."

"Or if I were to hear of a sudden improvement in your welfare now that our business is concluded . . . I know your bank balance, Hanne. I know where you keep your money. And if, suddenly, there was more of it, I would worry."

"There won't be. That's impossible. I know what you're saying."

"Do you? I wonder."

"You're saying—" She gasped suddenly, as if the breath had been knocked from her.

"Not out loud, Hanne. Okay? Not out loud. Look at me. No. Look . . . You see? There is no need for words. You and I know exactly what the other means. Don't we?"

"We do."

"The bastard," John said. "He grabbed her. Did you hear that?" He was pacing—three steps one way, three the other, his head bowed because the van wouldn't allow him to stand upright. "And he's not going to say enough."

"Sounds like he knows."

"He *suspects*. He doesn't know anything. But I still think he bought the phone call. He'll have to check it out, at the very least."

Petrovitch made a glib reference to the lights, how the glare from them was all wrong. If this was his joint, he said, then things would change. Des wondered aloud whether he might reach up and start fooling with the bulbs, and discover their microphone. Hanne was sniffing again, as if lunch had given her a cold.

"You need to take care of yourself," Petrovitch told her.

They were getting up from the table. So little had happened. A trap set, perhaps. A muted threat or two. Des was rubbing his hands together. The technician said, "You want me to wrap it up?"

"Not until they leave," Des said.

"They've gone. You didn't catch that?"

"Catch what?" John asked.

She smiled tolerantly. "Their footsteps on the carpet."

"Now you're showing off, Suzie," Des told her, and she looked away, pleased with herself. Des spoke into a hand-held: "He's coming out. I want to know where he goes."

John pushed his nose against the black glass. Petrovitch passed within two feet of him. John wanted to burst out and throw him to the ground. He wanted to batter the truth out of the man. Make him say everything he had been too cagey to discuss in the restaurant. He felt like they had miked the wrong table, so little had been uttered. Now they would have to wait until Christmas.

"You'll fog up the glass," Des hissed. "He'll see you."

"He's already gone," John said. "Let's just hope we see him again."

DECEMBER 21

John rode shotgun to Des Boyle while they drove around and around Gananoque. Checking the motel lots and the waterfront, up behind Town Hall, along the river, and behind the corrugated walls of the steel factory. Others were patrolling the Parkway and one cruiser was stationed in Rockport. Yet another officer had secreted herself in the trees near the entrance to Granite.

They decided to try Kingston, and for another hour they hunted Adams Denver on the side streets and in the taverns of that old city. They ate lunch together at a tiny Cambodian joint with six tables, watching a man who had obviously spent most of his life staring into a wok. John borrowed a newspaper from the counter and read that the police investigation into the deaths of Bill Sumner and Hinton Cowley were progressing well. The police were hunting a suspect but were releasing no further details at this time. "'It is speculated, however, that this is a cooperative effort, involving law enforcement agencies from both Canada and the United States,'" he read aloud.

Boyle said, "You've got more than a small soft spot for this woman, John."

Selby stared at the green cans of coconut juice lined up in the cooler next to the cash register. He chewed shrimp away from the tail. When he cleared his throat to speak, Des Boyle just laughed at him.

"Maybe you shouldn't incriminate yourself," he said.

After lunch John made feeble excuses and drove to Hanne's house. There was no obvious police presence, but John knew that in an apartment opposite, as well as in the next-door neighbour's and in a garage in the laneway behind the house, heavily armed teams waited for Nikolai Petrovitch to punish Hanne Kristiansen for her telephone betrayal. John darted up the crooked front walk.

Hanne dragged him through the house and out again. There was a long, thin garden, mostly buried under snow. An ancient wheelbarrow with a rusted-out bucket. A black squirrel tore into a peeling birch. A blue plastic line looped from an iron hook screwed into the largest of the cedars.

"My secret garden," she told him. "Do you remember the allotments in Germany?"

John saw, as clearly as if he had just turned away, the thin strips of stony ground next to the railway line in East Berlin, each tended lovingly by mostly Muslim gardeners. "I do. You could see them from the road."

"That's right. Well, this reminds me a lot of those. In summer I let the lawn go and concentrate on my vegetables and my wildflowers. It's the garden that sold me on this place."

Back inside she made him a salad, and they sat on the floor in front of the couch. "So Germany meant something to you," he said. He had trouble believing her. More and more he thought that Hanne was more interested in his protection than his affection. Now, as then, she was looking for a way out of a jam.

"John, we met in an all-night bar and moved in together right away. I was painting. You were a spy, sort of. I was watching German films in the afternoons and recognizing the locations. I was living the most romantic life ever. You have no idea how sad I was."

"No, I don't. You're right."

"Well, I was. The garden is proof of how much it meant. That's why I showed you."

They climbed the stairs and undressed with the curtains drawn and the stereo playing something ambient that Hanne said afterwards was called "The Pearl," and she *loved* it—didn't he?

John said to be honest he wasn't listening to it. "You're keeping me pretty busy," he reminded her, wiping a finger across her sweat-beaded stomach. "And besides, the street's full of cops, the Seaway's hiding a murderer, and you, my love, are at the heart of it all." He meant it kindly, but she curled away from him. After a minute or two he heard her sniffing and so he slotted behind her and mused on how the sheets were so much thicker than the threadbare set they had lived with in Germany. He brought his hand up between her breasts and slipped his foot between hers and they fell asleep.

When they awoke the light was failing. Hanne lay with her head on his chest and said that his heartbeat was incredibly slow. She took her watch from the carpet and measured his pulse at fifty-eight. "Isn't that dangerous?" she said. "Come on, get on the floor. Do some push-ups for me. Let's see if it climbs."

"You know," John said, thinking he needed to be serious, "it could very easily be many millions of dollars' worth of diamonds. There will be consequences for you."

Hanne lifted her head. "Oh." Her voice was flat, defeated. "You know those stones are probably long gone by now, right? They're history."

"I do know that."

"Good."

He got dressed sadly. The circumstances held so little promise for them. They were under surveillance. The RCMP wanted to arrest Hanne. And John still wasn't convinced she wouldn't disappear again, or abandon him even after he had done everything he could. She trod lightly around the bed, picking up clothes as she went. He grabbed for her and she fell on top of him, laughing.

*

Two hours later he entered the RCMP station just outside Gananoque. He had just been questioning Hanne Kristiansen, he said to the desk sergeant. He wanted to see Michael Hollins' BMW. No, he wouldn't disturb anything. It was just something she had said.

He took the man's directions and his thoughtfully offered flash-light and drove out to the wrecking yard. A German shepherd put its front paws against the wire fence. A bearded man came out of his trailer and threatened to kick the dog's skull in if it didn't shut up.

Hollins' car was half its original length. The hood had disap-peared and there was no space between the driver's seat and the dashboard. Ragged triangles of windshield clung to the rubber frame. The passenger-side front wheel lay on the ground beside the car. The glove compartment was open and empty. A white powdery residue lay all over the dash.

John took a knife from his pocket and slashed through the uphol-stery, put a long, deep cut in each cushion. He thrust his fist into each gash and felt around inside. And then he walked briskly away. There was nothing there, and nowhere left to hide anything.

DECEMBER 22

The air was clogged with snow. It was hard to breathe. Great soft plates of it sifted down. It was eight o'clock in the evening, three days before Christmas. Snow crept up the sides of the buildings and roads disappeared.

Tim and Rebecca drove slowly, wipers on uselessly and headlights punching softly ahead. Offshore a dim huddle of trees and a lone light from Goose Island. Behind it and above, like a crown, the string of lights on the Canadian span of the Thousand Islands Bridge.

They had been invited to dinner by Donald Graves and his wife, Mae. Tim was hesitant, but Rebecca said, What else would they do? They would worry themselves silly, that's what. Or cower somewhere, waiting for Adams Denver to burst in. And neither option appealed to her as much as decent, relaxed conversation in front of a fire. And so they'd set out. Tim remembered en route that Michael used to make lame excuses to come down here to see Donald, and it made him doubly glad they had accepted the invitation.

They turned off the Parkway and bumped onto a narrow lane that wound through the trees. There was no road any more, just a road-sized gap.

Tim stopped. "I don't know if we should go any farther," he said.

Rebecca laughed at him. There was something wrong with the heater and her breath fogged the glass.

He pressed on, feeling the Toyota sink as well as move forward, trying always to strike a balance between haste and caution. A shout went up and Tim realized it was because someone had seen them coming. He pushed a little harder and felt the back end slide out. He eased off and tried again, more gently, and in this stop-start way they made it the last fifty yards.

The house was one of four along the shore beneath the bridge. Traffic moved through the sky twenty-four hours a day. The road passed more than two hundred feet overhead. Tim knew he couldn't live in the shadow of that much busyness. He had said as much to Donald

Graves one night when driving him home, but Graves had been drunk then and waved him off. "The stairway to heaven," he'd said. "Who wouldn't want to see that climbing from their own backyard?"

A pretty wooden porch was piled high at one end with firewood. At the other, to the left of the door, a rocking chair and a barbecue. The lid on the barbecue was closed but smoke hissed from it anyway, then curled out from under the porch roof and poured into the sky. Tim opened his window. He smelled lamb, and heard the rumble of trucks. A wind chime of seashells and fishing line tinkled gaily.

"Well, no question they're alive," Rebecca said.

Graves appeared at the side of the house, his arms loaded with kindling. Tim thought of Bill Sumner's Jeep, the wood in the back seat.

"Hello there," Graves called. "We saw you coming down the drive. How are you, Tim?"

"I'm fine, Mr. Graves."

Graves stopped at the bottom step of his porch. "It's Donald, Tim. Donald." He dropped the kindling and marched out to meet them. "And you, Rebecca, how are you, my dear?" He put an arm around her. "This woman's food," he said to Tim. "More than once I drove home from your father's restaurant in tears. Weeping, I tell you. You are a wonderful artist," he said to Rebecca. "The rest of us are barbarians." He waved an arm theatrically in the air. "We burn things. We kill them and then we forget about them." He sniffed the air. "Mae!" he called. "Mae. The hound is well done, I think."

The front door flew open. Mae belonged, Tim thought for the hundredth time, in film. European film. She wore an ankle-length blond fur but no shoes. Her toenails were scarlet, her lips were plum. She came to the top of the steps and waved a foot at them. "It's as far as I go," she said. "They're still wet." She lifted the lid of the barbecue and smoke engulfed her. But rather than coughing, staggering away, beating the air wildly, she bent backwards at the waist, smoothly, calmly, as if about to embark on a great experiment in limbo dancing, and backed away from the cloud. "You're right, Donny," she said, straightening gracefully. "The dog is most definitely done."

They were shown into the house and Mae unbuttoned her fur. She sat them around a table and positioned a platter of meat at its centre. She brought glasses and decanted wine into a porcelain jug decorated with folksy images of porcupines with bulging green eyes and long, bendy quills. The wine went next to the meat, and Mae returned to the kitchen for vegetables that steamed on the stove. The inside of the house was open; all the walls had been removed. A wood stove heated the place and its stovepipe rose into the ceiling like a periscope. A stairway zigzagged up a back wall.

"We've meant to call before now," Graves said. "It's easy to say, I know, but we have."

"It's okay. Really." Tim played with a lamb chop. He held it by the bone and pushed it around his plate. He wasn't hungry; he couldn't do it.

Graves put his hand on top of Mae's. There was a shuffling under the table. They liked their privacy. You would, out here, at the edge of the world, Tim thought. In the space between two worlds. You would have to like it.

"Your father was never a yes-man," Donald said. "You put something in front of him and if *he* didn't want it, he'd tell you. He stood his ground."

"That might be overstating things, dear," Mae said. They all looked at her. Her utterance seemed to need an annotation, or a translator, someone to dig into the words.

"I don't think so," Donald said. He looked at his wife. Was it sternly or pleadingly? Was there anything in the gaze—a caution, an order? Tim couldn't tell.

"How are you, Tim?" Mae said. She smiled. Underneath her coat she wore the flimsiest of summer dresses. A gauzy film of leaf patterns, leaves and stems falling around her feet. "We heard the police were looking for someone, and Donald said whoever it was had stayed with you."

"I also said I didn't know if that was true, Tim," Donald said. "It was just what people were saying." He was clad in thick winter denims, a rough suede vest over a flannel shirt. They were a mismatched couple, and yet they clearly adored each other, whatever tensions were simmering.

"He was staying at the house," Tim admitted. "You're right. But it's complicated." He looked at Mae. "And yes, I'm okay," he told her. "I'm learning not to expect my father around every corner."

A light swept through the room and Donald pushed his chair away from the table. He went to the window. "Just a snowmobile," he said. "Damn fool kids, I bet. They're always tearing up and down here."

"Are you sure?" Tim scraped his chair away from the table and stood behind Donald. A distant white light, the size of a soccer ball, was visible between the trees.

"Snowmobile it is," Donald said.

He made to turn away but Tim took hold of his sleeve. "Then, what's that?" A second, more feeble light separated itself from the first and floated right.

"A flashlight is what it looks like," Donald said. Mae and Rebecca joined them at the window.

"That's weird, isn't it, Donny?" Mae said. "What would they be up to out there?"

"It's kids, I tell you," Donald said, clearly resistant to any darker possibility. "You people have to calm down." The second light was stationary now, hovering waist-high between slim birches, but then it moved to rejoin the main beam. That brighter light then disappeared. "He's turned it off," Donald said.

They watched then as the flashlight grew steadily brighter. "He's coming this way," Rebecca said.

"Well, we'll see who it is any second, then," Donald said. "Won't we?"

Before they could identify the figure, though, he moved off again to the right. To Tim's mind, it was as if someone was circling the house.

Mae wrapped an arm around her husband's waist. Donald, though, broke away and began to clear the table, as if in a few minutes they might all gather around the fire's heat for liqueurs. Tim remained where he was; he cocked his head, strained to gather in anything just beyond the range of everyone else in the room.

"Maybe he's right," Rebecca whispered in his ear. "I'm sure it's just a kid. Come on."

"It's gone," Tim said. "He turned it off."

"He went away," Mae said. She sighed and lifted the wine jug from between the lamb and the mint sauce. "I'll refill this. I'm sure we could all use another drink. We've all become edgy. The slightest thing . . ."

"Wait," Tim said.

"Tim," Donald said harshly. "That's enough."

But they could all hear it now. The whine of the snowmobile being restarted. Then they saw the jiggling, dancing flight of headlights on the wall.

Donald strode back to the window and peered through the gap in the curtain without pulling it back. "He's stopped on the road. Some forty, fifty yards down."

Mae said, "I shouldn't worry, Donny, right?" The high gloss of her early enthusiasm had dulled substantially. Worry worked at the corner of her mouth.

"The telephone," Tim said. "Dial 9-1-1."

"Don't be stupid," Donald chastised him. "You'll make a fool of yourself."

Mae, though, lifted the receiver. "It's down," she said, holding it out in front of her as if for them all to witness its silence.

Donald shook his head. "That means nothing. It happens all the time here." He turned his back on the window but stood there framed by it, as if daring someone to shoot him.

The engine revved again. Mae tiptoed to the door and turned the lock, then she slipped a bolt home. Donald told her, "I don't think that'll stop him, my dear."

Tim was nearly frantic. Without any proof, he was now convinced that Adams was out there.

"I know it won't," Mae said. "But we have to try."

"Of course we do." Donald stepped away from the window. "You're right." He leaned heavily against the table.

"Move the table," Rebecca commanded, and she and Tim dragged it across the floor and positioned it in front of the door.

"There's not a hope in hell that'll stop him," Donald said. "Even if you were right, which you're not."

The snowmobile rushed towards the house. There was nothing they could do now, Tim thought. He slipped along the wall and pulled back the curtain. The snow that fell on the cooling barbecue was turned instantly to boiling water and then steam.

The snowmobiler had seen Tim peering out and he raised his arm in greeting, then pointed at the house. It was so plainly an innocent gesture and such a shock that Tim's pulse first soared and then plunged. It was nothing, after all. He was wrong, and Donald was right; he looked a fool. But that was okay, he could live with that.

He was about to grab his wineglass—because Mae was right, he could use another drink—when the window next to his face shattered. Glass sprayed the table. Shards cartwheeled. A second later another shot rang off the barbecue. Rebecca screamed and Tim heard something hit the ground. Someone must have been hit by a bullet. But Rebecca and Mae were climbing the stairs, scrabbling desperately at the wooden planks with their hands, as if to pull themselves higher faster, and Donald was on his knees at a long cupboard next to the sink.

Donald looked over his shoulder. "Is it him?"

"I couldn't tell."

"Well, this will slow him down, whoever it is." He tossed away a broom, then reached in to the cupboard again. Tim saw sacks of flour and rice, a four-litre green-and-gold tin of olive oil. Donald, though, had found what he was looking for and brandished it enthusiastically. A shotgun. An honest-to-God weapon.

Donald crawled across the floor to join Tim at the window. "Is he out there?"

"I don't suppose he's left, if that's what you mean," Tim said. He got to his knees and peeked above the glass-strewn sill. A snowsuited figure lumbered heavily across the car tracks Tim had made and took shelter behind a thick oak. Tim thought he could make out a pant leg to one side of the tree, the toe of a boot. He brought Donald's head next to his own. "The oak," he said. "He's behind it."

Donald slid down the wall below the window and frantically fed shells into the shotgun. He was panting. He snapped the gun closed, stood, and poked its snout through the broken window. He fired blindly and the recoil knocked him off his feet. To Tim, it felt as if the blast had ripped all the membranes in his ears and nose. Donald said something, but Tim couldn't distinguish one word from another. He stared at Donald's mouth, thinking to lip-read, thinking to focus for a second on anything at all.

"Is he still there?" Donald said. The words reached Tim this time, but as if accompanied by a deafening orchestra of tambourines and triangles.

Tim shook his head and, as he lifted himself from the ground to see what was happening, he imagined that Adams would, at any second, poke his arm through the window and fire a bullet into each of their skulls. Instead he saw that Adams was retreating, weaving from tree to tree.

"Fire again," Tim told Donald. "Away from him, though. Into the air."

"Where is he?"

"Back towards the snowmobile. He obviously didn't bank on you having a gun, or fighting back."

Donald brought his gun round again and fired into the pines. The snowmobile's light burst on and in its concentrated beam snow sifted down between the illuminated tree trunks. Adams—if it was indeed Adams—shot deliberately again at the house. Once. Twice. The first bullet went clear through the door, ricocheted off the wood stove's hard black flank, and clattered into a drawer full of cutlery. The second chased it home.

Mae and Rebecca had advanced as far as the top of the stairs. At the sound of the shots they threw their arms around each other.

"He's leaving," Donald said. "We chased the bastard off, I think."

And it did look that way. The snowmobile was turning, its headlight sweeping over the Thousand Islands Bridge and then brightening the snowy trail back to the main road.

"I don't think he's finished with us yet," Tim said. "I don't picture him giving up this easily. He'll double back."

Donald pointed at the roof. "You're forgetting where we are," he said. They were both on the ground still, beneath the window. Donald was ferreting through his pockets for more shells. When he found two he cracked open the gun. "The border," he said, jamming the yellow cases into the twin barrels. "The bridge."

"I don't follow."

"At Hallowe'en kids let off some firecrackers down here. Next thing, there were cops all over. They had a helicopter out there on the water, aiming its light at us." He chuckled at the memory. "Never seen kids so scared. Anyway, this guy must've known all the shooting would draw attention. Look at that, he's on the run now."

Tim stood up this time instead of hauling himself up over the sill.

He moved to one side of the window and, as Rebecca and Mae crept down into the living room, he watched the snowmobile fishtail away, the brake light flickering on and off as the shooter negotiated the pot-holes and tree roots.

"He's fucked," Rebecca said. Her hands were shaking but she seemed as furious as she did scared.

"I'm still worried," Tim said. "He has to know this is the last shot he'll get at us." He took a breath, as if about to dive into deep waters, and heaved the table away from the door. Rebecca grabbed his sleeve and tried to stop him, but Tim plunged outside.

He crouched on the porch, then shuffled to the end. The barbecue sat sentry beside him, warming him, as he stared into the darkness and the trees, down the road that ran under the bridge, which climbed sharply over the trees, trailing its garland of lights. A mon-ster, he thought. A beast moving past.

Adams' snowmobile—Tim was convinced it was him—burned along the shore. There was no way to catch up, and anyway, Tim had no inclination to even attempt that.

Rebecca and Mae and Donald had edged onto the porch. Mae had her fur on again, and she'd wrapped an arm around her husband. Donald cradled the shotgun like a child.

"What do we do now?" Rebecca said. "Can we use the phone at one of these other places?"

Donald said that wouldn't work. "Summer homes," he said. "No winter service. Just us. We need to get out of here."

Mae nodded. "We'll drive away."

"Well, we should do it now," Tim said. "We have to go to the police."

Donald had his hands on his hips. "Where will you go, Tim?"

"Like I said—the police."

Donald said Adams would surely expect them to run to the police, and there was only one sensible route there. He suggested they meet at The Apple instead, an old-fashioned inn in Gananoque. "Three roads converge there," he said. "He can't cover all of them. We can phone from there."

Mae disappeared inside and then returned with her fur fastened. She wore boots now, knee-length tan suede. She seemed calm, determined. "Thank you, Tim," she said. "But I think we shall have to postpone dessert. Some other time."

Tim felt a great warmth for her. The brave front was more than he was capable of.

Donald's car was parked around back under a corrugated lean-to. Snowshoes hung on the wall, and some tools they wouldn't need for a long time—a rake and some rusted hedge clippers.

Mae climbed into the driver's seat. Rebecca leaned in to receive a kiss on her cheek. She said to Tim, "Do we know where we're going?"

"Donald and I were just discussing that."

"Good."

Mae looked up at them. "You look so cold," she said. "Do hurry." She reversed out of the makeshift garage. The tires slipped on the greasy slope but then took hold. She gave an elegant toot on the horn, as if they were only embarking on a Sunday drive, and crawled slowly forward in Adams Denver's tracks.

"Watch he isn't waiting at the road," Tim called. "Try to get some speed going."

"Let's follow them," Rebecca said, "before I throw up."

Tim grinned as cheerfully as he was able and hurried around to his car to open the passenger door for her. "We'll be okay," he said.

"I don't know about that. Was it really Denver?"

"Had to be."

"I know," she said, suddenly convinced. "That *fucker!* If you see him on the road just fucking run the prick over. Okay?"

Tim laughed. His stomach was churning, but he knew exactly what she meant; together, he thought, they were capable of anything. It was a laughable sentiment rather than a funny one, but as he shifted into reverse and worked to get the car turned around without getting them shot, he thought it might provide at least enough courage and impetus to get them safely out to the highway.

*

Oh, I'm fucked now, Adams thought. He was roadside, kicking snow out of the snowmobile's packed tracks. There was way too much adrenaline left in his system. Those dim bastards firing back at him were responsible for that. Well, they got the juices flowing, no fucking doubt. And then there was the small business of not finishing the job. That was plain embarrassing, that was.

But yeah, it was all over, near enough. And he wasn't fucked permanently, no sir. He'd hunt them down in Kingston. Put Donald in his grave. Mae too, if he had to. Finish the job properly and then hit the highway. Tim and Rebecca he didn't give a toss about, really. Unless they were in the way. He'd go down Toronto way, see Niagara Falls frozen; he'd like that. Stay in a fucking honeymoon suite. Spread-eagle himself on the bed. Play some darts, see the waxworks. And wasn't there a casino? He fucking hoped so. He'd spin the sodding wheel. Feel the breeze coming off of it. It was just days away. It was inevitable. It had risen up marvellously from the great pool of possibilities. He could feel it coming at him. The end, the fucking *end*, he thought, is nigh.

It would be more complicated now, of course. The cops would be all over him. Or if not that, they would be all over Donald and Mae. He'd have to bide his time. Hole up. That, or try to strike before the force got too organized. Ah, it was a fucking mess. And Petrovitch would be busting his balls, he knew he would. He'd suggest sending Oleg, that turtlenecked and humourless bastard, to finish the job, impugning Adams' professionalism in the process. Well, there'd be none of that. Once Adams signed on the dotted line, he was committed, thank you very much. And he worked alone. No exceptions.

He thought about lying in wait off to the side of the highway. But this place would be crawling with cops once Donald got to a telephone. And Adams had seen lights up on the bridge even before he'd left. Some idiot shining his flashlight down off the footpath, the pathetic beam not even cutting into the tops of the trees. No, it was better he hide up. Read the newspapers for clues, see how much they gave away. He was a patient man. More and more he was able to hold off doing the impetuous thing. He loved that word: *impetuous*. It would make a great tattoo, he thought. No, he would wait for them to come out of their hole. And then *bang*! Game over.

Fuck Petrovitch, too, he thought, throwing a leg over the machine like it was a very short horse. Sure, he'd finish the job, but fuck him anyway. And Tim too. Rebecca he wasn't so sure about. Him and her, it wasn't the worst pairing in the world. But fuck it. What was he thinking? He got the snowmobile started again. Then, jerkily, he was covering ground. It was always the same, Adams thought: he was either spinning his fucking wheels or he was climbing a fucking hill. He was killing someone or he was hunting them down. That was it, over and over.

*

Tim and Rebecca were silent until they made it back to the main road. Tim saw the house in the rear-view, all lit up and abandoned. Rebecca held her hands in her lap, and every time Tim looked over they were wrestling each other into submission.

He blanked. It was along here somewhere that he and his father had walked together and found the remains of a deer, and seen in the distance wild dogs. He had often seen deer crossing the ice between islands. Sometimes the deer stopped at the unfrozen main channel and just stared disbelievingly at the boats. Other times they ran right off the edge and thrashed to the other side. Or else drowned.

"Where are we going?" Rebecca asked.

"Donald mentioned The Apple. Because it's not on the strip."

"I can't believe he killed Bill and Hinton," she said.

They weren't listening to each other, he realized, just saying whatever came into their heads.

"I want to get some things from my place," Rebecca said. "Do you think we can risk it?"

Ten minutes later Tim pulled up outside her building. Bellini's was closed. The video store too, but a figure moved about inside, re-shelving cassettes.

"I'll come up," he said.

They moved through her apartment like thieves. Rebecca took a chair from the dining room and put it beside the wardrobe. She passed down to him a metal box with a ring in it, a camera, and then a final package—a velvet cushion, he thought, and pretty, but when she passed it to him he felt its solid heft and knew he was wrong.

Tim followed her into the kitchen. He held the package flat in the palm of his hand, for fear of squeezing a trigger. He knew nothing about weapons.

"That's it," she said. "That's all I need." They locked the apartment door and trundled noisily down the stairs like a normal couple off to dinner. If only it were that easy, he thought.

In the car Rebecca slid the revolver from its soft envelope. It lay in her hand, platinum grey. It was small and curiously beautiful.

"Jesus, where did you get that?" he said.

"My dad. He's a gun nut. He said if I was going to work in the hospitality industry, and particularly in this part of the world, then people were going to offer me stuff."

"What sort of stuff?"

"Cigarettes, booze, drugs. Smuggled shit. My dad watched all the reports on television about the boats zipping over the St. Lawrence stuffed to the gills with cigarettes and he saw men in masks and he said I had to have a gun. Kingston has too many prisons. Too many crazies. He said he wouldn't leave until I accepted it."

"That's a stupid way for him to think."

"It's absolutely nuts."

"What is it?"

"Glock," she said. "Semi-automatic. Muzzle velocity 360 metres per."

"Per what?"

"Second."

"Shit."

"I know. It's a foreign language." She blushed. Slid it back inside the cushion and then slid that into the gym bag she had filled with clothes, her wallet, the bottle of gin she had glimpsed as they were leaving her apartment.

They parked behind the cinema near the water. They cut through alleys strewn with Coke cans and coffee cups, leaflets advertising a winter fair. At The Apple they checked in as a couple. It felt illicit in all the wrong, non-pleasurable ways, and when Tim scrawled their names in the guest book he did it nervously and illegibly. On the floor behind the counter several years of the *National Geographic* were discreetly stacked. On an old teak buffet was an aquarium filled with soil, a maze of tunnels pressed against the glass.

The teenage girl behind the counter had blue hair cut so that it stood up straight at the crown and fell forward into her eyes and over her ears. "You'll have it nice and quiet," she said. "There's only one other couple here. And I've put them in the Rolfe suite, other end of the hall."

"The what suite?"

The girl launched, with little enthusiasm, into her spiel. "All four suites are named after apples," she said. "Apples that are, um, very rare now. They're actually extinct, but, well, you know." She winked extravagantly. "I'm putting you in the Spitzenberg."

"I've never heard of it," Tim said.

"Exactly."

Rebecca described Donald and Mae. "Is that the other couple?"

The girl nodded severely, smacked her gum. "Uh-huh," she said. "That's them. Are they, like, your friends?"

Their room was wood-panelled and dim, dominated by a canopy bed. The bulb in the bedside lamp was weak so Rebecca removed the shade. She stared at the naked light a few seconds and then declared, "I can't stand it," and replaced the shade. They lay on the bed letting their eyes get accustomed to the murk. The chenille bedspread had a cigarette burn through its centre. The lace curtains were stiff, papery. The tiles in the shower stall were cracked and the cracks had gone brown, black. There was a layer of dust in the bottom of all the drawers, as if they had sat open for many months, filtering the air. They were, the girl had said as she followed them up the stairs, the only guests she had had this week.

Tim showered quickly, rubbing at his body with the brittle mould of rose-scented soap. The overhead fan rumbled heavily. When he was done, Rebecca took a turn and then they sat on the bed next to each other. They regarded themselves in the silvering mirror over the dresser.

"Is that us?" Rebecca said. "We look so haggard."

"You just have to look harder to see us," Tim said. "We're still in there somewhere."

They tiptoed down the hall to the other occupied room. The word "Rolfe" had long ago been scratched into the door. When they knocked, Donald answered without asking who they were.

Mae sat in a wicker chair in the farthest corner. Her fur coat lay on one of the two double beds, a *People* magazine beside it. "You try to forget what is happening to you," she explained. "You pretend you have all the time in the world."

"You shouldn't stay here long," Graves said. He perched on the edge of a bed, his socked feet crossed over each other. He nodded gently, as if confirming to himself that what he had said made sense, and it caused his body to rise and fall a little.

"I'm still surprised he didn't succeed in killing us all, right then," Donald said. "It would have made sense."

"It makes no sense," Tim said. "What are you talking about?"

Mae said, "Go easy, Donald. It's not his fault."

"We should call Des Boyle now," Rebecca said. "The RCMP detective."

Donald shook his head.

Mae said, "She's right, Donny. It's time."

"Not tonight, thank you very much."

Mae said, "They can guard us. They can take us somewhere safer."

"They can also decide to put us in a cell. No. If you like, I suggest you go somewhere else and call for yourself."

"Donny. Don't say such a thing." She looked wounded, smaller.

Rebecca took her side and pleaded with Donald, but finally Mae scolded her. "You cannot divide us, Rebecca. My husband knows better than I. If we are in the darkness I trust him to find the way out."

Tim wanted Donald to come clean, at least. There had to be more here. Some scheme Donald and his father had worked on. It made the most sense. "Why would they put you in a cell?"

"I think you should return to your room," Mae sputtered. "Are you staying here?"

"Other end of the hall."

"Good. Then I think you should try to sleep. I don't think he'll find us here."

"He may even fuck off. Who knows?" Donald said.

"No, hold on a second," Tim said. "Why would they put you in jail?"

Mae put her arms around her husband's shoulders and tried to dissuade him from speaking. "What's done is done," she cooed. "It won't do any good. It's not Tim's fault."

"But it is his father's. If he hadn't been so damned greedy."

"We were greedy too," Mae reminded him.

"What did he do?" Tim asked.

"He stole from Petrovitch," Donald said.

Tim said, "How do you know this?"

"We helped him," Donald spat. "We were greedy and stupid. *I* was greedy and stupid. My wife tried to talk me out of it."

"We were in it together," Mae said.

"In what?" Rebecca said.

"We ferried Mr. Petrovitch's people to an island a few times," Mae said. "Michael recruited us."

Rebecca began to pace. "All this is about smuggling? Smuggling what?"

"Diamonds," Tim said. "Right?"

"Yes, diamonds," Donald said sullenly.

Mae pushed away from him so she could look him in the eye. "You knew what it was, Donny?"

Donald nodded. "Michael told me one night."

"And you didn't tell me?"

"I didn't want to scare you. And the less you know, the better I felt."

Rebecca said, "Where did he get the diamonds?"

Mae looked at her husband, who was fussing with the edge of the bedspread. "Well, Donny? I think you owe us all an explanation."

"They were Russian. Hanne Kristiansen got them into Canada. They were sold in New York."

"Hanne? I like Hanne," Mae blurted. "How could she?"

Tim said, "Let me get this straight. My dad got you and Mae to smuggle diamonds across the St. Lawrence for Nikolai Petrovitch."

Donald nodded but kept his gaze fixed on the bedspread. "We took them to an island just over the border. But that's just half of it. He got greedy. He started stealing diamonds from Nikolai. Skimming stones."

"And now Nikolai is taking his revenge."

"Looks like," Donald said.

"Only, you weren't involved."

"Right again."

"So how do you know about it?"

"Your dad asked me to help him. He offered me a cut."

Mae grabbed his knee. "You never told me that."

"Well, he did," Donald said. He sounded irritated. Defeated maybe, but also angry. "Would you have wanted to know? Would you really? What would you have done? You would have worried yourself to death, that's what. That's why I didn't tell you."

"You had no right."

Rebecca was still pacing and massaging the back of her neck.

Tim's head was spinning.

Donald said, "I turned him down, Mae. It was a lot of money. I said no. I said he'd get us all killed."

Tim said to Donald, "So how did he do it?"

Donald shrugged. "No idea. I told him I didn't want to hear about it. I was angry with him. I still am. And we still had to do more runs for Nikolai. It was awful. I thought one of his goons would shoot us out there. I was convinced he knew."

Tim said, "And Bill and Hinton?"

Donald's lower lip began to shudder; his eyes filled with tears. "Maybe Michael went to them when I said no to the idea of stealing from Petrovitch. I don't know what help Hinton could have been. He doesn't have a boat, for Christ's sake. The poor man. But Bill at least had a speedboat. Maybe that's it."

"Why not me as well, then?" Tim said.

"I've thought about that, Tim. Petrovitch had good reason to believe you weren't involved. Your father was always adamant about keeping you in the dark. But my guess is he thought you might lead him to the stones. Or that they were hidden somewhere. It was better for him to infiltrate your house than kill you and find himself locked out and the place guarded by police. Your dad had just died, too. If you were to follow suit it would raise suspicions about Michael's death, wouldn't it? Nikolai wouldn't want that."

"And Hanne? Why isn't she dead?"

"She operates the pipeline. Maybe that's all she does. It probably wasn't easy to set that up."

"Listen to yourself," Mae said. "*The stones!* You've been thinking about this, Donny. Whenever you were staring out the window or into the fire, I have to think now that you were thinking about *this*. I hate that."

"I hate it too."

Rebecca said, "We don't have to tell the police any of this tonight. We just need them to get Denver. We need to say what we saw, that's all."

"And Adams eventually says why he was after us and we get put in our cells." Donald faced his wife. "Separate cells, Mae."

"But we have no choice," Rebecca said. "It's stupid to think we can hide here forever."

"We can hide here tonight, though," Donald said.

"And do what?"

"Think."

Tim looked at Rebecca. He didn't know if the diamonds were still in her car. He was inclined to grant Donald his stay, but it was impossible and impossibly stupid.

Rebecca was exasperated. "It's stupid not to call," she said. "We'll all end up dead."

Donald suggested they could keep watch, each of them taking a couple of hours in the hall.

"Oh, Donny, this is terrible," Mae said. She leaned back on the bed as if she might never get up again.

"But it's workable," he said. "It's that or jail."

"You can say you were forced to do it," Tim said. "By my dad."

Rebecca squinted at him.

"That's generous of you, Tim," Donald said. "And perhaps we go that route. But not yet."

He stood up and wanted them gone. Mae looked at him as if on any other night she might tell him he was being rude.

They all stood at the closed door. Donald had his hand on the knob. Tim thought about how you could throw a pretty short rope around them. They took up so little space, seemed so benign; it seemed incomprehensible that someone could want them dead.

"I'll take the first watch and wake you, Tim, in a few hours," Donald said. "And in the morning let's put some people around us. We'll meet downstairs. Say, eight?"

"We're the only people staying here," Tim said.

"The waiter, then. And that punk girl at the desk."

He opened the door a crack and Rebecca and Tim slipped through.

They lay fully clothed on the bed in their room. The television flickered noiselessly. A man on a stage, his hair tousled and his rumpled face running with sweat, pushed the palm of his hand into the forehead of a frightened girl. She fainted away from him and was caught by two black women in blue dresses who had clearly seen it coming.

Tim asked her: "Where are they?"

"They're here. In my bag. I thought ... I don't know what I thought." She smiled. It was an arrangement of muscles that suggested to him that she would not break under the strain. It also embodied suggestions of tenderness and sadness. Her face contained hints, he thought—his heart rushing blood into his own face—of a world he would gladly lose himself in.

"Let's see them."

Rebecca dug through her things and tossed the baggie onto the bed as casually as if it contained nothing more than a late-night snack. Tim nudged the stones free of the tissue, pushed them around on the quilt. "Like broken marbles," he said.

Rebecca held one up close to her face. "They're so ordinary," she said. "What a waste."

Tim gathered up the remainder and shook them in his fist like dice. "Two sixes," he forecast, and rolled them out. The tiny constellation gathered in the quilt's hollows and seams.

Rebecca looked away; she focused on the television. "Put them away," she said. "They confuse me all to hell."

Tim did as he was told. "I can still see him, my dad, waving that spatula around," he said, hoping to distract her. "He was so happy in front of that stove at the restaurant."

The television evangelist had summoned another victim. A bookish young man in a tweed jacket and chinos handed his spectacles to one of the women in blue and then stood expectantly, awaiting the thunderbolt.

"People are frightened of being alone," Rebecca said.

It was something he had thought himself, watching other shows like this one. She draped a leg over one of his. He revelled in its warm pressure. The boy in the tweed jacket received his smack but remained upright. He stared ahead glassily, wore a sheepish smile. The evangelist bellowed something into the rafters, into the banks of television lights and dull grey scaffolding. He hit the boy again. It was a blow hard enough to unbalance an ox. With a closed fist he might have knocked the boy out. The boy tipped back as if felled with an axe. The women lowered him gently to the floor and he quivered there a while.

Rebecca said, "This really is the wrong thing to do, you know. We're sitting ducks. But you feel responsible, don't you."

"We can leave, if that's what you want," Tim said. "We can leave and go to the police. We'll take those damn stones with us. We'll just leave Donald and Mae out of it."

"It's too late for that. And anyway, you would hate me if I made you leave them."

"I would never hate you."

"I need the gin," Rebecca said. "I can't think straight." She lifted her leg from his and sat up. Her face was visible in the mirror. She closed her eyes slowly, opened them and saw him watching her. "Whatever happens, I like that we're together," she said.

She passed the gin to him. It was tepid and foul in his mouth. He swallowed and waited for the burn. The chemical rush of juniper and licorice. Rebecca laughed and said, "I know, isn't it disgusting?" She lay down and again threw her leg over his. He passed her the bottle and she stared into its mouth. Wind rushed through the courtyard and must have worried an antenna because the religious program warped on the television screen; the ghost impressions of a shoot-'em-up cop show came through, then receded.

Tim sighed. He saw again his father leaning against the counter in the kitchen, sipping his wine. Watching Rebecca work. Often, the next day would find Michael trying to duplicate whatever it was Rebecca had served the night before. Getting a sauce to the right consistency. The way she moved a pan over a flame. Tim told that to Rebecca. He asked her, did she know how lucky they'd both felt to have her at the restaurant?

"I think I knew. Whenever I came through the door and the two of you were there, I never worried that you had been talking about me."

"I hate that he wasn't who he seemed to be," Tim said. "But you know, I watched him on the news for a dozen years. I saw him say one thing in front of a camera, and then he'd phone me to crow about what a great snow job it was."

"That's so sad."

He placed an arm across her hip, felt the jut of it under his hand. Her thigh across his. The way their breathing had synchronized.

The religious program ended after a period of singing and tears. It was replaced by a grainy montage of the Royal Canadian Mounted Police and the Rocky Mountains, great swooping aerial shots of Newfoundland fjords and Ottawa fireworks, the Niagara deluge in summer and then in winter, and the sapphire and emerald beauty of the Thousand Islands. Finally the Canadian flag snapped against a cloudless sky. Their lives reduced to postcards. Tim heard only the faintest intimations of the national anthem, and then the station cut off. The lurid horizontal bands of the test card popped onto the screen, and he even watched those for a while, saw how other programs moved faintly across that late-night background.

Rebecca's breathing slowed and she nuzzled into him. He had touched her skin only for fleeting moments. He felt her hair against his chin, how his hand was slotted in the space between her ribs and her waist. Her foot resting on his shin just above the ankle. He held her more tightly and she acknowledged his grip with a murmur. He stared at the ceiling, its yellowing stipple, and concentrated on the sound of the wind and the intermittent traffic. Adams was in one of those cars. And he had probably been inside Bill Sumner's place the night Tim was there. This lout had gained access to all of them. All except Rebecca. Tim felt protective of her in an old-fashioned way that embarrassed him and would have annoyed her. But as he felt her around him, the edges of her mingling with his, he knew that she probably felt the same way about keeping him safe.

He stretched to see the alarm clock on the bedside table. It was old; the numbers clicked heavily into place: 2:17. He leaned over and whispered in her ear. "I'm going to call Des," he said. "You're right."

She pulled him around so they were facing each other. "Thank you," she said, and she lifted her head slightly from the pillow so she could kiss him.

DECEMBER 23

John dreamt this time of whales, and fish-littered coral that heaved and settled, and of a body opened from neck to waist, its entrails wafting in the current, trapped under water. He dreamt that when he rose to the surface he inhaled wave instead of air and sank, knocked his head against the reef.

Hanne was shaking him awake. The unpleasantness of being stirred while it was so dark mingled with the altogether delicious realization of where he was. For the moment, he was refusing to believe that Hanne was less interested than he was in fully resuming their sexual relationship. But she was able to switch her affections on and off; he knew that. For her, this was an episode, a phase, a fling rekindled. Nothing more. John didn't work that way. It was one of their basic differences, and one of the reasons she'd left him so sharply.

"What time is it?" He clung to the sensation on his skin of warm water, the colours of tropical fish.

"It's nearly five. Someone's hammering at the door."

"_____"

"John!" she said.

He abandoned his dream. Listened.

"That's the third time," Hanne said, when the thumping started up again.

John worked frantically into his pants; he thrashed around on his back. Hanne handed him his shirt. He wanted his shoes on; it was important he not go out there with bare feet.

He trotted down the carpeted stairs in Hanne's house. There were dark shadows behind the front door's glass. It was one of the security detail, it had to be that. Probably a raccoon had set off a motion sensor and a cautious rookie wanted to make sure they hadn't been killed in their sleep.

He yanked open the door.

Des Boyle seemed more embarrassed than John. He cleared his throat, shuffled awkwardly on the front step. His black overcoat was hiked up around red ears. Behind him, two uniformed constables squinted into the dark house.

"It couldn't wait, not really," Des said sheepishly. "If there was another way . . ."

John shrugged. "You've got nothing to apologize for."

"No," Des said. "I don't."

John did up another button on his shirt, ran a hand over his chin. Christ, it was cold out there. He didn't have any socks on with his shoes and he was acutely aware—more aware than he had been when he'd first opened the door—of how totally unprofessional he appeared. "So what's happened?" he tried. The question felt awkward, as if he had no right to ask it.

"Tim Hollins is holed up in a Gananoque bed and breakfast with Rebecca Rae. They were visiting another couple for dinner—Donald and Mae Graves, I'll fill you in later—and Adams Denver showed up. We assume it was Denver, they didn't make a positive identification. We don't know whether he was after Tim or the others. But anyway there was a battle, and Adams ran for it."

"A battle?"

"Sounds like. Donald owns a shotgun."

"Okay. Let me . . ." John pointed behind him, at the stairs and the soft honeycomb of light at the top.

"Sure. We'll wait in the car."

Hanne gasped when he told her. She was sitting in the centre of the bed with her feet folded under her.

"Donald and Mae Graves, do you know them?" he asked.

"He's a guide or something," she said. "He and Michael got along well, I remember."

He waited for her to add more.

"That's it, I swear," she said. "That's all I know."

She went downstairs with him. She was scared, she said. That made sense, didn't it?

He told her it made perfect sense and he opened the door a crack. The night slipped in and chilled them.

Hanne kissed his cheek. "Fuck," she said, "it's nearly Christmas. This really sucks."

He put her back against the door and kissed her. He felt removed from the act, a man watching another man. "You hate Christmas," he reminded her. "'I *detest* Christmas.' I think those were your words."

"I was young," she said, pushing him away. "I'm different now."

"Not so different," he said, but she was already moving back into the warm depths of the house, away from him.

"Go," she said. "Go save the world."

*

"You did what?" Petrovitch asked.

It sounded to Adams as if Nikolai was having trouble believing his ears. "It's a temporary setback," he said, by way of reassurance. "Nothing I can't handle, Niki."

"Where are you?"

"Around," Adams said moodily, because it didn't matter where the fuck he was, did it, as long as he was in the vicinity of his target.

"So tell me again."

Adams ran through, one more time, the debacle out at Donald and Mae's. A task he resented. To ask a man to repeat the story of his failure was just rubbing salt in, there were no two ways about it. But he had woken Petrovitch up, which was asking for trouble, really. He had even heard Petrovitch ask someone, probably his girlfriend—though you never knew—to leave the room. A woman's voice had asked why, and Nikolai had had to repeat himself. Adams understood why Niki would be pissed at him. No man liked waking up to bad news. He understood. It was one of his strengths, he thought—being able to put himself in another man's shoes. It made him humble.

Nikolai whistled. "What a fucking mess!" he said.

Adams said he was inclined to agree.

"You should have hit Donald the minute Oleg returned to dry land after the last run. If I had known you would fuck this up, I would have had him do it that night. I cannot believe this."

"But it's not his line of work, particularly, is it?" Adams said. "Not his specialty, really."

"Apparently it is not yours, either," Petrovitch sneered.

Which set Adams off. He was cold, hungry, and bedraggled. He was at the telephone next to the washroom at the all-night Tim Horton's, a large double-double in his free hand. But any minute now the place could fill up with cops. He needed instructions or a dismissal. He didn't particularly care which.

"Don't fucking lecture me, all right? You're not down here."

"Donald knows more than anyone out there. He knows enough to do me harm, and he may well know what Hollins did with my fucking diamonds. What you had to do wasn't complicated."

"I appreciate that."

"Where did they go?"

"I haven't figured that out yet."

"To the police?"

"Nah, they didn't go there. I sat on the road for an hour, Niki. That's the one place they didn't go. And no cops went busting out of there either, so I'm thinking maybe they went to ground, you know?"

"Then, fucking find them. Now! And then get out."

"You were going to arrange my transport actually, Niki. Remember?"

"And I will. When you need it, it will be there for you."

"Where, Niki?"

"At the casino. You will be met at the casino. Someone will take you to the airport."

"My schedule, though. It could be any time."

"He will go there now and wait for you."

"That sounds all right. That sounds reasonable."

"I am a reasonable man, Adams. But finish the fucking job."

Adams nodded. "Right, then." He hung up the phone and swilled back the rest of his coffee. If there was any relief in the situation it was that the sparse crowd comprised layabouts like himself, people paying no attention. Which was perfect. He was able to waltz right back onto the street without anyone lifting their head.

He supposed he should stash his yellow Volvo, because it stuck out like a neon sign. Which meant if they had left town he was fucked, well and truly. He hadn't said that to Nikolai, but chances of finding them were pretty slim. He'd best present himself at the casino in the morning and take a lift to the airport. Nikolai could finish up himself; he said he was prepared to do that. But Adams would give it until daybreak; he'd check the motels along the strip and down by the water. He'd risk one last drive along the Parkway, stick his head in at Granite. Indulge in some decidedly risky behaviour because he was a man dedicated to finishing the job. But as soon as the sun came up he was gone, that was it for Gananoque, Gateway to the Thousand Islands. It was good fucking riddance.

*

A century ago, The Charlotte Bistro, on the inn's grounds, would have housed carriages, but shortly after six in the morning, when Rebecca pulled back the glass door, a bell tinkled gaily and all of them were swamped with the scents of cinnamon and coffee and lavender. A rack of postcards hung from the wall. The Thousand Islands. Kingston's waterfront at night. A grizzly bear snagging salmon from a furious stream. The tables were circular, with square white tablecloths arranged at their hearts. Rebecca made for one of the booths that ran along the back limestone wall. The seats were high-backed and uncomfortable. The waitress moved a piece of gum around in her mouth and her white dress rustled. A fleck of dried egg had stuck to the chrome post of a coat stand. An RCMP officer perched uncomfortably on a stool next to the door, his arms folded across his chest.

John Selby helped himself to a cup of coffee. The waitress smiled warmly. "You go right ahead, love," she said, and John raised his cup to her.

Rebecca played with the salt shaker, moved it around the pepper as if the two were hesitant lovers, or enemies looking for an opening, while Tim stared out towards the road, kept his eye on the distant bend, the point at which Adams would become visible if he came for them. John pulled an extra chair across the floor and put it at the head of the table.

"I can't believe you pretended to be a friend of my father's," Tim said.

"I thought you had nothing to do with any of this," John said. "And your father had just died. I didn't want to come across as if I was accusing him of something. I thought that would be needlessly hard on you. I thought if we were only to have one conversation I should try to make it as harmless as possible."

"But you're an American agent," Rebecca said.

"What, so I shouldn't act in a considerate way?"

"That's not what I mean. I don't know what I mean. Just that I had no idea this was so *huge*."

"You must also have been trying to trap me," Tim said. "You must have suspected me of something."

The waitress arrived with more coffee, and Rebecca ordered toast. Tim held his fingers against the side of the thin white cup as long as he could, until the heat became too much to bear. A young American couple had set their baby in a high chair. While the mother fed the infant tiny spoonfuls of an orange pulp from a Gerber jar, the father made hideous contortions of his face.

Donald and Mae set the bell dancing again. John had met them ten minutes earlier in their room. Donald had been belligerent and Mae had made excuses for him. A second officer joined the first at the entrance.

"I hate booths," Mae said. "Look at this." She passed a hand through the small space between her stomach and the lip of the table. "This is what I'm talking about."

Donald squeezed in next to Tim, and although he had more reason to complain—his stomach rested snug against the tabletop—he remained silent. When they were offered coffee he nodded, and Mae requested tea. They were wearing their same rumpled clothes.

"I told you," Donald said at last. He pursed his lips.

"Mr. Selby is here to catch Adams," Tim said. "And to protect us. He knows you have nothing to do with this."

John said Tim was jumping the gun; there were a hundred questions. And Des Boyle would have a hundred more, he said, "given that Donald and Mae have already admitted to some serious mistakes."

"We know Des Boyle," Mae said. "Don't we, Donny? He's a nice man."

"Maybe that'll help you, then," John said.

Donald stared belligerently at him. "Tim says you pretended you were one of Michael's friends. He says you gave a lousy performance. Who's to say this isn't just another act?"

John shrugged. "Look around you. You don't need me to answer that," he said.

Donald huffed something about men of the shadows and Mae regarded him fondly. She could be Rebecca's mother, Tim thought. The profile was similar, and also their strength, their resolve.

"I'm not annoyed at you, Tim," Donald said after a while. "Just annoyed at myself for believing I should be able to control everything. So what do we do now?"

"We stay put until after breakfast," John said. "And you talk."

"Put" sounded to Tim like a made-up word.

Donald patted his chest pocket. "Oh, hell. After all that, I forgot to take my pills," he said. "Isn't that odd." He worked his way out of the booth. "I never forget. I'll be right back."

"Someone will come with you," John said.

"No, they won't, Mr. Selby. Not unless you're worried I might swim down the St. Lawrence and from there to Europe. I'm going to my room, that's it."

As Donald walked past the counter, one of the officers caught Selby's eye and John shook his head. "Let him go," he mouthed.

Rebecca said, "Is he okay?"

"He's fine. His heart races sometimes. But it's nothing."

They all watched Donald pace lightly along the path between coach house and main building, twirling his room key on its red plastic fob. Another man, with an army-green toque pulled low, approached from the other direction, absorbed in a newspaper. They were both preoccupied. If they weren't careful . . . Tim laughed out loud as the two of them ran into each other. Rebecca and Mae craned to see. The man clung to Donald as they swung around each other, performed a clumsy tango. Tim was about to explain what had happened, tell them how he had seen it unfold. But the two men weren't separating, and Donald had slumped against the wall, next to the inn's main door. The other man still had hold of him, was drawing his arm back. Then the glint of a knife as it disappeared again between Donald's ribs.

Mae screamed. The composure that had so impressed him, that had held them all together, vanished.

Donald managed to push the man away, but he collapsed into the door, which swung open. The attacker spun around and saw police pouring from the café. He leapt over Donald's curled body and disappeared into the black shadows.

John was the first to give chase, bursting between the two officers, who had frozen and were looking for instruction rather than taking initiative. Tim followed him. Rebecca would tell him later that he also bashed into the waitress on his way out, that coffee shot from her carafe and landed all at once, as if a brown cloth had been thrown to the floor, and he would shake his head, not remembering.

Tim sprinted along the footpath. Donald's attacker reappeared in the doorway and shot at John. John crumpled.

John was dead, that was Tim's first thought. His world had changed to the point where a man lying horizontal on the ground was most likely deceased. But then Selby rolled onto his side and clutched, in obvious agony, at his knee. There was blood on his pant leg and the snow around his knee was filling with it.

"Holy shit," Tim said.

Selby, his teeth gritted, said, "Donald."

"He shot you!"

"Donald," John said. "Go!"

Tim dashed to the main building, a cop right behind him, and found the blue-haired receptionist behind the counter, her eyes watering, her hand held shakily in front of her face. Donald was in the fetal position on the oriental carpet in front of her, his face contorted, eyes wide, hands clutching his stomach. The knife embedded there, poking between his fists. There was blood on them and on his clothes, blood also at his neck and smeared across his face. So different, this, from the dry clotting on Cowley's shirt. Tim took it in in a fraction of a second. Also the sick, jaundiced light that was thrown onto the wood panelling, the sound of a tap dripping.

"Where?" Tim yelled.

The girl looked at him uncomprehendingly, but then slowly she raised a hand and pointed upstairs.

At the top of the stairs Tim made for the only open door. The police officer went the other way, and the moment Tim entered the dishevelled room he wished he hadn't—Donald's attacker was still there, struggling with the back window. A newspaper was strewn on the floor. He heard Mae scream downstairs—she must have reached her husband. Tim yelled. At the same instant the window gave and the man yanked it open, thumped at the already ripped screen, which fell away, tumbled like a fouled kite onto the fire escape. Tim realized it was Adams Denver only as he drew level with the bed. Adams, though, gazed at him as if he were a complete stranger. Their relationship had changed.

Adams leaned through the window, his stomach on its peeling frame. He tipped over its axis and fell head first onto the fire escape. Tim got to the window and Adams was righting himself, then clambering down. The cop entered the room with his gun drawn, but Adams was already halfway to the ground.

Tim nearly dove through the window, the cop still behind him like a shadow he couldn't shake. He heard his name and looked up. Rebecca was there, partially obscured by the back and forth of the old staircase, the tips of her fingers lined up along the bottom of the window frame. He and the cop clattered down the metal stairs and Tim leapt from the bottom of them, still three metres off the ground. The cop did the same thing but landed poorly and yelped, grasped for his ankle. So this was what they meant by protection, Tim thought. Where the fuck was the other one? And weren't there cruisers somewhere, and SWAT teams? He stopped long enough to realize that helping the man to his feet wouldn't result in any real assistance, and then he ran after Adams.

They sprinted one after the other down the centre of Water Street, a lane of one-storey, ramshackle, wood-frame cottages with plywood hammered over some of the windows and frayed lace strung up in many of the others. A chained Rottweiler reared up on its hind legs and pawed the air. Tim was gaining. Maybe Adams was waiting for an alley-bound moment to pull his gun.

But then Adams rounded the corner onto Ontario Street. His head dipped and he charged away. The houses here were larger, red-brick Victorians, on large lots and with cars in front of them. There were frozen playsets and the lake was visible between them. In the summer there would be docks, and boats tied up. A police siren sounded and then passed, one street up, in a blur of red and blue lights. The same thing happened again.

Ahead was King Street. A closed beer store. A maroon station wagon. Tim made the corner as Adams ducked into an open-air pedestrian mall. He was only thirty metres ahead.

"Denver," he shouted. He chased him past Versailles Jewellers and the Pajo's Coffee kiosk. It was too early. There was no one on these streets yet.

Adams tripped, sprawled on the iced cobblestones. A grunt escaped him and he struggled to get up. Tim dove at him, took him down again next to the Sports Experts window. A mannequin in a Speedo stared blindly. A woman in a blue wool coat, sipping from a paper cup, peered out from Pajo's. Tim yelled, but she simply turned her back.

Adams gained the upper hand. He straddled Tim. "Ya fucking git," he said. He smacked the heel of his fist into Tim's face. Tim felt his mouth fill up with blood. Adams rolled off and Tim put his hands up to his nose, felt the give in it, the sideways movement, and tasted warm, sweet blood at the back of his mouth.

Adams was on his feet. He kicked Tim in the ribs, the hip, the knee. "I don't fucking need to kill you," he yelled. He leaned over Tim. "Stay down," he screamed. "Stay the fuck down."

Blood ran into Tim's eyes and he rubbed an arm across his face.

Adams ran off, moving sideways, skipping nearly, so he could keep an eye on Tim. When he was too far away to have it make sense to come back, Tim rolled to a sitting position. The woman was in the window of Pajo's again. She held her cup to her lips, nibbled nervously at its soft edge. He showed her his bloody hands and still she didn't move. He wobbled to his feet, stood in the indentation he had made in the snow.

"You're dead, then, mate," Adams shouted back. "It's your fucking choice."

Tim, to the accompaniment of yet another siren, began painfully to run.

They leapt, one after the other, down several flights of steps. Adams had his hands out, almost as if he thought he might get lucky, catch an updraft and fly. Tim was reminded of a hapless British ski jumper he had seen on television: Eddie the Eagle had landed in that same uncertain, unstable way. But Adams was pulling away now. Tim kept putting his hands to his nose, and he had to breathe through his mouth.

At the bottom of the fourth flight of stairs, the mall ended. Adams chose to gallop up the hill and across the main road, into the parking lot of the IGA supermarket. A corral of shopping carts sat quiet at the centre, a chain looped through their red handles. A hunched man was sweeping the entrance. Adams ran past and the man looked up. He stopped sweeping and stared open-mouthed. "Call the cops," Tim said. "Get out to the road and flag them down." The man nodded, but then he began to sweep again.

The store windows held signs for 99¢ chicken legs and $2.99 Tropicana. Adams' Volvo was there, hidden between Dumpsters piled with flattened boxes. A crate of tangerines had broken and the perfect rounds surrounded the car, as if it were the tree that had dropped them.

Adams yanked at the door. He yelled at Tim, "I'm gone. I'm out of your frozen fucking wilderness."

A man stepped from behind the Dumpster. A humourless, pock-marked face. A brush cut and black high-necked sweater. A long black wool coat. His hands invisible and his shoulders drawn up close to his face as if he'd been waiting a long time in the cold. The appearance was that of a monk.

Adams looked surprised. "Oleg. Beautiful. Right, then. Get this fucking idiot away from me," he said.

Tim stopped dead.

The new arrival grimaced. He pulled his right hand free of the overcoat, calmly aimed a long black gun at Adams, and pulled the trigger. There was almost no sound; it was more like someone sucking water through a straw than firing a bullet into a body. Adams thumped against the car. The man fired again. Adams' head whipped back and smacked off the roof. He ricocheted forward and slumped. The man strode ahead and opened the back door. He pulled Adams' body off the frame and dragged him to the back, both of them knocking oranges around with their boots. He bundled Adams in and slammed the door.

Tim wanted to throw up. His turn was coming. Blood was melting the snow.

Oleg looked around his feet. He kicked at a tangerine and it skidded Tim's way. "Blood oranges," he said. He sounded pleased. Tim blinked. Oleg kicked at the ground, scuffed some snow into the air. He rapped with a bent knuckle against the window of the car. Adams' bloody head rested against the other side of the glass. "He was out of his depth."

"You're not . . ."

"Going to shoot *you* now?" He shook his head. He bent to look inside. "It is a mess in here. There's no room for you."

The sweeper came to the corner of the building.

Tim's knees gave out. The fall he had expected minutes ago came now.

Whoever Oleg was, he climbed into the bloody Volvo. He started it up and adjusted the mirror. "Time to go."

"I don't get it," Tim said weakly.

"You're not supposed to. Get on with your life."

Tim spat, then wiped his chin. His spit was bloody. He fell forward onto all fours.

"You are dog," the man said. "Bark for me."

Tim didn't know what to do. Any second he was going to throw up.

Oleg revved the engine. He threw it into gear and laughed. "See, you are strong. You didn't do it. That is important," he said. He rolled smoothly away, crushing oranges. Tim threw up, and then he collapsed into the snow.

There were footsteps. The sweeper was standing over him, leaning on his broom. "You okay, mister? I thought I heard something."

Tim closed his eyes. He lay there and waited for the sirens.

PART iii

DECEMBER 25

The piss pouring into the bird's body thins, then falls short. The pool around the corpse burns into the frozen ground. A voice Tim has not heard before floats down.

"Hey, look at this." There is a general grumbling and then more footsteps on the rock. Four of them gather above. Tim imagines the one pointing. "Down there."

"Where?"

"Right there."

"I don't see it."

"In the piss."

"That's disgusting."

"It's a bird. Look at its wing."

"Maybe you stained it."

"Funny."

Tim presses back more firmly against the rock face. Holds his breath as if it might pass through the rock and cause the men to rise and fall. He cannot see Rebecca and he dares not turn or shift.

"It's not the most amazing thing I've ever seen," one of them says. There is movement. "I'm going down."

It is an incomprehensible plan. Tim wants him more than anything to change his mind. Whoever it is. You pissed into a decayed finch, he thinks. What can possibly make you want to come down for a closer look?

He braces, and the still air fills suddenly with the shape of a man descending feet first. He has jumped from the rock and comes down like a cumbersome crow. His jacket billows out behind him. His arms out to the sides like thin wings, he seems to hang in the air. But when he lands he emits a low animal grunt and tips to one side. It is like the policeman from The Apple all over again. No one is able to land on their feet any more.

The men above laugh down at him. "Stupid," one of them says. "Do you realize, if you broke your ankle we'd have to shoot you?" The man rolls onto his back. His legs are apart and Tim can clearly see the knobs of his kneecaps, the tight bunching of his penis and balls.

"I'm fine." He rolls again, onto his side. The bird is beside his head.

"I've never known a man who would jump off a cliff to lie in his own piss," someone says.

"Fuck off. It's fascinating. The insides have been eaten away." The man is absorbed by the tiny amalgam of feathers and dried gut.

"Get up. For Christ's sake." It is a new voice. "This isn't *National Geographic*. Come on."

The man sits up with a sigh. He is perhaps forty years old. The collar of his shirt, visible under his jacket, is white, the sort one might wear to an office. His pants are well creased and his shoes shine. The soles are leather. He might have been a bank manager.

"The trouble with you . . ." the man begins. But he doesn't finish the thought. He has seen them.

Everything after that happens at once. There is no discerning the order of things. The sounds arrive before the visuals; the world is turned on its head. Tim tries to move and for an instant he is trapped by the rock because he has tried to sit up rather than moving forward. Rebecca is also trying to get away from the rock that would hold them in place. It is as if the world conspires against them.

The man straightens his legs and his backside rises like a sprinter's in the starting blocks. Finally his hands come free and he is upright. Tim is a shade behind in his evolution. He has to stay hunched under the rock. He tries to move into an upright position and also to move up the slope, to climb and move free. Rebecca is right behind him.

The man laughs. He points at them. His face is flushed; he cannot believe his luck. "They're right here." He points ahead. "Cut them off!"

The air fills with figures, with vultures landing heavily, inexpertly. Tim tries to break between them. It is his only chance. He has no idea if Rebecca will be able to follow. Perhaps the men will be thrown to either side and Rebecca will slip through that gap. Or they will turn to go after him and she will run down, towards the lake, into the arms of fishermen. Everything he does is about Rebecca, for her. But there is no time to evaluate the moves. He rushes for the space between two of the men. They are still struggling to regain their balance after their drop and he hopes to seize the advantage. He makes it through. The air screams in his lungs. The slope is steep and slippery; he knows he will fall, but so will his pursuers.

Rebecca pulls even with him and then ahead. She moves more lightly through the trees, seems to stay on top of the snow while he sinks into it. He chases after her. The four men are all around him; they seem to move as Rebecca does, as if a special dispensation has been made for everyone but him. Something hits him between the shoulders and he falls into his own shadow. Rebecca screams. He tries to get up and one of the figures moves in from his left and kicks him in the ribs. Again Rebecca cries out. He sees one of the men grab her arm. She wrestles free but only makes it another step or two. He is kicked again. His face in the snow, snow in his ears. It feels as if one or more of his ribs has already broken. He has trouble inhaling. Then his hand is stamped on and he draws it into his body. He tries for a fetal position but someone is pulling at his legs. He kicks out and connects; someone falls back and swears. He scrambles a few feet up the slope. They are like hyenas around him.

Rebecca calls his name and he catches a glimpse of her leg pumping, seeking traction on the slope, a man advancing on her, his gun in his hand like a baton, as if this really is a race. He intends to say something but is suddenly aware of a foot swinging at his face and then impacting. The world buzzes, spins. He opens his eyes and again the foot comes in. He has time only to screw up his features. And then it is black.

*

John Selby is furious. He cannot remember being more angry. His anger is matched only by that of Tim Hollins, who is in the passenger seat.

John tries to explain. "They should have identified themselves, I admit. But you shouldn't have run. Everyone looks suspicious at this point. They were supposed to babysit you until the end of the day, that was all."

Tim is unapologetic. "For fuck's sake. You must know what I was thinking when they arrived. An hour ago I thought I was going to die."

John says he can imagine how awful it was, yes, and those men will be talked to. He cannot believe they didn't identify themselves. He cannot believe what they have done to Tim's face, and John would not be a bit surprised if one of the kid's ribs was broken. He explains to Tim what is happening this morning. Because he feels sorry for him, he tells him some of what is planned, how at Chez Piggy, Hanne set up Nikolai Petrovitch. It is a way of saying he is sorry, he supposes.

Sonny Rockliff raps on the window and John climbs out, closes the door behind him. The hood on Sonny's parka is pulled tight around his face, which is red and windburnt.

"How's your leg?" Sonny asks.

The truth is John's knee pains him and makes it difficult to concentrate. Adam's bullet took only skin, but it was much more than a graze. The doctor had to do a lot of pulling to get the two sides to meet. There are twenty-five stitches knotted along that crooked red line, and he has little mobility in the joint. He also has a cane, and feels old.

"Nothing to worry about. Bit of stiffness" is all he says.

"And the old man?"

"Donald? He'll be okay. It was touch and go for a while, but . . . he's lucky."

"Good. And how's the son?" Sonny indicates Tim.

"He'll be okay. But the optics are awful—a gang of U.S. agents beating the crap out of an innocent Canadian on Christmas Day."

"They were overzealous, but that's the price of freedom, John. And anyway, why did he run?"

"Run? He could have run off a goddamn cliff. They put the girl in the hospital."

Sonny inclines his head, but only so he can say, "It's a shame you had to bring him here," without looking John in the eye.

"Don't lecture me. There was no time to talk him down and still get here."

"Fair enough."

In summer this would be a picnic area. There are toilets hidden behind cedar fences and wooden benches have been stood on end. The Seaway is visible where mighty pines have been cut away. There are several police cars and unmarked sedans, but there are no reporters, no TV crews. Men and women rush about like ants. A pretty woman unwraps a silk scarf in black and gold. She pulls it over her head so she resembles, when she laughs and tips her head alluringly, Audrey Hepburn being swept along in a convertible.

"Where's Hanne?" Sonny says. "I thought we agreed she would be here, so we could keep an eye on her. For her own protection," he adds, although both of them know that is not what Sonny means.

John considers, very briefly, lying to his superior. It would be easy to say she was mentally exhausted, and that John thought it best she stay at home, under guard. Because he is embarrassed. The truth is he doesn't know where Hanne is. An officer knocked on her door this morning and got no response. Their feeling is that Hanne escaped out the back door and fled down the laneway. John is still inclined to believe there is a simple explanation. Hanne will be discovered at the gallery, catching up on work that has been allowed to pile up. Or she will return from an introspective walk along Kingston's frigid but picturesque waterfront. But there is no time to prove that her disappearance is innocent and temporary. A team of Kingston police officers is searching for her. John doesn't trust his instincts completely with respect to Hanne. He will find it hard to look Des Boyle in the eye.

"She slipped below radar this morning," he says, hoping to be vague but not too vague, hoping Sonny will read it to mean she is simply staying out of the way.

"You don't know where she is."

"No."

Sonny regards him with the faintly masked impatience of a father registering a fatal disappointment in his son. John wants nothing more than to spit at his feet. Sonny barks an order to a woman running from one vehicle to another and then he says, "But you're working on it."

"I'm sure she's frightened," John says. "She's independent. She's taken responsibility for her own safety, that's all."

"I hope so, John. I sincerely hope so." He adds that John can choose whether or not to be a part of the takedown. There are plenty of good people here if he decides against it. If he wants to look for Hanne.

John doesn't appreciate the implication that he is expendable, or even interchangeable, and that he has compromised the investigation somehow. "Of course I want in. How do we stand?"

Sonny explains that Des Boyle and a special response team from the RCMP have set up on two islands on the Canadian side of the border. "They stay there unless Petrovitch gets away from us—which he won't—and makes a run for it. Our people are on an island on the U.S. side. Six people are on Manhattan Island already. We're lucky. There's forest between his house and the direction we approach from. He can't see a damn thing." Sonny wheels around and checks for his own vehicle, a tan Explorer. "Do you want to see a map?"

"I know where it is. I set this up, remember? A short sprint from the Canadian border. Is Mossine in there?"

"Yep." Sonny is pleased with himself, obviously. His enthusiasm for the morning's work will not be diminished by John's insubordination. "He doesn't have a clue," Sonny says. "He's wandering around in a smoking jacket sipping on eggnog."

"All good news. And any squeak from Petrovitch?"

"As we speak, he's driving to Kingston. You remember Matt Hart and the Pernice fellow from RCMP? They were out at the dump site when we went through the trailer? Anyway, they've been tailing him the last twenty-four hours. Right now they're around Belleville, stuck in a traffic slowdown—I guess there was a nasty accident. We're expecting him to make for the airport. There's a chopper on standby there. The listed renter is the nephew of a pilot Petrovitch has used before, so I think we're pretty safe in assuming it's him. Although," Sonny says reflectively, "he could damn near walk if he wanted. It's solid all the way. I personally find it very frightening, and so does the White House, that this joker has been able to move unhindered across the border."

"Well, Hanne's convinced a chopper is how it will work. There's way too much ice to risk a boat. And Mossine has a pad he uses. Petrovitch has used it once before. How about us? How are we getting there?"

"We fly to the airstrip on Wellesley Island—taking the scenic route so as not to spook the man—and then they've got some hovercraft type thing waiting for us. You ready?"

John nods.

"And we got Oleg. Last night."

"You did? Where?"

"Toronto. He was getting a massage. Full body. We don't think Petrovitch knows yet."

"Caught with his pants down, then." Thinking to be lighthearted, conciliatory.

"He actually put up quite a struggle. Threw a loveseat at one of the Canadians."

"Jesus! And do we think he'll be cooperative now?"

"He thinks we're considering extradition."

"For what?"

"We led him to believe we like him for all the murders. And it turns out Bill Sumner is an American. An old draft dodger. Which would get Oleg a place on death row, or so we've told him."

"So he will talk."

"I think so. If he doesn't disappear."

"I don't follow," John says.

"Laevsky split. Caught a flight to Moscow last night. The Canadians twigged about an hour after takeoff."

"They'll be able to bring him back, won't they?"

But Sonny is noncommittal. He seems to want John to feel responsible.

John tells him Oleg won't get bail, though, surely. "So it's not something we need to worry about, is it?" He points at the car, and at Tim behind the glass. They don't have time to squabble over lost opportunities.

"Get someone to take him home," Sonny says, as a chopper buzzes in low over the water, "FBI" stencilled on its navy-blue flank. The TV people would have a field day, John thinks. When was the last time the FBI assembled on Canadian soil? On Christmas Day, no less?

"Let's go," Sonny says, like a director calling for action. He claps his hands together and bends at the waist; he scuttles towards the helicopter, ducks below its black rotors.

John returns to the Jaguar. Tim tells him he gets the picture, and John apologizes. "When it's over I'll call you." He summons another American and directs that Tim should be taken home.

"No, to the hospital," Tim says. "Not home."

"They tell me it's just a couple of stitches on her shoulder."

"Then, I'll be able to leave with her," Tim says.

John says fine. It's a good idea they stick together. Just until they get the all-clear.

Sonny is yelling from the helicopter. Windmilling with his arm.

"Do you know where Hanne is, by any chance?" John says. "I want to talk to her."

"You don't know where she is?"

Another accusation is how it sounds. John is trying to break away. The chopper is louder now. Sonny has instructed the pilot to give John no more time.

"She was supposed to stay home," he says. "But it wasn't an order, just good advice. So no, I don't know where she is, unfortunately." He backs away. "Maybe Jamaica," he says to Tim flippantly, and then laughs. "Last I heard, she said she wanted to spend Christmas in Jamaica."

"That's a weird thing for her to say."

John shakes his head. "I'm joking. She said it to Petrovitch at the restaurant. She was just trying to be funny." He is still backing away and has to yell now. "Stay safe." He runs below the thrashing blades and is pulled through the door. Sonny gives the pilot the thumbs-up and the bird lurches again into the air. Tim follows it out over the ice.

*

Tim explains it to Rebecca in the car. He is speeding towards Granite and making her slightly nervous. She has to keep telling him to slow down, or to back up a bit in his explanation, because she hasn't understood something. She holds her right arm stiffly and Tim sees her wince occasionally, even though she insists she is fine.

"It makes sense," he tells her.

"Nothing makes sense. He told you all this? She's in *Jamaica*? Don't the FBI only reveal things under pain of death?"

Tim blushes. "I don't think he understood what she meant."

Rebecca shifts in her seat to face him more directly and to get her arm away from the door. "And what *did* she mean?"

Tim swings off the highway and then into the restaurant parking lot. He pulls up as close to the door as he can. "Wait here," he tells her. He runs inside and fetches a map. He unfolds it between them.

"What's going on, Tim?"

"Probably nothing," he says. "I'm undoubtedly wrong about this."

"Just tell me what's going on this morning, or else *I'll* shoot you. What did John Selby tell you? What are they all doing?"

He tells her what he knows. "Hanne wore a wire," he says. "At Chez Piggy. And she faked a phone call when Petrovitch was in a position to overhear. She made like she was going to off-load some of the stolen diamonds on Christmas Day."

"An honest-to-God sting operation," Rebecca says.

"Exactly. And that's where they are today." He tells her about the FBI helicopter. How it made him shiver. How it seemed surreal. Like if he became the most successful actor in the world he would still never experience another moment quite so cinematic.

"I wish I'd been there," she says. "But I still don't get—"

"It's something John said. He said Hanne wanted to spend Christmas in Jamaica."

"I don't get it."

"Hanne has disappeared," Tim tells her. He knows that is to over-state the case, but he needs her to trust him.

"Does Selby think something has happened to her?"

Tim shakes his head. "He thinks she wants privacy."

"But you don't."

"I'd just like to make sure."

"Of what? Tim, she said she wanted to be in Jamaica, where it's hot and sunny, and a few thousand kilometres from here, where it's freez-ing and everyone's dying. That doesn't sound too alarming to me." Rebecca's voice is high-pitched. She looks at Tim as if the painkiller she has taken has robbed him of a hard outline. As if every word from his mouth is nonsense.

"But it's not Jamaica she was talking about," he tells her. "It's Jamaica Point." He stabs at the map. "Dad used to make the same joke."

"He did?"

"When he went out sometimes. I thought he was being mysterious, or being a bit of a prick. But now . . ."

"Now you think . . .?"

"I think it's possible."

"And you want to go there. Right now?"

He says he does, and Rebecca wants to know why he didn't tell any of this to John Selby. She is annoyed with him. And frightened, he thinks.

"It didn't occur to me until afterwards."

"Call him now, then," she says. "I'm tired, Tim. It's been a rough morning, in case you hadn't noticed. I thought we could, I don't know, build a fire or something. I thought we could pretend the world doesn't exist."

"Half an hour," he tells her. He sticks a finger to the map. "It's not even eight kilometres."

"You'll get us killed," she says, but it is half-hearted, he can tell she doesn't believe that. Tim has his hand on the key and is looking at her expectantly. "Turn it, fine," she says. "But I can't believe this is how you want to spend the rest of Christmas Day."

*

At the southern edge of Maple Island, Sonny guides John into a run-down fishing cabin converted for the morning into a war room. It smells of old paperbacks and of worms. There is an excitement in everyone that John finds unsettling. Sonny is like a boy on his first field trip. There are two men in combat fatigues. They have rifles trained on the more elaborate winterized home that is visible on Manhattan, just across the thin, frozen passage. It is clear to John that he is expected to stay in the background. His active role in the investigation is over. Sonny sits him down on a folding camp chair and squats beside him. A battery-powered heater purrs on the ground between them. On a low table is a radio receiver turned down low. Christmas carols issue from it, as well as the sound of a man singing along tunelessly.

"That's him?" John says.

"Has a hell of a voice, doesn't he?"

John peers across the strait. Occasionally Fenton Mossine is visible, moving through his island retreat. "Looks pretty damn lonely," he says. "I wouldn't want this. Not for all the money."

Mossine's awful warble, made worse by its satellite transport to them, fills up the wormy room. There is the rush of a tap being turned on, a toaster popping.

"You should take a look at yourself about now," Sonny says. "It isn't pretty. At least he's warm in there. We might freeze to death before your Petrovitch shows up. I just heard that Hart and Pernice lost him coming out of that traffic jam. They think he might have exited at Napanee and taken the old road into Kingston. I hope so. We'll have to wait for him to show at the airport."

Your Petrovitch. That is what sticks. The bastard. Sonny is already preparing for the worst. Making it clear who will be blamed if this operation comes to an ignominious end.

*

Jamaica Point is off the Thousand Islands Parkway, somewhere beyond Rockport. A kilometre or two, Tim says. He is almost positive. The Parkway is deserted; they have the perfect road to themselves.

"It's in here somewhere," Tim says. "I remember seeing the sign." They slow down as they pass signs for Smugglers Cove and Lost Man's Point, Lyon's View and Mussel Beach. "It must be just up ahead."

Tim can see that Rebecca is still nursing her shoulder. He feels guilty for dragging her out this way. He would much rather be at home with her; he hopes she understands that. He doesn't like the look on her face. It is unreadable, which means that in the last couple of kilometres Tim has interpreted it as an expression of disappointment and sadness. As mild tolerance or simple fatigue and pain.

They drive another couple of kilometres without finding the right turn. Finally Tim pulls off to the shoulder. He checks his mirror and then swings the car around. "We'll go back," he says. "You're dead right. If we don't see it on the way back, we'll forget about it. I'll call John Selby from home."

Rebecca kisses his cheek; she squeezes his arm. "Thank you." She leans back against the headrest and closes her eyes. Tim is so intent on watching her, the way her eyelids flutter and her chest rises and falls, that he nearly drives off the road.

*

Hanne's life has just been threatened, she is sure. She was stupid to come to Jamaica Point, stupid to think Petrovitch would appreciate her gesture of penitence, and stupid most of all to believe that she was better to appease Petrovitch than cooperate with John. How did she convince herself that this was her best option? That this would offer her the best chance at freedom, at staying alive?

They are inside the small lighthouse that warns boats away from the Tar Island Narrows. A tiny white room, perfectly circular and without furnishings, other than the camping stool he has made her sit on, so he can prowl around her. There is just a rickety staircase with one of the risers recently replaced, and on the bare wall a grey fuse box with the door hanging open.

She has been here before. Both times to meet with Nikolai and Michael, away from prying eyes. Michael wanted to protect his friends and his son from what he was doing, and Nikolai was more than happy to get away from the tourists with their telephoto lenses and their too-curious stares.

She has already given him the diamonds. The eight small stones that she has collected from the four deliveries of Russian art. She stole two stones each time, because she was positive he would never know, not if she replaced the screws properly in the frames, and the frames in the packages. She was meticulous in her theft. Choosing nondescript diamonds, and wearing latex gloves. Working in the very early morning, with the gallery locked and the alarm set. She told no one. Not even Michael. Especially not Michael, who would eventually have betrayed her, she is positive, and who insisted on keeping the diamonds they stole together (repeating the exact process she had perfected on her own) rather than selling them, because he thought Nikolai would suspect their treachery and would be looking for signs. She has no idea where those diamonds ended up. She has been secretly hoping that John would find them in Tim's home, so that guilt would attach concretely to Michael and she might be spared by Nikolai. But then men began to die indiscriminately and she felt she needed to act more forcefully. She wanted to control her own fate.

She has told Petrovitch she merely found these eight among possessions Michael had left with her the day he died. That she found them in a briefcase and, because she knows Nikolai might well ask to see that case, she has already bought a battered bag from an antique store and filled it with what might pass for Michael's things: a couple of recipes clipped from *Gourmet* magazine, a pair of leather driving gloves, a notebook (new), and a fountain pen (old). Her plan was to add in her own defence that not only has she returned what is rightfully Nikolai's and which she is appalled Michael would steal, but she has also saved him from FBI and RCMP ensnarement. Her part in that ensnarement, she wants him to understand, was performed under extreme duress, and she hopes that Nikolai appreciates how well she was able to subvert the authorities' plan. In essence, she wants him to believe that they are a team, that they are on the same side in that neither of them wants to go to jail.

And now she has said her piece. Nikolai has accepted the diamonds without expression or outward sign of surprise. He has pocketed them without even tugging loose the yellow drawstring on the small velvet pouch she brought them in. He listened seriously and without interruption to her explanation of why and how. But now, rather than letting her go—so she can smuggle herself back into her house before John becomes too suspicious—Nikolai is circling her. Every time he disappears behind her she cringes, convinced that he will grab her hair and pull her to the ground, or he will hit her, or even shoot her. He is working himself into a fury. She thinks he has probably been rehearsing the things he will say to her, all the way from Toronto. He has already told her that he had to drive here rather than fly, because he thought they would be waiting for him at the airport. "I am on the run," he said to her, melodramatically, when he arrived. She had been waiting for twenty minutes and was shivering. She thought she might throw up. She had no idea what he would do next.

He is building up speed, she thinks, as he circles her. Like a gyroscope, he could spin off in any direction. "Stupid," he is saying. "The two of you were stupid to think you could pull this off."

She nods and bites her lip. She braces herself for the blow she is certain must be imminent. "I didn't know," she protests. "If I had known—"

"You *did* know," he tells her. "I am sure you knew."

He crouches in front of her. She looks at the floor. Someone has swept in here. There is dust against one wall, a collection of twigs, the empty husks of earwigs and beetles. "You know why I came," he says.

She isn't at all sure if it is a question. She shakes her head. For an instant she holds his gaze.

"I knew there would be this," Petrovitch says. He shakes the bag in front of her. "It is stupid to try to placate a man with his own possessions, but I knew you would try."

"I shouldn't have warned you, then," Hanne says. "I should have let you go. When we met that day, the restaurant was full of cops, American agents." She might as well paint him a more detailed picture, is what she thinks. "They want you to enter the United States illegally. That alone would get you a long sentence. And they thought you would yell and scream at Fenton Mossine. That you would admit things. I saved you from that. Don't you understand? They don't have enough to prosecute you and so they're setting you up. They figure the rest of their case will come together while they let you rot in jail. But I've saved you from that, too. We have nothing to worry about now."

"I know what they thought." He puts his hands on her knees. "And now all that remains is to discover what story you told them."

She shakes her head and he squeezes the muscle above her knees. She grabs at his hands but he doesn't release her, and she tips back her head and screams.

*

Tim edges away from the lighthouse. When he is thirty metres away he sprints down the driveway and around the curve to where Rebecca is waiting. "Get to a phone," he instructs her. "Call the number John gave me. It's on the front dash. He's here."

"Nikolai?"

"And Hanne. He's got her in there. I can't see them. I didn't want to risk looking in the window, but . . ." He is forgetting to breathe. "He was yelling."

She takes a step away from him, and he hates seeing her do it. She is reluctant, frightened all over again, and he feels that it is his fault. He has made this happen. He is to blame, whatever the outcome.

She backs up towards the car. "What are you going to do?"

He tells her he doesn't know. He looks over his shoulder, but then he runs to join her. He rushes her to the car and opens the door for her. "Your gun," he says, "it's back there, right?" and he reaches for her bag. "Will I be able to figure it out?"

Rebecca's hands are shaking. "I hate you for this," she says, and he smiles weakly, wraps her in his arms. She pushes into him for a second but then wriggles free. "Pay attention," she says. "This is the safety. I'm taking it off. Is that what you want?"

He tells her it is and can't look at her when he says it.

*

"It was a stupid accident, right?" Hanne insists hopefully. "That's all. Michael's death was *so* different from the others."

Petrovitch shakes his head. "I should have had Oleg do all the work," he says ruefully. "Not just the one job. Michael's was the only perfect death. The other man was a fool." He still towers over her.

Hanne's knees are together; she rests her elbows on them and puts her head in her hands. "So you did kill him?"

Petrovitch moves away, leans against the wall. He crosses his arms. When Hanne lifts her head enough to look at him through the veil of her hair she sees that he is pleased with the way this is going. She is convinced he intends to kill her, too. "But I saved you," she says. "I am the opposite of the others. You think they were out to ruin you, but I'm not. I'm returning the diamonds Michael stole. Christ, I even betrayed John in order to save you."

"John?"

"John Selby. He's with the FBI, or the BVC, something to do with the border. And he was here to trap you. Frank Coleman is the other name he used. I used to date him. I think that might be why he was assigned to you. But it didn't work. It worked against them. I'm *here*, aren't I?" she says. "I'm not there, with them."

He laughs at her, cuts her off. "So you've known about this for how long? You cooperated with the fucking FBI to set me up?"

"I just told you, that's not what I was doing. They forced me."

But Petrovitch is done talking. She is stupid, she realizes, for the last time. She invited this. A meeting where no one would think to look. A confrontation while the rest of the land gathers around great piles of gifts.

He strides past her and opens the door. It is a brilliant morning. She thinks she can feel the heat of the sun on the side of her head. But her head is also throbbing. Her eyes are wet and her knee is bobbing up and down. She is an unreliable witness to her own sensations. She has no control any more. She thought she did, but it has gone.

He tells her, "This is it. You know that, don't you? I want you to know."

*

No one can believe what they are looking at. No one wants even to look. Sonny Rockliff says, "This is truly the saddest way to spend Christmas."

"For us or him?" one of the operatives wants to know. He leans his rifle against the porous wall of the cabin and raises a set of binoculars. "That is fucking horrible. I should be with my wife and kids, not watching some sad-sack asshole flick through the porn channels."

"I'm with you," Sonny says. He paces the cabin, which amounts to not much more than simply turning around. "What do you think, John?"

"I think it's pretty clear Mr. Mossine isn't expecting company for the holidays," John tells him. He feels oddly guilty about the way they are all witnessing Fenton's lurid morning routine. At first, when Fenton sat down on the couch and began to scan through dozens of channels, John thought it was a positive sign. The man was waiting for something to happen. He was killing the little free time he had, rather than launching into a more substantial project. But then Fenton found what he was looking for, and Maple Island began to fill up with groans and suppressed giggling.

John is also restless. They could be here for hours. He looks around, looks into the sky for an approaching chopper. Maybe there was good reason for Sonny to be doubtful so quickly. Maybe Petrovitch did hear of Oleg's arrest and has fled. Perhaps they should have let Oleg alone for another day or two. They have fucked up. As for Hanne's disappearance and what it might mean, he cannot even begin to contemplate those things yet.

His telephone begins to hum against his ribs. He doesn't register it immediately. Or rather he registers it, but it never occurs to him that he should answer it. Finally he tugs it out. Sonny shushes everyone else.

"Where is that, exactly?" John says into the receiver. "Someone in here has a map, right?" He looks expectantly at Sonny, who spins on the ball of his left foot while snapping his fingers as if in accompaniment to Mossine's low grunting. Someone hands him a map. "Jamaica Point," John says. ". . . West of Rockport." Sonny holds the map up so John can see he has located the place. "And where are *you*?" John says, facing the blank wooden wall so he can concentrate. "Okay . . . Okay . . . Fine . . . Yes." He snaps the phone shut. "He's not coming," he says. "He's on the other side."

Sonny shifts into a higher gear. He wants the helicopter to collect them, right now. "And get Mossine out of there," he yells into a walkie-talkie. "Just get him to the mainland . . . Stateside, you idiot . . . No, I don't care. But when we get Petrovitch I want Mossine in the next room corroborating everything . . . Yes, now . . . I don't care what he's doing."

Men stream from the trees. They run together across the ice. There are men already at Mossine's window and a hovercraft rounding the east end of Maple Island. John stays at the telescope long enough to see the astonished and embarrassed and completely puzzled expression on Fenton Mossine's face as he voluntarily draws back the glass door to let his accusers in. Even as he backs into the room, his hands in the air, John sees Mossine craning for more information: just how many men did they send out to arrest him? And shit, look at all this firepower!

*

Tim presses his back to the lighthouse. He slips away from the door, makes it to the opposite side by the time Petrovitch has pushed Hanne Kristiansen out. He doesn't know what you do in these circumstances. There are ice crystals on his fingers. He is aware of the absurdities piling up. Petrovitch has just admitted to ordering his father's murder. He has a gun in his hand, and looking down at it, the hand seems not to belong to him. It is Christmas Day. The FBI and the RCMP have an island across the St. Lawrence surrounded. He has always wanted to act in larger dramas and this feels like a dream role, and yet all he can think is: this is the last place on earth.

He moves towards them, unsure of anything. Who he is protecting, and from what. What he will do when he rounds the lighthouse curve enough that they see him. What he wants to do, and what he is actually capable of. And then they see him and none of that matters.

A startled Nikolai Petrovitch jumps a step backwards. It is almost funny. He is, for an instant, a man about to have a heart attack. Tim raises the gun and points it. Nikolai grabs at Hanne and has hold of her sleeve, but she manages to twist away and makes it inside the lighthouse. A latch is thrown and Nikolai thumps uselessly at the door. Tim points his own weapon squarely at Petrovitch's chest. He is aware of the pulse in his temples, and how his head seems to move slightly with each new rush of blood. The air seems thicker than it should, as if it is full of water, or is beginning somehow to set hard. All of this in the half second it takes Nikolai to slump nonchalantly against the door.

"It has been too long," the Russian says. He smiles bitterly.

Tim waves the gun from side to side. It is his way of saying, No, I can't hear any of this. Don't talk to me, whatever you do. Not after what you just said. At the same time he is wondering if the gun is even loaded. He never thought to check; he wouldn't know how. And Rebecca never told him.

"Now, what are you going to do with that thing?" Petrovitch says.

It is a decent enough question, Tim thinks. One that leaves him stumped. He tries to summon spit enough to say something. He hates this man, wants more than anything to shoot him. To put a *plug* in him. But he doesn't want to *talk* to him. He doesn't want to have to listen. The very thought of it makes him wince.

"We're going to wait," Tim says.

"For the cavalry, Tim? How sweet."

Nikolai bolts for the cars, his feet slipping out from under him. He makes it to the black BMW, and when he discovers that Tim has already removed the keys and locked the doors he curses and advances on him.

"I thought you might leave," Tim explains, "and I'd rather you didn't, really. Your gun was in there too and, well, I'd rather you didn't have that either."

"Give me the fucking keys," Nikolai barks.

Tim points out onto the frozen river. "They're out there."

"Bullshit."

Tim shrugs.

"The gun, then."

Tim retreats uncertainly. Nikolai has his hand stretched out, as calmly as if to receive change in a coffee shop. Tim squeezes the trigger and the gun leaps in his hand. The kick is like that of a rabbit against his palm. The bullet smacks into the gravel a body's length from Nikolai and buries itself. Nikolai stops. Tim aims at Petrovitch's Lexus and takes out a tire. Petrovitch yells at him to stop, but Tim aims again and punctures the driver's side front tire on Hanne's green Volkswagen.

Petrovitch advances on Tim. "You think this will stop me?"

Tim aims into the distant mess of alder and leafless birch and fires randomly. He squeezes the trigger until he has emptied the magazine. He waves the gun uselessly, not sure whether to toss it aside or jam it into a pocket.

Petrovitch turns abruptly and makes for the rocks that are piled from the lighthouse down to the ice. He begins the climb down. He is not even looking at Tim, who warns him, ludicrously, to stop. He follows Nikolai down to the ice. The keys really are out there. Forty, fifty metres. As far as a throw would take them. Invisible from the shore, but if Petrovitch walks directly out, which he does, he may well find them.

Tim decides the only option he has, if Selby doesn't show immediately, or Des Boyle, is to get to the keys before Petrovitch does. He calls to Nikolai, who is charging hard away from shore, hoping to distract him, send him off course. But Nikolai ignores him, bends triumphantly and then jangles the keys above his head. Christ, that was way too easy. They are sixty metres from each other. Tim races for the shore and scrambles back up the rocks to the gravel lot. Hanne is completely silent.

He doesn't know what to do next. Petrovitch will drive away with a flat tire. It seems inevitable. Perhaps he will attack the two of them. Tim's heroics will amount to nothing.

But then everything changes. Behind him, Petrovitch crashes through the ice sheet. Tim doesn't see it happen but the noise of the ice cracking and the body smashing into gelid water is unmistakable. It is Bill Sumner's buffalo all over again. The fear that Tim had this morning, when he and Rebecca were running away from Selby's men, has come true for Petrovitch. He spins, and sure enough Nikolai is floundering at the centre of a hole perhaps two and a half metres wide. The water in there is black, the hole seemingly bottomless. Nikolai grabs at the front lip and tries to haul himself onto the white ledge. But the lip breaks away. He tries again and the same thing happens.

Tim smashes on the lighthouse door. He screams that Hanne must help him. There is a pause and then the door opens. Hanne peers around its edge as if she would be able to close it again if this were a trap. When she sees that he is telling the truth she limps outside. She is dishevelled and her hands are shaking. Her face is very white. "Oh my God."

"I know," he says.

He scrambles down the rocks again, expecting her to follow, but when he steps onto the ice and checks for her, she is still in the doorway, a hand over her mouth. "I need your help," he yells. "I can't do it without you."

She says something he doesn't catch. He checks the ice beneath his feet. It is solid. There is an obvious fault line running across the Seaway, and Petrovitch has fallen through it. Now he is working his way around the hole, smacking at its edge, trying to bash through to a solid area. But he is tiring. His gasps are more desperate.

"Let him drown."

There is no mistaking what she says.

"I'm not coming down there," she says. "Let him drown. For God's sake, just let him go."

Rebecca fishtails into the clearing, her Lada screaming in too low a gear. And even though her return makes sense, she is the last person he expected to see. It seems to Tim that she is out and running before her car has even stopped moving.

"How?" is all she says. She sees Hanne, immobile still and leaning against the door jamb, and she skids to a stop, holds Hanne by the shoulders. "You okay?" Hanne nods, bites deeply at her lip, and so Rebecca leaves her, climbs down to the ice.

When she is beside Tim the two of them proceed together, hand in hand. Neither of them lifts a foot off the ice, they just slide across its surface. "There's too much weight with the two of us," he says. He knows it contradicts his calls for help but everything is happening so fast. And losing Rebecca is something he cannot contemplate. He lets go of her hand and moves six feet away from her.

Petrovitch has stopped struggling. He is treading water, trying to stay calm. His head is tipped back so that his mouth doesn't fill up with water. "Quickly," he gasps, as if they are his children, people who work for him.

"What are you going to do?" Rebecca says.

"Lie down, I guess. You hold my ankles. Something like that."

Rebecca doesn't say anything. He checks to make sure she has heard him. Surely she can't think the way Hanne does. They would be no better than Petrovitch.

Finally she says, "I'm not prepared to lose you."

"I know," he says.

"Or to risk my life for him. We need a stick, a branch or something." She scans the shoreline but it is all granite and gravel. The nearest trees are back towards the main road.

"You go," he tells her, knowing she won't leave him. They are stuck there together. Neither of them wanting to get any closer to the hole.

Nikolai disappears but then pops back to the surface, spluttering. Hanne is crying now. She is squatting, her arms wrapped about her knees. Nikolai tries to say something but his strength has gone; he swallows water and disappears again. His face when he surfaces is panic-stricken and blue. They stand and watch him. They should do something, but perhaps they have done all that can be expected of them. You killed my father, is what Tim thinks. You fucking killed him and now look at you.

Rebecca hears the FBI helicopter first. And then Tim sees it, flying low, tipping left and right as it swoops between islands. In seconds it is a roar directly above them and they drop into a crouch. Snow is blasted into the air and the surface of the water is worried into thick white ruffles that obscure half of Petrovitch's face like an Elizabethan collar. The chopper tips right and peels off so it can land next to the lighthouse.

John Selby is the first man down onto the ice and he hobbles past them, swinging a brown cane. He stops, though, well short of the hole. Tim imagines that Selby must have arrived in time to see Nikolai disappear, his hand rising over his head as if to wave good-bye. They wait for him to bob back to the surface but it doesn't happen. A half dozen men leap from the helicopter, weapons already aimed into the deep, as if they expect a monster to come for them.

"Do we have divers?" John screams. Hanne catches his eye, but he turns deliberately away from her.

"Not here," someone replies.

John stamps his foot in exasperation and Tim feels the vibration in his boots.

Rebecca takes his arm. "I can't look," she says, and buries her face in his chest, while Tim watches a stillness and a calm return to the water, and is glad.

DECEMBER 29

It is not the worst place to conclude a debriefing. Sonny Rockliff has brought John Selby and Des Boyle from the Border Vigilance Commission's offices to his Newark home. It has snowed overnight. The three of them have apple cider. They also have mincemeat pies with pastry hearts for lids. Outside, Lara, in a fur hat and lime-green ski jacket, is happily cutting sprigs of holly from a shining bush.

John has been in Newark for two days now and is oddly reassured by the unfamiliar room Sonny has given him, with its chintzy flourishes and ill-lit portraits of people he has no wish ever to meet. Wrapped in its utter strangeness he is rendered anonymous, unworthy of attention. Which is what he wants. He has even, in the halogen-bright evenings, wandered to a shopping area a mile from their house. Stared into windows full of clothes, his reflection a curious ghost among displays of wedding gowns and model fighter planes.

He and Sonny will never be friends. They are too different. Sonny is too aware of his relative youth and of the blame he was ready to assign if things went sour. His every action seems driven by personal motive as much as by national need. It is the conclusion John has come to, and it has settled in him as an undeniable truth. For his part, Sonny recognizes that this has not been a perfect month, but he is pleased with the outcome. Even John's participation, with its air of personal conflict, is sitting well with Sonny's superiors. *It was a risk worth taking* seems to be the consensus. It is further agreed that John will recuperate and then return to duty with the FBI. Sonny says he reserves the right to borrow John, and John has agreed, hoping the necessity never arises. They have settled into the amicable banter of two men who don't much care for each other but who have survived weeks adrift in a small boat.

Today, though, they have decided it is time to close the book on Nikolai Petrovitch. Sonny and John and Des have exchanged compliments about the grand state of international cooperation. They have settled at the modest oval table in the modest rectangular dining room that gives onto the gentle garden and they have begun to hash it out. And until now it has been straightforward. This is when you went *here*; this is what you reported *then*; this is when we decided to do *this*.

"We put some accounts wizards into the Bank of Montreal," Des says.

"That's where Petrovitch's girlfriend works. Ruby."

"*Worked*, John. Past tense. More than $20 million has arrived from Russia in the last six months. Deposited as profits from Nikolai's Russian business interests. But a new look suggests those 'interests' don't exist. It looks like Ruby invented them for him."

"Where did the money come from?"

Sonny says, "We think it was taken from New York to Moscow. Remember those suits we arrested after that punch-up in the bar? Their empty suitcases? We think they were going to collect payment. Presumably a cut went to Petrovitch's insiders, those who provided security at Laevsky's mine, and then the rest was transferred, with Ruby's help, to Canada."

"So he steals diamonds, smuggles them via Fenton Mossine to New York, and then smuggles the cash back to Russia so he can have it return to Canada looking clean," John says.

"That's about how it adds up, yes."

"It's a relief to know all the steps in the chain, anyway," John says.

"It's nice not to have loose ends," Sonny agrees. He watches Madison tumble from her sled and roll down the slope. Her laughter pierces the house and Sonny beams.

Des tells them that Petrovitch's business interests will be dissolved, including the haulage business.

"And who benefits?"

"The Government of Canada mostly," Des says. "Ill-gotten gains go straight into federal coffers."

"Glad to hear it," John says. "Is there any indication yet how he was intending to use those millions? We still need to make sure that getting the money together wasn't just step one in a larger plan."

"Looks like personal gain was his only motive," Des says. "We'll dig plenty deep before we say that categorically, but yeah, he's a greedy guy. Plain and simple."

"That's a hell of a relief," Sonny says. "We need more of those in the world." On the day after Christmas he had worked himself into a cold sweat worrying that, with Petrovitch gone, the profits from the sales would be difficult to track. The higher-ups, he suggested to John, would come to him full of nightmares involving gunrunners and drug traffickers, or even worse.

John says, "And what about the restaurant, Granite? Petrovitch had a big piece of that, too."

"We'll work with Tim Hollins on that issue. It doesn't serve anyone's interests to have him lose that place."

John laughs. "He's damn lucky he gave you the diamonds, or it would be a different story. Nice Christmas present, that. How long ago do you think he actually found those?"

Des smiles. "He says they just turned up. I didn't think it was worth pushing him on that point. Two hundred thousand is what they're worth."

"That's a shitload of trouble his father caused, for a couple of hundred grand," Sonny says. "A family destroyed. Two nations ringing all the alarms."

They stare out at Lara, with her pruning shears and her red cheeks. A jet is climbing in the sky.

"Hanne will have to serve time," Des says. "And I'm sorry about that, John. But there's no avoiding it."

"What the hell was she thinking? That's what I'd like to know," Sonny says. "What was she hoping to accomplish out there?"

Des says, "She claims to have realized at the last minute that she might have given him the wrong impression at the Chez Piggy meeting."

"That's the stupidest thing I've heard yet," Sonny says. He wipes pastry crumbs from the table onto the carpet.

"She damn well *should* serve time," John blurts. "She set us up to fail. She did it to save her own skin and could have got herself killed." He is angry with her still. The wound she has inflicted is the one that will last longest. Her betrayal of him, he thinks, will change him more than anything else about this case.

Sonny, cognizant of his responsibility here, looks away, and Des frowns at his own indiscretion in bringing up the subject. They lapse into an embarrassed silence. Lara is stamping the snow off her boots, holding on to the window frame to keep her balance. Her wedding ring catches John's eye—the sizable diamond clutched in its gold talons.

"At least she's not a target now," Sonny says, scratching the back of his hand. "If he'd just gone to jail it would have been like a time bomb ticking away."

Des blows across the surface of his cider. "There is some other, better news," he says. It is plain that he hopes only to change the subject, but John invites him to continue. "It's about Viktor Laevsky. The Russians won't force him to return, but they intend to try him for vehicular manslaughter on the evidence we provide."

Sonny regards him skeptically.

"No, we're optimistic," Des tells him. "We think it's a positive development."

John is still thinking about Hanne. He couldn't give a damn about Viktor Laevsky. She will not fare well in prison. She knows that, he thinks, and everything she did was in a misguided attempt to avoid that fate: destroy the case against Petrovitch, and so destroy the case against her.

Des says he is needed at home. "I've got a new dog that shits on the carpet," he confesses. "And my wife is petrified it's going to happen on New Year's Eve. We have friends coming for dinner. The stern disciplinarian in me is required."

John, though, stays with Sonny and Lara that night, and when Madison is asleep they tell each other jokes. None of them is very good at it and the jokes aren't very funny. Mostly they laugh at their collective lack of talent. Lara produces a bottle of bourbon and they work though half of it before Sonny pleads fatigue. In the morning, John says goodbye to them and climbs into a taxi.

DECEMBER 31

Rebecca has on a sleeveless black dress, ready for their New Year's Eve dinner, but for now she is still in the kitchen, getting things ready. When Tim asks her if she is in mourning she glares at him in mock-anger and then swats him on the shoulder with a steel spatula. "Exactly the opposite," she says. He grins, and she moves around the thick counter at the centre of their kitchen so she is opposite him. She picks up a mushroom cap and tosses it at him. He catches it in his mouth, which pleases her, and she tips back her head and laughs.

Tim told her an hour ago that they are partners now, that the restaurant belongs to her as much as it does to him. He will put it in writing if she likes. She was with Tim when Des Boyle came by to explain the government's position. As Des understood it, Petrovitch's interest in Granito would be sold to them, at no interest. She is clearly still buzzing from the idea, and astonished, she says, that so much good has come out of these terrible few weeks. "Out of this *shit*" is what she said, and Tim thinks he will never forget the mild shock and extreme delight he felt at hearing that word leap so energetically from her.

Together they carry the platters of prosciutto and pear, of olives and cheese, through to the dining room where Donald and Mae are waiting. They have established Donald in an upright armchair so that he will be more comfortable. He moves stiffly, like a man in a strait-jacket. His guts are full of stitches that will eventually dissolve, and staples that won't, and he is in some pain, but tonight he is congenial and reaches constantly for Mae's hand. Rebecca places the antipasti in the centre of the table and the four of them gather around it. Tim pours wine while Mae jokes that Donald will be easily seduced once the Merlot mixes with the painkillers.

"I've always been easily seduced," he tells her, and she laughs, says yes, that was always your problem.

"It's your fatal flaw," Tim says. "There's one in every tragedy. Hamlet's flaw was his constant hesitation. Yours is that you're so easily seduced."

Rebecca says she thinks that she would pick a Donald over a Hamlet any day.

"Thank you, dear," Mae says. "And we're alive, after all. It's hardly a tragedy."

Donald nods at this, and grimaces.

Donald and Mae have been formally charged in Canada with smuggling, but at John Selby's recommendation the Americans have declined to seek further punishment. It is thought that this decision will result in Donald receiving a fine rather than jail time. His lawyer says that the court will take his age into account, and the argument that Donald was preyed upon is a strong one, particularly given that Petrovitch tried eventually to have Donald killed. The promise of a positive outcome has left Mae relieved and radiant. All evening she has been beaming, moving between the empty tables so smoothly it is as if she is dancing with them, being passed from one to another.

After dinner, although it is cold, they put on their coats and huddle on the deck so that Donald can smoke. Rebecca points out the footprints that belong to John's men, and their own tracks down on the ice, preserved like fossils.

Mae says, "All this running about," and Rebecca nods as if she knows exactly what Mae means.

"I hear you had a secret of your own," Donald says to Tim. "Rebecca told me. A bag of them, eh?"

Mae says, "I wouldn't have told anyone either, Tim."

"Oh, I'm not suggesting you should have, lad," Donald says. He leans against the railing, keeping his free hand wrapped across his stomach. He has a tuxedo shirt on under his open coat and the white frills move like waves in the breeze. A goose flies over, its dry flap transfixing them all.

"I didn't know what to do," Tim says. "I had no idea. There were so many ways to play it. Trust me, I thought about trying to sell them. The money would have solved a lot of problems. I couldn't pull the trigger, though."

Rebecca wonders aloud whether this makes Tim more like Hamlet than Donald, and everyone laughs.

"God, this is so *good*," Mae says. "I really didn't think we'd all make it."

Tim doesn't want to say so out loud, but he agrees with her. When they were at The Apple in Gananoque, and Donald was on the ground, Tim thought it would end badly for all of them. And again down there, around the point and below the Whale Back, he was convinced they would die. There seemed no reason to think their fate would be any different than Bill's, or Hinton's. Than his father's. He isn't sure what to do yet with the knowledge that his father was murdered. He doesn't think they will ever know how it happened. There were no bullets. No sign of trauma other than that involved with the car going off the road. The BMW has been towed to Toronto to undergo further tests. Oleg, though, is denying any involvement. Des Boyle says that is because he senses they have no evidence. When some is found, then Oleg will probably confess. But it is also a possibility, Des thinks, that Petrovitch was lying and he wanted only to scare Hanne. "We'll find out, though," Des said, sensing, Tim thought, that a lingering uncertainty would be dismaying.

But Des is wrong. Tim is of the opinion that it doesn't matter how his father died. Petrovitch is dead, and good riddance to him. Oleg will go to prison and serve a life sentence. Nothing will change for either of them. Whether the brake line was cut in his father's BMW or whether he simply slid from the road seems the least important fact. He knows others would disagree with him. Rebecca, even. And he can't articulate his reasons, but he feels peaceful. He feels some of what he sees in Mae's face: a near-giddy relief that it is over and that they made it. His own need for absolute truths seems to pale in the face of that fact.

Tim reaches around in his pocket and displays for them all what he has kept.

They crowd round to see the diamond that rests in his palm like a tiny bird's egg. It seems fragile, insignificant. It is the root of everything that has happened, and yet it is dull in the moonlight.

"You devil," Rebecca says.

But he shakes his head and draws his arm back. He fires the stone out over the Seaway. He follows its arc for a short distance but then loses it against the background of glittering stars and glowing planets. A second later he thinks perhaps he hears the soft plop of it burying itself out there.

"Best place for it," Mae says.

"In the spring, you know, it'll sink to the bottom," Donald says. "Be there forever."

Rebecca disagrees with him. "It might get carried out to the ocean eventually," she says.

It is their new mystery. Tim suggests to Donald that he'll have to bring the tourists along this channel now. "You have a new story for them," he says.

Donald grins. "I've got a few new stories for them," he says. He drops his cigarette to the ground and sparks break free and flutter more brightly than the diamond, down onto the slope where they are extinguished. He twists his foot on top of the butt. "We all do."

They stand for a while, the four of them in a line. Tim has his arm draped over Rebecca's shoulder. He kisses the side of her head. They look, all of them, for the brighter gleam that is the diamond in the brilliant snow sparkle. It's an impossible job; there is no retrieving it now.

"Just be sure to tell them we serve some fine food up here," Tim says. "See if you can't drum us up some business so we can pay the mortgage."

"Do I get a commission on that recommendation?" Donald says. He coughs, and the spasm of it has him clutching his stomach.

"That serves you right," Mae says to him. "Come on." She bundles him indoors. "I want to get you home," she says, "so I can punish you properly."

Within minutes Tim and Rebecca are alone. They carry the clutter of dishes back into the kitchen. "We'll be doing a lot of this the next few years," Tim says, scraping the scraps into the garbage can. "Are you okay with that?"

Rebecca says she isn't; no way. "We hire someone for this sort of thing," she says. "We recruit an army of underlings to do our bidding. We save only the glory work for ourselves. The creation of fantastic new dishes. We accept accolades from all over the world and fill our guest book with eloquent raves."

"What else?"

"Maybe a cookbook," she says.

"And?"

"God, I don't know," she tells him. "It's early days. But it'll be fantastic, won't it? Seriously. I mean, you and me. We'll be great together."

They load the dishwasher and Tim pulls shut its silver door so they can leave it humming and thrashing. "You're right," he says. "We'll be the best." He turns out the light and takes her hand. He leads her away from the work and the cooling ovens.

"This is our room," he tells her. "If you want." They are in the bedroom. There is still a picture on the bureau of his father, and another of his mother. Those will have to go, but he means what he says.

She looks at him curiously. He is hanging his shirt on the back of the door.

"Not just mine," he says. "*Ours*. But only . . ."

She screws up her face.

"We don't have to," he says, suddenly alarmed. Perhaps it is too fast. Has he misread her?

But then she laughs, and comes at him around the bed. She throws her arms about his neck and kisses him. "You were going to save him, if you could," she says quietly. "Weren't you?" They sink onto the bed and lie side by side staring up at the ceiling, its godawful light fixture.

"I suppose I was."

"I think that's a remarkable thing," she tells him. She reaches for his hand.

"Hardly. I just wanted him to suffer for many more years," he says. "It was the sadist in me."

Rebecca shakes her head. "I don't believe that. You were trying to save him. Despite everything. You hadn't thought about what it might mean. Well, it means you're good."

He doesn't know whether she is right. Or how many conflicting thoughts were computed as he skated and slithered towards the thrashing body in the water. All he knows is what he did. Which was to act as most people would—to preserve life, whoever it belongs to, and not to extinguish it. He is determined not to believe he did anything that was exceptional. He distinguished himself from Adams Denver and Nikolai Petrovitch, but not from Rebecca, or from Donald and Mae, from Bill Sumner or Hinton Cowley.

He slips the dress strap from her shoulder. He reaches across her and releases the other strap. He runs his hand over the smooth ball of her shoulder and down the outside of her arm to the elbow. He is much more interested in her body right now than he is in philosophy and ethics. Rebecca bends her leg so that the dress falls from the knee and over her thigh. "I really don't know if I'm that good," he says.

She draws his hand down across her stomach and he feels the tensing of her muscles as she rolls towards him. "I think you're about to prove otherwise," she says.

ACKNOWLEDGEMENTS

I owe thanks to many, but none more than Samantha Mussells, who not only inspires me and is my first reader, but also has to live with me. Iris Tupholme, my editor and publisher, bought the book and has helped work wonders. Anne McDermid nudged me into some pretty unfamiliar corners and made me write my way out. Then she sold the book. I am grateful twice over. Joanna Lyon and my parents, Clive and Jennifer Sinnett, were unstinting in their support and enthusiasm. Many at HarperCollins have been patient and helpful. They include Noelle Zitzer, Siobhan Blessing, Kevin Hanson, Allyson Latta, Catherine Marjoribanks, Michaela Cornell, Lisa Zaritzky and Lorissa Sengara.

The Canada Council provided a grant and I gratefully acknowledge its importance.

Among the books I read, *Diamond* by Matthew Hart and *Discovering the Thousand Islands* by Don Ross stand out as particularly relevant. There were also articles: Jane Kramer's "Private Lives," about Germany's war on terrorism, and Victor Erofeyev's "Dirty Words," about profanity in Russia, both appeared in *The New Yorker* and both contain information that improved this book.